Annalise St. John thought life wasn't worth living—
until a sexy stranger gave her something to live for....

Charity Williams's close call with disaster might have
terrified her—if her gorgeous guardian angel hadn't insisted
on getting even closer....

When rebel Travis Morgan rode to Angie Brady's rescue,
he never dreamed he'd be driving away with her heart....

Angel
in your
EYES

*It takes a special man
to save a woman's heart....*

Relive the romance...

Three complete novels by one of your favorite authors

Dallas Schulze sold her first book when she was twenty-four, and is eternally grateful to the publishing world for saving her from having to find a "real" job. The bestselling author of more than forty books, she's won many awards, including a Lifetime Achievement Award from *Romantic Times Magazine,* and two bestselling book awards from Waldenbooks. She lives in California with her husband, one very spoiled calico cat, a couple thousand books, lots of rosebushes and enough quilting fabric to cover half the earth's surface.

DALLAS SCHULZE

Angel in your EYES

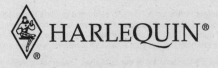

HARLEQUIN®

TORONTO • NEW YORK • LONDON
AMSTERDAM • PARIS • SYDNEY • HAMBURG
STOCKHOLM • ATHENS • TOKYO • MILAN • MADRID
PRAGUE • WARSAW • BUDAPEST • AUCKLAND

HARLEQUIN BOOKS

by Request—ANGEL IN YOUR EYES

Copyright © 2000 by Harlequin Books S.A.

ISBN 0-373-20175-3

The publisher acknowledges the copyright holder of the individual works as follows:
EVERYTHING BUT MARRIAGE
Copyright © 1992 by Dallas Schulze
CHARITY'S ANGEL
Copyright © 1992 by Dallas Schulze
ANGEL AND THE BAD MAN
Copyright © 1992 Dallas Schulze

This edition published by arrangement with Harlequin Books S.A.

Visit us at www.eHarlequin.com

Printed in U.S.A.

CONTENTS

He saved her life,
but she taught him to live....

Everything but Marriage

Prologue

"We find the defendant guilty."

Reed Hall felt the impact of the words strike the man standing beside him, but a quick glance showed absolutely no expression in Devlin Russell's face. He might have been listening to someone reading from a newspaper rather than hearing himself convicted of first-degree murder.

Reed listened to the sentencing, listened to the judge wipe out the next twenty years of a man's life. Devlin was twenty-two. After twenty years in prison, his youth would be gone, stolen not just by the years but by hard experience. If he survived.

Reed glanced at his client again. Something told him Devlin Russell would survive. There was no give in him. Reed didn't think prison was going to change that.

There was a buzz in the courtroom as the judge finished speaking. Reed turned to Devlin, speaking quickly before the guards came to remove the younger man.

"This isn't the end of it, Russell. We can appeal."

The eyes Devlin turned to him were steel gray and full of icy bitterness. "Save your breath, Hall. The evidence was overwhelming. You know it and I know it."

"It was circumstantial," Reed said stubbornly.

"And that's the only reason I'm not facing time on death row," Devlin said harshly. "Don't waste energy on me. Save it for the next poor bastard."

The guards stopped next to the table, and for an instant, Reed thought he saw a wild despair in Devlin's eyes. But it was gone so quickly he might have imagined it. Without another word, Devlin turned, holding out his hands for handcuffs to be snapped over his wrists.

Reed's gaze followed him as he was led from the courtroom. Devlin didn't look back. The attorney snapped his briefcase closed as the door shut behind his client. No one had ever told him that being a public defender was an easy task. He didn't expect it to be easy. In the five years he'd spent at the job, he thought he'd developed a certain hardness, a shell that was practically impenetrable.

But something about Devlin Russell had gotten through that shell. It wasn't anything Reed could put his finger on. There was certainly nothing soft or vulnerable about the young man. He hadn't made any extravagant claims to innocence.

He'd admitted to sleeping with his employer's young wife. He'd made no apologies for that. But he hadn't killed her. His eyes hadn't pleaded with Reed to believe him. In fact, he didn't really seem to give a damn what anybody thought, which hadn't helped him with the jury, Reed acknowledged with a sigh.

He lifted his briefcase, but his eyes lingered on the door through which they'd taken Devlin. He should drop this one. Devlin was right. The evidence against him had been overwhelming. He should just chalk this up as one of those things. You couldn't win them all. You had to learn to live with the failures.

The problem was, he believed Devlin Russell was innocent. How did you live with seeing an innocent man sent to prison?

Eight years later…

"You can tell his lawyers to take the money and burn it. I don't want it." Devlin Russell paced from one side of Reed's small office to the other.

"Think about it, Devlin," Reed suggested quietly. "I know how you feel but—"

"You *don't* know how I feel," Devlin interrupted harshly. "I just spent eight years in that hellhole. Eight years of my life gone forever. Eight years doing time for a crime I didn't commit.

"And now that old bastard thinks he can make up for it by leaving me his money. Well, nothing can make up for what he did to me."

"I didn't say it could." Reed leaned back in his desk chair, watching Devlin through narrowed eyes.

It was the first time he'd seen Devlin since he'd been released from prison less than a week before. Over the past eight years, Reed had made it a point to visit the other man. But seeing him outside the thick gray walls, he was struck by how much the years inside had changed Devlin.

Eight years ago, there'd still been traces of youth about him—a certain lankiness that hadn't yet disappeared, maybe a trace of softness around the mouth. But there was none of that now. The man in front of him was all hard muscle and barely contained anger.

"Think about it before you turn the money down," Reed said again.

"I don't want Sampson's money," Devlin said flatly. "Dead or alive, he can't buy my forgiveness. I hope he rots in hell."

"I don't think he was trying to buy your forgiveness. From what his lawyers told me, he was looking for forgiveness from a higher source." Reed's mouth twisted cynically.

"Eight years of my life gone. You can't wipe the slate clean that easily."

"Maybe not. Thankfully, that's not our decision." Reed tapped the small stack of papers in front of him. "When Harold Sampson made a deathbed confession to murdering his wife, he made you a free man. His will makes you a very rich one. In the letter he dictated, he said that he couldn't die with your conviction on his conscience."

"He didn't have much trouble living with it for eight years," Devlin said cynically.

"I'll admit that his sudden religious streak seems conveniently timed for him to meet his maker with a clear conscience, but that's not the point. The point is that you are now, not only exonerated of the crime, but independently wealthy."

"I already told you I don't want his money."

"And I'll tell you again that I think you're cutting off your nose to spite Sampson's face. The money can't give you back the last eight years, but it can make the rest of your life a hell of a lot easier. If you don't take it, what are you going to do?

"A prison record, even on an unjust conviction, isn't likely to make most employers all that eager to hire you. What kind of a job do you think you'll get? Construction? Heavy labor? I'd think you'd have had enough of that."

Devlin's shoulders shifted uneasily under the cheap nylon jacket he was wearing. Despite himself, he was starting to listen to Reed's arguments. What the hell was he going to do with the rest of his life?

"You've got a sister somewhere up north, don't you?"

"Kelly," Devlin murmured. A cloudy image of a gap-toothed, eight-year-old came to mind. An entire decade had passed since he'd seen her. She'd be eighteen or nineteen now. He'd received letters from her over the years, though he stopped writing after he was arrested for Laura Sampson's murder.

"Well, think what the money could do for her," Reed suggested. "You could become something of a philanthropist if you'd like."

"I don't think I'm the philanthropist type."

"So spend it all on yourself. Don't look on this as money to buy your forgiveness, Devlin. Look on it as the least Sampson owed you. He stole eight years of your life. The money can't give that back to you, I know. But think about what it *can* do for you."

"What happens if I refuse it?"

"The courts will have to decide what to do with it. It will probably take years because there are no obvious heirs. The expenses will mount while the will lies frozen in probate, which will make a lot of lawyers very happy. Or you can save the courts a lot of time and accept it.''

"Bloody hell." Devlin shoved his hands into the pockets of his jeans and turned to stare out the window. He'd been released less than two weeks ago, and he still hadn't quite gotten used to his freedom. The idea that he could not only look at the thick carpet of lawn across the street but actually go and walk on it if he chose was still hard to absorb.

If he didn't take the money, he was going to have to find work immediately, and he wasn't going to be able to be too choosy about what he took, either. One thing he knew, he couldn't ever work indoors again. He'd had enough of walls and closed doors to last him a lifetime.

If he took the money, he wouldn't have to worry about finding work. He could go see Kelly, go home. Not that there was much left for him in Indiana anymore. But Kelly was still there.

She was all the family he had, unless you counted his crazy old man, and Devlin hadn't counted him in a long time. With this money, he would be able to buy Kelly anything she wanted, take her anywhere she wished to go. He had a chance to make up for all the years he hadn't been there for her.

Listen to him. He was as bad as Sampson, thinking money could make up for lost time. But Reed was right. It could make life a lot easier from here on out. And he could always give the damn stuff away later.

"I'll take it," he said without turning from the window.

Reed stifled a grin and reached for the papers on his desk. The mills of the gods not only ground slow and fine, they ground out some pretty peculiar stuff. But it seemed as if they did get around to providing justice eventually.

Chapter 1

The building was little more than a shell—four walls and a roof. The exterior was still plywood, the interior contained only enough walls to provide structural support, and those walls were bare studs and exposed wiring.

Devlin Russell stood in the middle of the room that would eventually be the living room. Hands on his hips, he surveyed his new home, feeling satisfaction well up inside him. It was exactly the way he'd envisioned it.

He hadn't been sure he could explain what he wanted well enough for anyone to draw up usable plans. But Kelly's husband, Dan Remington, had suggested Michael Sinclair, and Michael had given him just what he'd asked for. Plenty of open space and lots of windows. The only doors would be on the bathroom and the closets. Other than that, one room flowed easily into the next.

Dan's company, Remington Construction, had put up the shell, but Devlin planned to do most of the remaining work himself. It paid to have relatives in the business.

The idea of having family was still new. When he'd come back to Remembrance last summer, he'd practically walked in on the middle of his sister's wedding. He'd found himself not only a brother-in-law, but about to become an uncle.

Thinking about his nephew, Clay Remington, aged nine months brought a rare smile to Devlin's lean features. He'd never thought of himself as particularly fond of children, but that was before he'd discovered his nephew's toothless smile.

Thunder cracked in the distance, breaking into his thoughts. A cool wind danced through the open doorway, smelling of rain. Devlin turned to face it, inhaling the damp scent as if it were a fine perfume. After eight years in prison, it was far more precious than any perfume.

If the scent could be bottled, it would sell for a fortune on the inside. Men who'd stab each other over a tube of toothpaste would have committed murder in the blink of an eye for just one breath of the air he was breathing now. Air that didn't smell of concrete and unwashed bodies, fear and despair.

He shook his head, forcing the memories back, locking them in a deep corner of his mind. That was behind him now. He was never going to be closed in again, never going to be shut away from the smell of rain and growing things.

Lightning flashed, an eye-searing bolt of white that lightened the twilight sky. Thunder crashed hard on its heels, bringing with it the near-silent rush of rain.

Without a moment's hesitation, Devlin walked outside, pulling the door shut behind him. Lightning split
the sky again, so close he could almost smell the
ozone. He thought briefly that it might be wiser to
stay inside. But he'd spent too many years on the
inside, too many years missing the clean feel of falling rain. Even after almost a year, being able to walk
in the rain felt like something approaching a miracle.

He shoved his hands into the pockets of his jeans,
circling around the house toward the overgrown field
that only the most optimistic individual would have
called a yard.

The rain fell in soft, heavy drops, soaking him to
the skin in a matter of minutes. The earth drank in
the moisture, sending up a dark, musty scent.

A river ran along the bottom of the field, one of
the features that had persuaded Devlin to buy the
property. The real estate agent had been careful to
point out that the water was too deep and too swift
at this particular spot to offer decent fishing. But Devlin wasn't interested in the fishing. He just liked the
idea of having a stretch of free-flowing water practically at his back door.

He'd almost reached the riverbank when he realized he wasn't the only one foolish enough to come
out in a rainstorm. Across the river from Devlin's
property was another field and beyond that, a little-
used country road. He guessed the other storm wor-
shiper had left a car on the road and walked across
the field, a long, soggy hike through knee-high grass
and weeds.

The driving rain and the approaching darkness
made it difficult to distinguish much more than a
vague shape on the opposite bank. A woman, judging

from the white dress she was wearing. She was coatless and bareheaded.

Standing too close to the edge of the bank, he thought critically, particularly with the ground soaking up the rain like it was. The ground near the edge of the river was less than stable, as evidenced by the muddy scars of innumerable small cave-ins.

Devlin started to call across to her, warn her that she was too close to the edge. But he shut his mouth without speaking. There was something in her posture that made it seem as if it would be an intolerable intrusion to speak to her.

She stood staring down at the water, her arms hanging loose at her sides, her shoulders hunched slightly forward as if bent under some burden. Something in the posture spoke to him through the careful walls he'd built around himself. Even through the driving rain, he recognized a soul deep in despair. He'd been there often enough himself to be able to see it in someone else.

He took a step back, thinking to leave her alone with her thoughts. But she was still too close to the edge of the river. Maybe she wasn't aware of it, couldn't see how unstable the bank was from where she stood.

"Hey!" She responded sluggishly to his call, her head lifting slowly, as if it were too heavy for her neck to support. Her face was a pale oval in the growing darkness, her eyes smudgy shadows.

Her despair seemed to reach across the yards that separated them, grabbing him by the throat, choking off the words of warning he'd intended to offer. She looked like a ghost, her pale face and hair taking on an otherworldly gleam in the rainy darkness.

For the space of several heartbeats, they stared at each other. Devlin blinked, forcing aside the fanciful idea that she was a figment of his imagination. She was just another lost soul. And she was standing too close to the edge of the river.

He started to call out to her again, to tell her to move back from the water. But before he could say anything, she moved, lifting one hand—toward him?

Afterward Devlin could never be sure what happened next. Did the bank crumble under her feet? Did she start to move back and lose her footing? Or did she quite deliberately step off the bank? The only thing he was sure of was that she didn't cry out. She tumbled into the rushing water as silently as if she were indeed nothing more than a figment of his imagination.

Even as the water closed over her, Devlin was wrenching his shoes off, letting them fall to the wet grass. Taking two running steps forward, he jumped off the bank after her.

He hit the water feet first, feeling the icy shock of it penetrate his jeans instantly. The current promptly tumbled him headfirst into the river. He surfaced, gasping for air, his arms flailing to keep his head above water.

He let the current sweep him along, squinting ahead for some sign of the woman. There. Only a few yards away, he caught a glimpse of something pale. He swam toward her, using the force of the current to help him.

She went under an instant before he reached her. Devlin launched himself forward, plunging his hands under the water where he'd seen her disappear. His left hand tangled in something soft and flowing, whether it was her hair or her dress, he couldn't tell. As he locked his fingers around it, the water took him under with a malicious gurgle.

He surfaced, gulping in air. One-handed, he floundered toward the edge of the river. The water was probably no more than chest deep, but the river narrowed here and the current was swift, making it impossible for him to get his feet under him for more than an instant at a time.

He grabbed hold of a tree root that protruded from the bank, pulling himself and his burden to the water's edge. So far, he'd felt no movement from the woman. She'd neither struggled against him nor aided his efforts. He wondered briefly if he was dragging a body out of the water, but there was no time to worry about it. Alive or dead, he wasn't leaving her in the river.

By the time he'd manhandled her limp form up onto the riverbank, he wasn't sure he had the energy to accomplish the same for himself. The river tugged at him, trying to drag him back under as he pulled himself out of its deceptively soft embrace.

Devlin collapsed onto the wet grass next to the woman, feeling the rain beating down on his back. It was coming in torrents now, making him wonder if they weren't just as likely to be drowned here as they had been in the river.

If she wasn't drowned already. The thought sent a spurt of energy through his tired muscles. Getting to his knees, he bent over her, pressing his fingers to her throat, seeking a pulse. He couldn't feel anything but her chilled skin.

His face grim, he ripped open her blouse and laid his ear against her chest. For a moment, he thought all his struggles had been in vain—that he'd accomplished nothing more than pulling a corpse from the rushing water. Then, so faint he almost dismissed it as his imagination, he heard a heartbeat.

Lifting his head, he watched her chest rise as she drew in a breath. She coughed weakly and he turned her onto her side, rubbing her back as she coughed up the river water she'd swallowed. What were you supposed to do for someone who'd almost drowned?

Her skin felt like ice beneath his hands. The first thing to do was to get her warm. Devlin lifted his head, peering through the rainy darkness, trying to orient himself. There were no lights to be seen. The storm clouds were so thick that no moonlight shone through.

He didn't know how far downstream the river had swept them. He shivered as a gust of wind blew the rain almost horizontally. The one thing he did know was that they needed to get some shelter and warmth.

Devlin got to his feet, pulling the woman up with him. She was limp in his hold, apparently unconscious. He bent, putting his shoulder against her midriff. Grunting with effort, he stood upright with her slung over his shoulder.

Unless the current had swept them a great deal farther than he thought likely, the house was the nearest shelter to be found.

He put his head down and started walking.

One thing eight years in prison had taught him was endurance. And determination. He didn't think about how tired he was or how far he might have to walk. He didn't think about the stones that bruised his bare feet. And he never considered the possibility that his strength might give out.

He simply walked steadily forward, using the sound of the river as a guide to make sure he didn't wander too far off his path. He'd left a light on in the kitchen. Another hundred steps and he'd be able to see it. And if not, then he'd take a hundred more and a hundred beyond that, if necessary.

The woman was a dead weight on his shoulder. He could feel her arms swing limply against his back with each step he took. He could only assume that she was still breathing.

His legs were beginning to tremble with exhaustion. Devlin lifted his head, peering through the rain. Was that a light, or was it his imagination that put it there? He took a few more steps but the light remained steady. The sight of it poured new strength into him.

Veering away from the river, he kept his eyes on the light, half afraid it might vanish as he drew closer. But it didn't vanish, and he could make out the sturdy outline of the house.

Pushing open the back door, Devlin stumbled inside. He leaned against the wall for a moment, savoring the feeling of being in and out of the rain and darkness. If he'd been alone, he would have let himself slide down the wall and collapse in a heap on the floor.

But he wasn't alone. Besides, now that he was inside, he could feel a bone-deep chill. They both needed to get warm.

Forcing his aching legs to move again, he carried his burden into the bathroom, the one room in the house that was completely finished. He bent, letting her slide off his shoulder, his hands guiding her to the floor. Stepping over her limp body, he turned the

water on in the shower stall, testing it cautiously until
he was sure he wasn't going to scald both of them.

Once the temperature was adjusted to his satisfaction, he turned his attention to his unknown guest.
Kneeling beside her on the tile floor, he began stripping her clothes off. She was breathing but still unconscious. He didn't know if that was a bad sign or
not, but he did know that she needed to get warm.

She was too thin, he noted absently. Her ribs were
plainly visible along her side, and her hipbones were
much too prominent. Her hair was long, pulled back
by a rubber band that had survived her tumble into
the river. Devlin snapped it, feeling the heavy wet
strands spill over his hands.

Once he had her naked, he stood and stripped off
his jeans and shirt. He hesitated over his briefs, wondering how she'd react if she regained consciousness
to find herself locked in a shower stall with a naked
man. On the other hand, the briefs were cold and wet
and hardly enough to reassure a frightened woman.
Shrugging, he stepped out of them, dropping them
onto the floor with the rest of their clothing.

Bending, he picked the woman up. Elbowing open
the shower door, he stepped beneath the warm spray
with her in his arms. The water sluiced over them.
Devlin lowered her feet to the floor, sliding one arm
around her waist to support her against his body.

Under other circumstances, it could have been a
highly erotic moment. A man and a woman naked in
the shower together could hardly be anything else.
Unless of course, both of them were chilled to the
bone and one of them was unconscious.

Devlin kept them both under the water until he felt
warm again. The woman had stirred once or twice,

her features puckering as if she felt the pain of returning warmth. But she didn't wake up. Devlin had the odd feeling that she didn't particularly want to wake up.

He turned the water off and lifted her out of the shower stall, holding her braced against his hip while he reached for a towel to wrap around her. Grabbing another towel for himself, he lifted her against his chest and carried her into the bedroom.

Since furniture hadn't been a major priority up until now, his bed was the only place he could put her. He set her on the mattress, easing the towel away before pulling the sheet and blanket up over her. Clumsily he wrapped the towel around her hair, thinking it would be better than letting it soak the pillow.

He toweled himself dry and pulled on fresh jeans and a sweatshirt before returning to stare down at his guest. Who was she? Had she fallen into the river or jumped? Remembering those seconds before she'd disappeared into the water, Devlin couldn't be sure which it had been. Was she going to thank him for saving her life or curse him?

Shrugging, he found a heavy sweatshirt and sat down next to her on the bed. Whether she liked it or not, she was alive. And he had no intention of damn near getting himself killed fishing her out of the river only to see her catch pneumonia.

Easing her into a sitting position, he pulled the sweatshirt over her head, stuffing her arms into the sleeves, lifting her to pull the hem down over her hips. It was miles too big for her, in length as well as width, covering her past her thighs.

He noticed again how thin she was and wondered

if she was making a fashion statement or simply hadn't been able to eat. No money?

He took the damp towel from her hair and wrapped the heavy length in a dry one. From the length of it, he guessed it would fall past her waist, and he found himself wondering what color it would be when it dried.

When he stood up, he noticed the bloodstains he'd left on the floor everywhere he walked. He hadn't realized his feet were bleeding until he saw the smears of red. He remembered feeling stones biting into his feet on the walk home, although after the first ten yards, he'd stopped noticing the pain, concentrating all his thoughts on moving forward.

Now that he had a chance to think about it, his feet hurt like hell. Devlin went into the bathroom and examined the bottoms of his feet. For the most part the cuts were small, but there were quite a few of them. He put bandages on one or two larger cuts and then pulled on a pair of heavy white socks.

Leaving the woman sleeping in his bed, he went out to the kitchen and put water on for coffee. While it heated, he used a towel to mop up the water he'd tracked through the house earlier. His feet had bled everywhere he walked, leaving stains on the floor. But since it was nothing but a plywood subfloor, Devlin wasn't concerned. Carpet and oak flooring would cover the marks eventually.

His guest still hadn't stirred by the time the coffee was ready. Devlin checked her pulse. It was steady, but did it seem a little too fast? Too shallow, maybe? She should probably see a doctor. For all he knew, there was something wrong with her besides being too thin and, what, judging by the smudgy shadows under her eyes, he'd guessed was a pretty bad case of exhaustion.

He could put her in the car and take her into town, drop her off at the emergency room and wash his hands of her. But wouldn't she be terrified to wake up in a hospital, surrounded by strangers?

"Yeah, right, Russell. Like she knows you so well," he muttered aloud. Still, something in him resisted the idea of taking her to the hospital.

Before he could make a decision, the soft chimes of the doorbell broke into his thoughts. Giving his visitor a last glance, he left the bedroom. He was too far off the beaten track to get many unexpected visitors. His sister Kelly was the only person who might drop in on him, and she wasn't likely to have driven so far out in the middle of a storm.

Devlin pulled the door open, staring blankly at the man on the doorstep. His thoughts had been so caught up in the woman in his bedroom, it took him a second to shift his focus and realize who he was looking at.

'Ben.'

Ben's smile took on a quizzical edge. "Have I got the wrong night? I thought you asked me to come out tonight."

"Tonight." Devlin shook his head, his mouth twisting in a smile. "No, you don't have the wrong night. I'd forgotten. Come in."

"I could come back another time," Ben offered.

"No. This is fine. In fact, your timing is great."

Devlin took Ben's wet coat and hung it up on one of the nails that served as a coat hook until he could get around to putting a real coat closet in.

"Everyone tells me that," Ben commented, following Devlin into the kitchen. He nodded in answer to

Devlin's offer of coffee. "Why is my timing particularly great this time?"

"I have a problem." Devlin handed him a cup of coffee. He'd forgotten all about asking Ben Masters to come see him. *Dr.* Ben Masters. He'd planned on discussing a donation to the clinic that was Ben's pet project, but the other man's arrival was too fortuitous to ignore.

"Problems are my medical specialty," Ben said.

"There's a woman in my bedroom."

Ben's brows rose. "We should all have such problems."

"Yeah, well this one really is a problem. I fished her out of the river earlier tonight. She seems okay, but she hasn't regained consciousness."

"Any sign of a head injury?" Ben asked, all traces of flippancy gone. He was suddenly the complete professional.

"None that I can see."

"How long was she in the water?"

"Not long before I got to her and pulled her head up. It took a little while longer to get both of us out of the water. And it was a while after that before I got her home. She was cold, so I put her in a warm shower and then put her in bed."

"Sounds good so far. I'd like to see her."

"Be my guest." Devlin circled the breakfast bar and led the way into the bedroom.

The woman was still lying where he'd left her, but when he stopped beside the bed, he saw that her eyes were open. He'd grown so accustomed to her being unconscious that it was a shock to see her awake.

He'd turned on a lamp near the bed earlier, and in its light, he could see that her eyes were large, the color hovering somewhere between blue and green. At another time, he might have thought them beautiful. At the moment, he was struck by their complete lack of expression.

She didn't seem at all disturbed to find herself in an unfamiliar bed, with two strange men standing over her. She stared at him for a long, silent moment before her eyes shifted over his shoulder to Ben. She gave him the same silent scrutiny and then closed her eyes as if losing interest in keeping them open.

It was left to Ben to speak. Something in that wide blue-green gaze had left Devlin voiceless. He stepped back automatically as Ben edged by him and sat on the side of the bed. The woman's eyes opened again as she felt the bed dip, but she only stared at Ben with that same emptiness in her eyes.

"Hi. How are you feeling?" Ben's voice was low and soothing. He reached for her arm, which was lying on top of the covers, his fingers searching for her pulse. She watched him for a moment, as if debating whether or not to answer him.

"I'm okay," she said at last. Her voice was so low Devlin had to strain to hear it.

"Good. Do you remember your name?"

"Annalise," she said slowly, frowning as if it were an effort to remember. "Annalise St. John."

"Do you remember falling in the river a little while ago?"

"No."

"Devlin pulled you out." Ben gestured over his shoulder to where Devlin stood silently watching. Her gaze shifted to Devlin, but there was no visible change in her expression, nothing to tell Devlin that she was glad he'd saved her life.

"I'm Ben Masters and I'm a doctor," Ben continued when she offered no response. "Would you mind if I checked you over? Made sure everything was in working order?" His friendly smile got no response. Her thin shoulders lifted in a gesture of indifference.

Taking that for consent, Ben glanced at Devlin. "Can you get my bag? It's in the front seat."

"Sure." Devlin left, glad of an excuse to leave the room. Something about that blank gaze made him uneasy. It was like looking at someone whose soul had abandoned her.

Who was Annalise St. John, and what had happened to drive all the life from her eyes?

Chapter 2

"Well, it would be a good idea to run a few tests—a blood workup, maybe. But I don't think there's anything physically wrong with her that about a week's worth of sleep and three square meals a day won't fix."

Ben and Devlin were seated at the breakfast bar, fresh mugs of coffee in front of them. Outside, the rain had gone from a downpour to a steady drizzle that slanted past the windows.

Annalise St. John was asleep again. She'd allowed Ben to examine her and then drifted off to sleep, apparently indifferent to his findings.

"So what's wrong with her?" Devlin asked, cradling his palms around his coffee.

"She's exhausted and undernourished. Could be anorexia," he said, more to himself than Devlin. He shook his head. "I don't think that's it, though. If I had to guess—which I do—I'd say she either hasn't had the money for food or doesn't care enough to bother eating.''

"Doesn't care enough?" Devlin raised his brows. "I'd never really thought of food as something you had to care about to eat."

"Well, I can't be sure without seeing more of her, but I'd say your Annalise has a pretty nasty case of depression."

Devlin nearly protested Ben designating her as "his" Annalise, but it wasn't important enough to argue. "Depressed enough to commit suicide?" he asked slowly, remembering those moments when she'd stood on the riverbank across from him.

Ben shot him a quick look, his dark eyes sharp with interest. "Hard to say. Depression affects different people different ways. She seems very passive now, too passive to bother killing herself, I'd say. But that's not to say it's not possible. Is that what you think happened? She jumped in the river?"

"I don't know." Devlin lifted his shoulder in a shrug, half sorry he'd mentioned the possibility. It seemed like an intrusion into her privacy somehow. "It was getting dark, and the rain made it nearly impossible to see."

"Well, no one could say for sure but Annalise, and I'm not even sure she'd remember. She doesn't seem to remember much of anything."

"Amnesia?" Devlin questioned, startled.

"No. More like an immense indifference. Or maybe she thought I was being too nosy for my own good," he added with a grin.

Devlin's smile was perfunctory. Remembering those empty eyes, he didn't think Annalise cared what questions Ben asked. He didn't think she cared about anything.

"I can arrange to have her admitted to the hospital," Ben said briskly.

"The hospital? I thought you said there was nothing physically wrong with her."

"Depression is a treatable medical condition," Ben said.

"So she needs drugs or therapy to recover?"

"Not necessarily. There's no one treatment for depression. We'd have to do some testing. Hopefully, we could get some cooperation from her."

"Did you suggest this to her?"

"She fell asleep on me before I could mention it."

Devlin frowned down into his coffee cup. Ben was offering the obvious solution. Annalise St. John would be taken off his hands, given into the care of competent professionals who could help her deal with her problems. He could forget all about her and get on with finishing his house.

"I think I'll just let her sleep here tonight," he said slowly. "If she wants to go to the hospital tomorrow, I'll bring her in."

"Okay. Let me know how she's doing one way or another and don't hesitate to call if you need me." He drank the last of his coffee and slid off the high stool. "I've got early appointments in the morning so I'm going to head home. I'll give you a call tomorrow."

"Yeah. Thanks." Devlin stood up and held out his hand. "Thanks for everything. Send me a bill."

"I will." Ben grinned. "I make it a point to send bills to patients I figure can pay them."

"That reminds me," Devlin said, remembering the

reason he'd asked Ben to come out in the first place. "I wanted to give you a check for your clinic. Kelly tells me you're doing some really worthwhile work."

"Kelly's prejudiced because she works there part-time," Ben said lightly, watching as Devlin dug through a drawer full of screwdrivers, cupboard handles and screws of assorted sizes until he finally came up with a checkbook.

"I feel we're doing some good," he continued. "People don't think of the poor as being a problem in a small town. But Rememberance has grown a lot in the last few years, and the problems have grown along with the town."

"Well, I've been hard up against it in my time," Devlin said, ripping the check out and handing it to Ben.

"Thanks. I really appreciate this." Ben's voice trailed off, his eyes widening in shock as he took in the size of the check. He looked at Devlin. "I was about to say that every little bit helps," he said with a shaken laugh. "But this definitely qualifies as more than a little bit. Thank you."

Devlin shrugged, wishing that he'd just made the donation anonymously, as he'd done with the other donations he'd made to various charities this past year. Maybe it was because he knew Ben through Kelly that he'd felt the urge to give him the check personally. Besides, Kelly had told him the clinic needed money urgently, and arranging anonymous donations took a little time.

"I'd appreciate it if you don't mention this to anyone. Including Kelly." Especially Kelly, he thought. The last thing he wanted was for her to start asking questions about how he came to have that kind of money to give away.

"Sure." Ben folded the check and slipped it into his pocket. "I really appreciate this. To tell the truth, I was wondering how we were going to pay the lease next week. This should take care of that worry for quite a while."

Devlin shrugged, ignoring the curiosity in the other man's eyes. "Like I said, I've been up against it a time or two myself."

He shut the door behind Ben, leaving his hand on the knob as he listened to the sound of Ben's rickety old sedan disappearing down the long driveway toward the road. From the condition of the doctor's car, he thought that perhaps he should have given him a donation toward a vehicle fund.

He hoped he hadn't misjudged Ben's discretion. He hadn't told his younger sister much of what he'd done since leaving home ten years before, turning her questions aside with vague answers about traveling a lot and offering thin excuses for why he hadn't written.

She'd finally stopped asking, glad enough to have him back in her life that she was willing to accept him without question. Devlin didn't need anyone to tell him that her husband didn't feel quite the same. Dan had never said anything, but it was obvious that he hadn't bought Devlin's vague explanations.

As far as Dan was concerned, there was no excuse for the way Devlin had simply disappeared from his sister's life, ignoring the letters, leaving her to deal with their mother's death and their father's abuse.

Looking at it from Dan's point of view, Devlin couldn't blame him for feeling the way he did. The fact that he hadn't known Seth Russell was abusing

Kelly didn't excuse him, even in his own eyes. He *should* have known. He should have been able to read between the lines of Kelly's letters and see what was happening.

He shrugged, as if the physical gesture could ease the invisible burden of his thoughts. He couldn't have done anything to help Kelly even if he had known, but it didn't change the guilt he felt that he hadn't been there for her.

But the past was the past and he had other, more urgent concerns at the moment. Like an unconscious woman with possible suicidal tendencies. And the fact that he hadn't eaten since lunch, which was nearly eight hours ago.

If the former was a problem with no immediate solution, the latter was at least easily dealt with. Getting some leftover stew out of the refrigerator, he placed it on the stove and turned the burner to a low heat before going to check on his guest.

She didn't stir when Devlin stopped beside the bed. If it hadn't been for the barely perceptible rise and fall of her breathing, he would have been convinced that she was dead.

His hands in his pockets, Devlin looked down at her. There was nothing to be read from her features, nothing to tell him whether her fall into the river had been deliberate or accidental. Not that he'd expected a visible sign.

Annalise St. John. It was a pretty name—unusual. If he hadn't been there to pull her out of the river, would anyone have known what name to put on the body? Or would she simply have been buried in some graveyard, records of her death filed under the name

Jane Doe? And would anyone have cared, one way or another, including her?

She was too thin. Her pale skin was stretched taut over cheekbones that were too sharp. One arm lay on top of the blanket, and the bones in her wrist were clearly visible. He pulled one hand out of his pocket and reached down to circle her wrist, frowning when he saw how much his finger overlapped his thumb.

How long had it been since she'd eaten a decent meal? She'd had nothing with her but the clothes on her back—no purse, no jewelry, no identification. Maybe she was one of the growing number of homeless, unable to find work, slipping through the cracks in the welfare system.

Her skin was cool to the touch. Only the faint but steady beat of her pulse under his finger reminded him that he was touching a living, breathing woman and not a pale statue.

How had she gotten out here, so far from town? It didn't seem likely that she'd walked this far. Unless she'd caught a ride from someone. Or maybe his original speculation had been right. She'd left a car somewhere across the river. Tomorrow he'd go look for it, tow it back here if necessary.

He released her arm, straightening slowly, his eyes still on her face. She was fine boned. Even with the added pounds she should be carrying, he suspected she'd have a fragile look about her. Was she attractive? He tilted his head, trying to picture her with a little more flesh on her bones, a touch of color in her cheeks.

But the image wouldn't quite come into focus. He kept seeing those blue-green eyes, completely empty of expression.

He'd seen a lot of misery during his time in prison. His first cell mate had hung himself a year after Devlin arrived. But he couldn't remember seeing quite that same emptiness in Sal's eyes before he killed himself.

He shrugged the memories off and turned away from the bed. Whatever had happened to bring the woman to this low, it wasn't his problem. He'd fished her out of the river, given her a place to spend the night.

In the morning, he'd feed her breakfast and take her to the hospital or any other place she wanted to go. He'd provide her with money for a fresh start if that was what she needed. Money was the one thing he had plenty of these days. But that was as deep as his involvement was going to go.

Devlin ate the reheated stew, listening to the light patter of the rain on the roof. The weather report on the radio was promising clear skies by morning, which meant he could start on the redwood shingles that would cover the exterior of the house. And if the rain continued, there were plenty of things that needed doing inside. That was the thing about building a house, there was always work to do.

By the time he'd finished rinsing off his plate, the rain had stopped. Looking out the window over the sink, he could get an occasional glimpse of stars through the tattered cloud cover. That meant he'd be able to work outside tomorrow.

After he'd gotten the St. John woman settled, he reminded himself. He felt a mild twinge of annoyance. One thing he'd done his best to avoid, in the year since he'd left prison, was involvements of any sort.

He hadn't sought out friendships, hadn't gone looking for female companionship to ease an occasional endless night. Bitter experience had taught him that such ties, no matter how fleeting they were, could extract a higher price than he wanted to pay. Bedding Laura Sampson had cost him eight years of his life.

Not that he expected every such experience to end in a prison sentence. But it lingered in the back of his mind that he'd paid a high price for indulging a fleeting sexual urge.

It wasn't just sexual involvement he'd avoided. He'd even kept a certain distance from Kelly. She didn't know where he'd been or what he'd done in the years since he left home, and Devlin preferred to keep it that way. It was enough that he was back in her life.

Reed Hall was as close to a friend as he had. The lawyer had believed in him during the trial and had visited him despite Devlin's lack of encouragement. Reed had helped him get his bearings when he was released. But he couldn't let his guard drop completely, even with Reed.

The reserve that had been a part of him even before the trial, the wariness that was a partial legacy of his childhood, had hardened into a thick wall during his years in prison. Sometimes Devlin wondered if it was even possible to get through that wall. Cynically he doubted it was worth trying.

But apparently, you couldn't lock the world out completely, no matter how hard you tried. The world, in the form of one Annalise St. John, had arrived more or less on his doorstep.

He sighed, reaching up one hand to rub the back of his neck. By this time tomorrow, she'd be gone. He'd get her settled somewhere else first thing in the morning. Soon she'd be nothing more than a quickly fading memory. An anecdote he'd probably never tell anyone.

But at the moment she was occupying his bed, the only bed in the half-finished house. Which meant that he was going to have to find somewhere else to sleep.

An hour later, Devlin crawled into the sleeping bag he'd unrolled on the living room floor. With an air mattress under it, it made an adequate if not luxurious bed. Before he got the bed his unexpected guest was now occupying, he'd spent several weeks sleeping just like this, unrolling the sleeping bag in whichever room was least cluttered with construction debris.

Stretching out on his back, he linked his hands beneath his head and stared up at the open beams above him. He was tired. A full day's work followed by rescuing a woman from the river had left his body more than ready for a solid night's sleep. But his mind wasn't in the mood to cooperate.

His thoughts kept drifting to the woman in the next room. Who was she? He knew her name, but he didn't know anything else about her. How old was she? Somewhere in her twenties, maybe. Certainly not more than thirty. Just what had happened to drive all the life from her eyes?

It was none of his business, he reminded himself firmly. She was simply passing through his life. A week from now, he wouldn't even be able to remember her name. But he wondered how long it would take to forget those eyes. They followed him into sleep, their very emptiness asking for something he could never give.

Devlin had no idea what time it was when he woke. One thing his years in prison had taught him was the ability to go from sleep to fully awake in the blink of an eye. Sometimes your life could depend on how quickly you woke up.

His eyes snapped open, one hand groping for the crude knife that had rarely been far from his side during his years of incarceration. His fingers found nothing but the soft flannel of the sleeping bag. He blinked and drew in a quick breath. The clean scent of damp wood and open space banished the remembered mustiness of a prison cell.

His fingers relaxed and he breathed in again, slower and deeper this time. Whatever had awakened him, it wasn't immediately life threatening. He sat up, pushing the top layer of the sleeping bag away, listening to the night sounds.

There was nothing out of the ordinary. Crickets scratched out a mating call. Close by, an owl hooted, a lonely sound.

And somewhere, the sound of someone crying softly.

Devlin pushed the sleeping bag aside and stood up. The soles of his feet sent up an annoyed protest at being put to use again, but he ignored the discomfort. He'd left his jeans on when he went to bed but removed his shirt, and the air was cool against his bare chest. The crying had stopped by the time he reached the bedroom and he hesitated in the doorway.

She was still in bed. There was just enough light to make out the shape of her under the covers. As far as he could tell, she hadn't moved since the last time he'd looked in on her.

Maybe he should just go back to bed. It wasn't likely she'd want some stranger intruding on her. Devlin's fingers tightened over the edge of the doorway as the soft sobbing started again.

Go back to bed. It's not your problem. Mind your own business.

But he couldn't turn away. There was something so completely hopeless in the sound of her tears. It tugged at emotions he'd thought beaten out of him a long time ago.

She was nothing to him. A stranger. Tomorrow she'd be gone, and the day after, forgotten. Whatever her sorrows, they were nothing to do with him.

His knuckles turned white with strain as he stood in the doorway. The sound of her crying brought back all the empty, frightened nights he'd spent in his life. Starting when he was a boy, lying in bed, smarting from the bite of his father's belt and gritting his teeth against the tears he was too stubborn to shed.

He knew what it was to be alone, to feel hopeless. He'd felt the despair he could hear in her tears. And he couldn't just walk away and leave her alone.

His movements stiff, Devlin crossed the room to the bed. She seemed unaware that she was no longer alone. The quiet crying continued. He half expected her to tell him to go away. The sort of grief expressed in her tears was not the sort that invited company.

But she said nothing when he stopped beside the bed, made no acknowledgment of his presence. In the moonlight that filtered through the dissipating cloud cover, Devlin understood why.

She was still asleep. Her face was twisted with anguish, her fingers knotted on the light blanket, but her eyes were closed and it was obvious that she was not awake.

Devlin reached out to wake her but drew his hand back without touching her. Somehow, knowing that she was asleep made her tears seem more poignant. Her pain must run very deep to follow her past the boundaries of sleep.

Hardly knowing why he did it, Devlin found himself bending to gather her slight figure up off the bed. Blanket and all, he lifted her into his arms. The sobbing stopped on a caught breath. He waited for her to wake, perhaps frightened or angry at finding herself held by a strange man.

But she didn't wake. After a moment's stillness, she turned her face into his collarbone, her thin body relaxing in his hold. One hand came up to rest against his bare chest, her fingers cool on his skin. There was so much trust in the small movement that Devlin felt a quick catch in his heartbeat. His arms tightened protectively around her.

"Fool," he whispered. She didn't know whose arms were around her. She didn't know him at all. Perhaps she sensed that she was no longer alone, but it didn't matter whether it was Devlin Russell who held her or Joe Smith.

Cursing the soft streak that should have been smothered years ago, Devlin eased down onto the bed with her still in his arms. She didn't wake as he bunched the pillows up behind his back. In fact, she simply relaxed more fully, her breathing deeper now, though still shaken by an occasional half sob.

Devlin leaned his head back against the wall and stared into the darkness. Twenty-four hours ago, he'd never heard of Annalise St. John. Twenty-four hours from now, she'd be out of his life forever and forgotten soon after that. But for now, he was willing to stand between her and whatever darkness was threatening her.

Chapter 3

Annalise woke slowly, aware of the soft comfort of clean sheets, the warmth of sunshine spilling across the bed. It had been weeks since she'd slept in a real bed. She felt a vague curiosity about her surroundings, but it faded before it could really take hold.

Her eyes still closed, she tried to retreat back into the comfort of sleep, but her body wouldn't cooperate. She was awake, whether she liked it or not. Not that it made an enormous difference. Awake or asleep, the world felt more or less the same.

She opened her eyes and stared up at the open beams above her. Open as in unfinished ceilings, she noted, her gaze skimming over the unfinished plywood and two-by-fours. The walls were in the same condition. Wherever she was, the building, or at least this room, was still under construction.

Vaguely she was aware that she should feel some curiosity about where she was and how she'd come to be there. With very little interest, she cast her thoughts back to the last thing she remembered. It wasn't much. Her car had died on a country road.

She'd left it and started walking. Like everything else lately, it hadn't seemed to matter whether or not her car ran. She hadn't been going to or coming from anywhere.

There'd been a storm. She could remember the rain soaking her clothes. Then she'd been inside—in this bed, perhaps?—and there'd been a man—or was it two?

Her tentative interest faded and she let the faint memories go. What difference did it make anyway? Yesterday paled into the same gray mist that had filled most of her days since—

No. She wasn't going to think about that. The hurt still lay under that soothing gray curtain, waiting to jump out at her. It would swallow her whole if it could. She wouldn't think about it. Better if she thought of nothing at all. That was safest.

Annalise sat up and swung her legs off the bed. Her head swam momentarily and she closed her eyes until the sensation abated. She frowned. She didn't like it when she felt things. Not even physical things, like dizziness. It was best not to think, not to feel.

Opening her eyes, she stared at the room without much interest. That it was a bedroom could be assumed from the presence of the bed she sat on. Beyond that, it was mainly bare walls and huge windows. There was an archway that led to a hall on one side of the room. On the other was a door, the only one in sight. She assumed that led to a bathroom.

She was wearing a man's sweatshirt beneath the sheets, her clothes nowhere in sight. She didn't wonder how she'd come to be that way. Whoever had put her in the big bed had obviously done her no harm. There was a white terry bathrobe draped across the foot of the bed and Annalise reached for it.

She'd just as soon stay where she was, but she doubted she'd be left alone for long. Experience told her that someone always came along, poking and prodding, asking her how she felt, wanting to know what she was thinking. She'd learned to avoid the county shelters for just that reason. It was easier to sleep in her car than to have to deal with all the questions and concerned looks.

The robe was large enough to go twice around her thin body. The hem dragged on the floor around her feet. It had been a long time since she'd concerned herself with how she looked. She cinched the belt tightly about her waist, pulling her thick hair out of the collar to let it straggle down her back.

Once the robe was secured, she hesitated over what to do next. What would she be expected to do? She puzzled over that for a moment. It was important to act like other people. If you acted different, it drew attention. And it was best not to draw attention.

She could smell coffee. She followed the scent toward the archway, her step reduced to an awkward shuffle by the hem of the robe.

A sixth sense had told Devlin his guest was awake even before she appeared across the breakfast bar from where he was sitting. Though it was barely eight o'clock, he'd been up since five. He'd had three hours to convince himself that the woman sleeping in his bed—who'd spent a good portion of the night in his arms—was nothing more than a minor inconvenience in his life. As soon as she woke, he'd find out where she'd come from or where she'd been going and see her on her way. End of story.

Which didn't explain the odd tightness he felt in his chest when he heard her stirring in the bedroom. He scowled at the book he'd been reading over breakfast. He'd found the biography of Catherine the Great quite enough to absorb his attention until now. Suddenly, a long-dead empress couldn't keep his attention from drifting to the waif he'd fished out of the river the night before.

He knew the precise instant that she left the bedroom, but he didn't lift his head from the book. He'd had plenty of time to familiarize himself with his guest's features over the past twelve hours or so, still he was reluctant to see her awake. Alive. It might make her real in a way he'd prefer not to see. He didn't want to see her as a real person. It was much simpler to view her as a package he had temporary care of.

He couldn't just pretend she wasn't there. Devlin lifted his head slowly as she stopped on the other side of the breakfast bar. His robe was ludicrously big on her. It wrapped around her thin torso more like a blanket than a garment. One side had slipped down to reveal her collarbone. There was something very vulnerable about that wedge of pale skin covering the too-prominent bone.

His eyes lifted to her face. He realized he'd made a mistake in assuming that seeing her awake and conscious was the same as seeing her *alive*. Except for the fact that her eyes were open, her face was the same pale, emotionless oval it had been.

The eyes that should have given her features life

were just as empty as they had been the night before when Ben Masters had been here. They were blue-green, widely spaced and thickly lashed. The kind of eyes a man could drown in.

He'd heard that one's eyes were windows to their soul, revealing who the person was. Annalise St. John's eyes were nothing but beautiful mirrors, reflecting only his own image back at him.

He blinked and drew his eyes away, uncomfortable under that expressionless gaze.

"Have some coffee," he said, by way of greeting. He reached out to snag the pot. He lifted a cup off the rack that sat on the tiled bar and poured it full of steaming black brew, pushing it toward her. "Black okay?"

"Yes." She stared at the cup as if not quite certain what to do with it.

"Pull up a stool," Devlin suggested. She did as he suggested, pulling a stool from under the counter and sitting down across from him. He waited, but she didn't say anything. She just sat there, her hands in her lap, her eyes on the coffee cup.

"I've got tea, if you'd prefer it," he said, when the silence had stretched.

She reacted slowly, lifting her head to stare at him with those beautiful, expressionless eyes. "Coffee is fine."

She reached for the cup, lifting it to take a sip. He had the feeling she'd taken a drink more because he seemed to expect it rather than because she had any interest in the coffee.

"How are you feeling?"

"I'm fine, thank you."

"You could have taken a chill," Devlin said, watching for some reaction.

"I'm fine," she repeated as if it were a phrase she'd learned from an English translation book.

"From the river, I mean."

"River?" The word rose at the end, indicating a question, but there was no flicker of interest in those smooth features.

"Don't you remember?"

"I'm not sure." This time, her look was wary. It made him think of a small animal who'd learned to suspect a trap close on the heels of any kindness.

"You fell in the river yesterday. Last night, really. Or you jumped," he added deliberately, thinking to spark some reaction.

But she only blinked slowly, digesting his words as if they were about someone else. "I don't remember."

It was left to Devlin to interpret just what it was she didn't remember. Did she not remember being in the water at all? Or not remember whether she'd jumped?

"I pulled you out."

"Oh. Thank you," she added politely.

And that seemed to be the extent of her interest in the whole subject. Devlin wanted to take her by the shoulders and shake her out of the apathy that seemed to have swallowed every spark of life in her.

He wanted to call Ben and tell him to come get Ms. Annalise St. John. Take her to the hospital. Take her and sell her to white slavers. He just wanted her off his hands and out of his life. He didn't need the kind of aggravation she provided. He didn't need anything or anyone disturbing the hard-won tranquility he'd achieved in his life.

"You look like you could use something to eat," he said abruptly.

He got up without waiting for a response, if she had one. It was obvious that, for the moment at least, the best way to deal with his houseguest was to simply take charge. He didn't know whether she'd ever been capable of making decisions, but she didn't show any ability in that direction right now.

He'd get some food into her and then decide what the next step should be. One thing was certain, he wanted her off his hands as soon as possible.

Annalise dabbled her spoon in the bowl of hot cereal Devlin sat in front of her. He'd told her his name while he was preparing the cereal. Maybe she should have asked before that. Devlin Russell. She should remember that. He'd think it odd if she didn't.

She knew her responses hadn't been what he'd expected. She could see that much in his eyes. She tried to remember how she should act. How she would have reacted a year or two ago. But that time seemed centuries ago. It was hard to stretch her memory back that far. She abandoned the effort.

She caught Devlin's eyes on her and dipped into the cereal, spooning up a mouthful and swallowing it without tasting it. He'd been kind to her. The thought penetrated the haze of confusion that seemed to surround her these days.

He'd pulled her out of a river, he'd said. That had been kind of him. He couldn't have known that it really didn't matter one way or another. There was no one to care, no one to mourn her death. Least of all her.

There'd been times when she'd thought it would be nice if the haze simply deepened and darkened, sucking her into its depths, swallowing her forever. He'd said she might have jumped into the river.

She frowned down at the cooling cereal, trying to remember the night before. But she couldn't remember anything clearly beyond her car dying. And then there'd been the rain. Or had it been more than rain? Did she remember being in the water? A strong arm snatching her up into the air?

She shook her head. She was tangling memories with imagination. She didn't remember falling into the river. Or jumping? No. She didn't think she'd jumped. If she'd wanted to take that way out, she could have done it a long time ago. It wasn't a fear of death that had stopped her. It was just a feeling that killing herself would hardly be worth the effort. She was all but dead anyway.

Wasn't she?

Devlin watched the faint expressions chase across her face, but he couldn't read anything from them. At least they proved she wasn't an android. He'd begun to wonder, half expecting her to turn down the cereal in favor of a lube and an oil change.

He shook his head at the absurdity of the thought. Maybe he'd been spending too much time alone lately. Maybe he'd just forgotten what the rest of the world was like. But he didn't think Annalise's reactions were normal, no matter how long he'd been away from the real world.

She seemed to sense him watching her. She looked

up, a faint frown creasing her wide forehead. Devlin waited for her to speak, but she returned her attention to the cereal without saying anything.

As soon as she was done eating, he'd ask her what she wanted to do, where she wanted to go. If she didn't know, then he'd call Ben Masters and let him come deal with the problem.

But somehow, once she was done eating, he found himself providing her with an old shirt of his and a pair of sweatpants to put on. She accepted the clothes with the same polite thank-you she'd offered for his saving her life. One seemed to mean just as much as the other to her.

And then, he really did want to get started on the shingles. There was no rush to call Ben. He certainly wouldn't be able to dash out right away. It would probably be better to wait until lunchtime anyway.

Maybe all Annalise needed was a little time. Maybe she was still feeling the effects from her fall into the river, though she didn't even seem to remember it. A few hours one way or another wouldn't make any difference.

Devlin kept an eye on her from his perch on the ladder. Certainly no host could complain about her being an overly demanding guest, he thought with a half smile. She'd put on the clothes he gave her and settled herself on the half-finished front porch. She'd been there for two hours now, and as near as he could tell, she hadn't moved in all that time.

She hadn't questioned his allowing her to stay. There wasn't any arrogance about her acceptance of his hospitality. If he'd told her to leave, he was sure she'd have accepted that with the same indifference. She just didn't care where she was.

She sat in the lawn chair that constituted his full supply of outdoor furniture, her hands in her lap, her feet neatly together, and stared at nothing in particular. For a while, it had been interesting to try to guess how long it would be before she moved. But for the past hour, he'd found himself watching to see if she was still breathing.

Depression, Ben had suggested. Comatose seemed like a better description. Devlin set a shingle in place and steadied a nail for the hammer blow. Out of the corner of his eye, he could see Annalise, still as a statue. Was it possible for someone to sit down and simply go into a coma?

Distracted by the thought, he brought the hammer down, missing the nail by an inch and his thumb by a much less comfortable margin. Startled, he released the nail, and both it and the shingle dropped past the ladder to join the debris on the ground.

The curse he muttered was succinct and obscene. He glared at Annalise. She couldn't just sit there. That was all there was to it.

She didn't stir as he climbed down the ladder. It wasn't until he stopped on the porch directly in front of her that she seemed to become aware of his presence. She blinked slowly and tilted her head to look up at him.

"Can you do me a favor?"

The question seemed to confuse her. He didn't know if it was because she didn't understand him or because she couldn't imagine what favor she could do him.

"A favor." It was more a flat repetition than an agreement, but Devlin took it as such. Maybe if she had a reason to do something, she'd come out of that damned shell a little.

"I'm expecting something in the mail," he lied without hesitation. "Could you walk down to the end of the road and see if it's here yet?"

She blinked at him again, her eyes going from his face to the smooth dirt road that stretched out behind him.

"I'd appreciate it," he said, in case she was thinking of refusing. In truth, he doubted she was thinking anything at all.

After a moment, she nodded. It took a moment more for her to stand up and move uncertainly off the porch. She seemed slightly confused to find herself doing something more than staring into space.

Devlin frowned, wondering if he should have left her alone. He probably should have called Ben first thing this morning. It was obvious she had real problems. Maybe a hospital would be the best place for her, someplace where people understood what she was thinking, what she was feeling. But he couldn't quite separate hospital and prison in his mind. And the last thing he wanted was to be a part of anyone being committed—institutionalized.

It wasn't as if he'd sent her on a walk across the continent, he reminded himself. From the ladder, he could see the half mile to the end of the road, so he could keep an eye on her. And since he didn't know of any dangerous animals lurking in the fields of Indiana, the worst that was likely to happen to her was that she'd have a walk on a beautiful spring day.

Part of Annalise was aware of the beauty around her. Sunshine poured down on the empty fields, a warm golden shower that bathed everything in sight. She could feel the same sunshine on her shoulders, warming her face. But the warmth couldn't penetrate to the chill she carried deep inside.

When she'd locked away the part of her that felt pain, she seemed to have slammed the door on every other feeling. She sighed, scuffing her bare feet over the surface of the road, which was still damp from last night's rain.

She'd seen the way Devlin Russell looked at her, sensed the puzzlement in his eyes. She couldn't blame him. Sometimes she felt a sort of puzzlement herself. She could remember another Annalise, someone who'd laughed much more than she cried, someone who'd thrown her arms open to life.

She shook her head, pushing the memories away. That Annalise was gone. It was like remembering someone she'd known a long time ago. It was safer not to remember, not to feel.

The mailbox was empty. Annalise stared at it for a moment before slowly closing the door. She pushed her hands into the pockets of the baggy sweatpants and looked up and down the empty road. Should she wait for the mail carrier or go back to the house?

Before she could make a decision, a rustling in the tall grass beside the mailbox drew her attention. It seemed more than the light breeze could account for. She would have ignored the movement, as indifferent to it as she was to virtually everything else around her, but some small sound accompanied it. Not quite a whimper, nothing as demanding as a cry, it held a plaintive note that pierced straight to feelings Annalise had thought all but dead.

She moved closer and crouched down, peering into

the growth of weeds and grasses. It was impossible to see anything, nevertheless she knew the sound hadn't been a product of her imagination. She held out her hand, rubbing her fingers together coaxingly.

"Hello in there," she whispered. She scooted closer. "Who are you?"

There was silence and then a scratchy mew of inquiry.

"A cat, huh?" She rubbed her fingers together again. "Why don't you come out and let me take a look at you?"

Another silence answered her. She waited patiently, aware that her heart was beating much too fast. She was prepared to kneel beside the road all day, if necessary. She hadn't thought she had it in her to care about anything anymore, but she could no more have walked away from the animal than she could have flapped her arms and taken flight.

Another hesitant inquiry, a little louder this time, gave Annalise new hope. The grass stirred, and a pair of golden eyes peered unblinkingly out at her. There was something in that gaze, an almost human wariness that brought a tightness to her chest, as if a fist were squeezing at her heart. Or perhaps as if a terrible pressure were suddenly being eased.

"Come here, kitty. I won't hurt you. Are you all alone out here?" She kept her hand extended and continued the soft patter.

It seemed terribly important that the cat come to her. She couldn't have said quite why. Maybe something in that lonely little cry, in the need that underlay the animal's suspicious gaze, had spoken to some part of her that she'd thought numb forever.

She'd felt a tiny crack in that wall this morning

when she'd looked into Devlin Russell's eyes. He'd provided her with food, clothing and saved her life, even if she didn't recall that. He'd asked few questions, made no demands.

The cat crept a few inches closer and Annalise felt the crack widen. She'd never been proof against someone else's need, whether that someone was human or animal. It was one of the things Bill had said he loved about her and part of what had eventually destroyed their marriage.

But she didn't want to think about Bill right now. He was part of another life, part of the hurt she'd tried so hard to lock away. Right now, she was only concerned with the cat, with convincing it to trust her. Maybe she could help the cat even though she'd failed so miserably at helping herself.

Devlin looked over his shoulder and saw Annalise walking back up the driveway. She'd been gone so long, he'd begun to wonder if she'd just kept walking. He'd told himself that it was fine with him if she didn't come back—it would certainly eliminate the problem of what to do with her. But he couldn't deny the relief he felt when he saw her slight figure returning.

Maybe it was the fact that he'd saved her life; maybe it was just that she seemed so helplessly inadequate when it came to taking care of herself— whatever it was, he seemed to feel responsible for her. He didn't *want* to feel that way, but he didn't appear to have much choice in the matter.

Devlin drove a nail into a shingle and turned to look at her again. Her arms appeared to be crossed in front of her body. Her head was bent downward over them. He frowned. Had she injured herself? Fallen maybe?

He slid the hammer through a loop on his leather tool belt and started down the ladder. He was going to feel guilty as hell if he'd sent her off to get the mail he'd known wasn't there and she'd managed to hurt herself.

Devlin reached the ground at the same time that Annalise entered the yard. He started toward her, his quick, urgent strides slowing when he saw that she was uninjured.

Instead of clutching the hideously bleeding wound of his imagination, she was holding a cat. Devlin stopped, letting her cover the remaining distance between them.

Annalise stopped in front of him, lifting her eyes from the cat to meet his. Devlin felt the impact of that look like a blow to the solar plexus. This wasn't the blank stare he'd seen all morning. Her eyes were dark with concern.

"She was down by the mailbox," she said.

"She?" He had to drag his eyes from hers. He stared at the unprepossessing lump of scruffy gray fur in her arms. So she had beautiful eyes. So what. They were just eyes. Blue-green and deep as the ocean, but they were still merely eyes.

"I couldn't simply leave her there," Annalise said, her voice uncertain. "I'm sure she's hungry."

Devlin forced his attention to the cat, who was regarding him with deep suspicion from the safe harbor of Annalise's arms.

"I've got some tuna," he offered, holding out his hand to allow the cat to sniff his fingers. "She's pregnant."

"I know. Do you think someone abandoned her because of that?"

"Probably."

Distress flared in her eyes. Devlin lowered his hand, clenching his fingers against the urge to smooth the frown from her forehead. He'd thought nothing could be more disturbing than the blank lack of expression she'd worn since waking. But he was discovering that Annalise St. John was infinitely more disturbing with life in those wide-set eyes.

Annalise followed him into the house, her attention all for the cat. Devlin opened a can of tuna and emptied it onto a saucer that he set on the kitchen floor. Aside from the obvious bulge of her stomach, the cat was hardly more than skin and bones, but when Annalise lowered her on the floor, she didn't immediately rush toward the food.

She stayed just where she was, her thin body stiff, her eyes wary. She eyed Devlin, weighing the potential hazard he represented. Obligingly he moved back from the food. She hesitated a moment longer and then slinked slowly across the floor. She sniffed at the tuna and then lifted her head to give the surroundings one last careful look before she finally took a bite.

"How long do you think it's been since she last ate?" Annalise asked softly.

Devlin shrugged. "A few days, probably. She's not in bad shape, aside from being a little scrawny."

"How could someone just abandon her like that? When she needed help?"

Devlin looked at her, wondering who had abandoned her when she needed help. Her interest was focused on the cat, who was devouring the tuna with dainty greed.

"They probably told themselves that she'd hunt her own food. People like to believe that lie, especially about cats."

Annalise lifted her eyes from the cat, catching him by surprise as her gaze met his. "Do you mind that I brought her here? I should have asked."

"I don't mind." With those big eyes looking at him uncertainly, he'd probably have said he didn't mind if she wanted to pull his fingernails out.

"I've got to get back to work," he said abruptly, dragging his gaze from hers. What he really needed was some fresh air to blow away the unwelcome realization that Annalise St. John just might be a very attractive woman.

Chapter 4

Annalise spent what remained of the morning and most of the afternoon fussing over the cat. Devlin spent the same period of time trying not to watch Annalise.

It wasn't easy.

There was something remarkably appealing about the picture she and the cat made. Both of them needed more meat on their bones. Both of them had a certain bruised look, as if life had battered them a little too often. Not that it mattered to him what treatment life had handed out to either the woman or the cat.

Devlin tightened his jaw and focused doggedly on the task at hand. Up until today, he'd had no trouble concentrating on whatever needed doing on the house. In fact, he'd enjoyed the vast majority of the work, no matter how repetitive some of it was. It felt good to be building something with his own hands, something strong and enduring.

But when Annalise had tumbled into the river, she'd also tumbled right into the middle of his life. It should have been easy to ignore her. It wasn't as if she demanded attention or chattered his ear off. In fact, she was so quiet, he should have been able to forget her presence completely.

It didn't seem to work that way, however. Thoughts of his houseguest occupied more of his time than Devlin wanted to admit. He kept telling himself that he was going to ask her where she wanted to go— make it clear that he didn't mind fishing her out of the river, but that didn't make her a permanent part of his life.

He could take her into Remembrance and find her a place to stay. Or maybe she'd want to go to the hospital. Just because she was showing signs of life didn't mean all her problems were solved. She might actually welcome a chance to get some medical help.

Somehow, lunch came and went and the afternoon slowly drifted by, and he still hadn't said anything to her about leaving. He told himself that he didn't want to do anything that might turn her back into the un-responsive lump she'd been before finding the cat.

The truth was, she intrigued him. She'd responded with total indifference to the idea that she might have tried to commit suicide, yet she'd nearly cried over the plight of an abandoned animal. She hadn't both-ered to wash her face or brush her hair, but she'd carefully bathed the cat with a warm washcloth and spent hours combing knots out of the animal's knotted fur.

Maybe he missed humanity more than he was will-ing to admit. When he'd left prison, he'd wanted nothing more than to be alone. After so many years spent in forced proximity with hundreds of other men, the very idea that he didn't have to see or hear anyone else for days on end had been paradise.

He'd been content with the way he'd arranged his life. He was close enough to Remembrance to see his sister and his young nephew, the only people he had any interest in. Yet he was away from the hustle and bustle, stuck out in the country, where he might not see anyone but the mail carrier for weeks at a time.

Now, suddenly, Annalise had been dropped into his life, and he was finding that he wasn't as eager to see the last of her as he'd have liked.

Devlin let the day drift by without saying anything about finding her another place to stay. It didn't seem to occur to Annalise to worry about it. If it was someone else, he might have thought she was assuming a bit much, but he didn't think Annalise was being presumptuous.

He didn't think she'd given any thought to the matter at all. From the looks of her, he suspected it had been a long time since she'd thought much about the little details of life, like where she was going to spend the night or where the next meal might be coming from. Especially the meal part of it.

For someone who looked as if they hadn't had a solid meal in weeks, Annalise showed little interest in food. She'd eaten less than half of the roast beef sandwich he'd put in front of her at lunch. She'd fed the rest of its contents to the cat, who showed no hesitation at all about making up for lost dinners.

The sun was starting to sink as Devlin put away the ladder and his tools. It was too late to do anything about settling Annalise somewhere else. She'd have to spend the night. But tomorrow, first thing, he'd tell her that other arrangements had to be made.

When he entered the kitchen, Annalise was sitting on the floor next to the cat, who was polishing off a saucer of tuna. As far as Devlin could tell, the animal had done nothing but eat since her arrival in his home. It didn't seem possible that such a small animal could hold so much food.

Annalise climbed to her feet as he walked to the sink and started to scrub the day's dirt from his hands.

"I hope you don't mind that I opened another can of tuna. Beauty was hungry."

"Beauty?" Devlin gave the scruffy cat a doubting look. True, fed and bathed and combed, she looked considerably better than she had when she first arrived, but the word *beauty* was hardly the first thing that sprang to mind when he saw her.

"She needed a name," Annalise said. "I thought it suited her."

"She's welcome to all the tuna she wants." Devlin answered the original question and sidestepped the necessity for comment on the name.

"Thank you." Annalise watched him work soap into his hands and forearms. He had strong hands, widely palmed with long, blunt fingers. The kind of hands that made you feel safe and protected.

She looked away, focusing on Beauty, who'd finished her meal and had settled down to take a thorough bath. Watching the little cat earnestly cleaning her dull fur, Annalise was suddenly aware of what her hair must look like. She hadn't bothered to comb it, hadn't even looked in a mirror.

How long had it been since she'd cared enough about her appearance to look in a mirror? Weeks?

Months, perhaps? She reached up to pat her fingers over her hair. Glancing at Devlin, she saw that he was watching her as he dried his hands. What did he see when he looked at her? A pale, unkempt woman who was too thin, she answered herself promptly.

"I must look pretty awful," she murmured.

"I've seen worse." One corner of his mouth kicked up in a half smile. "You're welcome to use the shower and a comb if you'd like."

"Thank you." Annalise smoothed her hands over the baggy sweatpants, aware that they weren't quite steady. "You've done a great deal for me."

"Not that much." He shrugged. "I've been down on my luck a time or two myself. I ran your clothes through the washer and dryer. They're on the foot of the bed."

"Thank you." She felt as if there should be something more to say, but she couldn't find the words.

"Dinner's in an hour," Devlin said, making it clear that, as far as he was concerned, the conversation was closed.

Annalise took the hint. She wasn't sure what exactly she'd wanted to say anyway.

The bathroom was huge, with a tub the size of a small swimming pool and a separate shower stall. This room seemed the most complete of any she'd seen in the house. Ivory tile covered the shower, as well as surrounding the tub. The walls that weren't tile were painted a matching shade of ivory.

The floor was also tile, a slightly darker shade of gray. The faucets and towel racks were all brass, the golden gleam a warm contrast to the pale ivory. The towels, the bath mat and the fixtures were all a stark black. It was a striking combination. Rather stark but not cold.

Annalise showered, lathering the heavy length of her hair several times. She tried to remember the last time she'd had access to a shower and all the hot water she could stand. The last time she'd been able to afford a motel room, she thought. That had been weeks ago. She'd had that part-time job stocking shelves in a supermarket. Where had that been? Chicago?

She wasn't sure. She'd drifted in and out of so many different places this past year. Ever since— No. It didn't matter since when. She wasn't going to think about that. Not now. Not when she felt a lightening of the misty fog that had all but smothered her these past few months.

When she was at last satisfied that her hair was clean, she shut off the shower and stepped out onto the bath mat. She wrapped her hair in one thick ebony towel and wrapped another sarong-style over her breasts.

She felt warm. The hot shower accounted for only part of that feeling. This was a warmth that was more than skin-deep. Somewhere inside, a thawing had begun. The chill that had gripped her soul for the past year had eased its hold.

Maybe it was Devlin's kindness; maybe it was his asking if she might have jumped into the river the day before. Certainly the thaw owed something to feeling Beauty's small furry body in her arms, to knowing that someone or something needed her.

Annalise stared into the mirror, really looking at herself for the first time in months. She almost regretted her bravery. The mirror reflected her image back to her with merciless clarity. There was no softening of the too-prominent angles of her cheekbones, nothing to add color to her pale skin.

She looked older than she was. She was twenty-five, but she could have passed for ten years older. It wasn't anything as obvious as wrinkles that added years to her age. It was a certain worn look about her skin and the emptiness in her eyes. They looked as empty as her arms felt.

She pushed the thought away and turned from the mirror. What difference did it make how she looked? There was no one to care, no one to even notice.

Devlin was finishing up dinner when Annalise entered the kitchen. He shot her a quick glance as he slid two steaks under the broiler. It took a conscious effort to drag his eyes away. Cleaned up and with a spark of life in her eyes, she was dangerously close to beautiful.

He slammed the broiler door shut. She was still much too thin, of course. The white dress she'd been wearing when she tumbled into the river was too large. It wasn't a particularly attractive dress to begin with. A loose bodice attached to a full skirt that drooped at the waist. It looked old and worn.

But it couldn't detract from the startling improvement in Annalise's appearance. She'd washed her hair and toweled it nearly dry before combing it out. Last night he'd wondered what color it would be when it was dry. Today, he'd noticed little more than that it was lighter than he'd expected. Now he could see that it was a sort of ash blond. It hung thick and straight almost to her waist. It was the kind of hair a man could lose himself in, the kind that was made to be spread over a pillow.

"Is there anything I can do to help?" The question made Devlin realize that he'd been staring at her.

"You can finish setting the table." His tone was abrupt, made more so by the realization that it wasn't as hard as he would have liked to picture Annalise's hair spread across a pillow—his pillow specifically.

They worked in silence broken only by Devlin pointing out the location of plates and silverware. The last of the sunlight disappeared just as they were sitting down to eat. The kitchen was an oasis of light, tucked between the twilight outside and the rest of the house, which was all in darkness.

Devlin cut off a slice of steak and put it into his mouth, chewing slowly. He didn't think he'd ever be able to take good food for granted. A year on the outside and he was still deriving enormous pleasure from something as simple as a well-cooked steak.

"It's very good." Annalise's comment drew his attention to her. "Thank you," she added shyly.

"You're welcome."

She took a few small bites and set her fork down.

"I don't think I thanked you for getting me out of the river," she said slowly.

"You thanked me. Don't let your dinner get cold."

She picked up her fork and ate a little more, but he didn't need to be a mind reader to know her thoughts weren't on her meal.

"I didn't jump," she said abruptly. He shot her a quick glance, but she wasn't looking at him. There didn't seem to be much he could say in reply, so he said nothing, letting her work out her thoughts.

"At least, I don't think I did," she added, as if she felt she should be scrupulously honest.

"You don't owe me any explanations."

"Don't I?" She eyed him uncertainly. "It seems to me that you ought to know, one way or another. The thing is, I'm not a hundred percent certain myself." She toyed with her fork. "I wish I were," she said, her voice hardly more than a whisper.

He was just going to let the subject drop, Devlin thought. He didn't want to get into an emotionally loaded conversation. Whether or not she'd tried to kill herself was a matter of almost complete indifference to him.

"Were you thinking about killing yourself?"

The abrupt question seemed to startle her. She looked at him, her eyes uncertain.

"I don't know." The promptness of the answer made it clear that it was no more or less than the truth. She really didn't know what had been on her mind, in her heart.

"Does it really matter at all that much, one way or the other?"

"I should know, shouldn't I?"

"Why?"

She stared at him, groping for an answer to the simple question. *Of course,* it was important for her to know what had really happened. After all, you couldn't attempt to kill yourself and not know it. Could you? She frowned and looked away from that cool blue gaze. What did he know, anyway?

"It's just important. That's all." Her answer carried a hint of peevishness that almost made Devlin smile.

"Do you want to die, now?"

''No.'' Her eyes swept to his again.

''Then does it really matter all that much what you did yesterday? Knowing isn't going to change what happened, whether you fell or jumped. And it isn't going to change how you feel now.''

''No, but I'd still like to know.''

Devlin took his time chewing and swallowing his last bite of steak and then pushed the plate away. Crossing his forearms on the table in front of him, he looked at her, his eyes unreadable.

''That riverbank isn't all that stable at the best of times. In the midst of a heavy rain, it's even more prone to crumble. You were standing close to the edge. In fact, I was just about to call over to you and warn you when you slipped.''

Annalise digested this, feeling a burden lift from her shoulders. ''Then you don't think I jumped?''

He shrugged. ''I think it's pretty likely that the bank crumbled under you.''

''Thank you.'' Her smile was wider this time, a bit uncertain, as if it had been a long time since she'd used it.

Devlin didn't like the odd little pain that smile caused in his chest. ''Your dinner's getting cold,'' he said brusquely.

Annalise picked up her fork, more to be polite, he suspected, than because she was interested in the food. Whatever the reason, it wouldn't hurt her to eat a bit more.

God, listen to him. He was beginning to sound like a mother hen. He'd never thought of himself as a particularly paternal type, but something about Annalise brought out a long-buried urge to fuss. He'd just as soon bury it again, he thought sourly.

"Where do you live?"

Annalise's fork hit the plate with a snap.

"Live?" She repeated the word as if unsure of its meaning.

"I was just wondering if there was someone who'd be worried about you."

He was watching her face carefully and he thought he saw a tinge of relief, as if the second question was easier to answer than the first.

"No, there's no one." She hesitated but seemed to feel the need to add something. "I've been traveling for a while, actually. I don't really have a permanent address."

Or a temporary one, either, he'd be willing to bet. It would have been cruel to ask her why she'd been traveling or what she'd been doing. He might be many things, but cruel was not one of them.

"Do you have a car?" She blinked at him, as if the question was a difficult one.

"Yes," she said slowly, frowning as if the memory were vague. "It died. I didn't know what to do. So far from town and all."

He didn't believe for one minute that she had any idea of how far she was from Remembrance. He doubted she even knew where the nearest town was. But he didn't pursue the question. He neither expected nor wanted her to spill her guts to him. She was welcome to her secrets, whatever they were.

"Oh!" The sudden exclamation brought Devlin's eyes to her.

"What's wrong?"

"It just occurred to me that I haven't even asked you if you'll let me spend the night here again."

The embarrassed color that flooded her cheeks was

really rather attractive, he decided. It made her eyes seem darker, wider.

"You're welcome to stay the night."

"You must think I'm a dreadful person." She pushed her half-eaten dinner away, her distress obvious. "I've barely thanked you for saving my life. I hardly even acknowledge your kindness and then I presume on your hospitality. You should have gotten rid of me hours ago."

"Don't worry about it." Devlin ignored the fact that, hours ago, he'd been thinking exactly the same thing. "Everybody needs a little help now and then."

"But I shouldn't have just assumed I could stay here."

"I don't mind." He reached across the table, closing his hand over the fingers she was twisting together. The impact of the small touch was more than he'd expected. Her hands felt so delicate beneath his, as fragile and vulnerable as a child's.

He was torn between conflicting urges. He wanted to put his arms around her and tell her everything would be all right, that he'd keep the world from hurting her again. And he wanted to carry her into the bedroom and see just exactly what that heavy length of hair looked like spread across his pillow.

"You're welcome to stay the night," he said again. He drew his hand away casually. Annalise didn't seem to have noticed anything unusual about the moment.

"I can't offer to pay you," she said with difficulty.

"Good. Because I wouldn't accept it." He pushed back from the table and stacked their plates. He felt her eyes following him as he moved to the counter. After a moment, she stood up and cleared the table of their glasses. Devlin took them from her and placed them in the dishwasher.

"I really do appreciate everything you've done for me," she said.

"I haven't done all that much." He snapped shut the latch on the dishwasher and turned to look back at her. He really wished she didn't look so vulnerable and so uncertain. The protective shell she'd locked herself inside of was breaking up around her.

"Tomorrow, I'll get myself out of your hair," she said.

"We'll worry about it tomorrow." Devlin pretended not to see the uncertainty in her eyes. He knew as well as she did that getting her out of his hair was going to be more than a matter of simply waving goodbye as she disappeared into the sunset.

Hours later, hands beneath his head, Devlin stared up at the ceiling. The exposed beams were nothing more than deeper shadows in the darkness above him. He'd considered, briefly, putting in a ceiling, but he liked the feeling of spaciousness that the open beams gave.

But his thoughts weren't on the architecture. And they weren't on the next day's tasks. Since the day he'd decided to build a home, the house had occupied most of his waking hours, either thinking about it or working on it.

Tonight his thoughts weren't on plaster versus drywall or whether to build a deck or pour a patio. Instead, he was thinking about the woman who now occupied his bed—his comfortable bed, he amended, taking note of just how hard the floor was, even with an air mattress beneath him.

It didn't take a genius to guess that Annalise had hit rock bottom. The emptiness that had been in her eyes this morning had told of someone who no longer cared what became of them. She hadn't reacted when he'd asked her if she'd tried to commit suicide, because it really hadn't mattered to her.

When she awakened to find herself alone with a strange man, she hadn't shown any of the normal concern a woman might have been expected to feel. And he didn't believe it was because he had a particularly winning smile. She hadn't been worried about what he might do to her, because nothing could be worse than whatever she'd already experienced.

What had happened to her to drive her so low? Rape? The thought brought a slow flush of anger to his face. He'd long believed that a man who'd force a woman was something less than human. But the thought that someone might have raped Annalise brought that contempt into focus, sharpened it with a more personal rage.

He forced his tight muscles to relax. He didn't know that that was what had happened to drive all the life from her. Time enough to find the son of a bitch and castrate him if he found out that was the case.

Odd how she'd literally dropped into his life less than twenty-four hours ago, and here he was lying awake wondering about her. He frowned into the darkness. He had the feeling that he should have let Ben take her to the hospital the night before. Already he was getting involved. No matter how tenuous that involvement, it wasn't for him.

But he couldn't just walk away from her. His mouth twisted in rueful acceptance. Like it or not, he cared what happened to Annalise. She'd brought out feelings he'd thought only Kelly could stir in him. Feelings of protectiveness and concern, things he didn't particularly want to feel.

Maybe it was the fact that he'd saved her life. Maybe you couldn't save someone's life without them becoming real to you. Perhaps it was the vulnerability in her eyes. He couldn't ignore that look, the fragility of her. Physically she looked as if a stiff breeze could carry her away. But it was the uncertainty in her eyes that spoke to him.

Finding the cat seemed to have cracked her shell. Beauty. He grinned into the darkness. The name was pure wishful thinking. The cat looked like a scruffy, furry gray basketball. But Annalise had looked at her and called her Beauty. There was something ineffably poignant about that.

Thirty-six hours ago, he'd had nothing more on his mind than what color to paint the window trim. Now he had a woman who needed a lot of careful handling if she wasn't to retreat back into whatever hell she'd been hiding in when he found her; and a cat who looked as if she were about to deliver a litter of fifty any minute and in the meantime was threatening to eat him out of house and home.

Devlin shook his head and closed his eyes. Time enough to worry about both of them in the morning.

He might have been more concerned if he could have seen the half smile that softened his mouth as he drifted off to sleep. He didn't look at all like a man who'd taken on unsolicited burdens.

Chapter 5

When Annalise awoke, the first thing she was aware of was that she didn't feel as if a heavy weight were sitting on her chest, making every breath almost more of an effort than it was worth. She snuggled her head deeper into the pillow, keeping her eyes closed as she took a mental inventory.

She sensed that it was still early, probably not much past dawn. But she didn't feel like going back to sleep. She was awake and she wanted to stay awake. For the first time in months, she felt a sense of anticipation for the coming day.

A small movement alerted her to the fact that she wasn't the bed's only occupant. She opened her eyes, her mouth curving in a soft smile when she saw Beauty stretched out beside her. Annalise stroked her fingers over the little cat's head. Beauty opened her eyes, giving her an unreadable look before closing them again. The rumble of her purr made it clear that Annalise's attentions were acceptable.

Annalise's smile widened. The cat felt full of life, content with her lot. Of course, her lot was pretty darned good at the moment. She had tuna for breakfast, lunch and dinner and a comfortable bed to spend her nights in. Much the same as her own lot, Annalise thought, her smile fading.

Maybe it was time to look ahead, to try to put some order into her life. These past few months were little more than a smoky blur. She'd probably never remember all the places she'd been. But as Devlin had said, the past was past. She couldn't go back and change things. She could only move on from here.

Devlin. She'd known him only a day and still knew virtually nothing about him; yet she had the feeling that she knew him well. Something deep inside her responded to him, telling her this was a man she could trust, not just with her life, which he'd already saved, but with her soul.

Odd, for the past year, she hadn't been entirely sure she still had a soul. She'd more than half believed it had died when she'd lost the only person in the world who meant anything to her. But it seemed it had just retreated away from the black pain that had gripped her for so long.

She scratched under Beauty's chin. Maybe what she'd needed all along was for someone or something to need her again. Or maybe, she'd had to go through a period of mourning before she'd be able to respond to that need.

When Devlin had asked her if she'd tried to kill herself, he'd chiseled the first small crack in the wall she'd built to protect herself. Life had held little value for a long time, but hearing that it had almost been taken from her, perhaps by her own actions, had struck her harder than she'd realized at the time.

She sat up, dislodging the cat, who gave her a huffy look before jumping from the bed, hitting the floor with a less than dainty thud. Annalise hardly noticed her indignant departure. She swung her legs off the bed and then sat without moving, staring at the bare plywood beneath her feet.

Just where was she going to go from here? It was all very well and good that she was starting to rejoin the living, but that didn't make all her problems go away. She had no money, no place to live, no job and no prospects of getting any of them.

She fought back the depression she could feel hovering in the background, ready to swoop down and swallow her whole. Squaring her shoulders, she stood up.

There'd been a time when her optimism had been so strong it might almost have been considered a character flaw. It might take a long time to recapture that optimism. She might never regain it. But she wasn't going back to the gray emptiness that had characterized her life for so long.

She had a long way to go before she had her life in order. But she could only take it one step at a time and hope to God that there was firm ground to step onto.

Devlin had showered and shaved in the second bathroom and was cooking breakfast when Annalise made an appearance.

"Good morning."

"Hi." Devlin returned his attention to the bacon, trying to ignore the sharp pinch of awareness he felt. Damn, why couldn't I have fished a ninety-year-old lady out of the river?

"Is there anything I can do to help?" In the face of his less-than-enthusiastic greeting, Annalise's smile faded, her eyes taking on the uncertain look that made his chest ache.

"Sure. You can tell me how you like your eggs and then you can butter the toast." Devlin made a conscious effort to soften his voice. It wasn't her fault that she made him think of hot nights and cool sheets.

A few minutes later, they sat down at the kitchen table. Ordinarily Devlin ate at the breakfast bar, but he preferred to have Annalise across the table from him than sitting inches away on a stool.

She had more appetite this morning, he noticed. She was doing justice to the bacon and eggs. He waited until they'd both finished eating before breaking the silence.

"Do you remember where your car is?"

"I think so." She frowned, trying to bring better focus to blurred memories. "It died and I pulled it off the road. I remember seeing an old barn. It looked like it was about to collapse."

Devlin nodded. "I think I know the place. It's a couple of miles from where I first saw you, though. Did you walk far?"

Annalise thought about it for a minute and then shook her head. "I don't know. I...wasn't thinking very clearly, I'm afraid."

"Don't worry about it. There aren't all that many dilapidated barns around. Chances are it's the one I'm thinking of." He rose from the table and picked up both their plates. "Why don't we go take a look at your car? If I can't get it running, we'll tow it back here."

Annalise started to protest that he'd already done more than enough for her, but she closed her mouth without speaking. Without a car, she couldn't go anywhere. No doubt, Devlin had already thought of that. He was probably anxious to get her car in running condition and get her out of his hair.

They left the house a few minutes later. Devlin stopped on the porch, frowning down at her bare feet. "You can't keep running around without shoes. With all the construction that's been done on this place, the whole area is probably full of nails and bits of wire and God knows what else."

Annalise curled her toes against the floorboards. "I don't have any shoes."

"No. I suspect they were lost in the river," he said absently, still frowning at her feet. "Hang on."

He disappeared back into the house, leaving Annalise to contemplate the embarrassment of being so completely incompetent in providing for herself that she was dependent on someone else for something as basic as shoes.

Devlin was gone only a minute, returning with a pair of white sneakers in his hand. "Here. See if these come close to fitting."

Annalise took the sneakers from him and sat down on the edge of the steps. A moment later, she stood up, flexing her toes inside the slightly stiff canvas.

"They fit."

"Good. Kelly left them last time she was here. I

should have thought of these yesterday before asking you to check the mail.''

''Kelly?'' Annalise hung back when he stepped off the porch. ''Are you sure she won't mind me borrowing her shoes?''

''Positive.'' Devlin turned back, narrowing his eyes against the bright morning sun. ''She'd be glad you could use them.''

''Oh.'' Annalise followed him to his truck, aware that the shoes didn't feel as nice as they had a moment ago. Who was Kelly? A girlfriend, no doubt. The thought caused an odd twinge of something that could have been, but wasn't, dislike.

''She sounds nice,'' she said as Devlin inserted the key in the ignition.

''Who?'' He glanced at her questioningly as he started the truck.

''Kelly. She sounds nice.''

''She is. Always has been, actually.'' He put the truck in gear and started down the driveway.

''So you've known her a long time?'' They were probably practically married, she thought. Maybe he was even building the house for the two of them.

''All my life.'' He shot her a curious look. ''She's my sister.''

''Your sister?'' Annalise felt her mood lighten. Not that it had anything to do with finding out that she was wearing his sister's shoes and not his lover's. ''She lives near here?''

''In Remembrance.''

He didn't seem interested in expanding on the barebones information, and Annalise didn't pursue the topic. She doubted if he'd have told her even that much if she hadn't questioned him.

It didn't take them long to find her car, pulled crookedly off to one side of the road. Annalise felt as if she were seeing the little compact for the first time in months.

The car had been a wedding present from Bill. His family had been wealthy, and by the time they married when she was nineteen and he was twenty-two, he'd already come into two trust funds. Buying a car for a wedding gift had been nothing out of the ordinary for the Stevens family.

She remembered how excited she'd been, examining every inch of shiny blue paint, polishing out imaginary smudges on the bumper with the hem of her shirt. Now the paint had faded to a dirty gray shade and the bumpers were pitted with rust. The little car looked unloved and unkempt. Reflecting its owner, she thought bleakly.

She smoothed her hand over the cheap cotton of her skirt. She hadn't taken any better care of the car this past year than she'd taken of herself. And they'd both suffered some wear and tear as a result.

Devlin pulled his truck in behind the car and got out. After a moment, Annalise followed him. She wasn't at all sure she wanted to get any closer to the car. It held so many memories. She'd gone from happily married to single to destitute in that car. For the past few months, she'd lived in it more often than not, sleeping curled awkwardly across the front seats.

As Annalise reached the rear of the car, Devlin opened the driver's side door and reached in to pull the keys out of the ignition.

"I guess I wasn't too worried about anyone stealing it," she said uneasily, though he hadn't, by so much as a look, commented on her carelessness.

"I guess." The look he ran over the car made it clear that he thought any such worries would have been close to delusional. He slid behind the wheel with some difficulty. The seat was adjusted for legs considerably shorter than his, and his efforts to push it back proved useless.

Annalise linked her hands together in front of her, watching as he cranked the engine without result. A look under the hood didn't produce any miraculous solution. Devlin lowered the hood and pulled a rag out of his back pocket, wiping his hands as he considered the battered little car.

"Is it something awful?" Annalise asked at last.

"I don't know. How long has it been since you had a tune-up done?" Her blank look told him it had been considerably longer than it should have been. "It could just be that it needs points and plugs." He shrugged. "Or it could be one of half a dozen other things."

"Oh." There didn't seem to be much she could add to that single word. She didn't need to tell him that she didn't have the money for a tune-up, let alone the half a dozen other things it might require. He hadn't asked about her financial state, but he had known it was nearly nonexistent.

If Devlin was aware of the blow his words had dealt to her fragile optimism, he didn't show it. He looked up and down the road, frowning in thought.

"There's no sense in trying to do anything with it here. I brought a tow chain. I'll tow it back to my place."

Annalise nibbled on her lower lip. She wanted to ask him to just tow it to the nearest service station and she'd deal with it from there. But the truth was, a service station was going to want money even to look at the car. And money was something she had all too little of.

While Devlin moved the truck around to the front of her car, Annalise opened the passenger door. Her purse was lying on the floor in front of the seat, an open invitation to anyone who'd happened by. On the other hand, the purse wouldn't have been much loss. When Shakespeare wrote that "Who steals my purse steals trash;" he could have been writing for her.

Even the purse itself wasn't worth stealing. It was cheap brown plastic that had started to crack on the corners, an advertisement that its contents were no more valuable than it was.

Perched on the edge of the seat, she opened it, examining its contents as if someone might have dropped a wad of one-hundred dollar bills in when she wasn't looking. But it was the same pathetic inventory she'd been seeing for months: a lipstick she hadn't used in weeks, a checkbook for an account she no longer had, a pocketknife that had gotten damp and rusted shut, a handful of small change and four tattered dollar bills.

Her fingers trembled on the edge of a leather photo wallet, its quality a contrast to its surroundings. She hadn't opened the wallet in almost a year. The images it held were just too painful. Not that she'd noticed the pain growing any less for avoiding the photos.

Suddenly she wanted desperately to open the wallet. What if her memories had grown dim? What if she was no longer remembering clearly? After all, her memories of forty-eight hours ago were blurred. She toyed with the clasp, feeling her pulse speed with something close to fear.

"I've got everything hooked up."

Annalise jumped, her hand jerking back from the wallet as if she'd just been caught shoplifting. She slipped out of the car and faced him, the purse clutched defensively in front of her.

"I was just looking at things."

Devlin lifted one brow in surprise. "They're your things," he said mildly.

"Of course. Of course they are." Annalise forced her fingers to relax their death grip on the cheap plastic purse. He must think she was a total idiot. Not that he could have had much doubt even before this latest demonstration.

"I've got the tow chain hooked up," Devlin said, offering no comment on her odd reaction.

Annalise followed him back to the truck. She had to get herself under control. A tall order when she hadn't managed anything close to that in months.

Devlin was aware of his passenger's tension as he towed the battered compact back to his house. He wasn't quite sure what had triggered it, whether it was seeing the car or something in the ugly purse she clutched with white-knuckled fingers.

From the looks of her car, he'd consider it a miracle if it didn't need everything from the chassis up replaced. And he wouldn't bet much on the condition of the chassis. It was a wonder it had run as long as it had.

So much for getting her off his hands today. But he couldn't pretend to feel the disappointment he wanted to at that thought. The truth was, it had been rather pleasant to go out to the kitchen this morning and see that scruffy cat waiting to be fed. And it had felt good to lean against the counter and watch the sun coming up, cup of coffee in hand, and know that there was someone else in the house, someone else to concern himself with.

If he was honest, he had to admit that maybe Annalise provided the same thing for him that the cat had given her—a chance to be needed. Maybe he was lying to himself in thinking that he could make his life away from the rest of the world, that he didn't miss occasional human contact.

Not that he was particularly anxious to open his doors to the entire world or even to a tiny portion of it on a permanent basis. But it wouldn't be so bad having a houseguest for a while. She'd have time to put her life back together, and he'd get the chance to feel as if he were helping her out.

One thing he'd learned was that there wasn't much personal satisfaction in handing out sums of money to worthy charities. Oh, it helped to soothe his conscience, which still pinched over his accepting the money in the first place.

It didn't matter how logical Reed's arguments had been or how right he was, there was still a part of Devlin that regarded Sampson's fortune as nothing more than the biblical thirty pieces of silver, only he'd somehow sold himself down the river.

But Annalise didn't need his money. Or at least, that wasn't all she needed, he amended, glancing in the rearview mirror of her car. It seemed to him that what she needed, more than money, was time. Time to rest, time to heal.

Who knows, maybe in helping Annalise St. John to heal her wounds, he'd find a way to heal some of his own.

* * *

After Devlin maneuvered her dead car into position near the house and unhooked the tow chain, Annalise pulled a cardboard box of clothing out of the narrow back seat. She'd sold her suitcase to a pawnshop months ago—in Saint Louis, she thought.

She set the box on the ground and looked at the remaining items in the car. Everything she owned in the world was in that car. She doubted if all of it, including the car, would bring more than fifty dollars.

She was twenty-five years old, with no marketable skills, emotions that seesawed between optimism and despair and no idea of where she was going to sleep tonight.

No, that wasn't quite true. She hadn't known Devlin long, but it was long enough to be sure that he wasn't going to throw her out in the street. Or in this case, the field. He'd see her settled somewhere. But where?

"There's a washer and dryer in the utility room behind the kitchen. You're welcome to use them." Devlin had come up behind her with that quiet walk she was coming to associate with him. He stood looking over her shoulder at the car's rather meager contents, his expression unreadable.

"I was just thinking that it's not a lot to show for a quarter of a century." She forced lightness into her tone. Devlin's gaze shifted from the car to her.

"I've never thought it was a good idea to measure success by what you have. Possessions are the easiest thing in the world to take away."

"True. So I suppose I'm in a pretty good position since I've got nothing left to lose."

"That's one way of looking at it," he said with a half smile. He glanced down at the box of clothing.

"There's soap in the cupboard over the washer. If you need anything else, let me know."

Annalise's eyes followed him as he walked away. She bent down to pick up the box, but her thoughts followed Devlin. Did he ever smile all the way? Something more than that cautious upturn at one corner of his mouth?

It wasn't any of her business if Devlin Russell never smiled again, of course. But something about him suggested a hard-won reserve. As if he'd found that being open was too painful, that caring too often ended in hurting.

"I suppose I'm the last one to tell him different," she said, addressing the remark to Beauty, who'd risen from her corner of the kitchen to follow Annalise into the utility room.

"I'm hardly a walking advertisement for the benefits of caring about people." She dumped the clothes into the washer and started the machine. Beauty beat a hasty retreat from the sound of the water. Annalise followed her into the kitchen, bending to pick up the rotund little animal, cradling her against her chest. Beauty immediately began to rumble her approval of this treatment, kneading her paws against Annalise's arm.

Annalise carried the cat with her as she left the kitchen. For the first time since her rather unorthodox arrival, she really looked at the house, trying to envision it with the walls finished and proper flooring laid down. With furniture and curtains and pictures on the wall.

It had the potential to be a beautiful home. The rooms were big and airy, the windows occupied almost as much space as the walls, bringing the outside in, making the rooms seem even larger than they were.

Was he building this house for himself? Did he plan to share it with someone? Just because Kelly had turned out to be his sister didn't mean there wasn't a woman in his life, someone who'd had a say in designing the open floor plan, in picking out the tile in the bathroom, the kitchen cupboards.

"I don't think so," she murmured to the cat, whose eyes were nearly closed. There was something about Devlin that spoke of aloofness—an indefinable reserve that made it hard for her to believe that there was a special someone in his life, someone he let down his guard with. Someone who'd seen him really smile.

She sighed and set Beauty down. Whether he smiled and whether he had someone to share this house with were not her concern. Her concern was figuring out where to go from here. One of her foster mothers had once told her that every journey began with the first step—a useful truism. The problem was figuring out in which direction that first step should be.

With the vague idea that taking an inventory of her belongings might bring some inspiration, Annalise went back outside. She'd assumed Devlin was working on the section of the house he'd been shingling the day before. Instead, she found him bent over the engine compartment of her car, wrench in hand. Two spark plugs lay beside him on the fender already.

He looked up as she stopped across the car from him. "Well, the plugs definitely aren't helping things any. And the points are badly burned. The oil is low and it's also filthy. It has to be changed. Your plug wires could use replacing, too. Until I can get it running, it's hard to say what else might be wrong. Maybe a tune-up is all it really needs.''

He set a third spark plug beside the other two and reached for the next one. ''I've got some things I need to pick up in town this afternoon. I'll get the parts while I'm there.''

''You can't!'' The worlds came out more forcefully than she'd intended. Devlin straightened away from the car, resting his greasy hands on the fender as he looked at her.

''If you're worried about the money, forget it.''

''I can't forget it. You've already done so much for me.''

''I haven't done that much, and the cost of a few parts isn't going to cause me any problems.''

''That's not the point,'' she insisted, her voice nearly strangled with embarrassment. ''I can't just keep on taking and taking from you. You saved my life. You've taken care of me. You don't even know me.''

''Look, we went over this before. You thanked me for saving your life. And as far as taking care of you goes, I haven't done anything incredible. A place to sleep and a little food aren't going to get me nominated for sainthood.''

Annalise twisted her hands together in front of her, struggling for the words to make him see how she felt. All her life, she'd always taken her fair share of any work that was to be done. Her parents had been killed in a car wreck when she was eight and she'd been put in foster care. One thing she'd quickly learned was that it made her life easier if she did her best not to be a burden to anyone.

It was a lesson that had carried on into her adult life. She'd continue to work after she and Bill were married, not because they needed the money but because she had to know that she was pulling her own weight, even if it was in low-end secretarial jobs that didn't pay that much.

Bill had laughed and said he didn't care what she did as long as she as happy. But she didn't think Bill had ever understood just why she needed her "little job," as he'd called it. If Bill hadn't been able to understand, even when he'd loved her, how was she supposed to make Devlin understand?

But Devlin did understand. More than she could have imagined. The need to be beholden to no one was something he understood very well. From early childhood on, he'd known what it was to have only himself to depend on. His father had been abusive. His mother had simply retreated into another world where unpleasant things didn't happen, and Devlin had learned to survive without depending on either of them.

"I wasn't going to mention this yet, but it looks like now is as good a time as any." He tossed the greasy rag down and leaned one hip against the front of the car, crossing his arms over his chest and fixing her with a cool blue gaze.

"Mention what?" He was probably going to tell her that he'd really hoped to get her out of his hair by now or that her car positively needed a complete overhaul. She dropped her hands to her sides, concealing their trembling in the folds of her skirt.

"How are you at organizing?"

"Organizing?" The question was so far from what

she'd been expecting that he might have been speaking a foreign language.

"And dealing with people on the phone?"

"I...I used to do secretarial work," she said slowly. "And I worked as a receptionist for six months."

Devlin nodded thoughtfully. "Sounds good."

"Good for what?" She hardly dared to hope that it might be what it sounded like. If he knew of a job...

"Are you interested in going to work?"

"Yes." She gripped the folds of her skirt, trying to contain the hope that was welling up inside. Just because he knew of a possible job, it didn't mean she'd be qualified for it. After all, she hadn't worked steadily in almost three years. And it wasn't as if her qualifications had been stunning before that.

"Good. I need someone to deal with suppliers for me and to organize the paperwork on building the house. I've been throwing everything in a drawer. I can offer you room and board and a reasonable salary."

The figure he named seemed more than reasonable, when you added in room and board. Annalise swallowed the urge to shout an acceptance.

"You don't have to invent a job for me," she told him, her chin lifting in an unconscious gesture of pride. "If there's something I can help you with, I'd be happy to do it. There's no need to pay me."

"Not very practical of you," he commented, arching one brow. "Besides, I always believe in paying someone who works for me."

"But you've already done so much for me," she protested.

"We've already talked about that." He waved one

hand to dismiss the issue. "I could use someone to handle the paperwork and the suppliers. Do you think you could do it?"

"Yes." She nodded slowly. The kind of work he was describing wasn't difficult, and it was similar to jobs she'd held in the past.

"But you don't have to pay me for it. Room and board would be more than enough."

"The salary goes with it," he said flatly. "That's my offer, take it or leave it."

Annalise stared at him, wondering how it was possible to feel so much gratitude toward someone and, at the same time, have the urge to smack them. He knew she didn't have a real choice. What else could she do? It occurred to her to wonder if she was crazy to be upset with him for being *too* generous.

"All right," she said at last. "But don't think I'm not going to earn my keep."

"I wouldn't think that." Though his expression was solemn, Annalise could see the smile in his eyes. He held out his hand and she put her own into it. His fingers closed over hers, warm and strong.

Annalise smiled, hoping he couldn't feel the way her pulse had accelerated. Nerves, she told herself. It was just nerves.

Chapter 6

When Devlin got back from town that afternoon, he had not only car parts and the nails he'd needed for the shingling, but also a new bed and a small chest of drawers.

Annalise had started out with great plans to begin work immediately on the rather large box of papers he'd handed her before he left, but sometime around one o'clock, she'd found herself nodding off at the table. She'd settled onto the sofa to rest just for a moment and didn't wake until Devlin pushed open the front door two hours later.

Startled, she jerked upright, staring at him dazedly as he carried a mattress through the living room and into one of the unfinished rooms off it. He passed by her again, nodding to her as he disappeared out the door.

Annalise pushed her hair off her face, trying to shake off the thickheaded feeling that was an inevitable result of sleeping in the middle of the day. She had only partially succeeded when Devlin entered the house again, this time with a box spring balanced on his back.

She cleared her throat as he reappeared. "What was that?"

"A bed," he said, and disappeared out the front door.

Annalise blinked. A bed. Of course. Why hadn't that occurred to her? She'd thought it might be a rhinoceros.

This time, when he came back in carrying pieces of a bed frame, she followed him. He put the pieces on the floor and pulled a screwdriver out of his pocket before kneeling down to begin assembling the frame.

"What are you doing?"

He shot her a look that said he was beginning to have doubts about her intelligence. "I'm putting together a bed frame."

"I know that. *Why* are you doing it?"

"Because it won't hold the box spring and mattress unless it's put together."

He was being deliberately obtuse. She knew it and he knew it. He was hoping she'd drop the subject and the argument he sensed she was going to offer.

"Did you buy this bed for me?" Obviously the only way she was going to get a real answer was to ask the real question.

"Generally, when you're offered room and board, the room includes a bed," he said without looking up from the task at hand.

"I could have slept on the sofa," she protested, distressed that he'd spent money on her.

"No, you couldn't."

"Then, you can take the cost of the bed out of my salary."

"No."

The blunt refusal silenced her momentarily. She stared at him, searching for something to say. When the silence stretched, Devlin looked up. Seeing the distress in her face, he put down the screwdriver and stood up.

"Look, don't make a bigger deal out of this than it is. I'd planned on this being a spare bedroom," he lied without hesitation. In truth, he'd been thinking of putting exercise equipment in this room. "It can't be a spare bedroom without a bed. I just bought the bed a little sooner, that's all."

"It seems like I've already taken so much from you," she said unhappily.

"Like what? You don't eat as much as that cat. Besides a few ounces of food, what have I given you?"

"It's not material things I'm talking about."

"Well, the bed is very material and I'm not taking it back and you're not sleeping on the sofa. I'm going to put this together and then you can sleep standing up in the closet if you'd prefer."

Annalise recognized defeat. "At least, let me cook dinner."

"Can you cook?"

"Yes."

"Then the kitchen is all yours."

It wasn't until she went to bed that she realized that a bed wasn't the only thing Devlin had bought. A small chest of drawers sat against one wall and a thick throw rug had been placed next to the bed so that her feet wouldn't encounter the wooden subfloor first thing in the morning.

There was a set of sheets and two pillows placed neatly in the middle of the new mattress. And not just plain white sheets, either, she saw when she opened them. They were off-white with a delicate sprinkling of lavender flowers scattered over them. There was a night table and a simple porcelain lamp beside the bed.

The small bathroom that opened off the room had been stocked with soap, shampoo and towels. There was even a bottle of bubble bath sitting on the edge of the tub.

Annalise picked the bottle up and opened it, inhaling the light floral scent. She put the lid back on, feeling tears sting the backs of her eyes. It was too much. The job, buying parts for her car, furnishing a room for her, buying her bubble bath. He'd just done too much.

She knew better than to argue with him anymore, though. It wouldn't get her anywhere. He could hardly return the bubble bath, anyway. She was just going to have to make sure she proved worthy of the efforts he'd gone to. She didn't want him to ever have cause to regret all he'd done for her.

She bent to turn on the taps, adjusting the water to something just short of scalding. It had been a long time since she'd had a chance to soak in a luxuriously full tub.

Sprawled in a big leather recliner in the master bedroom, Devlin heard the hum in the pipes as Annalise turned the water on. He was aware of an almost imperceptible easing of tension. He'd more than half expected her to protest when she saw that there was more than a bed in the room.

Actually, a bed was all he'd planned to buy, but it had occurred to him that she could hardly keep her clothes in that pathetic cardboard box. As an inveterate reader, he considered a lamp by the bed to be essential, which meant he had to get a table to put it on.

The bed required sheets, and while he was buying sheets, he'd realized that the bathroom had no towels. From there, it had been an easy step to soap and shampoo.

He leaned his head back, his book forgotten. He couldn't quite remember when he'd enjoyed shopping as much as he had this afternoon. Not that he hadn't derived a definite satisfaction in choosing the things that had gone into the house right from the start. But it hadn't been quite the same.

He'd found himself wondering what Annalise's taste was like. Would she prefer a floral design on her sheets or did she like the sharp edges of geometrics? What colors did she like?

He heard her shut the water off. She'd be stepping into the tub now. She'd probably pinned her hair up on top of her head, but there'd be a few tendrils that managed to escape. The bathroom would be slightly steamy, lending a soft-focus look to her pale skin.

He closed his eyes, wishing he didn't know quite so clearly what she looked like without her clothes. Odd, how when he'd had her naked in the shower with him, he'd felt not the slightest trace of sexual awareness. His only concern had been to get her warm, and he'd thought he noticed little more than that she was too thin.

But suddenly, he was remembering other things. Like the softness of her breasts pressed against his arm, the sleek length of her legs, the intriguing triangle of curls at the top of her thighs.

He shifted uncomfortably in the chair, his eyes snapping open. His jeans were suddenly too tight. With a groan, he stood up, dropping the book onto the bed as he strode to the window.

He was acting like a randy teenager, getting hard just because a woman happened to be taking a bath a couple of rooms away. He'd had eight years to conquer his random sexual urges, eight years to contemplate the high cost of his carelessness about whom he slept with.

And in the year since leaving prison, he'd managed to maintain that iron control. Sexual release wasn't worth the potential price it extracted. He'd channeled everything he had into building this house, into purging himself of eight years of hell.

It wasn't as if he hadn't seen women he found attractive this past year. He'd contemplated the advantages of establishing a pleasant, no-strings-attached relationship with some mature woman, based on little more than satisfying a mutual physical need.

But he hadn't quite figured out how to go about establishing such a relationship—he could hardly take out an ad. Besides, sooner or later, most women wanted something more. They generally craved the kind of emotional ties he could never give.

So he'd clamped the lid on his sexual needs. He hadn't found it all that difficult. Until now. Maybe it was the vulnerability in Annalise's eyes or the way she nibbled on her lower lip when she was thinking. Or maybe it was the fragile build of her that made him want to see if his hands could span her waist or just how neatly her breast would fit his palm.

He wanted to see her wearing nothing but that extravagant length of hair draped over her body. He wanted to wind his fingers in it and pull her close. He wanted to feel her mouth parting under his and her thighs opening to accept him into her.

"Damn!" The word was a groan. Devlin spun away from the window, forcing the images from his mind. He had to think of something else. Like whether or not he had enough shingles to finish the house or what color to paint the living room.

Or the soft glow of Annalise's skin as she stepped from the bath.

Growling a low, frustrated curse, he strode from the bedroom, turning toward the back door. Once outside, he drew in a deep lungful of cool night air. A brisk walk. That was what he needed. A nice brisk walk. In ten or twelve miles he'd have managed to forget all about the woman he'd just asked to live in his house for an indefinite period of time.

Annalise awoke to discover she was sharing her pillow with a purring cat. Seeing that she was awake, Beauty stood up, chirped a greeting and jumped off the bed, hitting the floor with a thump. The sound made Annalise smile. So much for the silent slink of the cat. Of course, Beauty was at a bit of a disadvantage at the moment. It was probably pretty hard to slink with a belly the size of hers.

Her smile faded, one hand creeping to her flat stomach. She snatched her fingers away, forcing her thoughts to focus solely on the coming day. Today she was going to get started on proving to Devlin that

she was something more than a charity case. He'd
hired her to organize his records and deal with suppliers, and that was just what she was going to do.

It was the most content day Annalise had spent in
months. Not only did she have a roof over her head
and a job, she felt as if she were getting herself back.
She was starting to recover the determined optimism
that had kept her going through assorted foster homes
and life's assorted curves.

She'd fallen about as low as it was possible to get
this past year, but she wasn't going to dwell on the
past. Neither was she quite ready to look too far into
the future. But she could focus on each day as it
came, which was a step up from where she'd been
for so long, when one day had meant nothing more
or less than the last.

She spent the morning sorting receipts into neat
little piles on the breakfast bar. She paused long
enough to make sandwiches for lunch, taking Devlin's out to him when he showed no sign of stopping
for the meal. He accepted the plate from her with a
quiet thank-you. Annalise didn't linger, sensing that
he preferred to eat alone.

The afternoon was a continuance of the morning,
with stacks of receipts soon covering the tiled bar. It
was starting to register that Devlin had already spent
a small fortune on the house. Everything had been
paid for outright, whether it cost three dollars or three
thousand.

Just where had he gotten this kind of money? she
thought, fingering the bill for the fixtures in the master
bath. She hadn't given it much thought until now, but

he'd made no mention of going to work. His only work seemed to be on the house.

Maybe he just happened to be on vacation at the moment and was using the time to get some work done on his house? She frowned. Possible, but she didn't think so. Wouldn't he have made some mention of that when he asked her to work for him?

And come to think of it, how many people could afford to hire someone to sort receipts and deal with suppliers? She didn't doubt that he'd invented the job to help her get on her feet and she appreciated the generosity, nevertheless that sort of generosity didn't come cheap. The salary he had offered her wasn't extravagant, but it was more than a pittance.

It was none of her business, of course, where his money came from. Yet she couldn't help but be a bit curious. An inheritance, perhaps? Maybe his parents had been wealthy, like Bill's.

But Devlin didn't have any of the vaguely privileged air that had been so much a part of Bill. There'd been a sort of naiveté about her former husband that stemmed from his inability to believe that life didn't just naturally go the way he wanted it to. Bill had always been surprised and a little hurt when things went wrong.

There was nothing of that about Devlin. On the contrary, there was a certain wariness about him, as if he regarded life as more of an adversary, something he couldn't really afford to trust.

She put down the receipt, reminding herself again that Devlin's finances were not her concern. He'd asked her to organize his receipts, not handle his checkbook. But a little judicious probing couldn't do any harm.

* * *

"You really can cook." Devlin took another bite of fried chicken as if confirming the truth of his comment.

"You seemed to enjoy the pasta salad last night," Annalise reminded him. "Did you think that was all I could make?"

"Well, it could have been a fluke."

Perched on a ladder ten feet off the ground for most of the day, Devlin had had plenty of time to consider his understandable but unwanted reaction to Annalise. And he'd decided that the only way to handle it was to ignore it.

Part of the problem was simply that he wasn't accustomed to having an attractive woman constantly underfoot. Familiarity didn't only breed contempt. It also bred—well, familiarity. In a few days, he'd hardly notice Annalise as a woman.

It had all sounded quite simple when he was thinking about it this afternoon. Now, looking at the soft oval of her face, he felt a twinge of doubt. Maybe the air was thinner near the roofline and it had affected his brain.

It was hard to envision noticing Annalise St. John as anything other than a woman. There was something so feminine about her. It was there in the soft line of her jaw, in the delicate line of her neck.

He dragged his eyes away from her, frowning down at his plate. It was a simple matter of mind over libido.

"Do you have any family besides your sister?"

Annalise's question dragged Devlin's attention from his increasingly tangled thoughts. She was looking at him expectantly.

"Besides Kelly?" It took him a moment to shift

gears. "No. Our mother died when Kelly was twelve."

"That's a tough age to lose a mother. How old were you?"

"Twenty-two. I'd already left home." *And had just started serving time for murder.* But there was no need to tell her that.

"What about your father? Did your sister stay with him?"

"What is this? Twenty questions?" Devlin pushed his plate away, contained violence in the gesture. He didn't like being reminded that Kelly had been left alone with that crazy old man. He didn't like remembering how badly he'd failed her when she'd needed him.

"I'm sorry." Annalise set her fork down, her appetite vanishing at his quick flare of anger. "I didn't mean to be nosy."

"No, wait." Devlin's hand closed over her wrist when she started to rise. "I'm the one who's sorry. I shouldn't have snarled at you like that."

"I didn't mean to pry." The smile she gave him held an edge of uncertainty that made Devlin's anger turn inward.

"You asked a perfectly normal question. You just...touched a nerve. That's all."

"I'm sorry."

She didn't say anything else, didn't give him an anticipatory look, didn't do anything to imply that she expected more of an explanation than he'd given. So why was it that he found himself talking again?

"Kelly was left with our...father." It was hard to say the word, hard to connect it with the harsh old man he remembered.

As far back as he could recall, it had been impossible to think of Seth Russell as his father. Fathers played softball with their sons and taught them how to drive. They didn't beat six-year-olds nearly unconscious, purging them of their sins.

"He was abusive," he said.

"How awful. Did he abuse you?"

"Yes." The simple word held a wealth of old memories, old hurts. "But he never hit Kelly. I stayed as long as I did because of Kelly, and he never hit her in all those years."

"How old were you when you left?"

"Eighteen." Devlin was hardly aware of Annalise's hand closing over his, her slender fingers trying to soothe the pain she sensed in him. "Kelly was eight. I didn't think she knew what had been happening, but she didn't cry when I told her I was leaving. She didn't ask me to stay."

"You were close?"

"Very. Mother was...well, she wasn't really around, even though she was physically there. I practically raised Kelly. I shouldn't have left. But I was afraid that if I stayed, I was going to kill him."

"I'm sure Kelly understood."

"Yeah. But that didn't do her a lot of good."

"Did he abuse her? After you left?"

"After Mother died." Devlin stood up, his rage too deep to allow him to stay still. He paced over to the back door, staring out the screen at the darkness beyond the porch light. "She doesn't talk about it much."

Annalise watched him, her eyes dark with compassion. She knew what it was to blame yourself when someone you loved was hurt. That deep-down feeling that you could have prevented it somehow. If only you'd said or done the right thing. If only...

And all the "if onlys" in the world couldn't change what had happened. She'd felt that way when her parents died, sure that if she'd just eaten her broccoli like her mother had asked her to do that last night, then their car wouldn't have skidded on a patch of ice and slammed into a telephone pole.

"You can't blame yourself," she said finally, wishing she had the right to go over and smooth the tension from his shoulders, to put her arms around him and help ease his pain.

"I can't?" He turned to look at her, his eyes dark and bitter. "I left her there. She was my little sister. She trusted me. I should have been there for her."

"Did you know what was happening?"

"No."

No, Kelly had written him cheerful little letters that never hinted at the hell she was living. She'd continued to write even when he'd stopped replying. He couldn't bear to tell her he was in prison, and he'd convinced himself that she would be better off thinking he'd forgotten her. But he hadn't been able to bring himself to cancel the post office box to which Kelly was writing. Nor to tell Reed to stop forwarding her letters. Sooner or later, she'd quit writing, leaving him completely alone.

She hadn't quit writing and he'd treasured each letter, reading them over and over again until they'd threatened to fall apart in his hands. He'd tried to imagine what she looked like as she grew from the freckled eight-year-old he'd left behind into a young woman. He'd pictured her going to dances, laughing with her friends, graduating high school.

Instead, she'd quit school rather than deal with their father's anger at her wasting her time getting an education. She'd endured his religious fanaticism, his periodic attempts to cleanse her of the devil that dwelled within every female by beating the sins from her.

She'd survived and managed to escape. She had a husband who worshiped the ground she walked on and a beautiful baby. When Clay started school, she planned to go to college.

"Where is Kelly now?' Annalise's question shook him out of his thoughts.

"She lives in Remembrance."

"Is she happy?"

"Yes." He could answer that without hesitation. "She's married and very happy."

"But you still blame yourself for what your father did."

"I should have been there," he said flatly, allowing no room for self-forgiveness.

"I seem to recall someone telling me recently that it didn't do much good to spend too much time worrying over the past," Annalise said thoughtfully. "Something about the past being past and nothing could change it."

Devlin stared at her, caught off guard by having his own words so neatly turned against him.

"Very clever," he said softly, his mouth starting to curve.

"I thought so." She looked so smug that his smile widened to something that might almost have been called a grin.

Annalise felt her breath catch. She'd wondered how he would look if he really smiled. She hadn't been prepared for the change the expression wrought in his lean features. If she'd thought him attractive before, she now realized the word was too anemic to apply. He was...devastating.

His smile revealed two deep dimples that creased his cheeks and banished the rather stern forbidding look he usually showed the world. He suddenly looked younger, approachable. The loneliness that haunted his eyes disappeared, replaced by a gleam that made them more blue than gray.

He looked altogether different, entirely too attractive. She felt a warming in the pit of her stomach that could have been, but wasn't, something perilously close to desire. She'd never felt anything quite like it before.

She swallowed hard and reminded herself that she had a life to get in order. And she certainly wasn't going to complicate the process by letting a mere sexual attraction get in the way.

"Okay, so now that you've heard my life story, what's yours?" Devlin leaned one hip against the counter and looked at her expectantly.

"Mine?" Annalise shrugged. "There isn't that much to tell." *At least not that much she was willing to tell.*

"Your parents?"

"Dead. They were killed in a car wreck when I was eight."

"That's tough."

"Yes. They didn't have any relatives who were willing to take me so I was put in a foster home." She ran her thumbnail along the edge of the table, remembering. "The Stomans. They were good people. I was with them for a year and then I went to live with the Polachecks. They had eight children of their own. Sometimes, it seemed as if they had so many kids in and out of that house that they hardly knew which were theirs, and which were friends. I'd never been part of a big family. It was nice.''

"How long were you with them?'' Devlin asked, trying to picture her as a child. Thin, long legged, her face dominated by those big blue-green eyes. She must have had long hair even then, but it would have been finer, more flyaway.

"I stayed with the Polachecks almost two years. I think they'd have kept me longer, but Mr. Polacheck's company transferred him to a new job in another state. So then I went to stay with the Johnsons. They were considering adoption. I heard them talking about it, but they decided they wanted to adopt a younger child, instead of one that was already half-grown.

"Then it was the Mannings. That was for three years. They had a horse. Then the Sanfords, but that was only for a few months. It turned out Mr. Sanford had been borrowing money from his company's retirement fund.

"I stayed in a county facility for a while until they could find another family who was willing to take me. I was pretty old by then, and it's not easy to find anyone willing to take on an older child.''

"You must have been ancient,'' Devlin agreed. "All of what, fourteen? Fifteen?''

She heard the anger he felt on behalf of the child she'd been and smiled. "It wasn't as bad as it sounds in the telling. All the families were nice to me. They did their best to make me feel at home.''

"It couldn't have been easy to pull up roots every year or two, especially for a child."

"I got used to it. After a while, you learn not to let your roots grow too deep."

Devlin made a sound in his throat that sounded suspiciously like a growl. Annalise grinned. "Don't picture me as a pathetic orphan like something out of an old melodramatic silent movie. I was always fed and clothed. No one treated me badly."

The look he gave her suggested that their definition of being treated badly might differ, but he didn't argue with her.

"So did they find another family willing to take on such an *old* child?"

"Yes. The Millers. They had two small children of their own. They used to let me baby-sit." Her smile took on a wistful edge. "They were great kids. Sara Ann was just a baby and I used to rock her for hours."

The image of Annalise with an infant in her arms was surprisingly vivid. He shook his head to dispel it.

"How long did you stay with them?"

"A year and a half. I would have stayed longer, but Mrs. Miller found out she was pregnant again and they just didn't have room for me anymore.

"I went to stay with the McCleans after that. They were an older couple and the money they got for taking in foster children helped supplement their retirement income. I stayed with them until I graduated from high school."

Devlin waited for her to tell him what she'd done after high school, but she didn't seem to have anything more to say. She was tracing aimless patterns on the table with her forefinger, her eyes on the movement.

Of course he wasn't going to ask her to continue. No one respected another person's right to privacy more than he did. On the other hand, he had to admit to being curious.

"What happened after high school?" he asked finally.

She hesitated for so long he thought she was going to ignore the question.

"I got married." She lifted her shoulders in a quick shrug, as if to indicate how dull this piece of information was.

"Married?" There was no reason he should find it so startling, he reminded himself. He knew people who'd been married and divorced more than once by the time they reached their mid-twenties.

"I was nineteen. Too young, I suppose."

"Divorced?"

"Yes. Two years ago."

Devlin hadn't realized how anxious he was to hear her answer until she gave it. The idea that she might still be married was less than appealing. Only because he wouldn't like to think of her still tied to a relationship that had obviously ended, of course. It didn't bother him from a personal angle.

No, there was nothing personal in his relief. Nothing at all.

Chapter 7

The difficulty in keeping his distance from Annalise wasn't simply because she was living in his house, Devlin discovered. What made it so hard was that he liked her. He enjoyed her company. She understood the value of silence and didn't try to fill every minute with conversation.

And the more time he spent with her, the more he wanted to spend. He told himself it was the novelty of it. It wouldn't be long before he tired of having someone sharing his home. He should start looking for alternatives. He needed to find somewhere else for her to stay, another job.

With every day that passed, it was harder to see the pale wraith he'd pulled out of the river. She'd put on weight, enough to fill the hollows in her cheeks and add to the slender curves that made it difficult for him to go to sleep at night. Her hair held rich highlights now, catching the sun and seeming to hold its warmth in the heavy length of it.

Sometimes it took a conscious effort of will to keep from sliding his fingers into her hair to see if it felt as warm and soft as it looked. No matter how hard he tamped down the sexual awareness he felt, he had only to look at her to feel it surging through him.

He was losing sleep, and there were times when he thought he might be losing his sanity. Obviously he had to get her settled somewhere else, a place where he didn't see her first thing in the morning, when the sleepy look of her eyes made him want to kiss her. Where he couldn't hear her run a bath every night and then torture himself with imagining her in that bath.

Ben Masters would be the person to call. He'd called him the day after Annalise's arrival and told him that she'd be staying with him for a few days. Ben had emphasized that Devlin was to call if there was anything he could do to help.

The cynical side of him suggested that the doctor's eagerness to help might have been aided by the size of the donation he'd made. But he didn't really believe that. Kelly had told him enough about Ben to make him willing to believe that the other man really cared. A man didn't spend as much time working with patients who couldn't pay as Ben did unless he was truly dedicated or running for political office.

He hadn't called Ben back, but he was sure the doctor would help him find a position for Annalise if he asked him to. That was the logical thing to do. He liked her and he'd miss her company, at least for a day or two. But the fact was, having her around was not conducive to the sort of peaceful life he'd spent almost a year establishing.

Still he didn't call Ben. And he didn't mention anything to Annalise about the possibility of finding her another place to stay. He told himself that he didn't want to upset her. She had come so far in such a short time. He didn't want to do anything that might bring that haunting emptiness to her eyes.

So he didn't do anything about getting her out of his life.

Though Devlin had driven into town three or four times to pick up things he needed for the house, Annalise didn't make the trip until after she'd been staying with him for nearly two weeks. Her car had been running for most of that time, but she hadn't felt any urge to leave the house that had become almost a sanctuary.

"I was thinking that some flowers along the drive right in front of the house would look nice," she said, glancing at Devlin uncertainly. She didn't want him to think she was pushing her way in where she didn't belong.

Devlin finished pulling the truck into a parking space before looking at her. He nodded. "That sounds nice. What have you got in mind?"

"I don't now for sure. I thought maybe, if you didn't mind, we could stop at a nursery. I noticed one on the way into town. We could take a look at what they've got."

"Sounds good." He glanced at his watch. "Will two hours give you enough time to get whatever you need?"

"I can buy a pair of jeans in less than two hours."

"Well, maybe you'll think of something else you need. There's a bookstore half a block down on the right. I've got an order to pick up there. Why don't we meet there in two hours?"

"Okay." Annalise climbed out of the truck, slamming the heavy door shut before moving around to the front of the vehicle. Devlin paused on the sidewalk, glancing at the list he'd just pulled out of his shirt pocket.

Standing there, wearing jeans and a soft gray cotton shirt with the sleeves rolled up over his forearms, he looked wonderfully solid. Annalise caught the inside of her lower lip between her teeth, holding back the urge to suggest that she could tag along with him. She could carry buckets of paint or bags of cement— whatever he liked. Just as long as he didn't leave her alone.

But that was ridiculous. He wasn't abandoning her in the middle of New York City. Remembrance, Indiana, was a peaceful, not very large town where the greatest danger likely to befall her was getting a ticket for jaywalking.

"You'll be all right?" As if he could read the doubts chasing one another around her mind, Devlin looked up from his list to pin her with eyes that saw more than they should.

"Sure," she said, forcing a bright smile. "It looks like a great little town."

"It's pretty peaceful." Devlin glanced at the shops that lined the street. "You should be able to find just about anything you need. There's a clothing store right across the street."

"Don't worry about me. I'll be fine."

When he hesitated, she gave him another smile,

hoping he couldn't read the stark terror she was feeling. She hadn't realized how much her sense of security had come to depend on his presence until she found herself about to be left alone in the middle of a strange town.

"You have enough money?" he asked abruptly.

"Yes. I already told you that the salary you're paying is too generous for what I'm doing. I have *plenty* of money."

"Good." He glanced at his watch again but made no move to leave. "Are you sure you'll be all right?"

It hit her suddenly that he had as many doubts about leaving her on her own as she did about being on her own. The knowledge stiffened her spine. Since when had she become so helpless that she couldn't buy a pair of jeans without a keeper?

Her fingers tightened on the strap of the cheap plastic purse, and her chin tilted up a fraction of an inch. Her smile lost some of its forced edge.

"I'll be fine," she told him again. "I'll meet you at the bookstore in two hours."

Lifting one hand in a casual wave, she turned and walked briskly off down the sidewalk. Devlin stayed where he was, watching her. She didn't look back, not even when she paused to check traffic before stepping into the crosswalk.

She looked very small and vulnerable. Maybe it was the way she was dressed. She was wearing a pair of jeans whose worn look had come from wear and not a designer's factory and one of his T-shirts, which was so large it made her look as if she were playing dress-up. Kelly's sneakers completed the outfit.

He forced himself to turn away, long strides carrying him in the opposite direction. Annalise was a

grown woman. She didn't need him to play body-
guard. She'd pulled herself together to an amazing
degree these past couple of weeks. He was sure a
couple of hours alone wasn't going to do her any
harm.

If only he could get it out of his head that she'd
looked absolutely terrified just before she walked
away.

"Actually, I really enjoyed myself." Annalise gave
him a shy smile. "I don't know if you could tell, but
I was scared to death there for a minute."

"It didn't show," Devlin told her without a second's hesitation. He didn't have to take his eyes off
the road to see her smile. He could feel it.

"Good." She rubbed her fingers absently over the
surface of her new purse, a scarlet canvas clutch. "I
felt really stupid. It isn't as if I've never been shopping alone before. I guess it's just that these last two
weeks, I've started putting myself back together
again. I wasn't sure I was ready to go out into the
real world, even for something as basic as shopping.
But it felt really good."

"Did you get everything you needed?" He cast a
doubtful look at the two sacks at her feet.

"I didn't need much." She was quiet for a moment, staring out at the fields that lined the road.
"You know, I'll never be able to repay you for all
you've done for me, Devlin. I don't now what I'd
have done if you hadn't—"

"One more word and you walk the rest of the
way," he interrupted.

"Okay." She slid him a quick glance and dared to

add one more sentence. "I just want to thank you," she said hurriedly.

"You've already thanked me." Her gratitude made him uncomfortable. He didn't want Annalise feeling grateful to him. He wanted her...hell, face it, jerk, you just plain want her.

His hands tightened on the wheel, the knuckles showing white for a moment before he forced his fingers to relax. Over the past two weeks, he'd gotten more experience than he'd ever hoped to have in quelling lustful thoughts.

There was little conversation during the remainder of the drive home. Annalise was content to savor the feeling that she'd faced a challenge and triumphed. Devlin was wondering how many cold showers a man could take before doing permanent physical damage. Something had to give soon. He only hoped it wouldn't be his sanity.

He parked the truck next to the house. He had to unload the truck bed, but he decided to change his shoes first. When the frame was first going up, he'd once dropped an armload of two-by-fours on his foot. The results had convinced him that the best way to move quantities of lumber was in a pair of sturdy boots.

Annalise preceded him into the house, going straight to the guest room to put away her purchases. She was snipping the tags from a crisp new pair of jeans when she heard Devlin call her name.

"Annalise? I think you should come look at this." There was a curious note in his voice, not exactly urgency but something more than a casual summons.

Annalise dropped the jeans onto the bed and left her room. Devlin was still talking, but he wasn't using any tone she'd ever heard from him. He was speaking too softly for her to make out words, but there was a low, soothing quality to his voice that was like stroking her hand over a warm blanket.

She followed the sound into his bedroom and saw him kneeling in front of the closet. She knew what was in the closet and who he was talking to even before she sank to her knees beside him.

Beauty lay on her side, smack in the center of the closet floor. She was lying on a dress shirt that had probably slipped off the hanger. It was a sure bet it was never going to be the same, but no one seemed to mind. Nestled against Beauty's stomach were four kittens, three grey like their mother and one a startling snowy white. All four were busily nursing with a concentration contrary to their size and helplessness.

Annalise felt tears come to her eyes, and her mouth curved upward in a foolish smile.

"Look," she said in a hushed voice, as if Devlin might not have seen his closet's new occupants. "She had her litter."

"It's about time. If she'd gotten any bigger, she would have popped like a balloon." Devlin's gruff words were at odds with the gentle finger he ran over Beauty's head. "What a good girl you are," he told the new mother. "Look at your beautiful babies."

Beauty regarded them with a look that could only be described as smug. She knew her kittens were beautiful, but she was pleased that these big, clumsy creatures were capable of seeing the obvious.

"They're so perfect," Annalise whispered, reaching out to stroke her fingertip over one tiny back. The kitten ignored her, intent on finishing her meal.

"Of course they're perfect. Look what a perfect

mom they've got.'' Beauty allowed Devlin to rub behind her ear, accepting his praise as her due.

If Annalise had had her doubts about whether or not Devlin minded that he'd acquired a houseguest and a pet in the same twenty-four-hour period, she was reassured now. He'd fed Beauty and never offered any objection to her presence, either by word or look, but he'd also never paid much attention to the cat. She'd thought that perhaps he was one of those people who were not entirely at ease with animals.

But he was perfectly comfortable with Beauty now, talking to her in that soft voice, making it clear that her efforts were not unappreciated.

Looking at the tiny kittens, Annalise felt fresh tears sting her eyes. Four new lives. It wouldn't be long before they'd be venturing out of their home in the closet and getting underfoot, making complete nuisances of themselves.

Life was a constant cycle of renewal. No matter what happened, there was always a new cycle beginning somewhere. It was a thought at once humbling and reassuring.

His attention drawn by her silence, Devlin turned his head to look at her. Their eyes met, his more open than usual with the simple pleasure he took in the new family, hers more green than blue with emotion.

He stared at her, caught by the hidden depths in her eyes. What was it about her eyes that always hinted at mysteries he'd never quite understand?

A strand of hair had fallen loose from the clip with which she'd drawn the heavy length back and lay against her cheek. He reached up to put it in place. Only somehow, his fingers were loosening the clasp.

It hit the floor with a sharp click. It could have exploded like dynamite and neither of them would have noticed.

Annalise's hair spilled over his fingers like living silk. Without taking his eyes from hers, he drew a handful of it forward so that it fell across her breast, a pale contrast to the navy T-shirt she wore.

Her eyes widened and he could hear an odd little catch to her breathing, but she didn't move back, didn't utter a word of protest as his hand closed over the sensitive nape of her neck.

His eyes locked on hers, Devlin drew her forward. Only in the last heartbeat before their lips met did her gaze flicker, her lashes coming down to shield her eyes from his.

But then his mouth was on hers, and he didn't have to read her reaction in her eyes. He could taste it in the way her lips softened beneath his, hear it in the barely audible sigh that escaped her.

Devlin had been fantasizing for almost two weeks about what kissing her would be like. But no fantasy could begin to compare with the reality. And the reality was that she was a taste of heaven on earth. And no fantasy could have prepared him for the explosion a simple kiss touched off between them.

His mouth firmed, his head tilting to deepen the kiss. Her lips opened to him, an invitation he didn't try to resist. Her tongue came up to meet his, her response as quick and hard as his own.

Still on his knees, he drew her closer, wanting to feel her with every pore of his being. Annalise's hands settled on his shoulders, hesitating uncertainly for a moment before her fingers crept into the thick darkness of his hair. She molded her fingers to the back of his skull, the simple touch fanning the flames of his need even higher.

Devlin left one hand buried in the irresistible silk of her hair. The other traveled down her back, tracing her spine through the thin knit of the T-shirt before coming to rest on her backside.

She complied easily when he pressed her closer, shifting his knees apart so that the cradle of her femininity pressed against the rock-hard proof of his desire.

His mouth caught the small gasp that escaped her as she felt the strength of his need. Devlin's mouth was avid on hers. All the hunger he'd been suppressing was battering at the doors of his control.

He wanted to press her back onto the floor and strip away the frustrating layers of clothing between them. He wanted to feel her thighs cradling him, feel her body accepting him in the most intimate of embraces.

He wanted to hear her cry out his name in her pleasure, to see her writhing beneath him, her body burning with the same need he felt.

The very strength of that need—the realization that he was within a millisecond of losing control— brought Devlin to his senses. He felt as if he were teetering on the brink of a huge chasm. On the other side lay as near to paradise as it was possible to find in the mortal world. But to get there, he had to risk giving up the control that had kept him sane through all the dark hours in his life.

That rigid refusal to give even a fraction of himself over into someone else's power had enabled him to survive his childhood and eight years in prison. And he couldn't possibly make love to Annalise and retain that control. He wanted her too badly.

Hammering down the screaming need in his gut, Devlin ended the kiss. His hands moved to grip her shoulders, drawing her away even though it felt as if he were pulling off a layer of his own skin.

Their eyes met, hers reflecting a startled wonder that made him ache to pull her back into his arms. But he wasn't going to do that.

For a moment, Annalise saw her own wonder reflected in Devlin's eyes and knew that the kiss had been as much of a revelation to him as it had been to her. Then the shutters came down, shutting her out, closing him inside.

"Annalise, I—"

She interrupted quickly. "Well, that was certainly a surprise." She scrambled to her feet as she spoke, quickly putting a little distance between them.

"A surprise," Devlin repeated. He stood more slowly, his feet slightly apart as if he were bracing for a fight. She forced herself to ignore the solid bulge at his fly that made it clear that he might have shut her out but his body hadn't quite gotten the message yet.

"Of course, it was only to be expected," she said brightly. She bent down to pick up her hair clip and swept her hair back into it with quick, nervous movements, hoping he couldn't see that her fingers were trembling.

"It was?"

"Of course. I'd been expecting it. Hadn't you? I mean, here we are, living here together. And you know what they say about proximity."

She edged toward the door, aware that she was babbling like an idiot. But she had to stop him from speaking. She couldn't bear to hear what he'd say, though she couldn't have said exactly what that might be.

''Proximity.'' He didn't seem capable of anything beyond repeating her words.

''Of course. Well, I'm glad that's out of the way. Now we can get on with things without wondering what it would be like to kiss one another. Thanks for calling me in to see the kittens.''

She could feel her inane smile starting to crack around the edges. ''I should finish putting away the things I bought today,'' she said, as if she'd brought back cartons of things instead of only two medium-sized sacks.

She darted out of the door before Devlin could say anything, though from the stunned look on his face she doubted he could have found any words.

Annalise reached the sanctuary of her bedroom, closing the door behind her and leaning up against it. The tight smile disappeared. She bit her lower lip when it threatened to tremble.

For all the nonsense she'd babbled to Devlin, no one could have been less prepared for what had just happened than she had been. Oh, she'd been aware of an occasional twinge of interest. You couldn't live with a man as attractive as Devlin Russell and not notice him.

She'd even had an occasional dreamy thought about what it might be like if he kissed her. But her vague imaginings of him gently pressing his lips to hers hadn't prepared her for the reality.

What had happened to her in there? She'd never felt that kind of blazing need in her life. Certainly never with Bill. She'd never even imagined she was capable of such feelings.

Bill had been her only lover, and she'd found sex with him a warm, friendly thing. Pleasant enough that she'd never had a reason to object to his advances, even if it hardly made the stars fall from the sky.

If she'd had her moments of wondering if there shouldn't be a little more to it than the vague pleasure of knowing that he'd found his satisfaction, she'd pushed the thoughts away, afraid to find any faults with her marriage. She'd lost too many people in her life to risk losing her husband by complaining about their sex life. She wasn't really the passionate sort anyway. Any lack she felt was undoubtedly in her.

But she couldn't believe that anymore. Moments ago, she'd discovered that she was very much the passionate sort. In Devlin's arms, in his kiss, a whole new side of her had been revealed. She hadn't just responded to his hunger. She'd felt a hunger all her own.

She pressed her fingers to her lips. If he'd wanted to take her right there on the floor, she'd have welcomed him. Even now, her body was still tingling with a new awareness.

"Forget it," she whispered fiercely. "You saw the look in his eyes. He doesn't want this any more than you do. You don't want it." The words were more order than statement.

Proximity. She'd been babbling when she'd told Devlin that was all it was, but the more she thought about it, the more sense it made. As she'd said, they were living here together, seeing each other constantly. It was only natural that a certain sexual tension would develop.

But that's all it was, and if they just ignored it, it would go away.

But if ignoring it was the cure, it was going to take longer than she'd hoped. Devlin wasn't the sort of man who was easy to ignore under any circumstances, but the kiss they'd shared made it almost impossible.

And as if to add to the problem, summer swept over Indiana, elbowing spring aside practically overnight. The temperatures rose accordingly. More often than not, Devlin's shirt disappeared sometime before noon, leaving Annalise with a fine, unwanted view of his muscled torso.

But the worst thing was not the sight of Devlin's truly splendid physique. The worst thing was the new tension that had sprung up between them. By tacit agreement, neither made any reference to the momentary madness they'd shared the day Beauty's kittens entered the world. But it was there in every glance that passed between them.

Beneath the most innocuous of conversations ran a fine tension, an awareness that didn't disappear with being ignored. The meals they shared were no longer relaxed interludes where the conversation might center on an idea Devlin had had for the house or a book one of them had read.

Conversation grew stilted, punctuated by long silences that neither wanted to break. It was the loss of Devlin's friendship that bothered her more than anything else. She hadn't realized how much she'd enjoyed the rather reserved companionship he offered until it was gone.

The sad thing was, she didn't know how to go

about regaining it. They couldn't go back and erase the kiss. It had happened. There was no changing that.

Sleeping together wasn't the answer, either. Though she was willing to admit, somewhat painfully, that if Devlin suggested it, she probably wouldn't hesitate very long.

But he wouldn't suggest it. Not unless he found a way to let her inside the wall he kept around himself, or at least partway in. She'd seen the look in his eyes when he ended the kiss. Dazed as she'd been, she recognized when someone was shutting her out.

It had hurt, but she knew it wasn't really personal with Devlin. She believed the wall was a deeply rooted part of him, a protection he let very few people inside. She knew what it was to put up walls. And she knew how badly it could hurt to let someone inside.

She was rather gloomily contemplating this thought a few days after The Kiss—she'd come to think of it in capitals. There was a storm building up; huge black thunderheads had been gathering all afternoon, making the air thick and muggy with the promise of rain.

It was the sort of weather that made your skin feel too tight, as if the electricity in the air had somehow gotten beneath it, drawing it closer about your bones.

Devlin was working outside. Annalise was supposedly entering figures into the accounting book he'd bought for that purpose when they visited Remembrance. Actually she'd spent a great deal more time staring at nothing than she had writing anything.

When she heard the sound of a car coming down the driveway, curiosity at least momentarily dislodged the frustrated circle of her thinking. She got up from the table and went to the front door.

A bright red compact had just pulled to a stop in front of the house, and a slender brunette was getting out. Annalise started to open the door, half thinking that the woman might be lost and hoping to get directions. Before she could push the screen open, the stranger's face broke into a grin.

"Dev!"

Devlin came into sight, shrugging into his shirt as he strode toward the woman. But it wasn't the sight of his bare chest that made Annalise's breath catch. It was the warmth of his smile—a genuine smile that lit up his entire face.

"Midget! What are you doing all the way out here?" Before Annalise had a chance to regain her breath, it was stolen from her again by seeing the taciturn, unapproachable Devlin Russell pick the brunette up and swing her around.

"Stop it, you fiend! You're all dirty." The reprimand might have been more effective if she hadn't been laughing up at him.

Midget? It didn't sound like the sort of pet name you'd give a lover. More like the kind of thing you might call a little sister. Was this Kelly?

She lingered in the doorway, watching shamelessly as Devlin lowered the other woman to the ground but kept his arm around her shoulders.

"I was visiting a site that Dan's working on, and on the way home, I realized that your place wasn't that far out of my way, so I thought I'd drop by. You don't mind, do you, Dev?"

"Of course not. You know you're always welcome."

"I've extended the same invitation to you," she said, a hint of tartness in the tone. "I haven't noticed you taking me up on it."

Devlin shrugged. "I've been busy. You know how it is, Kelly."

"I know exactly how it is. You're unsociable, Devlin Russell. Do you know how long it's been since you've been to see us? Clay is going to forget who you are."

"No, he won't. He's too smart. Is he with you?" Devlin dropped his arm from her shoulder, bending to look in the car window.

Clay? Who was Clay? The way the sun slanted across the windshield made it impossible for Annalise to see inside. It didn't prevent her from seeing the wriggling infant that Kelly lifted out of a car seat a moment later.

"Remember your Uncle Devlin, sweetie pie?"

"Of course he does. How's my favorite nephew?" Devlin held out his hands to take the baby from her, but Kelly held back.

"He needs to be changed," she warned.

"That's okay. We can change him in the house." He took the baby from her, holding him with none of the awkward self-consciousness that most men felt with an infant.

Annalise hardly noticed. When Kelly lifted the child from the car, the breath left her lungs with painful speed. She drew back from the door, feeling her skin flush and then pale.

She'd thought she was over the worst of it. She'd been so sure she'd moved beyond the agony that flooded her now. Oh, God, they were coming inside. Without giving it a second's thought, she darted across the living room and into her bedroom, shutting the door and leaning against it.

She heard Devlin and Kelly enter the house. She prayed that Devlin wouldn't feel it necessary to come and find her. She'd been curious about his sister and had thought it would be interesting to meet her. But that was before she knew Kelly had a baby. She couldn't meet her now. She couldn't go out there and smile and make polite conversation, trying not to look at Kelly's son.

Please, let Devlin just forget all about her.

"Whose car is that next to the house?" Kelly's curious voice carried easily through the door. Annalise held her breath, waiting for Devlin's reply. Let him say he'd bought it as a second car, that it had fallen out of the sky.

Devlin's answer seemed slow in coming, but it wasn't the one she'd been praying for. "It belongs to a...friend of mine. She's been staying with me for a couple of weeks."

"She?"

"Don't get any bright ideas, Midget. She's a friend."

Annalise pressed herself closer against the door as she heard Devlin's footsteps crossing the living room.

"Annalise?" He tapped lightly on the door. Obviously he thought she might be taking a nap. He couldn't possibly know that she was cowering here like someone about to be dragged before a firing squad. "Annalise?"

She could just pretend she was asleep. He'd go away then. Or he might open the door to check on her. And then she'd have to explain why she'd been pretending she didn't hear him.

"Yes?" The one word was almost impossible to force out.

"Kelly's here. My sister," he added, in case she'd forgotten.

"I'll...be right out," she managed.

Devlin lingered on the other side of the door, as if he'd heard something in her voice that didn't seem quite right.

She released her breath on a sigh that was only a hair's breadth away from being a sob. Straightening away from the door, she smoothed her hands over the soft pink T-shirt she wore over her jeans. She pinched her cheeks, knowing they must be too pale.

She could do this. All she had to do was go to out there and make a few minutes of polite conversation and then make some excuse to leave. Not for a moment, not even for a split second, would she look at Kelly's baby. Not everyone oohed and aahed over infants.

Her knees were trembling as she pulled open the bedroom door and stepped out into the living room. The first thing she saw was the baby, freshly diapered and overall clad, crawling across the floor in her direction.

It took every ounce of willpower she had to keep from darting back into the bedroom and shutting the door. She dragged her eyes from his small figure and forced a smile that she hoped didn't look as sickly as it felt.

Afterward she could remember very little of her meeting with Kelly Remington. She must have responded in all the right places and said the right things, because no one seemed to notice anything wrong.

When Kelly picked up Clay, Annalise felt an actual, physical ache. Her arms hurt. She couldn't keep her eyes from the infant, who seemed reasonably content to view the world from the safety of his mother's arms.

"Would you like to hold him?"

At Kelly's words, Annalise's eyes snapped up to meet hers, wondering if she'd somehow revealed the painful hunger the baby made her feel. But Kelly only gave her a friendly smile and held Clay out. Vaguely Annalise was aware of the questioning look Devlin sent her, as if he sensed something of the turmoil she was feeling.

She wasn't going to take the baby, of course. Holding him would only make the pain worse, add to the emptiness that gnawed at her. She'd smile and thank Kelly and shake her head. She really wasn't the baby type, she'd say.

She saw her hands go out as if they belonged to someone else. Clay's body felt strong and sturdy in her hands. He studied her with bright blue eyes and then gave her a wide grin, confident that the sight of his two brand-new front teeth would make her a slave for life, just as it had done with everyone else in his life.

Annalise felt her breath catch, remembering another baby, another toothy grin. She drew him closer. He smelled of baby powder and formula. He felt like heaven. If she closed her eyes, he could be another baby, a little less sturdy, her eyes a softer blue.

"He's...he's very sweet," she said, aware that the silence had stretched on too long and both Devlin and Kelly were looking at her.

"We like him," Kelly said lightly.

"He's so strong. So healthy." Annalise tugged his overalls into better order, aware that her fingers were visibly trembling. "So healthy," she said again.

"Yes, he is." Kelly glanced at her brother, her dark eyes questioning, but Devlin could only shrug. That something was very wrong was obvious, but he didn't know what it was any more than she did.

After a moment, Annalise handed the baby back to his mother, her hands dropping immediately to her sides, her fingers curling into her palms.

"He's wonderful," she told Kelly, her bright smile at odds with the tears she didn't seem to realize were trickling down her cheeks.

"Thank you," Kelly said. "Are you all right?"

"Yes. Yes, of course." Annalise looked around as if she weren't quite sure where she was. "I...excuse me. I have to...excuse me."

She all but ran from the room, darting through the kitchen and out the back door, the screen slamming behind her. As if it were a cue, thunder rumbled, the sound closer now. A cool breeze skipped through the back door, stirring the papers on the kitchen table, sending them drifting to the floor.

Chapter 8

"What was that all about?"

Devlin dragged his gaze from the back door to his sister's bewildered face.

"I don't know," he said slowly. And it was none of his business, he reminded himself. He was trying to put distance between himself and Annalise, not get even more deeply involved. But her pain had been so vivid.

"You probably ought to get on the road before the rain really gets started." He reached out to give his nephew an absent nudge on the chin.

"And maybe you should see what's wrong with Annalise."

"Maybe." He was going to let her work this out without him, he reminded himself.

"And don't think I don't still have a million questions about her," Kelly added, gathering up Clay's diaper bag on the way to the door.

"Fine." Devlin's gaze drifted to the back door.

He saw his sister off, watching her car until it turned onto the main road. The rain started as he headed back into the house. He stood in the middle of the living room, reminding himself that he didn't want to get any more involved in Annalise St. John's problems.

She was far from suicidal now. Whatever had set her off, it wasn't his problem. She probably wouldn't even welcome his concern.

He went into the kitchen and began to pick up the receipts that had landed on the floor, setting them on the table and putting the account book on top of them. Outside, the rain was increasing in intensity.

Annalise hadn't been wearing anything remotely suited to a rainstorm. She'd be soaked to the skin in minutes. Staring out at the rain, he remembered the night he'd first seen her, standing on the riverbank, her shoulders slumped as if the weight of the world rested on them. She was still so vulnerable.

Cursing, he strode across the kitchen and slammed out the back door. He was just going to make sure she was all right, he told himself. She was sort of his responsibility, wasn't she? He'd make sure she was all right, and then he was going to take a nice hot shower and let her deal with her own problems.

It wasn't a hard rain, but it was a steady downpour that soaked everything it touched almost immediately. Devlin's light shirt was drenched before he was half-way across the backyard.

Annalise wasn't hard to find. The pink of her T-shirt stood out like a beacon through the falling rain. She was standing at the bottom of the long yard, staring down at the river.

Devlin felt fear cut off his breathing. His long stride lengthened into a sprint. What if he'd been wrong in thinking she wouldn't kill herself? What if she jumped into the river before he reached her?

He slowed as he neared her, feeling his heart start to beat again. She was well back from the bank. She had her arms crossed around her waist and her shoulders were hunched as if her pain were an actual physical burden. But she didn't look as though she'd been contemplating drowning her sorrows.

Adrenaline still surged in him as he stopped beside her. At first he thought she was so wrapped in sorrow that she wasn't even aware of his presence. But then she turned her head to look at him, her tears mingling with the rain.

"It hurts," she said quietly.

The simple, almost childlike statement sent a shaft of pain through Devlin's heart. Acting on instinct, he reached out, putting his arms around her and drawing her to him.

"I know." And he did know. Not what had caused her pain specifically, but he knew what it was to hurt so much the pain was almost unbearable.

Turning, Annalise leaned against him like a tired child, her cheek resting against his wet shirt, her hands settling on his hips.

"It hurts so much. Sometimes, I feel as if I'm dead inside, as if all that's left of me is the pain."

Her words sliced into him, making him feel her pain as his own. With both hands he cupped her cheeks, tilting her face up until her eyes met his.

"You're not dead, Annalise. And the pain gets easier to bear."

There was no lightening of the darkness in her

eyes. "Make it go away, Devlin. Make it stop hurting." Her lower lip trembled and Devlin's heart broke into a thousand pieces.

Hardly conscious of what he was doing, wanting only to ease her hurt, even if it meant taking the hurt and making it his, he lowered his mouth to hers.

He intended the kiss as comfort. He intended it to show her that she wasn't alone. He wanted to make her see that she was alive, that she could feel more than the emptiness and disillusion.

But whatever his intentions had been, they were scattered to the winds by her response. Her arms came up to circle his neck, her body arching against his. He'd offered a way for her to forget the pain, if only temporarily, and she was grabbing at it with both hands.

Despite the kiss they'd already shared, Devlin was caught off balance by the way passion seemed to almost literally explode between them. In the space of a heartbeat, everything was forgotten but the feel of Annalise in his arms, the taste of her on his lips.

He caught her closer, his mouth slanting hungrily across hers. Her response was every bit as urgent. Her fingers curled into the damp thickness of his hair, dragging him closer still.

There was no time to think. No time to wonder if this was the right thing. No time to draw back. The only thing possible was to feel her with every fiber of his being.

The rain had soaked their clothes, plastering the fabric to their skin. Devlin's hands slid down to cup Annalise's hips, lifting her off her feet as he pulled her against his thighs. She whimpered low in her throat as she felt his need pressed against her. She arched into him, making him curse the fact that they were still dressed.

He started to ease her back down to her feet, intending to take her into the house. But she had no intention of letting him go, even for that long. Her legs parted and came up to circle his lean hips, even as her arms tightened around his neck.

Devlin groaned, his hands shifting automatically to support her. The only way they could have been more intimately entwined was if they'd been naked. He could feel the heart of her pressed against the aching bulge of him. In that instant, he'd have given a year of his life to have their clothing vanish, to be able to slide himself into her.

He started up to the house, Annalise wrapped around him like the most sensuous of blankets. By the time he pulled open the screen door, the blood was pounding in his temples. If the roof had collapsed at that moment, it wouldn't have made him slow his pace. He had to have her. Whether it was in his bed or standing in the middle of a rainstorm or on the floor, he had to have her or go mad.

He was no longer concerned with keeping his distance—it was too late for that. And he didn't care that he might be getting too involved. His involvement was already too deep. All that mattered at this moment was easing the burning ache in his loins.

He stopped next to his bed, easing Annalise to the floor. She would have protested, but he was already stripping her T-shirt over her head. When he fumbled with the front clasp of her bra, she disposed of it herself, tossing the garment into a corner.

Devlin's hands came up, cupping the sweet dampness of her breasts, feeling the nipples hard and taut against his palms. He wanted to taste them, wanting to lick the rain from them. But Annalise's hands were already unzipping her jeans, stripping them down off her hips and then reaching for his.

"Hurry," she whispered. When the buttons defeated her shaking fingers, she cupped her hand over him, drawing a guttural groan from him.

"Hurry," she said again.

Devlin's fingers worked the buttons of his jeans. He shoved them down, releasing the heavy length of his manhood. Annalise's fingers closed around him and he thought he'd surely explode.

"You're going to kill me," he said, only half-joking. His hands closed over her wrist, drawing her away.

He eased her back onto the bed, following her down. His hands stroked the length of her sides, savoring the silken feel of her skin. But Annalise twisted beneath him, opening her legs, her ankles coming up to press against his hips.

Devlin groaned and fought the urge to take her invitation. This wasn't how he wanted their first time to be. He wanted to slow the pace, savor every minute.

"We've got all the time in the world," he whispered.

She stared up at him, her eyes dark with need and some emotion he was too dazed to put a name to. She shook her head, scattering her damp hair across the covers.

"Now, Devlin. Please, now."

"Annalise...ah, sweetheart." She'd reached between them and closed her hand over the swollen length of him, drawing him forward until he rested against her dampness.

''Now,'' she whispered fiercely, her hips arching as if to force him to take her.

Devlin's control shattered into a million pieces. With a soft curse that was almost a prayer, he slid his burning length into her. She gasped as her body stretched to accommodate his.

She fit him as if made for him alone. Her softness surrounded him, changing what had been near pain to a painfully intense pleasure. Devlin pressed his forehead to the pillow beside her head, struggling for some shred of control.

Despite her eagerness, she hadn't been quite ready for him. He'd felt it in the sharp gasp, in the tightness of the flesh that sheathed him. He wanted to empty himself in her, to feel an easing of the ache that had gnawed at him for weeks. But he wanted her to feel that same pleasure. It was a journey much sweeter if they made it together.

But Annalise wasn't interested in him taking his time. She wanted only to rush headlong into the sweet oblivion she could feel just out of reach. Only that would take away her pain, ease the feeling that she'd never be wholly alive again. She arched her hips into his, drawing her legs up to circle his waist so that she took him even deeper.

''Don't.'' Devlin lifted himself on his arms, his fingers knotted over the blankets as he struggled for control. ''Slow down, sweetheart.''

''I don't want to slow down,'' she whispered, her hips arching again as her fingers trailed down the length of his spine. ''Please, Devlin. Please.''

She lifted her head to plant soft kisses across his

chest. Her mouth found the flat nub of his nipple and her tongue came out to taste it. Devlin shuddered, feeling his fragile control dissolving like mist before a hot sun. Her teeth scored him lightly and he surrendered with a groan.

His hips rose and fell, feeling her flesh enfold him in the sweetest of embraces. Through the pounding in his temples, he knew that something wasn't right. She was rushing him along, her hands and legs holding him, dragging him headlong into the madness. But somewhere he'd lost her and it was too late to stop now.

He arched against her, grinding his teeth together against a pleasure so intense it must surely approach death. But the intensity of his release was clouded by the knowledge that he'd reached it alone.

He lowered his head to the pillow beside her, his breath shuddering in and out of him. He felt her legs drop to the bed, releasing him from their sweet prison. As his mind slowly cleared, he was aware that a deep anger was rolling in to fill the spaces temporarily emptied of need.

He was angry with Annalise for rushing their lovemaking, for refusing to let him take the time to make sure she was with him all the way. Most of all he was furious with himself for letting her do it.

Devlin rolled away from her, sensing the slight discomfort his withdrawal caused her. It only added to his anger.

They lay there without speaking, the room completely silent but for the steady patter of the rain. It was left to Annalise to break the silence. With an inaudible excuse, she started to get off the bed.

Devlin's hand caught her before she'd managed to

sit up, pushing her implacably back against the pillow. He loomed over her, his shoulders blocking out her view of the room, leaving her with nothing to look at but his angry gray eyes.

"You want to tell me what the hell that was all about?" he demanded fiercely.

Annalise closed her eyes, but she couldn't shut out the knowledge that he had a right to be upset. She'd used him to try to blot out the pain.

"I'm sorry," she whispered.

"Sorry?" Illogically his anger immediately darted away from her, centering solely on what he saw as his own monumental failure. "You're sorry because I acted like a randy sixteen-year-old?" He released her, rolling away to sit on the edge of the bed, his shoulders taut.

"I pushed you," she said, sitting up. She tugged the sheet up over her breasts. "I had no right to use you like that."

"Use me?" Devlin turned to face her, drawing one knee up on the bed. "*You* used *me?*"

"Yes." She lowered her eyes.

Devlin sighed, feeling all his anger drain away. "You didn't use me, Annalise. I've been aching to make love to you practically from the moment I saw you. But this isn't exactly how I'd have liked it to go."

"It's all right." She reached out to touch his arm, withdrawing her fingers quickly.

"No, it isn't. I wanted you with me."

"With you? I was with you." She blinked at him, confused.

Devlin stared at her. She didn't even realize what she'd lost in her headlong rush.

"What do you mean?" she asked.

"Never mind." It wasn't something he could possibly sit here and explain to her. Maybe, with luck, he'd get a second chance to show her what he meant. Because there was no sense in pretending that he didn't want to make love to her again. And again.

"What happened, Annalise? Why were you so upset? What was it about seeing Kelly and the baby that hurt you so much?"

Her eyes dropped from his to stare at the rumpled covers between them. She owed him an explanation. No matter what he said about having wanted her— and she tucked that away to pull out and think about later—the fact remained that she'd used him.

"I told you I'd been married," she began quietly. "What I didn't tell you was that I had a baby."

She heard the quick rush of Devlin sucking in his breath but she didn't lift her gaze from the bed.

"When Bill and I got married, I think we were both looking for a family more than anything else. He came from a very wealthy background. His parents had never had much time for him and I think, in his own way, he was as lonely as I was.

"We were happy. He was kind and funny and we laughed a lot." Her face softened with the memories and Devlin felt an odd little stab of something that could have been jealousy but obviously wasn't.

"We wanted to start a family right away, even though we were both pretty young ourselves. Both of us wanted children. We wanted the sort of stability and balance that a family can give. So we started trying to have a baby. Only nothing happened. After a few months, we went to a doctor and they started running tests.''

She plucked at the sheet, her forehead puckering as she remembered the endless poking and probing, the intimate questions from doctors she'd never seen before and would never see again.

''They finally told us that it was my fault. That there was something wrong with my tubes and it would take surgery or a miracle for me to conceive. And even with the surgery, the miracle wouldn't hurt.''

''So you had the surgery.''

''No.'' She shook her head. ''Bill and I talked about it and decided that maybe this was some sort of sign. We were so young and so earnest about life. We decided maybe we were meant to adopt children instead. I mean, I knew firsthand what it was like to be bounced from place to place, never really belonging, never having anyone you could count on. So we decided that was what we'd do.''

''What happened?'' he prompted her when she fell silent.

''A miracle.'' Her mouth curved in a smile of such beauty Devlin looked away. ''I got pregnant before we had a chance to do more than just start looking into adoption. We were ecstatic. We decided to hold off on the adoption, and then, in a couple of years, we could start the process again and adopt the rest of our family.

''I had a wonderful pregnancy. It was as if all the trouble I'd had conceiving had somehow made the pregnancy go more smoothly. My labor was easy and Bill was there when Mary was born.''

Unconsciously she clasped her hands over her elbows, hugging herself almost as if she were holding a child.

"She was the most perfect baby you've ever seen. She hardly ever cried. She was always laughing and happy."

She glanced at him with a self-conscious laugh. "I know all parents say that, but Mary really was special."

"I believe you," he said gently. "What happened to her, Annalise?"

Her smile faded. "She started to have problems when she was not quite a year old. It didn't seem too serious at first but we took her to the doctor. We thought we were being overanxious parents. But we weren't. The doctor told us she had Tay-Sachs disease. It's a genetic disorder. A perfectly healthy parent can be a carrier and pass it on to their child."

She was silent, staring into the middle distance, her face without expression.

"By the time Mary was two, she was blind. She died just after her third birthday."

The stark recital only added to the impact of her words. Without any breast-beating, she expressed all the terrible anguish she must have suffered.

"I'm sorry." The words were hopelessly inadequate of course, but there didn't seem to be anything else he could say.

"Thank you."

"When...I mean, how long ago..." He let his voice trail off.

"A year ago. I had her cremated and I scattered her ashes over a lake we used to visit. She liked to watch the gulls before...before she lost her vision."

She had to stop to clear her throat and then she continued more briskly.

"And then I packed everything in my car and started driving. I got odd jobs here and there, but I couldn't seem to concentrate very well. I was fired a couple of times. Sometimes I just quit because I couldn't bear to be in one place for very long.

"I guess I thought if I just kept moving, the pain wouldn't find me. Only it always did."

That explained her frantic rush earlier. She hadn't been desperate for him to make love to her. She'd been desperate to try to forget. Seeing Clay had brought all the hurt rushing back over her. That's what she meant when she said she'd used him.

"Annalise, what about Bill? Where was he?"

"He left," she said simply.

"He left you and your daughter?" Devlin felt rage churn in his gut. "The son of a bitch just walked out?"

"It wasn't like that," she protested. "You mustn't think badly of him."

"Oh, mustn't I?" he muttered, wishing he had the man in front of him so he could slowly choke the life from his miserable body. He got up and stalked to the dresser, snatching a clean pair of shorts out of a drawer and stepping into them with a motion nothing short of violent. He grabbed a pair of jeans and jerked them on.

"What kind of man walks out with his wife and daughter just when they need him the most?"

"A good man." She held up one hand when he looked as if he might explode. "And a weak one, I suppose."

"You suppose?" Absently he handed her one of

his shirts to replace the sheet she was still holding over her breasts. When she hesitated, he half turned away, though it seemed a bit late in the day to be worrying about modesty.

"Bill wasn't a bad person," Annalise insisted as she buttoned the soft cotton over her breasts. "He felt terribly guilty about Mary being ill. When she was diagnosed, we had tests run and found out that Bill was the one who carried the gene for Tay-Sachs. He felt as if it was his fault that she was ill."

"I can understand that," Devlin admitted grudgingly. "But I can't understand how he could leave you alone to cope with it."

"Some people just aren't strong enough to deal with something like that," she said, smoothing the tail of the shirt across her thigh. "He tried. He really did. But after a while, he couldn't even bear to look at her."

"So he dumped you?" The incredible thing was that he couldn't hear so much as a hint of bitterness in her voice, not a trace of anger.

"No. He moved out and I filed for divorce. But he continued to support us. I couldn't work, of course. Taking care of Mary was a full-time job. He paid for a house and all the medical expenses. We didn't have to worry about anything."

"Conscience money." Devlin dismissed her ex-husband's motives without hesitation.

"Maybe. But it was all he could give us."

"It wasn't enough," he snapped, angry for her.

"You can't ask more of someone than they're capable of giving," she said softly. "I don't hate him. I know he felt guilty about not being there for me, for Mary. He'd have continued to take care of me for the rest of my life if I'd wanted.''

''Big deal.''

Annalise didn't try to argue any further. She couldn't really expect Devlin to understand Bill. Devlin faced the world square on, dealing with whatever life threw at him. Until Mary's illness, Bill had never had to deal with anything more challenging than choosing the color of a new car.

When he'd been faced with something that would have been hard for anyone to deal with, he hadn't had the strength to stand up to it. He'd run away. It was something he'd have to live with for the rest of his life. If he deserved a punishment, that was surely more than enough.

She released a slow breath, aware that she felt incredibly tired and, simultaneously, lighter than she had in months. It was as if, in talking about what had happened, she'd shed some of the burden of the grief she'd carried for so long. She stifled a yawn.

Devlin had been pacing the room with long, restless strides as if he needed to do something to wear off the tension. Now he stopped next to where she sat on the side of the bed. Annalise looked up at him, her eyes questioning.

Hesitantly he reached out to touch his fingertips to her cheek, the tender gesture slightly awkward. She wondered if she was aware of the conflict she could read so clearly in his eyes.

After a moment, his hand dropped back to his side and he half turned away, looking out the window where the rain was still falling in a steady patter. Darkness had fallen while they talked, hurried along a bit by the storm clouds.

"I guess I ought to shut the doors, make sure I didn't leave any tools out in the rain."

"Yes." It suddenly seemed too much of an effort to hold her head up.

"Are you hungry? I could heat up some soup."

"No, thank you." She yawned again. "I'm just so tired."

"Go to sleep, then. I'm going to check on... things," he said vaguely.

Annalise watched him leave. She wanted desperately to fight the drowziness. There were things that needed to be said. But she couldn't think what they were.

Sighing, she lay down, curling up on her side, her face buried in Devlin's pillow. She'd only rest her eyes for a few minutes and then she'd be ready to cope again.

Devlin stood in the living room, staring out the window at the steady fall of rain. Ice clinked against the side of his glass as he raised it and took a swallow of its contents. He felt the Chivas slide down his throat, creating a mellow warmth in the pit of his stomach.

He rarely drank and never more than one drink. He'd had too much to drink the night Harold Sampson had murdered his wife and left all the evidence pointing in Devlin's direction. The fact that he'd admitted as much hadn't helped his defence any. But tonight, the Scotch helped ease his inner chill.

He twisted the glass in his hands, watching the amber liquid shift around the clear ice cubes. There had been moments during the past few days when he'd entertained the thought that maybe, if he slept with

Annalise, it would solve a whole host of problems, enabling him to stop taking cold showers and start sleeping at night. If he could make love to her just once…

His soft laughter was self-directed and held little humor. Of all the hopeless male fantasies, that had to be one of the oldest and, apparently, one of the most enduring. Sex rarely solved more problems than it created. You would think he'd have known that.

Not that knowing it would have stopped him from making love to Annalise. Nothing short of a cataclysm of truly spectacular proportions could have stopped him once he'd felt the depth of her response.

Of course, that response hadn't been the result of anything likely to increase the size of his ego. Annalise hadn't been desperate for him to make love to her. She'd been desperate to forget, at least momentarily, the grief that gnawed at her.

Devlin's mouth twisted in a rueful smile. It wasn't the sort of thing a man liked to hear from a beautiful woman to whom he'd just made love. His smile faded and he took another swallow of Scotch.

For someone who didn't intend to get involved, he'd done a rather poor job of keeping his distance. He frowned uneasily. There was no more pretending that he didn't care about Annalise. But there was also no reason to let things get out of hand.

He'd known for a long time that he wasn't suited to deep, personal involvements. He would never marry, never have children. His frown grew brooding as he looked into a future that stretched out ahead of him like a long, lonely road.

But that was the way it had to be. There were risks you just didn't take in life. One of the ones he'd promised himself never to take was the chance of ever hurting people the way his father had. It was common knowledge that abused children grew up to become abusive parents. Not all of them certainly, but the statistics made it clear that the odds were against him.

He couldn't quite picture himself striking a woman or a child, but it wasn't a chance he was willing to take. He was capable of violence. He'd known that even before he went to prison. The years in prison had sharpened that side of him—he wouldn't have survived without it.

There were those who would argue that the situations were quite different. One was defending your life, the other was attacking a person smaller and weaker than yourself. Because he was capable of one didn't necessarily mean he was capable of the other.

But what if that edge was sharper than he knew? What if the violence was so deeply ingrained in him that it came out when he wasn't expecting it? He'd lived with violence in one form or another most of his life. You couldn't just walk away from that kind of heritage.

He downed the last of the Scotch, feeling it settle in the pit of his stomach, a smooth pool of fire that helped ease the ache.

It had been, God help him, a relief to learn that Annalise couldn't have children. Not that he wouldn't have given his right arm if it would give her back the child she'd lost. But it wouldn't be his child—never his. It was a measure of how crazed he'd been that the thought of using protection hadn't even crossed his mind. All he'd been able to think of was that he had to have her.

The truth was, he still wanted her. If he'd ever

thought that his craving would be permanently eased if he had her just once, he'd been wrong. Scant hours after making love to her, he wanted her as much as if he'd never had her.

Annalise came awake slowly, aware that, while her mind was still tangled with sleep, her body tingled with life. She shifted, moaning softly as she dragged her eyes open.

The room was filled with the odd half-light that came just before dawn, all gray shadows and softened angles. She was naked, the covers stripped down to the foot of the bed, yet her body felt heavy with warmth.

Devlin knelt beside her, his eyes intent as he looked down at her. She blinked, trying to clear the sleepy fog from her vision.

"Devlin?"

He didn't seem to hear her husky whisper. His hands settled lightly on her shoulders, stroking downward until they hovered over her breasts, almost but not quite touching. From the sensitized feel of her nipples, Annalise knew it wasn't the first time he'd touched her, literally stroking her awake.

She opened her mouth to offer a shaky protest, but his palms settled on her breasts, his work-calloused thumbs brushing across the peaks, and her protest emerged as a moan.

"Devlin—" He bent and covered her mouth with his, swallowing whatever she'd planned to say. His tongue traced the line of her lower lip, coaxing her to open for him. Helpless to resist—not at all sure she even wanted to resist—Annalise parted her lips, inviting him inside.

The first time they'd made love, she'd set the pace. She'd been running from her hurt more than reaching for the pleasure she'd half sensed he could give her. This time, Devlin was in control. As the minutes stretched, it seemed as if he were not only in control of himself but in control of her.

Her body responded to his touch as if she'd been waiting for him all her life, storing up all the passion she'd thought she didn't possess so that this man could release it.

He savored the time she'd denied him earlier, alternately coaxing and commanding as he led her down pathways she'd never traveled before. His fingers knew just where to stroke her, just when to touch as lightly as a butterfly's wing and when a firmer touch would set her shivering with need.

He soothed. He demanded. He pleaded. And she gave him every trembling response he asked for.

When the time came, she opened to him eagerly, her hunger as great as his. But even now, he wouldn't allow her to rush things. He caught her face between his hands, his eyes intent on hers as he lowered his head and closed his mouth over hers, his tongue plunging deep even as his hips sank into the cradle of her thighs. His mouth swallowed her cry of pleasure.

He made love to her with fierce tenderness. She met his every thrust. Her hands moved frantically up and down his sweat-dampened back, feeling the ripple of his muscles.

Inside her, a spring coiled tighter and tighter until her whole body was tuned into that building tension, until she knew she would surely shatter into a million pieces if he continued.

And then Devlin's hand cupped her bottom, tilting her hips to receive him more fully. Annalise's breath left her in a surprised cry as the spring suddenly broke loose and sent her spinning outward. For a moment, it seemed as if her heart would stop with the intensity of it.

She felt Devlin swell inside her and felt the pulse of his release. His hands tightened almost painfully on her hips. A guttural groan tore from his throat. Annalise felt her own pleasure sharpened in the knowledge that he trembled against her.

The only sound was the rasp of Devlin's breathing. Annalise ran her hands slowly up and down his back, exploring the ridged length of his spine. He was heavy, but she liked the feel of him on her, within her.

She felt at peace in a way she couldn't remember feeling in a very long time. Maybe it was the fact that she'd told Devlin about Mary last night. Maybe it was the wonderful feeling of physical fulfillment he'd just given her.

Whatever it was, she knew deep inside that she'd finally turned a corner. She was moving out of the darkness now, moving toward the light. She'd never stop grieving for her daughter, but she'd finally accepted the need to move on.

The healing had finally begun, and she owed it to the man she held in her arms.

Chapter 9

The next time Annalise woke, the sun was pouring in through the light curtains, cutting a warm golden path across the bed. Devlin's bed.

She stretched, her mouth curving in a smile. She felt several unfamiliar, delicious aches, and her smile softened with sensuous memories. She'd always thought the writers who described sex as stars bursting overhead had rather vivid imaginations. But last night, she'd seen more than a few bursting stars herself.

She sat up, reaching for the robe Devlin had draped across the foot of the bed. Her robe, she noticed, her smile deepening. Not only was he a devastating lover, he was thoughtful, too. All in all, a pretty terrific combination.

Annalise got out of bed and shrugged into the robe, pulling her hair out from under the collar. She could

smell coffee and bacon, and she was suddenly rav-
enously hungry.

She went into the bathroom. Her attention was
caught by her reflection in the mirror, and she paused
to look at herself. She looked different. Just like in
the books where everyone could tell the heroine had
let the hero have his wicked way with her, she could
see the difference in her own face.

She looked younger. The lines of tension that had
added years to her age were softened. Her eyes
seemed brighter. For the first time since hearing the
doctor pass sentence on her beautiful little girl, she
was looking forward without a sense of dread.

It didn't matter that her place in Devlin's life was
ill defined. She wasn't going to worry about the future. She'd been taking each day as it came, and the
results had been worthwhile so far. More than worthwhile, she amended, thinking how short a time ago it
had been that she was living in her car, beyond caring
how she'd make it to the next day.

Devlin was standing at the stove when she entered
the kitchen. Though she didn't make a sound, he must
have felt her presence. She saw his back stiffen in the
moment before he turned.

There was a certain wariness in his eyes, as if he
weren't quite sure what to expect from her. Which
made them even, she thought, toying with the belt on
her robe. Because she didn't know what to expect,
either.

"Hi." Devlin broke the silence.

"Hi."

"How are you feeling?"

"Okay."

She stared down at her bare feet, wishing she had

a little more experience with this sort of thing. Was there a proper thing to say or do at a moment like this? Should she pretend nothing had happened? Or should she throw her arms around him? Something in between the two seemed a likely bet, but just what, she couldn't have said.

"Look, I—"

"I hope—"

Both broke off and looked at each other.

"You first," Devlin said.

"No, you go first. I don't know what I was going to say, anyway," she admitted with a shy smile.

There was an almost invisible easing of his shoulders. "I'm not all that sure what I was going to say, either."

"Really?"

"Really." His mouth relaxed in something approaching a smile. "I was probably going to ask you how you were again."

"I guess there aren't any firm rules on what you're supposed to say when you've just—I mean, after..." The words trailed off and she felt color come up in her cheeks.

"When you've just become lovers?" he said softly, his eyes kindling with memories. He started forward, stopping squarely in front of her.

Annalise focused her eyes on the top button of his shirt, feeling a newly familiar warmth in the pit of her stomach.

"Is that what we are?" she whispered. "Lovers?"

"Is that what you want us to be?"

She lifted her eyes to his face, seeing the question in his gaze. He was just as uncertain about this as she was, she realized suddenly. It was a novel idea. She didn't think Devlin Russell was uncertain about very many things.

"Yes." There was no hesitation in her reply.

His hands settled on her shoulders, his thumbs stroking absently across her collarbone. His expression was still serious, his eyes still held that odd wariness.

"Annalise, I'm not making any promises for the future."

"I'm not asking for any."

"There are things you don't know about me."

"I know enough."

"I don't want to see you get hurt."

Her fingers touched his mouth, silencing him. "Let the future take care of itself. I'm not asking you for anything more than you want to give, Devlin."

He closed his eyes, remembering her saying that her husband had given all he could—that you couldn't ask more of anyone than that. He'd dismissed the man as a sniveling coward. But was he really so different? Wasn't he asking Annalise to be satisfied with what he could offer?

For her own sake, he should bundle her into her car and hustle her out of his life as quickly as possible. He opened his eyes and looked at her, seeing nothing but acceptance in her gaze.

His hands tightened on her slender shoulders, drawing her closer. He knew he should send her away, but knowing and doing were two different things. He'd been alone most of his life. Would it really be so terrible to let her ease the loneliness that sometimes gnawed at him?

If he was careful, if he didn't let it go too far, maybe they could each draw something from the other. And when the time came, they could walk away without regrets. There was no harm in being a little involved.

As he bent to kiss her, he shoved aside the small voice that whispered that being a little involved was rather like being a little dead. It wasn't something you could do halfway.

If Annalise had ever thought she wasn't a particularly sensuous woman, she quickly learned how wrong she'd been. In Devlin's bed, in his arms, she found out that she had depths of sensuality she'd never expected.

If she'd been asked, she would have said that her ex-husband was a good lover. He'd certainly been kind and considerate, never demanding.

Devlin demanded. He wasn't content to have her simply lie beneath him, accepting his possessions. He demanded her participation, coaxing it from her with his hands and mouth. *His* satisfaction wasn't enough. He wasn't satisfied until he felt her skin heating beneath his hands and heard the soft cries she was helpless to suppress.

Though she tried not to, it was impossible to avoid comparing the only two lovers she'd ever had. She told herself she was being unfair. Bill had been young when they married, with little more experience than she. He'd never hurt her, never tried to coerce her into having sex if she didn't wish to. Making love with him had been a moderately pleasant if not terribly exciting act.

It was only now that she realized just how much she'd missed out on. Sex with Devlin could never be described as "moderately pleasant." It was passionate, consuming, achingly tender. He was more attuned to her body than she was, teaching her that there were more erogenous zones than the obvious ones.

She'd never have imagined that the skin behind her knees was so sensitive or that having him kiss the inside of her elbow could send shivers of awareness through her.

He encouraged her to explore his body as thoroughly as he had hers. Annalise was hesitant at first. It wasn't that she was unfamiliar with the male anatomy. After all, she had been married. But it was a long step from knowing what a man looked like without his clothes and feeling the strength of him under her hands.

But his response encouraged her to overcome her shyness. And she discovered that there was something intensely erotic at feeling Devlin tremble and knowing it was because of her. It made her feel bold and deliciously wicked.

When she thought about it, she was amazed by how quickly and easily they made the shift from roommates to lovers. Though she left most of her things in the spare bedroom, Annalise never used the bed there. It felt natural to go to sleep in Devlin's arms, wonderful to wake up in his bed.

She wondered sometimes just where they were headed. He'd said he couldn't make her any promises, told her there were things she didn't know about him. She didn't doubt he was right.

She still hadn't the faintest idea how he'd come by the kind of money he was spending on the house, especially since he never made any mention of a job he'd had in the past or might return to in the future.

But she didn't really care where the money had come from.

She knew the most important things about Devlin Russell. She knew that he was kind and much softer than he'd probably willingly admit. He'd not only pulled her out of the river, he'd helped her put her life back together.

He pretended to be indifferent to Beauty and her offspring, but he never forgot to make sure there was plenty of cat food in her dish. When the kittens started leaving their home in his closet and venturing into the wide world beyond, Devlin never once showed the slightest sign of impatience at finding them constantly underfoot.

When pathetic wails emanated from the bathroom at two in the morning, Devlin was there hard on Beauty's heels. He fished one particularly daring explorer out of the empty bathtub, which had been easy enough to get into but proved impossible to escape from. Annalise watched sleepily from the bed.

"They like you," she said, cuddling up to his side as he slid under the sheet.

"They're a pain in the neck," he muttered. But the complaint lacked any real force.

She smiled in the darkness. It was funny how he always downplayed his softer side, as if it might make him vulnerable to admit it existed. But she knew it was there.

Devlin's sister showed up again a few days after her first meeting with Annalise. Devlin was in town picking up some lumber when Annalise heard the car coming up the driveway. She'd been shredding chicken for a salad. At first she thought it was Devlin returning, but the deep rumble of the truck's engine was missing.

Rinsing her hands in the sink, she pulled a towel off the rack and dried her hands as she went to the front door. She recognized the car immediately.

Color climbed her cheeks when she thought of Kelly's last visit. Devlin's sister must think she was insane. If Devlin had been home, she might have been tempted to duck out the back door rather than face Kelly again. But Devlin wasn't here and she could hardly ignore his sister.

Drawing in a deep breath, she pushed open the screen door and stepped onto the porch as Kelly crossed the yard. There was no sign of her baby and Annalise felt a twinge of relief. She knew she wouldn't fall apart again, but it would be a long time before she could look at a baby without feeling the pain of her own loss. Maybe that time would never come.

"Hello." Kelly's smile was friendly as she approached the porch.

"Hi." Annalise hoped her own smile didn't reflect her nervousness. "I'm afraid Devlin's not here."

"I figured that when I didn't see his truck." Kelly climbed the steps and stopped beside her, reaching up to take off the sunglasses that shaded her dark eyes. "Mind if I wait for him?"

"Of course not." Annalise was shocked that she felt she had to ask. She pulled open the screen. "I made some lemonade earlier today. Would you like some?"

"Sounds like heaven." Kelly followed her into the kitchen. "It looks like you were in the middle of something. Why don't you finish it and I'll pour the lemonade?''

Annalise hesitated, but Kelly was already pulling open the refrigerator.

''What are you making?''

''Sesame chicken salad.'' She returned to the task of stripping the chicken from its bones. ''It's been so hot, I thought a salad would be nice.''

''It looks like this summer is going to be a real scorcher, doesn't it? Have you been living with my brother very long?''

The question was asked in the same casual tone as her comment about the weather. It took Annalise a moment to register the change of subject.

''Not long. A few weeks.''

''How long have you known him?'' Kelly asked brightly. She filled two glasses with lemonade and set the pitcher down before fixing Annalise with inquiring eyes.

Annalise took her time about answering. She finished the last piece of chicken and scooped the meat into a bowl. She washed her hands and picked up the towel to dry them before turning to look at Kelly.

There was curiosity in the younger woman's eyes but no hostility. Annalise couldn't have blamed her if she'd been more than a little doubtful about her brother's houseguest, considering her performance when they'd met. But if Kelly had doubts, she was concealing them.

''Actually, I met your brother a few weeks ago,'' she said slowly, trying to decide how much to say. What would Devlin want his sister to know? There was no way of knowing, and since Devlin wasn't here, she was just going to have to go with her own instincts.

"I fell in the river, and he pulled me out."

Kelly's eyes widened. The glass she'd just lifted hit the table with a thump that threatened to slosh lemonade over the top.

"You're kidding."

"No." Annalise folded the towel with nervous precision and set it on the counter. She linked her hands in front of her. "I didn't have any money or anywhere to go so he let me stay here. I've been helping him with some records and doing most of the phone calls to suppliers."

"You don't have to explain to me." She stopped and gave Annalise a sheepish smile. "I suppose I more or less asked for an explanation," she admitted.

"I don't mind. I don't blame you for being curious."

"Well, I suspect Devlin wouldn't feel the same way. My big brother has a nasty habit of never telling me anything. Sometimes I think he must have been a superspy all those years he was gone."

Annalise smiled but didn't comment. She'd thought the same thing herself. She knew Devlin had left home at eighteen and that he hadn't come back to Indiana until a year ago, but he'd never mentioned what he'd done during the years in between. Just like he'd never mentioned where he'd gotten the money to build the house. But she didn't think he'd particularly appreciate her speculating about his past with his sister.

"I'm glad you came back," she said. "I wanted to apologize for my behavior the other day. I must have seemed like a crazy woman."

"No. You seemed like someone who was in pain. I've been there a time or two myself. You don't have to apologize."

Until that moment, Annalise hadn't seen much resemblance between Kelly and Devlin. But there was a certain look of acceptance in Kelly's eyes that suddenly made her think of the way Devlin had taken her in without asking questions, without demanding explanations. It was a rare quality but one the Russells seemed to have more than their share of.

"Thank you. But I want to apologize anyway. And I feel as if I should explain."

"Don't feel you have to."

"I want to." Annalise moved away from the counter to pull out a chair at the kitchen table. Kelly followed suit, sitting down across from her.

"A little over a year ago, my daughter...died."

There didn't seem to be any other way to say it, but the words sounded flat and harsh in contrast to the bright sunshine that filled the kitchen. It hurt to hear them. Saying it aloud seemed to sharpen her loss.

"How terrible." Kelly's sympathy was quick and warmly offered. "I'm so sorry."

"Thank you." Annalise gave her a shaky smile. "Mary was older than...your baby, but for a minute, when I saw him, it just brought it all back. But that's no reason for me to run out like such an idiot."

"Please. Don't apologize, Annalise. I can't even begin to imagine how you must feel. If something happened to Clay, I'd...I just don't know what I'd do." Kelly blinked against the sting of tears, unable to conceive how she'd go on if something happened to her son.

She reached across the table, her hand closing over

Annalise's. Though she'd promised herself that she wasn't going to cry, Annalise felt tears fill her eyes when she met Kelly's gaze. Maybe it was the fact that Kelly had a child of her own that made her sympathy seem so personal.

"Thank you." She turned her hand, returning Kelly's grip. Her smile was shaky but hardly more so than Kelly's.

The low rumble of Devlin's truck coming up the driveway interrupted before either of them could say anything more. Annalise felt a mixture of regret and relief. There was relief in having the too-intense moment broken, regret because it seemed as if she and Kelly might have made a start toward a friendship given a little more time.

Kelly watched her older brother's arrival with interest. It had only been a few days since she'd found out that Annalise was living with him, but that had been more than enough time for her to speculate endlessly over the sudden arrival of a woman in Devlin's life.

Since a lot of her speculating had been done out loud, it had been her husband's suggestion that she drop in on Devlin again. Actually Dan's suggestion had been more of a plea. He'd taken Clay with him for the day and all but ordered her to go see her brother and satisfy her curiosity.

Kelly had been relieved when she arrived to find only Annalise. She knew from past experience that she would get little satisfaction from trying to pry information out of Devlin. Better to question the furniture, it was more likely to answer.

In the year since he'd unexpectedly appeared on

her wedding day, he'd told her almost nothing of where he'd been or what he'd done in the ten years since he'd left home. She'd respected his right to privacy.

No one knew better than she what his childhood had been like. It wasn't the sort of background that encouraged a person to be open and forthcoming with other people, even with those who cared for them. The wariness in his eyes told her that the intervening years hadn't given him any reason to open up.

Kelly accepted his choice, even as she ached for the hurts that made him keep the world—including her—at a distance. She'd been completely unprepared to find that he had a woman living with him.

He'd said that Annalise was staying with him, making it sound as if she were more of a temporary boarder than anything else. Annalise had also implied that her staying with Devlin was little more than a case of him offering her a helping hand when she'd needed it.

But it didn't take more than a few moments of observing them together for Kelly to be sure that they were sharing a bed, as well as a house. It wasn't anything obvious. It was subtle things. A certain intimacy in the way they looked at each other, in the casual way Annalise straightened his shirt collar.

That Annalise cared for him was easily read in her eyes. What Devlin felt was harder to say. He didn't reveal his feelings easily. But it seemed as if there were a little less tension around his eyes, a subtle relaxation in the way he held his shoulders.

Kelly could only hope that, whatever was developing between the two of them, neither of them were going to get badly burned.

* * *

It was a few days after Kelly's second visit that the dog showed up. He was not a terribly prepossessing animal. Of a size approaching huge and a color best described as nondescript, he was shaggy, filthy and undoubtedly riddled with fleas.

The first time Annalise saw him, he was trying to tip over the trash cans. He darted off as soon as he saw her, and she thought that was the last she'd see of him. But he was back a few hours later, a gray shadow in the brush at the edge of the yard.

Her heart went out to him. He was so obviously starving. She got some hamburger from the refrigerator and put it on a plate that she carried out into the yard. The dog darted away as soon as she stepped into the yard, but she had the feeling he hadn't gone very far. She set the meat down a few yards away from the porch. She returned to the house but lingered at the back door to see what would happen.

It wasn't long before the dog reappeared. He approached the plate warily, his eyes darting back and forth as if looking for a trap. The food disappeared so quickly, she halfway expected him to eat the plate before he realized it wasn't edible.

She'd been feeding the dog for three days before Devlin noticed. Annalise had just put out another plate of hamburger and was standing on the back porch, watching the dog eat. He'd become a little more confident, no longer running as soon as he saw her. She'd been wondering how long it would take to get him to the point where he'd let her approach him and hadn't heard Devlin's approach.

"A friend of yours?"

She jumped and spun around guiltily. Devlin stood behind her, his eyes on the dog, who'd lifted his head

from the plate and was watching the two of them
warily. Annalise was one thing, but Devlin was an
added factor that he wasn't at all sure of.

"He was starving," she said, getting to the point
immediately.

"He looks like you should be feeding him hay instead of meat," Devlin suggested, eyeing the dog's
massive frame.

"He doesn't eat much." Since the dog was polishing off a pound of hamburger just then, it wasn't perhaps the most truthful thing she'd ever said.

Devlin's gaze settled on her face, his expression
unreadable. "I'd guess he doesn't eat any more than
a small pack of wolves."

"I couldn't let him go hungry," she said, nibbling
on her lower lip.

"Don't worry about it. I'll pick up some dog food
when I go into town this afternoon. Is there anything
else you need?"

And that seemed to be all he had to say about the
dog. He didn't offer any objections to the animal's
presence, any more than he'd objected when Beauty
joined his household or when her kittens had slowly
taken over the house, treating it as their own personal
playground.

Annalise named the dog Lobo, in honor of Devlin's
comment about him eating like a pack of wolves, and
invested considerable time in convincing him that she
could be a friend, as well as a source of food.

Devlin showed no real interest in the latest addition
to his former household of one. Annalise thought he
was completely indifferent until she came home from
a rare solo trip to Remembrance to find Devlin seated
cross-legged in the middle of the backyard, a plate of

hamburger a few feet away from him and Lobo crouched warily a little beyond it.

The house must have blocked the sound of her car from reaching Devlin. She had no doubt he wouldn't want her to know that he was trying to gain Lobo's trust. As she watched, Lobo crept a little closer to the meat, his shaggy belly dragging on the grass.

Devlin didn't move. She could hear the low rumble of his voice, though he was speaking too softly for her to make out any words. The words weren't as important as the tone. Lobo's ears pricked forward slightly, and he edged a little closer to the food.

Annalise couldn't have said how long she stood there watching, and she had no way of knowing how long Devlin had been waiting before she arrived, but he never showed a hint of impatience as Lobo slowly made his way to the food. Devlin didn't move as the dog ate, keeping up the same low-voiced conversation, which was answered by an occasional puzzled look from Lobo or a twitch of an ear.

When the plate was empty, Lobo didn't immediately dart away. Instead, he lifted his head to look at Devlin. He licked his muzzle, his eyes seeming to hold a question. Moving slowly, Devlin lifted his hand, stretching it out palm up. Lobo sniffed the air between them, and for a moment, Annalise thought he was going to take the man up on his invitation to come closer. But instead, he shook himself as if shaking away the urge to be too trusting and turned and trotted off.

She'd planned to get out of sight and pretend she hadn't seen anything of the interaction between man and dog, but Devlin turned his head suddenly, almost as if he sensed her presence. It would have been ridiculous to duck back out of sight.

Annalise pushed open the screen door as Devlin stood up. He retrieved the empty plate and walked toward her, his steps slow.

"For a minute there, I thought you had him," she said.

Devlin shrugged. "From the looks of him, I'd say he's been on his own quite a while. It isn't easy for him to trust."

Rather like himself, Annalise thought, but she didn't say as much. She took the plate from him as they entered the kitchen. She rinsed it and set it in the dishwasher, turning around in time to see one of the kittens launch a fierce attack on Devlin's shoe. Devlin bent down to pull his attacker loose from his shoelace, settling the infant in the palm of his hand, where it promptly began to chew on one of his fingers.

"You're very good with animals," she told him softly, watching him deal with the kitten.

"It doesn't take much." He deposited the kitten on the floor, where it promptly darted off in search of new mischief.

"You were very comfortable with your nephew," she added, remembering how easily he'd handled the infant, without any of the stiffness men usually showed when confronted by a baby. "You'd be a good father."

"No." The single word was flat and harsh. "That's something I'll never be."

He walked out without another word, leaving Annalise staring after him with a frown. What had she said to upset him?

* * *

Devlin strode out of the house, aware that he'd overreacted. Annalise's comment had been nothing more than the sort of casual remark anyone might make. She'd had no way of knowing that her words were going to touch a sore spot that he'd thought healed long ago.

Maybe he wouldn't have snapped at her if he hadn't suddenly had a picture of her stomach swollen with child—his child. He shook his head, dismissing the image. It was impossible for more reasons than one.

Even if Annalise could have children, she'd never have his child. No woman would ever have his baby. If there was any chance at all that the madness that had driven his father to abuse his children was buried somewhere inside him, he'd never take that risk.

There were moments when he lay awake at night, listening to Annalise's quiet breathing and thought of what it might be like to build a life with her as a permanent part of it. But he wasn't going to let himself be blinded to reality by a passing fantasy.

And reality was that he was a born loner. If only Annalise didn't make it so hard to remember that.

Chapter 10

It occurred to Annalise that there was a certain lack of justice in the fact that, though *she'd* been the one to start feeding Lobo, the first person he allowed to touch him was Devlin. Once that hurdle had been overcome, it wasn't long before the huge dog lost most of his wariness. But while he was tolerant of Annalise, he made his preference for Devlin's company quite clear.

Fortunately the dog's lack of appreciation was the only complaint she had with her life at the moment. She was living from day to day, putting the past behind her, not looking too far into the future.

Somewhere in the back of her mind was the knowledge that things couldn't continue as they were forever. She and Devlin were lovers, they were living together. Yet there'd been no mention of even the most rudimentary commitment between them. They'd simply drifted wordlessly from one stage to another, skipping more than a few stages in the middle.

But it felt right, and for now, that was enough. She'd lived with darkness for so long. Devlin had helped her bring light back into her life. Let the future take care of itself.

"Kelly called this afternoon," Annalise said as she scooped pasta salad onto her plate.

"Is everything all right?" Devlin set two glasses of iced tea on the table and took his seat.

"Yes. She called to invite you—well, us, I guess— to a party somebody is giving for her husband's firm. She said she could use a little moral support."

"Remington Construction was building a rather pricey batch of condos in Indianapolis," Devlin said.

"Maybe that's what it's for." She waited but he seemed more concerned with his dinner than with his sister's invitation. "What do you think?"

"I'm not really much of a party-goer. Unless you really wanted to go..." He let the question trail off. He looked up as he spoke, catching the fleeting look of disappointment, quickly smothered, in her blue-green eyes.

"No. Of course not. Do you want to call Kelly or should I?"

Devlin took his time in answering. He stabbed a curly noodle, frowning at it briefly before putting it in his mouth. He didn't taste the garlicky dressing that coated it.

Annalise had been living with him for over a month. She'd gone to Remembrance with him a few times, made the trip herself once or twice. Other than those trips and Kelly's two visits, she hadn't seen another person in all that time. It was hardly surprising if she had been looking forward to going somewhere.

It was different for him. He'd had more than his fair share of humanity after eight years in prison where privacy had been a nonexistent commodity. He could probably live the rest of his life without ever going to a town bigger than Remembrance.

A party with a bunch of people he didn't know and didn't want to know sounded just this side of hell. But there'd been that flash of disappointment in her eyes. She wanted to go and she couldn't go without him.

"Why don't you call and tell her we'll go?" he said slowly, knowing his conscience would nag at him if he suggested otherwise.

"Are you sure? You're not going because you think I want to go, are you?" she asked shrewdly.

"Of course not." He'd spent too many years in prison, he thought with a touch of black humor. He could lie without batting an eye. "Kelly is my sister and this sounds like something that's important to her. If she wants a little support, the least I can do is give it to her. You don't have to go if you don't want to," he added innocently.

"I don't mind. It sounds like it might be interesting." Annalise's mouth curved into a slow grin. "Actually, I really did want to go."

Devlin wondered if it was a dangerous sign to find himself wanting to lean across the table and kiss the smile from her lips.

Like Annalise, Devlin was living day to day. Unlike her, it was the way he'd had to live most of his life. Until recently, there'd never been a time when the future was more than a hazy picture in his mind.

When he was young, the future had consisted of surviving his father's unpredictable rages. After he left home, the future had started to take shape. He'd begun to think of what he might want to do with the rest of his life.

And then Harold Sampson had killed his wife and framed the last man who'd been fool enough to sleep with her for the crime. After that, there'd been no reason to think about the future. The state had his future all neatly wrapped up for quite a while to come.

Since leaving prison, he hadn't considered any further ahead than the next task on the house. He didn't know what he was going to do when the house was finished. Maybe he'd become one of those people who were forever adding onto their home, living in a constant state of construction. There were worse ways to spend your life. God knows, he knew that from personal experience.

Only recently, he'd begun to think that might not be enough. He'd started to wonder if there wasn't something else he'd like to do with his life. Of course, thanks to Harold Sampson's last minute surge of penitence, he didn't have to worry about earning a living.

But he didn't really like using the money. His distaste for it had grown rather than diminished. It didn't matter that, as Reed Hall had pointed out, it was the least the bastard had owed him. It still felt like blood money—paid for with his blood.

But as Reed had also pointed out, he had few marketable skills and eight years in prison would not make a good impression on his résumé.

He scowled at his reflection in the mirror. Why was

he suddenly giving so much thought to the future? Hadn't he learned a long time ago that plans for the future were nearly always derailed long before they came to fruition?

His eyes shifted to the bathroom door which stood open a crack. Annalise's voice drifted from behind it as she sang an old John Denver tune. Her voice was sightly off key and he found his mouth curving upward as he listened to her mangle the lyrics.

He didn't really have to look any further for the reason he was thinking about the future more than he liked to admit. There was something about Annalise that made him do a lot of things he wasn't accustomed to doing. Like adopting stray animals he thought as he reached down to peel loose the kitten that had climbed his pant leg almost to the knee.

And going to parties he had no wish to attend. He deposited the kitten in front of Beauty who promptly flatted it with one paw and began giving it a thorough and unappreciated bath.

Devlin straightened his tie, his frown deepening. Sometimes, he found it difficult to remember what his life had been like before the storm that had brought Annalise into his life. The picture seemed hazy around the edges, as if Annalise's presence had sharpened the focus somehow.

She'd switched to a show tune, humming the parts she didn't remember the words to. It felt good to be standing in his bedroom, listening to her getting ready just behind the bathroom door. A pair of kittens tumbled at his feet, doing their level best to tear each other to pieces. The scene was one of domestic tranquility.

That was what he felt. Tranquil. It wasn't something he'd known a great deal of during his lifetime. If asked, he might have said he didn't know what it felt like to be tranquil. But Annalise had brought that into his life.

"Do I look all right?"

Devlin had been so absorbed in his thoughts that he hadn't noticed her entrance until she spoke. He saw her reflection in the mirror and felt the breath leave his body.

Did she look all right? She looked like heaven, like every fantasy he'd ever had, like all the dreams he'd never let himself have. She looked like more than he could ever hope to possess.

He turned to face her, his expression carefully composed, revealing no hint of the tightness he felt in his stomach.

"I prefer your hair down," he said, reaching out to touch the sleek chignon that confined the heavy length.

"I thought it would look too casual," she said.

"It looks good this way," he said, banishing the slight hesitation from her expression. "You look really nice," he added, realizing immediately how hopelessly inadequate the comment was. "Beautiful," he amended. "You look beautiful."

"You really think so?" Her smile was at once pleased and shy. "Do you think this dress is okay?"

"It's fine."

It was more than fine. The style was deceptively simple. Sapphire blue fabric covered her from throat to knee and shoulder to wrist. But the soft fabric was so fluidly draped that it seemed to caress her body rather than simply conceal it. The skirt ended at her knee, floating softly around her long legs.

The color made her eyes seem more blue than green. Or maybe it was anticipation that made them look so bright and eager. He wished he'd thought of taking her out to dinner or a movie, rather than waiting for Kelly's invitation to make him realize that Annalise might crave something more than his company exclusively.

But taking her out to dinner made it seem as if they were dating. And dating was something you did when you were thinking about getting involved.

And of course you're not involved, his mind asked derisively. *You're only sleeping with her, you jerk. If that isn't involved, what is?*

"Ready to go?" He looked at his watch, as if concerned with the time. They had plenty of time, even considering the length of the drive ahead of them. But he didn't like the direction his thoughts were taking.

The sun was just disappearing from the sky as they reached Indianapolis. Devlin felt his hands tighten on the steering wheel and forced them to relax. He hated the feeling of being surrounded by so many people, so many buildings.

It was only for one evening, he reminded himself. He could tolerate anything for one evening.

But he wasn't so sure when he realized just where the party was being held. The developers hadn't spared any expense in giving the party. They'd rented one of the best restaurants in the city, which just happened to be on the top floor of one of the nicest hotels in the city. All thirty stories of it.

Standing in the beautifully decorated lobby, Devlin stared at the elevator, feeling beads of sweat break out on his forehead. The doors slid open, revealing a spacious, pleasantly lit elevator. All he saw were the boxlike proportions and the fact that there were no windows, no way to get out once those doors slid shut.

''They're holding the elevator for us,'' Annalise said, starting forward.

Devlin's hesitation was imperceptible as he followed her. It was an elevator, he told himself. People got on and off elevators all the time. He couldn't spend his entire life avoiding them.

He stepped into the cubicle. Immediately his tie felt too tight. His jacket seemed to have shrunk. There was only one other couple on the elevator, but he felt as if the air were being used up too quickly, as if suffocation was only a breath away.

He was unaware of Annalise glancing at him, her eyes showing sudden concern. She'd sensed his hesitation in the lobby and attributed it to a lingering reluctance to attend the party. She knew he'd only decided to go because he felt obligated to support his sister, and perhaps he'd sensed the interest she'd tried to conceal.

But the tension she felt radiating from him couldn't be explained away as a lack of sociability. His jaw was so tight she knew he had to be grinding his teeth together. Beads of sweat dampened his forehead.

Concerned, she reached out to take his hand. His fingers closed over hers, his grip too tight. She offered no objection but only moved closer so that her shoulder brushed against his. The elevator faltered for an instant, a hardly perceptible shift in speed. Devlin's fingers tightened so crushingly that she had to bite her lip to stifle a gasp.

When the elevator came to a halt and the doors slid open, his relief was palpable. He stepped out quickly, as if half-afraid the doors might slide shut, trapping him inside again.

Kelly had been watching for their arrival and she appeared before them immediately, sweeping them off to where she and Dan were seated. In the hustle of introductions and greetings, there was certainly no chance for Annalise to consider Devlin's behavior. But in odd moments during the evening, she found her thoughts drifting to those few seconds in the elevator when his hand had clung to hers as if he were a drowning man and she were a lifeline.

The answer wasn't hard to guess. In fact, it was a wonder it hadn't occurred to her before. The house he'd helped to design provided more than a few clues. Every room was full of windows. Even the bathrooms had large expanses of frosted glass that let in light and made the room seem larger, less enclosed.

The only doors were on the bathrooms. He'd had to install a door when he'd settled her into the guest room. Most of the rooms didn't even have a doorway that would take a door. Wide arches visually expanded the space, preventing any sense of being closed in, no matter where you were.

Devlin suffered from claustrophobia. Not an uncommon problem. A lot of people had it to some degree. Devlin obviously had more than just a mild touch of it. He'd been holding on to his control with nothing but willpower. The ride up in the elevator had obviously been a short stay in hell for him.

It was a rare show of vulnerability from a man who went to great pains to show only his strong side. Annalise felt a wave of tenderness. If he'd told her how he felt, she'd have happily volunteered to walk up all thirty flights with him. But of course he wouldn't admit to being afraid of closed-in places. And he wouldn't welcome any mention of it, either.

Despite his reluctance to attend the gathering, she noticed that Devlin didn't seem out of place. He didn't exactly circulate, but he made himself pleasant where necessary. He spent some time talking to Michael Sinclair, who'd designed, not only the project whose completion was being celebrated, but also Devlin's house.

Michael's wife, Brittany, was a friend of Kelly's, and Kelly made it a point to introduce Brittany and Annalise. The three of them chatted comfortably. By the end of the evening, Annalise felt as if she'd furthered her fledgling friendship with Devlin's sister and perhaps made a start toward another friendship with Brittany Sinclair.

In all her years of being moved from one foster home to another, she'd never had a chance to build friendships. After a while, she'd stopped trying. It simply hurt too much when the time came to give them up. Talking with Brittany and Kelly, she felt a deep regret for all the years she'd done without the sort of easy camaraderie she sensed between the two of them.

It was a pleasant evening, but Annalise wasn't sorry when Devlin touched her elbow and suggested that they had a long drive ahead of them. She'd had a nice time, but it had been a long time since she'd been around so many people all at once, and she'd forgotten what an exhausting experience it could be.

She felt Devlin tense as they stopped in front of the elevator, and she bit her lip, wishing she dared to suggest that walking down thirty flights of stairs was a long-time desire of hers. The doors slid open and Devlin stepped through them with all the enthusiasm of a man facing a firing squad.

They had the elevator to themselves. The doors had barely closed when Annalise turned and wound her arms around Devlin's neck, pulling his head down to hers until their lips met.

Devlin felt his mind go blank with surprise. Though he'd always encouraged her participation in bed, this was the first time Annalise had ever shown any hint of sexual aggression.

And this was more than a hint. He sucked in a quiet breath as she lowered one hand from his shoulder and boldly cupped her fingers over the growing bulge beneath his fly. Passion exploded in the pit of his stomach.

He forgot all about his hatred of enclosed places. In fact, he forgot where they were. His hands slid down her back to cup her bottom, drawing her forward. Annalise gasped. Her hand left him and she caught at his shoulders for balance as he lifted her off her feet to press her against his thighs, showing her just how successful her attempt at distraction had been.

His lips slanted over hers, his tongue plunging between her lips, taking possession of her mouth the way he longed to take possession of her body.

The elevator shuddered slightly as it arrived at the ground floor. Devlin's hands released her reluctantly, letting her feet touch the carpeted floor just as the door slid open.

Annalise stared up at him, her eyes dazed. Her impulsive attempt to distract him from his surroundings had been so successful she'd very nearly forgotten where they were.

"Shall we?" he murmured when she showed no signs of moving.

"Shall we what?" She sounded as dazed as she felt. Devlin's mouth curved in a smile, his eyes gleaming with purely masculine satisfaction.

"Go." He turned her in the direction of the doors and gave her a gentle push.

Neither of them said a word during the drive home. Not by so much as a word or a glance did either acknowledge those torrid moments in the elevator. They might have been completely unaware of each other.

But that wasn't the case. Annalise could feel the tension that hummed between them like a tautly pulled wire. If she'd thought the fire that had been ignited would die out during the long drive, she realized how wrong she'd been.

She didn't have to touch Devlin or even look at him to be acutely aware of him. He didn't have to put his hands on her to make her skin tingle with awareness. There was only one way for the evening to end, and the anticipation was the most arousing kind of foreplay. Proof positive that the mind was the most powerful erogenous zone.

By the time he stopped the truck beside the house, she wasn't sure her knees would support her. Devlin shut off the engine and thrust open his door without a word. Annalise pushed open her own door, but before she could slide to the ground, Devlin was there, his hands circling her waist. He lifted her easily to the ground.

Annalise had to lock her knees to keep from simply

collapsing at his feet. But even that didn't help when he slammed her door shut and then crowded her back against the truck.

"Do you know how much I want you?" he whispered raggedly.

If she hadn't already guessed, she would have now. Caught between the cool surface of the truck and the heat of his body, she could feel his arousal pressed against her stomach.

"All I could think about all the way home was how much I wanted to be inside you, feeling you close around me, all hot and damp."

She bit her lip to hold back a whimper of need, closing her eyes against the glittering intensity of his. His hands slid up from her waist to cup the weight of her breasts, his thumbs brushing over her nipples, bringing them to full arousal beneath the thin fabric of her dress.

Momentarily satisfied with her reaction, he shifted his attention to her hair, his fingers searching for and disposing of the pins that held it in place. It tumbled over his forearms in a heavy silk curtain. He buried his fingers in it, tilting her head up until his mouth could find hers in a quick, hard kiss.

He bent suddenly, lifting her in his arms with a movement so full of urgency that Annalise felt her breath stolen from her. Lobo lifted his head from his paws to watch them from the corner of the porch he'd claimed as his, but he seemed to sense that this was not a time to draw attention to himself.

They were barely inside the front door before Devlin was letting her slide to her feet, his fingers searching for the zipper at the back of her dress even as his mouth closed over hers.

Passion spiraled between them at a dizzying speed. The dress fell to the floor and he lifted her, arching her back over his arm so that her breasts were thrust upward. Annalise caught her breath on a sob as his mouth closed over her. He sucked strongly at her nipple. She felt the pressure deep inside, a hot liquid pool in the pit of her stomach.

Her fingers wound in his thick, dark hair, holding him to her as he switched his attention to her other breast. She twisted against him, seeking relief for the throbbing ache between her thighs.

She was only vaguely aware that he was moving, carrying her easily, never ceasing the sweet torment of his mouth on her breasts. By the time he at last allowed her to slide slowly the length of his body, she didn't have the strength to do more than cling to his shoulders. He eased her back and down. It wasn't until she felt the bed beneath her that she realized he'd brought her into the bedroom.

"My God, Annalise!" The words were torn from him as he realized for the first time that she was wearing nothing but a pair of scandalously small blue panties and a matching lacy garter belt that held up a pair of sheer stockings.

Seeing his stunned expression, she stretched, drawing up one leg and arching her back. For the second time that night she saw beads of sweat dampen his forehead, but for a very different reason this time.

"Do you like them?" she asked him, her voice husky and seductive. She'd felt deliciously naughty when she bought them and positively wicked when she put them on. Now she felt all woman, a temptress in sapphire silk.

"Like them?" He licked suddenly dry lips. "If I'd

know you had them on, I'd have been hard all night,"
he admitted.

"I bought them just for you." She ran the toes of
one foot down his leg. "Is that a gun in your pocket
or are you happy to see me?" As a Mae West imi-
tator, she wasn't likely to make it professionally. But
Devlin didn't seem to care.

"I'm *very* happy to see you," he said with a husky
laugh.

He disposed of his clothes in record time, popping
several buttons from his shirt when they refused to
yield to his shaking fingers. Annalise felt her body
flush in anticipation as the last of his clothes hit the
floor, revealing the magnificent strength of his
arousal.

She reached her arms up to him, needing to feel
him against her. She needed to feel him inside her,
driving away the emptiness. Not just the physical
emptiness but the emotional hollowness that only he
could fill.

At the sight of her reaching for him, Devlin felt his
pulse pound in his temples, batoning at all rational
thought beyond the primal need to feel her beneath
him, to feel her holding him.

His need was too great to allow time for dealing
with anything as complex as garters. The delicate silk
panties tore. Annalise didn't care. Her need was as
deep as his.

Her fingers clung to his shoulders as he came down
to her, his hips wedging her legs apart. He entered
her with one smooth, hard thrust, burying his aching
flesh in the damp heat of her.

She cried out as the deep ache in her was at once
eased and sharpened. It wasn't enough. It couldn't

ever be enough. She lifted her legs to take him deeper, wanting—needing—to feel him in every fiber of her being.

The feel of her long legs, still sheathed in the thin nylon stockings, pressed against his hips made Devlin groan. He surged heavily against her, feeling her nails dig into his shoulders as she met his every thrust, her breathing coming in deep sobbing gasps.

It was too intense to last very long. Devlin felt the delicate tightening of her body around him. He struggled to hold off his own climax, wanting it to last forever. But feeling Annalise shudder beneath him, hearing her call his name at the height of her pleasure, he felt himself dragged headlong into the vortex of her peak.

Annalise felt Devlin swell even larger inside her and then a guttural cry was torn from him. She clung to him, letting his shuddering completion drive her higher still until nothing existed in the universe but the two of them.

Devlin's body was heavy on hers, but it was a welcome weight. She'd never felt as complete in her life as she did when she held him in her arms. His breathing was still ragged when he moved to relieve her of his weight. She murmured a sleepy protest and clung to him.

"I'll crush you, sweetheart." The only time he used endearments was when they were in bed, another small intimacy that she savored. Reluctantly she loosened her arms, allowing him to ease to the side.

"You realize, of course, that you could have caused me permanent physical damage," he said conversationally. He slid his arm under her shoulders and drew her closer, tangling his fingers in her hair.

"What did I do?" She rubbed her hand over his muscled chest.

"Kissing me like that in the elevator," he reproached her huskily. "Especially when there wasn't anything I could do about it until I got you home."

"Gee, I'll try not to do it again."

"Things like that can do permanent damage to a guy." Since he was carefully arranging her hair across her breast as he spoke, his fingers lingering on the tender peak of her nipple, Annalise didn't think he was too upset.

"I'm sorry," she whispered, her back arching in an unconscious invitation as he stroked his thumb over her. She'd never have believed she could feel arousal so soon after the soul-shattering lovemaking they'd just experienced.

"I suppose I could be persuaded to forgive you," he said softly. He shifted so that he was leaning on one elbow next to her, his shoulders blocking out the dim light.

"You could?" Her voice was little more than a whisper as his fingers trailed across her stomach to find the lacy waistband of the garter belt.

"But it would take some pretty powerful persuasion," he warned her.

His mouth closed over hers, muffling the soft moan that suggested she was willing to be as persuasive as he liked.

Chapter 11

It was a scorchingly hot summer day when Reed Hall's rental car rumbled down the driveway. Annalise had spent the morning pulling weeds from the small flower bed she'd put in on the curve at the end of the driveway, but the heat had driven her to retreat to the shade afforded by the porch.

Devlin had invested in a glider to supplement the lawn chair that had been the porch's only furnishing. Annalise settled into its cushioned comfort, drawing one leg up under her, leaving the toe of her other foot on the floor to keep the glider in motion.

Beauty had joined her after directing a token hiss in Lobo's direction, a gesture that was greeted with magnificent indifference by the big dog. Annalise had worried about his reaction to Beauty and her kittens, but it had proved a groundless concern.

Lobo, for all his dangerous looks, had proved to be endlessly tolerant of assorted kitten-launched attacks.

In that respect, he reminded Annalise irresistibly of Devlin, hiding a marshmallow-soft interior behind a forbidding exterior.

The heat had a somnolent effect. She was drowsily contemplating whether or not to expend the energy required to go into the house and stretch out on the bed when she heard a car turn off the road onto the lane.

Devlin had been hanging drywall in the living room, but the sound of the car drew him out onto the porch.

''Are you expecting anyone?'' Annalise asked him, sitting up to watch the dust-covered sedan approach.

''No.'' He narrowed his eyes against the bright sun.

The man who slid out from behind the wheel nearly matched Devlin's six feet two inches, but any resemblance ended there. The sun caught in hair of such a pale blond it approached white. Where Devlin was broad shouldered and solid, this man was slender, though the casual knit shirt revealed the taut ripple of muscles in his arms. He moved with an easy grace that made Annalise think of athletes she'd seen on television.

''Reed.'' Devlin said the name under his breath. Annalise drew her eyes from the newcomer and looked up at him. As usual, it was impossible to read his expression, although she thought there was a certain tension in his shoulders that suggested the visitor was not entirely welcome.

''A friend of yours?''

''More or less.'' But he didn't move forward to greet the man. Reed crossed the yard, stopping at the foot of the steps, his head tilted to look up at Devlin.

"I was in the neighborhood. Hope you don't mind."

His voice was deep and slow, with the merest trace of a drawl to hint at a Southern background.

"Reed." For a moment, Devlin didn't seem to have anything to say beyond the flat greeting. Annalise's eyes darted between the two men, wondering just what a "more or less" friend was.

"It's good to see you," Devlin said at last. He stepped forward, extending his hand.

Reed's lean face features relaxed in a smile. He climbed the steps and took Devlin's hand, shaking it with unmistakable warmth.

"It's good to see you, Devlin. You're looking good."

"Well, I pretty well had to look better than I did the last time you saw me," Devlin said, his mouth twisting with a bitter humor Annalise didn't understand.

Before Reed could respond, Devlin turned to draw Annalise into the picture.

"Annalise, this is Reed Hall, a...friend of mine." The hesitation before the word *friend* did not go unnoticed by Reed, but he didn't seem disturbed. "Reed, this is Annalise St. John. She's staying with me."

Not, "She's living with me." Annalise noticed how he avoided making her presence seem too permanent. She swallowed the twinge of disappointment she felt and stood up.

"I didn't realize Devlin had such good taste," Reed said with an easy smile.

"Thank you." Up close, she realized that his eyes were an unusual shade of pure green, without the slightest hint of gold. The combination of that pale hair and brilliant eyes was striking.

"I made some lemonade earlier," she said as she withdrew her hand from his. "Would you like some?"

"Sounds wonderful. I was beginning to think I should have bought a canteen in the last town."

Annalise wondered just how good a friend Devlin considered Reed. Certainly he'd never mentioned the man to her. But then, though she thought they'd attained a certain closeness these past weeks, there was still a big part of himself that Devlin kept walled off. Most of his past was behind that wall.

Considering his rather wary greeting when Reed showed up, Annalise was surprised when Devlin invited the other man to use the spare bedroom, especially since he must have known that it meant she'd have to move her clothing and few personal possessions into the master bedroom. They might have been sharing a bed for weeks, but he'd never suggested that she move her belongings into his bedroom and she hadn't mentioned it.

While Devlin and Reed were talking, she excused herself and hastily gathered her clothing from the spare bedroom and deposited it on Devlin's bed.

There was no chance to discuss the move with Devlin until just before dinner when Reed took his suitcase into his room to clean up before the meal.

Devlin was slicing vegetables for a tossed salad while Annalise kept an eye on the marinated chicken she'd slipped into the broiler.

"I put my things in your room," she said. "I assumed that was what you wanted." She slid him a questioning look, wondering if he was going to feel that she'd stepped across that invisible barrier he kept around himself.

''Sure. Clear whatever closet and drawer space you need.''

Devlin sliced a cucumber with quick, sure strokes. Reed's unexpected visit had given him the excuse he needed to get Annalise moved into his bedroom. She shared his bed, but every morning she disappeared into the other bedroom to shower and dress.

At first, he'd thought it the perfect arrangement. It kept the true nature of their relationship perfectly clear. They were lovers but they weren't seriously involved. This was only a temporary arrangement for both of them, a chance to heal a few old wounds before moving on.

But lately, he'd started to realize that sharing a bed but not a bedroom was nothing more than a smoke screen he'd put up to try to convince himself of the ephemeral nature of their involvement. The fact was, he was more deeply involved with Annalise St. John than he'd ever expected, or wanted, to be with a woman. And he could debate the wisdom of that involvement from now till doomsday, but it wasn't going to change the reality of it.

As long as they *were* involved, he didn't want her sneaking out of his room to go to hers to shower and dress. Of course, he could have just suggested that she move her things into his room. But that might imply a commitment he wouldn't—couldn't—make.

Reed's visit had given him the perfect opportunity to get Annalise to move into his room without getting into a discussion of what the move *really* meant.

God, when had he become such a manipulative bastard?

He brought the knife down with too much force, causing it to slip sideways on the cutting board and nick the base of his thumb.

"Damn!" He lifted the injured hand to his mouth.

"Are you hurt?" Annalise darted to him, taking hold of his wrist to examine the injury.

"It's not bad."

"It should have a bandage. Here, rinse it off and I'll get the peroxide." Without waiting for his consent, she turned on the cold-water tap and thrust his hand under it.

With the cold water rushing over his hand, Devlin watched her rummage in the cupboard next to the sink, searching for the bottle of hydrogen peroxide and a box of adhesive strips. There was a small, concerned frown pleating her forehead. She was worried about him.

The thought flowed over him like a warm sunshine. In his life, there'd been few people who ever worried about him. His mother had never quite come into the real world long enough to worry about anyone but herself. And his father's only concern had been beating all traces of sin out of him.

Kelly cared enough to worry about him. Other than his sister, the only name that came to mind was Reed's. And even that had been largely because it was his job to worry about his client.

But Annalise wasn't his sister and she wasn't his lawyer. She wasn't bound by familial or professional obligations to be concerned. She just was.

"Here." She turned from the cupboard and shut off the water. Wrapping his hand in a soft cotton towel, she dried it gently. Devlin found himself regretting that it was such a minor cut. It seemed a pity for her to expend all that sweet concern on anything less than arterial bleeding. She examined the small cut, her frown easing.

"It really isn't too bad. Here, this may sting a little." She poured the hydrogen peroxide over the cut, lifting anxious eyes to his face as the liquid foamed into the injury.

"Waiting to see me writhe in agony?" His mouth quirked with humor.

"I just don't like hurting people, even in a good cause." She picked up an adhesive strip and opened it. "I always hated it when Mary injured herself. Sometimes, it was all I could do to keep from crying more than she did."

It was the first time he'd heard her mention her daughter since the night she'd told him about the child. She placed the strip across the cut, pressing the adhesive portion to his hand before lifting her eyes to his face again.

"I haven't thought about that in a long time," she said slowly. "It doesn't seem to hurt as much to think about her anymore. I guess maybe time really does heal all wounds."

"I guess so." Devlin lifted his newly bandaged hand to brush a lock of hair back from her face, his fingers lingering on her cheek. He wished suddenly that time could heal the wounds that had eaten into his soul, that he could believe the time would come when he'd feel whole, when he might be able to offer her something more than what he was now.

"Are you aware that you have a small squad of furred terrorists living in your house?" Reed's question preceded him. Devlin's hand dropped away from Annalise's face and he stepped back.

When Reed stepped on the other side of the breakfast bar, he had a gray kitten in his hand, one long finger rubbing absently between its ears.

"I should have warned you about them," Annalise said, when Devlin didn't seem to have a response. "They're at the mischievous age."

"Mischievous? After climbing my pant leg—while I was still in the pants, I'd like to point out—he proceeded to launch a vicious attack on one of my shoelaces."

"Yes. Well, we haven't quite managed to convince them that shoelaces aren't alien invaders." Annalise pulled the chicken out of the broiler and poked it experimentally. "I think supper's about ready."

Reed turned out to be a pleasant and undemanding guest. He was a lawyer. He'd been working as a court-appointed defender for the past ten years. He'd taken a few months off just to drive around the country, see all the sights he'd never had time to look at.

Annalise learned more from watching him than she did from what he said. He was easygoing, regarding the world with a sort of sleepy amusement. But after a day or two, she began to get the feeling that there were a lot of things Reed kept hidden, depths he shielded with a friendly smile and an easy laugh.

When she asked Devlin how he and Reed had met, he said only that they'd met quite a few years ago but hadn't really seen all that much of each other. He didn't volunteer any more information and she didn't try to pry it out of him, not that prying would have done her much good.

Reed didn't expect to be entertained. In fact, the first day he was there, he pitched in and helped Devlin put up drywall. He freely admitted that his experience as a handyman was limited to the ability to plug in a microwave oven and occasionally pump his own gas, but he wasn't afraid to get his hands dirty, and he didn't mind asking questions until he understood what had to be done.

Devlin would have sworn that the last thing he wanted was someone working with him. One of the joys in doing so much of the work himself was that it meant long, uninterrupted hours of solitude. But Reed proved to be an undemanding companion.

Their acquaintance over the past ten years had been brief, if eventful. Despite the fact that Devlin was willing to count Reed as one of the few people to whom he could apply the word *friend,* he couldn't really say that they knew each other well.

There hadn't been time to get to know each other well. When a man was on trial for first-degree murder, he was inclined to develop an immediate intimacy with the lawyer who was defending him.

When he'd been released from prison, there'd been the pressure of deciding what to do with his sudden, unwelcome inheritance. But there'd been more time for getting to know Reed as a man rather than simply as a lawyer.

Now, seeing Reed outside his familiar element, Devlin was able to confirm the fact that he liked the man. Reed appreciated the value of silence. If he didn't know how to do something, he watched Devlin until he figured it out. In fact, it was not unpleasant to share the labor with someone.

* * *

The small, oddly matched group rubbed along quite well together for nearly a week. Annalise had settled into Devlin's bedroom so easily it was sometimes difficult to remember that she hadn't always been there. She liked seeing her rather sparse wardrobe hanging next to Devlin's shirts.

Though she'd purchased a few things with the salary Devlin paid her, she'd put most of the money in an envelope she kept under her lingerie. Most of the time, she managed to pretend that things weren't going to change, that she was just going to continue living with Devlin, growing closer to him, gaining his trust.

But reality was something Annalise had learned to live with at an early age. And she couldn't completely overlook the possibility that, sooner or later, Devlin was going to want his house to himself.

If and when that time came, she was going to need the money she was carefully putting away now. Not that he'd throw her out into the metaphorical cold, but pride demanded that she be able to leave with some dignity. Even if she had severe doubts about whether or not she was earning the salary he was paying her, at least she had some claim to the money.

Her fingers lingered on the sleeve of the jacket Devlin had worn to the party in Indianapolis. Her cheeks warmed with memories of how that evening had ended. If she left, she'd take more than money with her.

Annalise shut the closet. Time enough to think about leaving if and when the time came. At the moment, she needed to check on dinner.

Dinner was a more lively affair since Reed's arrival. He was an amusing raconteur and his years of working in criminal justice had given him a better-than-average store of anecdotes.

Tonight he had Annalise laughing over the story of a drug dealer who'd shot a man for kicking the bumper of the dealer's Cadillac and then tried to claim it was self-defence because the car was like a part of him. The man had survived and the dealer had gone to jail, still protesting with apparent sincerity that his sentence was a gross miscarriage of justice. The absurd story even managed to draw a laugh out of Devlin.

But his smile vanished with Reed's next words.

"Cases like that are what help you keep your sanity," he said, pushing his empty plate away and tilting his chair back. "Thank God, all of them aren't like yours, Devlin."

Annalise's head jerked up, her eyes darting from Reed to Devlin. "Your case?" she questioned. "Reed defended you?"

"Damn." The front legs of Reed's chair hit the floor with a thunk. His eyes sought out Devlin's. "I'm sorry."

"It's okay." But Devlin's expression said it was far from okay. He looked at Annalise, his eyes shuttered. "Reed defended me."

Annalise bit her lip, swallowing the questions bubbling up in her throat. It was obvious that he didn't want to talk about it.

"I spent eight years in prison," Devlin said abruptly, shoving back his chair and standing up.

"Eight years?" Annalise couldn't prevent the startled exclamation or the question that followed. "What for?"

"First-degree murder." The words were flat. With-

out another word, he turned and walked out of the
kitchen. The screen door banged shut behind him as
he strode out into the gathering dusk.

He left a strained silence behind him. Annalise
stared at the chair he'd been sitting in, trying to absorb the impact of this new information. Devlin had
spent eight years in prison for murder. That was why
he never talked about the years after he'd left home.

"Me and my big mouth." Reed broke the silence,
his voice rough with regret. "I assumed you'd
know."

"No." She shook her head slowly. "I didn't know.
Devlin doesn't talk about himself very much."

"I remember. It made him difficult to defend. I
couldn't get anything out of him that would let me
play on the jury's sympathies."

"What happened?" She looked at him, her eyes
full of questions.

Reed hesitated and then slowly shook his head.
"I've already said too much. Let Devlin tell you
whatever he feels is right."

Annalise nodded. Of course he was right. It wasn't
fair to go behind Devlin's back. And if Devlin chose
to tell her nothing? Well, she'd live with that. It
wasn't as if it really mattered. Knowing he'd been in
prison didn't change him from the man she'd been
living with—the man she was very much afraid she
was falling in love with.

"The one thing I will tell you is that he was innocent," Reed said.

"Of course." The look she threw him said that he
didn't have to bother stating the obvious.

Reed watched her as she got up and began clearing

the table. He wondered if Devlin had any idea just how lucky he'd been to find a woman like Annalise.

Devlin still hadn't returned at ten o'clock. Reed had disappeared into the guest room early in the evening, commenting that he wasn't likely to be high on Devlin's list of people he was anxious to see. Annalise had stayed up, pretending to read a book.

But her mind couldn't focus on the printed page. She kept thinking about Devlin, how bleak his face had looked in those moments before he walked out. Did he think she'd turn away from him now that she knew about his time in prison? Did he even care?

At ten-thirty, she gave up and went to bed. She knew she wouldn't sleep, but maybe it would be better if she didn't blatantly wait up for Devlin.

She'd been absolutely sure that sleep would be impossible, but she'd been unusually tired lately and she drifted off not long after climbing between the sheets.

Annalise didn't know what time it was when she woke to the sound of thunder rumbling overhead. The weather report had been promising a storm for the following day. From the sounds of it, it had arrived early. She turned sleepily, reaching out for Devlin, but the bed was empty, the sheets cool.

Memories of the evening's events swept over her and she sat up, pushing the heavy weight of her hair back from her face. A glance at the clock told her it was a little after midnight. She was just about to swing her feet out of bed and go looking for Devlin, even if it meant trekking through the fields with a flashlight when she saw the still figure at the window.

She sagged with relief. He was home and safe. Nothing else was as important as that.

She started to go to him and then hesitated. The set
of his shoulders suggested that he wasn't in the mood
for company. Maybe she should lie back down and
pretend she hadn't wakened. But he looked so completely alone.

She slid off the bed and padded silently toward
him. Lightning flashed as she stopped next to him.
Thunder rumbled on its heels. He'd taken off his shirt
and draped it over a chair.

"Hi," she said softly. The muscles in his back
tensed as if expecting a blow.

"Go back to bed, Annalise." There was no anger
in the words. There was no emotion at all in them.

"Only if you come to bed, too."

"Later."

"Then I'll stay up with you."

He shrugged as if it were a matter of complete indifference.

Annalise hesitated. In the weeks she'd lived with
him, the one unspoken rule had been that neither had
invaded the other's privacy. He hadn't pushed her to
tell him about losing Mary, and she hadn't pushed
him to tell her about the past he so carefully avoided
mentioning. If she followed that pattern, then she'd
go back to bed and leave him alone.

But no one should be so completely alone. She'd
felt that way after losing her child. There'd been no
one she could turn to to share her grief, no one who
cared whether or not she lived or died. Eventually it
had nearly ceased to matter to her.

She slid her arms around Devlin's waist, pressing
her cheeks against the warm skin of his back. He
stiffened and she thought he might pull away.

"It doesn't matter, you know," she said softly.

"You don't have to talk about it, but I want you to know that it doesn't matter."

"Doesn't it?" He remained rigid in the circle of her arms, but he didn't pull away. "I spent eight years in prison. Doesn't that worry you?"

"You were innocent."

"Did Reed tell you that?"

"He didn't have to. And if you did kill someone, I'm sure you had a reason."

Her calm assumption of his innocence flowed over Devlin like a sweet benediction. His short laugh held pain.

"I could have used twelve people like you on the jury."

"Obviously, they were twelve very foolish people," she said lightly.

He turned suddenly, putting his arms around her and crushing her close. "Thank you."

"You don't have to thank me for having good sense." She rubbed her cheek against the mat of hair on his chest, saving the feel of him safe and warm in her arms.

She loved him. The thought slipped into her consciousness with hardly a ripple. It was as if it had been there all along, just waiting for her to notice it. How could she not love him?

Devlin's hand slid into her hair, tilting her head back. His eyes glittered down at her, their expression impossible to see. Lightning flashed behind him, and it occurred to her how many significant moments in their relationship had been played out with a storm as a backdrop.

"I have never in my life known anyone like you," he said, his voice hardly above a whisper.

''That makes us even, because I've never known anyone like you.''

He bent to kiss her, his mouth gentle. In the kiss, he tried to express all the things he couldn't find the words to say—how much it meant to him that she believed in him, the serenity she'd brought to his life.

Annalise felt the sting of tears, and she closed her eyes to conceal them from him. She wanted to tell him she loved him, that he'd made her life whole again, that she'd always believe him.

But now was not the time. Devlin wasn't ready to hear those words from her—might never be ready.

The eastern sky was just starting to turn gray when Devlin left Annalise sleeping in the bedroom. He hadn't slept. His thoughts were too jumbled to allow him to relax.

Annalise's unquestioning belief in his innocence had affected him more than he wanted to admit. He couldn't remember anyone ever having that sort of faith in him. It made him feel strong, humble and vulnerable. It was the feeling of vulnerability that made him frown.

''If you're anticipating the need to throw me out on my ear, I'll go without a fight.''

Startled, Devlin turned toward the dry voice, making out Reed's figure standing beside one of the windows.

''I was going to go on my own,'' Reed continued, ''but I'd be happy to give you the pleasure of tossing me down the steps.''

Devlin lifted his shoulders in an easy shrug as he walked forward, taking up a position on the opposite side of the window.

"I wasn't thinking about throwing you out."

"You should. I'm sorry for speaking out of turn last night." Reed offered the apology with simple sincerity.

"It's okay."

"No, it's not. I just assumed Annalise would know."

"Yeah. I hadn't gotten around to telling her." Devlin watched a thin gold edge appear on the eastern horizon. He hadn't planned on ever telling her, but there was no need to confide that to Reed. "No harm done."

"Good." Reed moved to perch on the back of the sofa. "But I'll be leaving today, anyway."

"You don't have to do that." Devlin glanced at the other man.

"Thanks. But it's time I was moving on."

Devlin didn't argue. He'd enjoyed Reed's company, but he wouldn't be completely sorry to see him go. He missed the easy space of evenings spent with no one but Annalise for company. It occurred to him that he didn't feel similar nostalgia for the many evenings he'd spent alone before Annalise's entry into his life. He pushed the thought aside.

"Why did you come?" he asked Reed. The question had been in the back of his mind ever since the lawyer's arrival.

Reed smiled, his teeth gleaming white in the near darkness. "I've asked myself that a few times."

"Did you come up with an answer?"

Reed shrugged. "I guess I needed to see that you were making out okay."

"Why wouldn't I be?"

"No reason." He shrugged again. "In the years

I've worked as a public defender, I haven't had very many cases that had happy endings. The ones who get off, more often than not, are back in court before long. The ones who do time usually get out and get in trouble again. It's not a really encouraging line of work.''

"Why stay with it?" Devlin leaned his shoulder against the wall, his eyes on Reed's face.

"For the few times when you know justice really has prevailed," Reed told him. "For the times when the client is innocent and you can prove it and you know they're going to stay clean." He stopped, his eyes bleak in the growing light. "But there don't seem to be very many cases like that anymore."

"So quit."

Reed's gaze jerked to his, his lean features breaking into a slow smile. "Actually, I have." The smile faded. "I've been thinking about it for a while. I had a case—" He broke off, shaking his head. "A nineteen-year-old kid. He was arrested on drug charges. He'd never been in trouble in his life."

"Was he guilty?"

"I don't think so. He said a friend of his must have left the drugs in his car. I believed him. Even if the judge didn't agree, it would have been a first offense and I could have gotten him off with nothing but probation. But just the arrest was enough to kill his chances of getting the basketball scholarship he'd been counting on to get him into college."

Reed stopped, his gaze focused on something only he could see.

"What happened?" Devlin prompted. He could guess what had happened, but he sensed that the other man needed to finish the story.

"He hung himself the night before the hearing," Reed said without emotion.

"It wasn't your fault," Devlin said after a moment.

"No. No, I know it wasn't my fault." He gave a quick half smile. "I told him he'd get probation at worst. I didn't quit because I believed Todd's death was my fault. I quit because I can't do it anymore."

"What are you going to do now?"

"I don't know." Reed hesitated a minute and then looked at him with a self-conscious grin. "Would you believe, I'm giving serious consideration to buying a ranch in Montana or Wyoming?"

"Sounds good." Devlin thought about how working to build something strong and lasting had helped heal his wounds. Maybe it could do the same for Reed.

Reed stood and stretched. "Well, I'm going to try and catch a couple hours sleep before I pack."

"You don't have to go," Devlin told him again.

"It's time. Wasn't it Ben Franklin who said that guests and fish both stink after three days? I've been here five and I think I'm beginning to detect a slight odor."

Devlin returned his grin, though he didn't argue. Reed turned toward the guest room, then he hesitated, turning back to look at his host.

"You've got one terrific lady in there," he said, nodding toward the master bedroom.

Devlin's smile faded, his expression suddenly wary. "It isn't exactly that kind of relationship," he said.

Reed's brows rose but, wisely, he didn't argue. "Well, whatever kind of relationship it is, you're damned lucky."

Devlin watched as he entered the spare bedroom. He continued to stare at the closed door, a frown tugging at his forehead. "Whatever kind of relationship it is." That was a damned good question.

Annalise reached out to take the hand Reed offered, her smile reflecting her regret at this goodbye. She liked Reed Hall. He was easy to like, but even without that, she liked the fact that he cared about Devlin.

Devlin had given her the bare outline of what had happened eight years ago, of how Reed had believed in him then. As far as she was concerned, that alone was reason enough to like the man.

"I enjoyed meeting you," she said. She wanted to say something about seeing him again someday. But her own relationship with Devlin was too uncertain. She didn't know how likely it was that she'd be here if Reed ever visited again.

"It was a great pleasure to meet you," he said, his soft drawl giving the words a courtly sound. His hand tightened over hers, his eyes taking on a serious edge.

"Have patience with him," he said abruptly, almost as if he'd read the doubts she hadn't voiced. "He's worth the effort."

Without waiting for her to come up with a reply, he bent to kiss her cheek. He released her hand, gave her a quick grin and disappeared out the door.

Annalise stared after him, listening to him exchanging a final few words with Devlin on the porch.

Have patience with him, he'd said.

She had all the patience in the world. The question was, would it do her any good?

Chapter 12

Devlin would have been happier if he could have defined Annalise's place in his life. He had to admit she had one. They were living together. When he looked around, he saw signs of her presence everywhere: a poster of a forest glade she'd tacked to two studs in the half that was drywalled living room; bright yellow curtains in the kitchen; flowers in the yard.

She'd made an impact in his life that went deeper than just sharing his bed. He'd smiled more, laughed more in the weeks she'd lived with him than he had in the ten years that had gone before.

She'd trusted him enough to share her grief, something more difficult than sharing his bed. She'd believed in him, asking no explanations. He'd told her the whole truth surrounding his conviction, holding back nothing. He hadn't killed Laura Sampson but he'd slept with her, knowing perfectly well that she was married. Annalise's eyes had offered no judgment, no reproach.

Life had left Devlin wary. Trust was something that he gave to very few people. He'd known most of his life that he'd never marry, never have children, never get deeply involved with a woman.

Yet here he was, involved with Annalise St. John, a woman who'd had more than her share of pain in life. He didn't want to add to that pain. He didn't love her, but he'd come to care for her. Yes, that was a good way to describe it. He *cared* for her.

That admission made it possible for him to admit that he'd begun to think it might be possible to have her in his life, perhaps for a long time to come.

It was all very logical. She needed a home. He had a home to offer. They got along, in and out of bed. When he thought about spending the next few years with her, it sounded like a good idea.

He couldn't offer her a grand, romantic passion. He didn't have that to offer. But he could give her security. Not marriage. He could offer everything but marriage. But she'd been that route once and he doubted she'd be interested in giving it another try.

And no children. He ached for the pain she'd suffered when she found she couldn't have children, but he couldn't pretend that he hadn't been relieved to know that was one thing he wouldn't have to worry about. And having lost her little girl, she wouldn't want to take that risk again, anyway.

She had plenty of reasons to want a gentler, more comfortable future. Maybe, just maybe, they could build that future together.

Annalise also thought a lot about the future in the days following Reed's departure. Her realization that she loved Devlin had changed everything.

After losing Mary, she'd never thought she'd be able to care deeply for another human being. The pain had been so terrible, it had been like acid eating into her soul. She'd never wanted to risk that kind of hurt again.

Devlin had proved how wrong she'd been. She'd cared for her first husband—thought she loved him. She saw now that what she'd felt for Bill had been nothing more than affection. They'd married more to assuage a mutual loneliness than because they felt a deep love.

What she felt for Devlin was nothing like her feelings for Bill. Her feelings for Devlin were so complex. She felt protected by him, but she also felt very protective of him. In his arms she felt safe, she also felt vividly alive.

Knowing how she felt didn't tell her how Devlin felt. that was the question that nagged at her now that she'd realized her own feelings.

He cared for her—that much she was aware of. But whether that caring went deeper than the concern he'd feel for anyone who was down on their luck, she couldn't be sure.

One thing she knew was that he had an enormous amount to give, if only he was willing to do so. It didn't take a psychic to tell her that he was wary of involvement. That he'd gotten as involved with her as he had was a hopeful sign.

Be patient, Reed had said. Patience was one thing she had plenty of. She was willing to give Devlin all the time in the world to realize that they could build something together, something as strong and lasting as the house on which he was lavishing such care.

She'd wait as long as it took for him to realize the future would be much brighter if they faced it together.

But the future was rushing in much faster than Annalise realized.

"You look pale." Devlin's dark brows drew together as he frowned across the table at her.

"Thanks." When his expression didn't lighten, she let her smile fade. "I'm just a little tired."

"You were tired yesterday and the day before."

"Excuse me for being human," she snapped. Immediately she bit her lower lip, regretting the outburst. "I'm sorry."

"That's okay." His eyes were concerned. "You just seem a little out of sorts, that's all."

Annalise poked her fork listlessly into the chef's salad in front of her. While she'd been making it, she'd felt positively ravenous and had nibbled at the ham and cheese. Now that it was in front of her, it had lost its appeal. Maybe she'd nibbled more than she'd realized.

"I'm just tired," she repeated, summoning up a smile. Actually it was all she could do to keep her eyes open lately.

"You slept this afternoon," he pointed out, still frowning.

Annalise kept her lashes lowered, forcing back the sudden tears that stung her eyes. He wasn't being critical. He was concerned. It was wonderful that he cared enough to be concerned. So why did she feel like bursting into tears?

"Maybe I need to take more vitamins," she suggested, keeping her tone light.

"Maybe you need to see a doctor."

"I'm not sick." Her fork clattered on the table as she pushed her barely touched salad away. "It's probably just the heat."

"It hasn't been that hot."

"Well, maybe I think it's hot," she snapped, shoving back from the table.

Devlin watched her storm from the room. After a moment, he got up and began clearing the table. He hadn't talked to Ben Masters since telling him that Annalise was going to be staying with him for a day or two. He stacked the salad plates in the dishwasher and shut the door, his expression thoughtful.

He wasn't much inclined toward interfering in someone else's life. But he'd been noticing Annalise's unusual lethargy for a week now, since not long after Reed left. She slept later in the morning, went to bed earlier in the evenings and had taken more than one nap in the middle of the day.

It wouldn't hurt to call Ben and ask him to suggest a doctor—a woman. Not because he had felt any reluctance to have Annalise see a male doctor—no, that wasn't it at all. He just thought Annalise might be more comfortable with a woman.

Annalise was lying on the bed when he entered the bedroom. Beauty was seated beside her, getting her ears scratched. Two of the kittens were playing a game of tag on the bedspread.

"How are you feeling?" he asked quietly.

"Stupid." She stopped petting the cat and sat up, giving Devlin an apologetic smile. "I must be more tired than I thought to snap at you like that. I'm sorry.''

"Don't worry about it." He came over to sit on the edge of the bed, drawing one knee up so that he faced her. "Before you get too much in sympathy with me, I should warn you that I called Ben Masters and got a recommendation for a doctor."

"Ben Masters. He's the doctor who was here the night you rescued me from the river, isn't he?"

"Yes." He'd been prepared for her to be furious. Instead, she looked thoughtful. "He suggested that you see a Dr. Linden. He says she's very good. I think I've heard Kelly mention her. Maybe you could call and ask her."

"That's okay. I'll trust your friend." She sighed. "I suppose it won't hurt to see a doctor. I'm sure there's nothing wrong that some vitamins won't cure.''

"Sure." Devlin reached out to brush her hair back from her face, feeling a vague ache somewhere in the region of his heart. She looked so pale.

Maybe he was overreacting. No doubt she was right—she was probably just a little anemic. Woman got anemic all the time, right? But he couldn't deny that he'd feel better when the doctor confirmed it.

Devlin went with Annalise to Dr. Linden's office, though she insisted that she was perfectly capable of driving into Remembrance by herself. He had other things to do in town, he said vaguely. There was no reason to take two cars.

Secretly she rather liked having him with her. It made it seem as if they were a couple, as if there were more definite ties between them than he'd will-

ingly admit existed. Besides, though she hadn't admitted as much, the blanket of exhaustion that seemed
to be weighing her down lately had begun to worry
her a little.

Dr. Linden was a pleasant woman in her forties.
She had medium brown hair, lightly sprinkled with
gray and rather ordinary features. But her brown eyes
were kind and reassuring.

Annalise endured the examination and answered all
the questions she were asked. By the time the nurse
told her she could get dressed, she was starting to feel
foolish for having come in. Really, a spell of tiredness
didn't seem like a symptom worthy of taking up a
doctor's time.

It was wonderful that Devlin had been concerned
about her, but she shouldn't have let his concern push
her into making an appointment that her better judgment told her was unnecessary. She got dressed, feeling as if she should apologize to the doctor.

But Dr. Linden didn't seem to feel any apology was
necessary. The nurse showed Annalise into a pleasantly decorated office and told her to have a seat. She
had only a moment to wait before the doctor came in
and sat behind the desk. She spoke before Annalise
could launch into the apologetic speech she'd been
rehearsing.

"I think the source of your tiredness is obvious,
Annalise."

"You do?" The question reflected her surprise.
"What's wrong?"

"Nothing is wrong precisely." Dr. Linden folded
her hands on top of Annalise's file and fixed the
younger woman with a kind smile. "You're pregnant."

The words hit with sledgehammer force. Annalise stared at the doctor, her mind completely blank for the space of several heartbeats.

"I can't be."

"About eight weeks along, I'd say." Dr. Linden glanced at her notes again, giving her patient a chance to absorb the news.

"You're mistaken." There was absolute conviction behind the statement.

"You seem very sure of that."

"I can't have children."

Dr. Linden's brows rose in surprise. "It says here that you had a successful pregnancy." She glanced at the chart for confirmation.

"Yes, but the doctors told me it was virtually a miracle that I got pregnant that one time." She explained, calmly and thoroughly, just why it was that she couldn't be pregnant.

For one moment, when the doctor had said she was pregnant, she'd felt a fierce blaze of joy, but she'd controlled it immediately, knowing that there'd been a mistake.

Dr. Linden listened to her explanation politely, asking one or two questions to clarify the situation.

"So you understand why there's been a mistake," Annalise finished, trying to pretend that her chest wasn't so tight with pain that she could hardly breathe.

"I understand why you find it difficult to believe, Annalise, but I'd like to point out that medicine is not as exact a science as we'd all like it to be. Certainly, the conditions you're describing would make conception extremely difficult—almost impossible. But it's that 'almost' that's the key word here. You did conceive once.''

"But they said it was a miracle," Annalise whispered, terrified to let herself start believing that what the doctor had told her could be true—that she could be carrying Devlin's baby.

"It's possible to have two miracles in one lifetime," Dr. Linden said gently. "You seem to have been twice blessed."

Looking at her, Annalise felt the reality of it start to sink in. A baby. She was going to have another baby. Devlin's baby. Tears filled her eyes. She pressed her hand over her flat stomach, letting the miracle slowly become real.

When she rejoined Devlin in the waiting room, she had to swallow the urge to shout out the news. She'd stuffed all the brochures and pamphlets she'd been given into her purse and decided that tomorrow would be soon enough to fill the prescription for prenatal vitamins. At the moment, vitamins weren't as important as going home and breaking the news to Devlin that he was going to be a father.

She told him that the doctor had given her a clean bill of health—which wasn't a lie. A pregnancy wasn't the same thing as an illness. Devlin's relief was obvious and Annalise hugged that to her on the drive home.

Surely he couldn't be so concerned about her and not have deep feelings for her. Deep enough to want to have a child with her?

He'd once said that he would never be a father. She hadn't pursued the subject. It hadn't seemed relevant. How could she have known that it was going to become suddenly, wonderfully, very relevant?

Annalise was so absorbed in both savoring the miracle of carrying a child and worrying about Devlin's reaction to the news that she didn't notice the increasingly worried looks he threw her as they neared home.

He waited until they'd entered the house before speaking.

"What did Dr. Linden really say?" he asked abruptly. He tossed his keys onto the breakfast bar and turned to look at her, his shoulders taut.

"I told you what she said." Annalise set her purse down, keeping her face averted from his. She needed time to decide how to tell him.

"But that's not all she said, is it?"

She glanced at him, reading the concern in his eyes. Looking away, she nibbled on her lower lip. Obviously he'd picked up on her distraction. He thought she was concealing something from him and he was right. But it wasn't what he thought. Maybe this was the best time to tell him after all.

"Do you remember that I told you I couldn't have children, that getting pregnant with Mary was practically a miracle?"

"Yes. What's wrong? Do you need surgery?"

"No. Actually, nothing's wrong exactly." She swallowed hard and linked her hands together to control the trembling of her fingers. She met his eyes, her own shining with joy. "I'm pregnant."

"What?" Devlin stared at her, his expression as blank as she'd felt when Dr. Linden first told her the news.

"I'm pregnant," she said again, her voice trembling with happiness. "We're going to have a baby, Devlin."

This time, the words penetrated. Annalise saw their impact in his eyes. She held her breath. She was prepared for him to be angry. They'd never even discussed the possibility of having a future together, and suddenly they were going to be parents. Even in the midst of her own delight, she wasn't foolish enough to assume that Devlin was going to instantaneously find the same joy in his impending fatherhood.

Emotion flashed across his face, but it was gone too quickly for her to read, leaving his eyes slate gray and completely empty of expression.

"Is your health all right?" he asked in a neutral tone.

"Yes. The doctor says I'm fine." Her eyes searched his face, trying to read something behind the blank facade he'd put up. "Devlin..."

"I'm glad you're well," he interrupted without apology. He glanced at his watch. "I forgot to pick up some things in town. I'd better get going or it'll be too late. Is there anything you need me to pick up?"

"I...I have a prescription for vitamins," she said slowly, feeling as if she'd missed a part of the conversation somewhere.

"I'll fill it at Johnson's."

Since he seemed to be expecting it, she got her purse and found the prescription. He took it from her and put it into his shirt pocket without looking at it. "Is there anything else you need?" He might have been a room service waiter asking if she had everything she needed before he left the room.

She shook her head. Devlin nodded politely and

picked up his keys. A moment later, the door shut behind him, leaving her alone.

That appeared to be the end of matter, as far as Devlin was concerned. For three days, Annalise waited for him to mention the baby, waited for him to show some emotion about it. Anger, dislike, even hatred. Anything would have been better than the complete indifference he seemed to feel.

She couldn't complain about his treatment of her. He was perfectly polite. He inquired after her health each day. He thanked her for the meals she prepared, meals neither of them ate more than a few mouthfuls of.

He also came to bed every night after she was asleep and was up before she woke. His eyes never did more than skim across her face, as if he couldn't bear to look at her.

She told herself he needed time to adjust to the idea. It had been as big a shock to him as it had to her. Where she could greet the news of her pregnancy with unadulterated joy, it was understandable that his feelings were not so simple.

Time, that was what he needed. Once he'd gotten over the shock, they'd be able to talk about the baby. They'd be able to decide what lay in the future. Annalise never had a moment's concern that he'd refuse to help her in caring for the child. She knew Devlin well enough to know that he'd take his responsibility seriously.

But she wanted their child to be more than a responsibility. She wanted Devlin to want this baby as much as she did. If she just gave him a little time to come to terms with the news, everything would be all right.

After three days, when nothing had changed, she decided that perhaps time alone wasn't going to do it. If there'd been only herself to consider, she might have packed a bag and left, no matter how much it tore her heart to shreds to leave him. But it wasn't just her anymore.

She had a child to consider now, and she had to try to make the child's father understand just what an incredible miracle they'd been given.

"We need to talk." She hadn't planned on it coming out so abruptly. She'd planned on approaching the subject more obliquely, but it was hard to be oblique with a man who was doing a darned good job of avoiding her.

"I have things to do." He had his hand on the doorknob and he didn't turn to look at her.

"We need to talk about the baby," she said determinedly.

Devlin's shoulders stiffened as if the word *baby* was a lash laid across them.

"I don't think so," he said tightly, still without turning.

"You can't just pretend it doesn't exist," Annalise threw at him.

His hand dropped from the doorknob and he turned slowly, looking at her without expression. "I'm not pretending it doesn't exist."

"Aren't you? You haven't mentioned it."

"Perhaps that's because I have nothing to say."

"You're going to be a father," she said, her tone pleading.

"No!" The facade of indifference vanished in an instant, revealing a blazing anger that made his eyes almost silver. "That's something I will never be!"

Annalise gripped her hands together. She lifted her chin. "You can't possibly think this isn't your baby."

"No. I know you conceived it with me." He made it sound like a cold, clinical act, and Annalise felt hurt rise inside her.

"Then how can you say you're not the father?"

"I'm the father, but it won't be anything more than an empty title." He stepped away from the door, facing her, his eyes full of anger. "You don't have to worry that I won't support you. I'll make sure you and your child have everything you need. But that's as far as it's going to go."

Her child. The words made it clear that he was distancing himself as much as possible. She fought the urge to turn away from his anger, to give in to the tears that burned at the back of her eyes. Anger wasn't going to do them any good. God knows, he had enough for the two of them.

"Can't we talk about this?" She struggled for a reasonable tone.

"Talk? What shall we talk about?" he asked nastily. "Shall we talk about how you lied to me? How you told me you couldn't get pregnant?"

"I didn't lie!" She was shocked by the accusation. In all her thinking, it had never occurred to her that he might believe she'd lied about her inability to conceive.

"Pardon me if I find that a little hard to believe," he sneered.

"It's the truth! Why would I lie about that?"

"Because you wanted me to get you knocked up,"

he said crudely. "Because you wanted a baby to replace the one you lost."

Annalise wasn't even aware that she'd moved until she saw her hand arcing through the air. Her palm hit his cheek with enough force to jerk his head to the side. The sound of the slap echoed in the big house.

Her hand fell to her side. He looked at her, the imprint of her hand scarlet on his cheek.

"You got what you wanted," he said. "You've got your baby. I'll make sure you're taken care of, but I don't see any reason to smile about it."

She stared at him, seeing the deep anger he felt. At another time, she might have seen the fear that underlay the anger, but her own emotions were too tumultuous for her to see anything but the obvious, which was that he was looking at her as if he hated her.

Shaken and trembling, Annalise was incapable of putting together the words to defend herself. That he could believe she'd use him as he'd just said, cut to the bone.

When he turned and walked out, she didn't try to stop him. She stood frozen in place, listening to the roar of the truck's engine disappearing down the driveway. He was going too fast, she thought vaguely. He'd spin out in the gravel at the bottom of the driveway. But he'd get it under control again. Devlin always got things under control again.

Moving dazedly, she turned and went into the bedroom. Methodically she began removing her clothes from the closet. Beauty, sensing that all was not as it should be, leaped up onto the bed and sat down on top of the small stack of garments. Looking up at Annalise, she meowed inquiringly.

Annalise felt the ice that had encased her crack. Sinking onto the bed, she scooped the cat up in her arms. Rocking back and forth, she let the tears start. In the past few minutes, not only her world but her heart had shattered into a thousand pieces.

And she didn't know if she'd be able to put either back together.

Chapter 13

Devlin took the turn at the end of the driveway too quickly. The rear wheels slid on the loose gravel. His hands tightened on the wheel, and he wrenched the truck into line with brute force.

The road was, as usual, empty. It was just as well, because Devlin sent the truck down it as if all the demons in hell were speeding after him. The trouble was, he was carrying the demons with him. No matter how fast he went, he couldn't escape them. Instead of the country road in front of him, he saw Annalise's white face, the hurt in her eyes. The image made it hurt to draw a breath.

Cursing, he slowed the truck, pulling it off to the side of the road. His hands knotted on the steering wheel, he stared through the windshield.

He'd been a fool. Annalise was no more capable of using him to get her pregnant than she was of swimming the English Channel. He couldn't remember ever hearing her tell a lie. He'd wanted—needed—to believe that she'd lied to him, that she'd used him.

From the moment she'd told him that she was pregnant, he'd felt torn apart by conflicting emotions. There'd been a part of him that had felt utter joy. A child was something he'd never thought to have, and he'd told himself he felt no regrets at that decision. But when he pictured Annalise carrying his baby, holding his son or daughter in her arms, he'd realized how wrong he'd been to think it was something he didn't want.

But the joy was quickly swallowed up by fear. He didn't have to close his eyes to see his father standing over him, his thin face twisted with hatred, his belt raised. He'd sworn never to have a child, never to risk finding that insanity in himself.

And suddenly, there was Annalise, telling him she was carrying his child, making him confront his own worst nightmares. His reaction had been rage. He'd told himself that it was rage because she'd lied, because she'd used him. In reality, the anger was easier to deal with than the fear that boiled like acid inside him.

But that didn't give him the right to hurt her. What if she left?

He stared down the empty country road, seeing his life stretch ahead of him, equally empty, equally lonely. Since Annalise had come into his life, he'd known a contentment, a happiness, he'd never thought himself capable of feeling.

She'd had a childhood scarcely less painful than his own. Her marriage had broken up just when she'd needed support the most, and she'd had to stand by and watch a beloved child die. And she hadn't let any of it destroy her. Perhaps it had come close, he thought, remembering the lifeless woman he'd pulled from the river.

But all she'd needed was a little time, a little bit of security, and she'd pulled her life back together. She'd not only learned to laugh again, she'd taught him how to laugh. She'd opened her heart to Beauty and Lobo—and one Devlin Russell—unwanted strays, all of them.

She'd given them all a home. Not just a house but a home. He'd thought he was building a home this past year, but now he could see what he'd really been doing was building himself a wall to keep the world at bay. Another prison, only this one was to protect him from life—from living.

If she left, it would be like hearing those big iron doors slide shut behind him. Only this time, there would be no reprieve, no one to say he wasn't guilty after all. He'd have no one to blame but himself.

His fingers were not quite steady as he turned the key in the ignition. He had to talk to her, apologize. God, how could he offer an apology for the things he'd said to her? He'd been unforgivably cruel. But whether she forgave him or not, she had a right to hear the apology.

He drove back at the same breakneck pace at which he'd left. He had no idea how long he'd been sitting there staring at the empty fields, realizing what a fool he'd been. She could have had time to pack and leave by now.

If she was gone, he'd just have to find her, he told himself. He'd track her down no matter where she'd gone and tell her he was sorry. She'd no doubt kick him out of her life, but he couldn't let her think that he really believed the things he'd accused her of.

Her car was still beside the house, and Devlin felt the band around his chest ease slightly. She wasn't gone yet. He could talk to her, tell her how sorry he was, tell her he hadn't meant any of it.

He strode into the house, trying to think of what he was going to say to her. How did you begin to apologize for the kind of things he'd said? But he had to find the words. He owed her that much.

Annalise was in the bedroom. He felt an almost paralyzing stab of pain when he saw what she was doing. Her clothes were on the bed. She was folding them neatly and setting them in a cardboard box. The same damned box they'd been in when he towed her car home, he realized.

She glanced up, her eyes not quite touching on his still figure, settling somewhere just to the left of him instead.

"I'm almost done. I thought you'd be gone longer." There was no anger in her tone. No hurt. There was nothing there at all. She could have been talking to a stranger.

"Annalise, I'm sorry." He winced at the inadequacy of the words, but they were all he had to offer.

"That's quite all right," she said politely. She folded a pair of jeans and set them in the box. "Actually, it's probably just as well you did come back. I was hoping it would be all right if I left Beauty and the kittens here, just until I find an apartment. I know you didn't particularly want a cat and I'll take her off your hands as soon as possible."

"Fine." He watched as she took a blouse off a

hanger and began folding it. He felt as if he were breaking into a hundred tiny pieces inside.

"Lobo, too, if you'd like," she went on, setting the blouse on top of the jeans. "Although, he really considers himself more yours than mine. If you want, I'll take him, too. I don't want you to feel as if you're stuck with him."

Where did she think she was going to find an apartment that would let her have, not only a cat and four kittens, but a dog the size of a Shetland pony?

"He can stay. You can all stay."

"No!" For an instant, her careful calm wavered and her fingers knotted over the T-shirt she'd just picked up. "Thank you," she said politely, forcing her fingers to relax.

"I was wrong."

"Yes, you were." But there was no anger in her words.

"I know you didn't lie to me about thinking you couldn't have children. I think I knew all along."

"I'm glad." She folded the last garment and set it in the box. "Excuse me. I want to make sure I didn't leave anything in the bathroom."

Devlin watched her leave the bedroom, feeling a blackness rising up inside, threatening to swallow him whole. He couldn't let her leave like this. There were things that needed to be said.

She came back into the room with a bottle of shampoo in her hand and tucked it down along the side of the box. Her eyes skimmed over the room, as if checking to see if she'd missed anything. The fingers that rested on the sides of the box trembled slightly.

It was that trembling that gave him hope. He hadn't

managed to kill her feelings for him completely if the thought of leaving could make her tremble.

"Don't go."

The simple plea sounded loud in the quiet room. Annalise closed her eyes as if the words had a physical impact.

"Don't," she said softly. "I understand how you feel."

"Do you?"

"Yes. You made it clear you didn't want a child. You didn't truly want to get involved with me, did you?" For the first time, she squarely looked at him, her mouth quirked in a half smile. "I guess I shouldn't have thought that because you made an exception on one, you'd be able to make an exception on the other. A baby is a much bigger commitment than a lover, isn't it?"

"I didn't want to get involved," he admitted slowly. He tried to pick his words carefully. This might be the only chance he had to make her understand, to beg her forgiveness. "I've always known that I'd never have a serious relationship with a woman. I never thought I was capable of the kind of feelings that required."

"Oh, Devlin." Annalise looked at him, the compassion in her eyes sending a stab of pain through him. "You're capable of a great deal more than you give yourself credit for. I've never met anyone with so much to give. Look at the way you took me in. And Beauty and Lobo. Strays, all of us," she said, unknowingly echoing his earlier thoughts. "You shouldn't sell yourself short."

He felt hope surge up. Surely she couldn't look at

him like that, say that he had so much to give and not still feel something for him.

"Annalise, I—"

"I should get going." She looked away from him, her tone suddenly brisk. "I need to find a motel tonight."

"Please. Don't go."

Her finger knotted over the sides of the box. She felt a wave of pain wash over her. He sounded as if he meant it. There was need in his voice, in his eyes. She wanted desperately to respond to that need, but she couldn't.

Her chest still ached with the pain of his earlier words. He felt badly about having hurt her and he wanted a chance to make it right. But the only thing that could make it right was if he loved her. And he didn't. He couldn't have loved her and said those things to her.

"I have to go," she said tightly. "I accept your apology, but I have to go."

"I was afraid," he told her, taking a step away from the doorway.

"Afraid? Of what?" Despite herself, her eyes went to his face. She didn't want to listen to him, didn't want to care about what he had to say.

"Of being hurt."

"So you thought you'd strike first?"

"Of hurting you," he continued, ignoring her sharp question. "Of hurting the…the child."

"You did hurt me," she told him, anger and pain tangled together in her stomach.

"I don't mean that kind of hurt." He waved one hand in an impatient gesture.

"What other kind of hurt is…" Her voice trailed

off. She stared at him, suddenly realizing what he meant. He was talking about physical hurt. Maybe she should have thought of it before, considering what he'd told her of his childhood.

"You think you might hit me or our child?" she asked, incredulity colouring her tone.

"The capability is there."

"Nonsense." There was no hesitation in her brisk denial. "You're no more capable of hurting someone smaller than you than you are of...of leaping tall buildings in a single bound."

Devlin blinked at her, disconcerted by her instantaneous dismissal of a fear that had haunted him all his life.

"My father..."

"Your father was obviously a very sick man, but I don't think it was a genetic illness."

"I could..."

"No, you couldn't." She sounded so completely sure. Devlin stared at her, feeling her confidence nudge at the base of the fear lodged inside him. "I know all the statistics about abused children becoming abusive parents, but it doesn't happen every time, Devlin. You couldn't ever become a child abuser."

He shoved his hands into his pockets and half turned away, ashamed of the tears that burned in his eyes. Once again, her belief in him made him feel strong and, at the same time, achingly weak.

Annalise watched him, feeling some of her pain ease in the face of his. He truly believed he could have it in him to hurt his child the way his father had hurt him. No wonder he'd been so adamant about never being a father.

He'd hurt her deeply with his accusations. That

pain couldn't be completely wiped away because she now understood his motives. But her love for him couldn't be so easily destroyed, either. Through her own hurt, she felt his pain.

"Devlin, you'd be a wonderful father," she said softly. "I've always known that."

"Have you?" He turned to look at her. His eyes dropped to her stomach for a moment before lifting to her face. "Am I going to get a chance to find out?"

It was her turn to look away. She loved him. With all her heart, she wanted him to be a part of their child's life. A part of her life. But they couldn't go on as they had been, playing at house without some sort of commitment. She wanted to bring her child into a stable home, full of warmth. Full of love.

The old saying about half a loaf being better than none might apply to bread, but it didn't apply to love. Not for her. She'd thought she could go on indefinitely, waiting for him to see what they could have together. Maybe she could have if she hadn't gotten pregnant. But the baby changed everything.

"I want it all," she said softly. "I want a commitment. I want to know that you'll still be here no matter how rough it gets. I want to know that…that you love me as much as I love you."

She lifted her chin, her eyes meeting his with fierce pride.

Devlin felt his heart stop. She loved him. She loved him. Suddenly his heart was beating much too fast, making him feel almost light-headed. He'd never realized how desperately he wanted to hear those three little words from her. He'd never let himself realize how much he needed her to say them.

"Annalise." He took a step toward her and

stopped. He took his hands out of his pockets and reached for hers. She let him take her hands, but there was no give in her. He'd always known there was strength in her. It was part of what he'd admired from the start. It had never been more evident than it was at this minute.

"Annalise, I never planned on getting involved with a woman. I never thought I could…love anyone."

"Of course you can." Her fingers squeezed his. "If you'll just let yourself."

He stared down at their linked hands, searching for the words to make her understand. "I care for you," he said slowly. "Wait." His fingers tightened over hers, preventing her from pulling away. "I know that doesn't sound like much, but it's more than I ever thought I'd feel for someone."

"I know," she said softly, without anger. "But I need more than that."

"I want to wake up beside you every morning," he told her. He lifted his eyes to her face. "I want to know that you're there when I wake up in the middle of the night. I want to watch your stomach grow with our child. I want to be there when that child is born. I want to know that you'll always be there, no matter what."

He drew her closer, desperate to make her understand how much he needed her in his life. "You have to stay, Annalise. Without you, I…don't know what I'd do."

She looked at him, feeling the last traces of ice melt from around her heart. The words he couldn't seem to get out were written in his eyes. He loved her. It was there in the way he held her hands, in the near desperation in his eyes.

She freed one hand, reaching up to lay it against his jaw. "You're talking about love, Devlin. You're talking about needing someone else to make your life complete. About wanting to share the bad, as well as the good. What do you think love is?"

"I don't know," he said simply. She knew it was no less than the truth. How could he know? There'd been so little of it in his life.

"Oh, Devlin." She leaned into him, resting her cheek against his chest, feeling the strong beat of his heart. His arms closed convulsively around her, and he bent to put his face against her hair.

"Teach me, Annalise," he whispered. "I don't want to lose you."

"You're not going to." She tilted her head to look up into his face. "You're stuck with me."

"We'll get married."

"I'd like that," she said, seeing some of the anxiety fade from his eyes.

He didn't need her to teach him how to love. All she needed to teach him was that he didn't have to be afraid to love. As long as she could see the love in his eyes, she could wait for the words. They weren't as important as feeling his arms around her, holding her as if he'd never let her go.

* * * * *

Physical therapy is taking on
a whole new meaning....

Charity's Angel

Chapter One

"Honestly, Charity, I don't understand you. You're twenty-five but you act more like you're ninety-five. Look at this place." Diane Williams made a sweeping gesture with one manicured hand, indicating her sister's living room.

"What's wrong with it?" Charity's eyes followed the gesture, seeking some fault.

"It's so...so...neat." Diane managed to infuse considerable distaste into the simple word.

"I like it neat," Charity said, not bothering to hide her smile. "After sharing a room with you for fifteen years, a little neatness is a pleasant change."

"A touch of untidiness is a sign of creativity," Diane said, picking up the old argument.

"Or the sign of a congenital idiot."

They grinned at each other, remembering all the times they'd said the same words with more acrimony. From the time Charity was born until Diane left home at twenty, the two sisters had shared a room. Since they were as different as night and day, the arrangement had made for some memorable conflicts.

"I still say it's unnatural to keep everything so

tidy." Diane reached for the pot of tea, pouring herself another cup.

"So I'm a freak of nature." Charity lifted her shoulders in a shrug, not visibly disturbed.

"You needn't think that I've forgotten the original topic," Diane said. She leaned forward and picked up another of the rich butter cookies Charity had bought specifically for her sister's visit.

Charity suppressed a sigh of envy as she watched Diane bite into it without the least concern about the calories she was consuming. It was one of the great injustices of the world that Diane ate like a stevedore and never gained an ounce.

"What topic?" Charity broke a cookie in half, with the vague thought that if you only ate it half at a time, there were fewer calories.

"Your love life."

"What love life?"

"Exactly my point." Diane finished the cookie and wiped her fingers on a napkin. "You don't have a love life."

"I'm perfectly content," Charity said, aware that it wasn't quite the truth. "Have another cookie." She pushed the tray closer, hoping to distract her sister.

But Diane was capable of eating and keeping to her point at the same time.

"You're twenty-five, Charity."

"I know. You keep saying that like it should mean something." She nibbled the second half of the cookie, wondering if the calories might somehow evaporate if she ate slowly enough.

"A quarter of a century," Diane reminded her ruthlessly.

Charity winced. "You do have a gift for a flattering phrase."

"I'm not trying to be flattering. I'm trying to get you to wake up and smell the coffee before it's too late."

"Too late? You sound like the maiden aunt in a Victorian novel. Are you about to tell me that I'm in danger of being left on the shelf?" Charity resisted the temptation of another cookie and leaned back in her chair, cradling her teacup in her hands. "I thought you were a little more liberated than that. If marriage is the be-all and end-all, then why haven't you taken the plunge?"

"I'm not talking about marriage." Diane waved her hand dismissingly. "And don't think I couldn't have been married half a dozen times if I'd wanted."

"Half a dozen? Are you aware that there are bigamy laws in this country?"

"Don't try to distract me," Diane told her sternly, putting on her best older-sister expression—the one she rarely had a chance to use. "I'm worried about you."

"Don't be. I'm fine."

"You're not fine. You're…you're stagnant, like an old swamp or something."

"An old swamp? A quarter of a century?" Charity bit her lip against the urge to grin. "Really, Diane, you should be careful about flattering me like this."

"You can laugh if you want to," Diane said huffily, reaching for a cookie. "But you know I'm right. It's not natural that a young, beautiful woman like you never dates."

"I date," Charity protested.

"And I'm not talking about mercy dates with the

grandsons of the little old ladies who live in this apartment building.''

"They're not mercy dates."

"When was the last time you went out with a man?"

"Last week. Mrs. Willoby's grandson. And he was a perfectly nice man."

"Could he get a cab in the rain? Order a wine? Did he make you feel special?"

"It was a friendly date, not the prelude to an affair," Charity told her, shifting restlessly. "And it wasn't raining and we didn't have wine."

"I'll bet he was either tall, skinny and tongue-tied or short, stout and never stopped talking about himself. He had moist hands and acne scars. He took you to some hole-in-the-wall place where they keep the lights low so you won't be able to look at the food too closely. He either overtipped or undertipped and he either made a clumsy pass or didn't have the slightest idea of how to make a pass if he'd wanted to."

"He didn't have acne scars," Charity mumbled, staring into her nearly empty cup. Why was it that Diane always showed these amazing bursts of insight just when you didn't need them?

"But I'm pretty close on the rest, right?" Diane fixed her sister with shrewd green eyes, reading the truth in her silence. "You deserve better."

"It's easy for you to talk. You're beautiful. You've got men falling all over themselves to meet you."

"You're hardly chopped liver. You're pretty."

"You know what Mom and Dad always said. Brian got the brains, you got the beauty and I got all the common sense."

"Well, they never meant that you were a dog, Char. I mean, people always comment on how much we look alike. You can't look like me and not be attractive."

It was said without arrogance. Diane Williams had spent the past ten years near the top of the modeling field. She was a stunningly beautiful woman, and it would have been false modesty to pretend she didn't know it.

Charity studied her older sister, trying to place just what it was that set the two of them so far apart when it came to looks.

They were both blond, but where Diane's hair was a miraculous pale gold, Charity's was more of a honey shade. They both had green eyes. But Diane's were electric, heart-stopping green. Charity's were a softer, darker shade. They'd both been blessed with dark brows and lashes but Diane's brows had a natural, elegant curve and her lashes were thicker and longer.

Their short straight noses were nearly identical. In her more desperate teenage moments, Charity had managed to convince herself that she had Diane beat in the nose department. Diane's nose had the faintest bump, a reminder of the time she'd fallen out of a tree and broken it. But somehow the tiny imperfection only emphasized the symmetry of her features.

Diane's mouth was wide, but Charity's was just a fraction wider. And of course there was the fact that when the tall gene was handed out, Charity had been sleeping in the back of the room. Diane was a willowy five foot nine. Her younger sister was a far-from-willowy five feet two and a quarter inches. And while Charity had never been ashamed of her figure, it always seemed just a little too lush next to Diane's elegant slenderness.

Charity sighed and reached for another cookie. The fact was she would never be the beauty Diane was. It had been the bane of her youth. Now it only brought an occasional sigh.

"Face it, Diane, I may look like you but there's some vital element missing."

"You can't tell me that you're so unattractive that men don't want to be seen with you."

"No, it's not that." Charity wondered how she could make her sister understand. "There's something very…motherly about me," she said gloomily.

"Motherly?" Diane widened her perfect green eyes. "You don't look a bit motherly."

"Well then, you explain why men always tell me their troubles. I've heard more stories of romances gone wrong than a therapist. Sometimes I feel like the *Statue of Liberty*."

"The *Statue of Liberty?* You feel corroded?" Diane wrinkled her forehead, trying to find the connection.

"Not corroded. You know—bring me your tired, your poor. The huddled masses yearning to pour out their problems on some sucker's shoulder."

Diane's endearingly girlish giggle was one of the things that had always made it impossible to hate her. Charity picked up another cookie, biting into it morosely.

"It's easy for you to laugh. When was the last time a man took you out and told you how much he missed his ex-wife?"

"I can't say it's ever happened," Diane admitted. "But they can't all be that bad."

"Maybe not. But I've had it happen often enough that I've gotten a little leery of trying. Besides, I haven't even *met* a man who's interesting in ages."

"Well, there has to be someone you find attractive."

"You mean, besides Mel Gibson?"

"Come on, Char. You have to know somebody you'd like to date. Even working in that stodgy little jewelry store, you have to have met somebody."

"Nobody." But even as she said it, an image popped into her mind. Diane jumped on the quick flicker of expression.

"Who? Who is it? Come on, I'm your sister. You're supposed to confide in me." She leaned forward, her eyes sparkling with interest.

"There is a guy," Charity said reluctantly. "But I don't really *know* him. He's a customer, that's all."

"It's as good a start as any. You should ask him out."

"What!" Charity straightened so fast that tea slopped out of her cup and into the saucer. She fixed her older sister with a stunned gaze. "Are you crazy?"

"This is the nineties. Women don't have to wait for men to do the asking anymore."

"How many men have you asked out?" Charity asked suspiciously.

"Well, I would if I met someone I liked and he didn't ask me first. Besides, we're not talking about me. We're talking about you."

"I'm not asking Gabriel London for a date." The very thought made her feel as though she couldn't breathe.

"Gabriel." Diane rolled the name around on her tongue before giving a satisfied nod. "I like it."

"Good. *You* ask him for a date." Charity set her cup down with a sharp ping.

"I'm not the one who has the hots for him."

"I don't have 'the hots' for him," Charity protested, glaring at her sister.

"Sure you do. I recognize the look. Are you saying he isn't attractive?"

"Of course he's attractive. He's very attractive, which is precisely why I'm not going to ask him out."

"What? You only ask unattractive men out?"

"I don't ask *any* men out. And I don't care if it's unenlightened."

"We're only talking about asking him to lunch, not asking him to marry you," Diane said, secure in the knowledge that she'd never have to ask a man to do either one.

"Well, I'm not asking him anything except whether he wants to pay with a check or a credit card," Charity said flatly.

Diane shrugged, putting on an air of vague hurt. "Okay. It's your life."

"That's right. Have another cookie." Charity shoved the plate at her with a motion just short of violence, closing the topic.

Imagine suggesting that she ask a man out. Especially a man like Gabriel London. A man who probably didn't even notice that she was female. The idea was enough to make her break out in hives.

GABRIEL LONDON put his feet up on his desk, studying the toes of his rather worn boots. It was one of those rare moments when the station house was calm and quiet. There was nothing on his desk that couldn't wait five minutes, nowhere he had to go, nothing he had to do immediately.

He frowned at his boots, suddenly aware that the relative peace was not particularly welcome. The problem with peaceful moments was that there was nothing to do but think. And his thoughts lately had not been of the comfortable variety. He'd been thinking a lot about where his life was headed, and he wasn't sure he liked what he saw.

"Brooding again?" Annie Sarratt perched on the corner of his desk, giving him an amused look out of wide green eyes. "You remind me of..."

"Don't tell me I remind you of a chicken you had back in Alabama," Gabe interrupted her, giving her a frown that had no visible effect.

"You're thinkin' of *broody,* sugar. I said *brooding.* You know, sort of sulky. Pouty, maybe."

"You know, the reason I haven't asked for a different partner is because I don't think it would be right to inflict you on someone else," he told her.

Annie grinned. "The only reason you haven't asked for a different partner is you know you couldn't find anyone else who'd put up with your sulks, sugar."

She'd lived in California for fifteen years but her voice still held the slow drawl of the deep South. No one was ever going to mistake Annie for a Valley Girl.

"I wasn't sulking. I was thinking."

"The way you do it, there ain't much difference. So what're you sulking about now?"

Gabe poked her threateningly with the toe of his boot, hinting that she might like to go somewhere else. As usual Annie ignored him, shoving his feet out of the way to settle herself more comfortably on the corner of the desk. *His* desk, he noticed sourly. She never sat on the corner of *her* desk to harass him. Of course, that would have put her several feet away, which would have made it harder to really annoy him.

He looked at her through narrowed eyes. It never ceased to amaze him how such a delicate-looking little thing could be so tough. She was five foot five but looked smaller. Her skin was as pale and soft as a magnolia petal. Annie would never be found sunning herself on the beach. She didn't want skin like an old saddle, she'd say in that soft Dixie drawl.

She sat there wearing a slim little black skirt and a pale gray blouse, looking as if she should be off to a luncheon where the topic of conversation might be how to raise money for the local symphony. But she was one of the best cops on the force. In a tense situation there was no one Gabe would rather have at his back.

They'd worked together for six years now, and the only time he'd seen Annie lose her cool was when her husband had been badly injured in a freeway pileup. Other than that, nothing seemed to faze her, not gun-toting teenagers, belligerent drunks or family disputes, which could be as dangerous as anything a police officer had to face.

In six years they'd developed a mutual respect that had grown into friendship. He knew better than to treat her like an airhead, and she knew how to look behind the smile to his more serious side. But at the moment he didn't particularly feel like discussing his thoughts.

"How about we ditch this joint and find a cozy

motel somewhere?'' Gabe raised his eyebrows suggestively and gave her legs an exaggerated leer.

''I 'spose we could, sugar, but you know what a temper Bill has. He just might take it amiss, if he found out the two of us had been keeping company in a motel. I'd hate for him to have to break you in two.''

''For a moment in your arms, I'd take the risk.'' Gabe pressed a hand to his chest, giving her his best soulful look.

Annie giggled. ''You could take that act on the road, Gabriel. But it don't wash with me. And you ain't distracting me from the subject at hand, either. You gonna tell me what you're sulking about?''

''You're a hard woman, Annie.''

''I know. Now what's got you frowning?''

Gabe sighed and gave in. He knew Annie well enough to know that she wasn't going to give up. She was like a slim and very attractive bulldog. Once she'd latched hold of something, she just didn't let go.

''You ever think about where your life is going?''

''Sure do. I'm going to stay at this job another two years and then I'm going to quit and stay home and have me two or three babies. I'm going to eat lots of chocolates and shuffle around the house in slippers and a bathrobe and watch all the daytime soaps.''

Gabe grinned, trying to imagine his meticulous, immaculate partner letting herself go to hell. More likely, she'd have her babies precisely on schedule, and by the time they were six weeks old, they'd be organized within an inch of their lives.

''I'd like to see that,'' he commented.

''Well, you hang around long enough and you will.

But I don't think that plan is going to work for you,'' she added thoughtfully.

"Oh, I don't know. I could probably manage to become a slob as well as anyone."

"No. You'd either end up moping or you'd be fussing for something to do. That's the problem with you Yankees, you've never learned how to relax. The minute you don't have something to occupy every minute of your time, you start to brood."

"Are we back to that again?" Gabe rolled his eyes in exasperation. "I told you, I'm not brooding. I was just thinking."

"What about?"

"About the fact that I've been a cop for twelve years now."

"And a good one," Annie put in, nudging his knee with the toe of her pump.

"Twelve years and I don't see any difference out there. We're still arresting the same people for the same things. So what have I spent twelve years doing?"

"You've spent it being a damn good cop. You put away a few bad guys, helped a lot of people and made a difference in their lives."

"Yeah, right. I made a big difference in Danny Androte's life." He broke off, the words surprising him. He hadn't even been thinking about the old shooting. He'd thought he'd come to terms with it a long time ago.

"You stop that right now," Annie told him sternly. "That boy had a gun and he'd already shot a woman and was fixin' to shoot you. You did what you had to do."

"So the psychiatrist told me. But the psychiatrist

wasn't the one who killed a sixteen-year-old kid.'' Memories darkened his eyes to muddy green. He shook his head. ''Sixteen years old, Annie. He should have been playing basketball somewhere, not robbing a liquor store.''

''You didn't put him where he was. He was the one who made the choice to rob that store. Would you be happier if he'd killed you?''

''Of course not.'' Gabe shoved back from the desk and stood up, pushing his hands into the pockets of his jeans. ''The point is that he's dead.''

''And you're not,'' Annie reminded him pragmatically. ''You did the only thing you could.''

''Maybe. I don't even know what made me think of that.'' Gabe stared down at his desk, the shooting flickering through his mind in stiff, jerky images, like a badly wound tape. He shook his head, dismissing the memories. ''I got a letter from my dad yesterday.''

''He still want you to come to Wyoming and play cowboy?''

''Yeah. The ranch is doing fairly well but he'd like to expand. Says he's getting too old to handle it on his own.''

''You thinkin' about going?'' Annie asked, watching his face.

''No. Not really.'' But his eyes weren't as sure as his words. He shrugged. ''I haven't been on a horse since my last pony ride at the L.A. Fair when I was eight. Can you see me on a horse?''

''I think you'd look real cute. Sorta like a poor gal's John Travolta.''

''You mean John Wayne?''

"No, I mean John Travolta. Sorta *Urban Cowboy* goes to Wyoming," she suggested with a grin.

"Thanks. If you're going to be insulting, you can get off my desk."

"Whatever you say, Gabriel." Annie slid off the desk with easy grace. "But if you were thinking about joining your daddy, I'd be the first to wish you well."

"Trying to get rid of me?" Gabe asked with a half smile.

"No. I'd just like to see a little sparkle in those nice eyes of yours. 'Sides, it might be kind of fun to break in a new partner. Get a little new blood in here." Annie's teasing smile didn't hide the concern in her eyes.

Gabe watched her leave the room, his thoughts a couple of thousand miles away. He'd only visited his father's ranch once in the five years since he'd bought it. But the wide-open spaces and the vast expanse of sky had lingered in his mind, like a glimpse of heaven.

On days when the city seemed as close to hell as he could imagine, he'd think about the deep silence of the ranch...the sharp scent of sagebrush when you brushed against it.

The phone on his desk jangled, shaking him out of his thoughts. He shook his head and reached for it. He must be going through an early mid-life crisis. He couldn't be seriously thinking about giving up his career and moving to Wyoming. It was just a phase he was going through. In a few weeks he'd have forgotten the whole idea.

Chapter Two

Charity started the day by sleeping through her alarm—something she *never* did. In the rush to get to work at something close to on time, she'd broken a fingernail, burned the toast she didn't have time to eat and unthinkingly grabbed the most uncomfortable pair of shoes she owned.

She smiled at the couple across the counter and resisted the urge to look at the clock, knowing it had been less than five minutes since she'd looked at it last. Trying to ease her cramped toes inside the pearl-gray pumps, she listened as the man explained that he and Rosemary were getting married, and he wanted the perfect engagement ring.

Ordinarily this was the part of her job that she liked best. She'd worked at Hoffman's Jewelry for three years, and while Diane might see it as a stodgy little store, Charity enjoyed the customers.

Today, however, she was distracted by her aching feet and her empty stomach. Having missed breakfast, it had been inevitable that she hadn't had a chance to grab more than a container of yogurt for lunch.

Not to mention that the conversation with Diane kept playing in her head. She wished her sister hadn't

used the words *quarter of a century* to describe her
age. It sounded so antique. In less than five years
she'd be thirty, then forty would loom up faster than
she knew, and then where would she be?

Charity set a tray of wedding and engagement rings
on the counter, smiling at the young couple. Really,
today of all days, she was in no mood to deal with
happily engaged people. Especially when they looked
so young that she had the feeling the groom's mother
had had to drive them to the store.

Twenty-five wasn't that old, she told herself
briskly. The prime of life.

Or the beginning of the downhill slide.

She suppressed a shudder as the bride-to-be
reached for the gaudiest ring on the tray. A huge diamond surrounded by emeralds, it was one of the
most tasteless pieces in the shop. So tasteless that it
had been sitting in the case, unsold, for as long as she
could remember.

Within half an hour the ring had been lovingly
boxed and presented to the young man. Wasn't it for-
tunate that the ring just fit Rosemary's small hand,
he'd said with a smitten glance at his fiancée. Personally Charity thought the ring looked like a cheap
Christmas ornament, but she kept the opinion to herself.

After Rosemary and her fiancé left, the store was
momentarily without customers. Charity signaled to
Sally, the only other employee, to take her break.
With the manager, Al Kocek, hiding in the office,
probably sleeping, and Sally on break, Charity was
alone in the store.

She eased her right foot out of its shoe, sighing
with relief as she flexed her cramped toes. Rubbing a

polishing cloth idly over one of the glass cases, she found her thoughts drifting to the conversation she'd had with her sister the day before.

Maybe Diane was right. Maybe she *should* make an effort to get out more, to meet interesting men. But she'd have to do something about her image. She wasn't sure what it was that made men see her more as a sisterly confidante than a lover, but there had to be a way to change the picture.

Maybe she should try a red leather miniskirt. She could have her hair permed into wild curls and buy a pair of those huge dangling earrings that her brother always said looked like cheap fishing lures. Three-inch spikes to give her a little more height.

She narrowed her eyes, trying to bring the picture into focus, but all she saw was a short, well-rounded blonde who looked as if she was dressed for a Halloween party.

She sighed, dismissing the idea without regret. She might as well face it. She was never going to look like a femme fatale. She wasn't even going to look like a femme semi-fatale. She was cursed with a wholesome look, and she was just going to have to live with it.

It was easy for Diane to talk about getting out more. Men stumbled over themselves to take her out, and not to talk about their old girlfriends, either.

When the bell over the shop door pinged, she looked up, relieved to have her thoughts interrupted. When she saw who was entering, Charity felt her face grow warm. She slid her shoe back on, hardly noticing her pinched toes.

"Mr. London." She moved forward, trying to ignore the way her pulse skipped a beat when he smiled at her. She'd seen that wide smile in more than a few of her fantasies.

"Hi."

"We just got a new shipment of crystal last week," she said, stopping at the shelves near the front of the store where a series of delicate crystal creatures basked in the late-afternoon sun.

"I noticed. Let me see the Pegasus, would you?"

Charity handed him the small winged horse, oddly pleased that he'd chosen her favorite piece. He cupped it in his fingers, holding it up so that the sunlight poured through it. Charity studied him while he examined it.

It was odd how his face had come to mind while she was talking with Diane yesterday. It wasn't as if she really knew him, not on any personal level.

Gabriel London had been coming into Hoffman's for over a year. Every month or so he came in and bought one of the little crystal animals Mr. Hoffman imported from Europe. The small pieces were exquisitely crafted and priced accordingly. They had a number of customers who collected them but none who lingered in her thoughts like Gabriel London.

It was hard to say just what it was about him that made him so memorable. He wasn't enormously tall—an inch or so over six feet maybe. He was built on lean lines, all muscle and not much bulk.

His hair was medium brown, worn short but shaggy, as if he couldn't be bothered with keeping it tamed. His eyes were hazel, a rich amalgam of green and gold. His features were too long, too angular to be really handsome. His mouth was wide, bracketed by lines that said he smiled often. His chin was strong, stubbornly shaped. His nose was…well, rather noselike.

Nothing all that extraordinary. But somehow it all blended into a whole that was considerably greater than the sum of the parts. No mere physical catalog could capture the way his eyes wrinkled at the corners when he smiled. Or the way he moved with a sort of casual grace that made her heart beat just a little faster than it had any business doing.

"What do you think?"

Charity blinked. What did she think? She'd been so wrapped up in analyzing Gabriel London that for an instant she thought he was asking her opinion of himself.

"Think?"

"Of the Pegasus," he prompted.

"The Pegasus. Of course." She blinked at the small crystal figure in his hand, trying to shift her thinking.

"Mind on other things?" he asked.

"Just drifted off, I guess. Sorry."

"No problem. Daydreams are a sign of an intelligent mind."

"According to whom?"

"According to me," he said, giving her that grin that never failed to make her heart skip.

"I'm not sure my boss would buy that philosophy," she told him with a smile.

"A slave driver?" he asked sympathetically.

"No. But he's not much inclined to encourage daydreaming on the job."

"Too bad." He held the Pegasus up so that the sunlight streamed through it. The delicate wings seemed to quiver with life. If she narrowed her eyes,

Charity could almost believe it was about to take flight.

"It looks alive, doesn't it," he said, reading her thoughts.

"Yes. It's a lovely piece." She reached out to touch one finger to the proudly arched little head, half-surprised to feel cool glass beneath her touch, rather than the warmth of a living creature.

"It's hard to believe that a human being could create something so exquisite," he murmured, talking to himself as much as to her.

"It's nice to be reminded of the good things we're capable of."

"Yes."

He looked past the Pegasus, his eyes meeting hers. Charity felt her color rise, and she hoped he'd attribute it to the warmth of the sun that poured in the front windows. She could suddenly hear Diane's voice suggesting that she should ask him out to lunch. It was so loud in her mind, she would hardly have been surprised if he heard it, too.

Watching the color come into her cheeks, Gabe wondered at its cause. She was really a very attractive woman, he thought, not for the first time. If he were honest, he would have to admit that it was her smile that kept him coming back to this particular store. He could have gotten the little crystal figures at a better price elsewhere.

Twice he'd almost asked her out. Each time he'd changed his mind. She wore no rings, but he couldn't believe that a woman with a smile like that wasn't seriously involved with someone. Besides, what if she accepted his invitation and then turned out to have the personality of an angry pit bull once she was away from her job?

Gabe rather liked having her in the back of his mind as a gentle fantasy. He wasn't sure he wanted to risk spoiling it with reality. God knows he had plenty of reality in his job.

But seeing her standing there with the sun picking out gold highlights in her honey-colored hair, with those big green eyes smiling at him, Gabe decided it was worth taking a chance.

He opened his mouth to ask if she'd consider having dinner with him sometime. The sharp ping of his beeper interrupted him before he could say anything. Grimacing, he set the Pegasus on the counter and reached for the beeper at his belt, silencing the electronic demand.

"Is there a phone here that I could use?"

"In the employees' lounge," Charity said. "Well, it's only a little room, really. But there's a phone there."

It was strictly against the rules, of course. Mr. Hoffman would frown severely if he found out she'd allowed a customer into the inner sanctum. But this was hardly an ordinary customer, Charity told herself, as she led the way to the back of the store. Not only was Gabriel London a regular patron, he was a police officer of some sort. She'd seen the badge several times when he took out his wallet to pay for his purchases.

Sally was just leaving the small room that went by the rather grandiose title of employees' lounge when Charity led Gabe down the little hallway. There were boxes stacked in one corner, revealing its true use as a storeroom. But there was a narrow sofa crammed against the wall next to a table that held a coffee machine, a couple of magazines and the phone.

Sally gave Charity a surprised look as she showed Gabe into the room. He murmured his thanks and moved toward the phone. Charity wasn't surprised to find Sally waiting for her at the end of the narrow hallway.

"Hoffman'll be furious," Sally said, not without a certain amount of satisfaction. She resented the fact that though Charity didn't have the title, she had the authority that went with being a manager. If anyone should be unofficial manager, Sally felt it should be she. After all, she'd been with Hoffman's six months longer than Charity. Never mind that she couldn't manage her own checkbook, it was seniority that should count.

"Mr. Hoffman certainly wouldn't object to my lending a hand to a police officer," Charity said calmly.

"Who say's he's a cop?" Sally's tone was ripe with suspicion.

"I do." The calm statement was difficult to argue with, though Sally looked as if she'd like to give it a try. Luckily for Charity's patience, the soft ping of the bell over the door announced the arrival of a customer. The subject was dropped as both women moved toward the front of the store.

Sally took the first customers, an older couple looking for a gift for their granddaughter's graduation. Hard on their heels was a couple in their thirties who headed straight for the engagement rings. Charity wondered if everyone in the world but her was married or about to be. With a small sigh she moved toward them.

She'd just set a tray of rings on the counter when the bell pinged again. Glancing at Sally, she saw that she was still showing her customers a delicate diamond tennis bracelet. Unless Al bothered to come out of his office, the new customers were simply going to have to wait.

Charity looked at the new arrivals and felt her heart give a sudden, sickening bump. Three men had entered, all of them in their early to mid-twenties. Two were unshaven, their faces covered with a ragged growth of beard. A good bath and a delousing would go a long way toward improving their social standing.

They didn't look as if they were interested in buying an anniversary gift for their ailing mother, she thought, and then chided herself for being so judgmental. They were probably perfectly nice young men. Right. And pigs really could fly.

Charity murmured an apology to her customers and moved toward the newcomers. Stopping at the end of the counter, her hand dropped casually behind it, her fingers hovering over the silent alarm button. It might not be fair to judge them by their looks, but if that trio was here for anything but trouble, she'd eat her shoes, which couldn't possibly be more uncomfortable than wearing them.

"May I help you?"

The inquiry seemed to amuse them. They glanced at each other, mouths curving in smiles that did nothing to reassure Charity.

"Can you help us?" That was the clean-shaven one, the one with the pale blue eyes.

"Yes. Is there something I can do for you?" Charity kept her smile firmly in place, despite the shiver that was working its way up her spine.

"Well now, that all depends," he said mockingly. "It all depends on whether you got what we want." He turned toward her as he spoke and Charity felt her uneasiness crystalize into fear. Despite the warmth of the late-spring day outside, they were all wearing jackets. As he turned toward her, his jacket swung away from his body, giving her a clear look at the rather large gun tucked in his belt.

"What is it you're interested in?" she asked calmly. Her smile frozen in place, Charity's finger came down on the silent alarm. The signal would be relayed directly to the police department. And if she was misjudging these men and they were really undercover cops, she'd apologize later.

"Well, we're interested in a lot of things." The clean-shaven one must be the leader. He took a step toward her, a truly sickening smile on his thin face. But he didn't get a chance to continue.

Al Kocek, for whom quick wit could not be placed high on his list of attributes, chose this particular moment to demonstrate why that was the case. The silent alarm had triggered a red light and a discreet buzzer in his office. Charity speculated later that he'd probably been sleeping on the sofa when the alarm startled him awake. There were any number of intelligent reactions he could have had. Unfortunately he bypassed all of them.

"Who the hell triggered that alarm?" His bellow preceded him as he charged from the back hallway.

Everything seemed to happen in slow motion. The man who'd been approaching Charity spun around, his hand reaching inside his coat. When it came back out, the gun was clutched in his fist. She reached out, thinking to push him off balance, but he wasn't close enough. Her fingers barely brushed the sleeve of his coat. The gun lifted and she saw his finger tighten on the trigger.

The sound of the shot was deafening. Charity threw her hands up to cover her ears, turning her head to see Al Kocek's bulky body jerk with the impact of the bullet. Red bloomed on his shoulder. He staggered and fell back.

There was a moment of unbearable silence. It was broken by a scream. For a moment Charity thought the screaming in her mind had become audible. But then she saw Sally's mouth open, her eyes bulging with terror as she stared at Al's motionless body. She dropped her hands from her ears, not surprised to find them shaking.

Sally's scream broke off into loud sobs that filled the shocked silence.

ON THE PHONE at the back of the jewelry store, Gabe listened as Annie gave him a rundown of a report that had just come in. They'd been investigating an extortion racket for nearly three months and it looked as if they might finally be getting a break.

"Okay, I'll be there in a few minutes and we can go over it," he said. "Good thing I didn't have a hot date tonight."

It was probably just as well he hadn't had a chance to ask the saleswoman out, he thought ruefully. If she'd accepted and then he'd had to cancel, it would hardly get their relationship off to a good start. He'd ask her to hold the Pegasus for him. He could come in next week, strike up a conversation and then suggest dinner.

"You mean you'd prefer a hot date to an evening

with me, sugar?'' Annie's question pulled his thought back to the present.

"It's a tough choice, but duty calls."

"I think it'll be..." Gabe lost the thread of her words, his head jerking toward the open doorway as a large man ran by, his shoulder bouncing off the doorjamb. The contact didn't slow him.

"Who the hell triggered that alarm?" His angry demand came back to Gabe. The words were answered by the sharp, unmistakable crack of a .38.

Instinctively Gabe dropped to the floor, his right hand reaching for the gun tucked in the back of his waistband.

"Report a 211 in progress at Hoffman's Jewelry on Maple." His staccato words cut Annie off in midsentence. He heard her suck in a quick, startled breath before he continued in a low voice. "There's been a shot fired. I don't know if anyone's been hurt. We could have a hostage situation."

"Where are you, Gabe?" Her voice was all business, the slow Southern drawl gone.

"In the back. I'm going to try and get a look at what's happening."

"You be careful." Personal concern for him crept through her professional tone. "And don't do anything stupid."

"Believe me, I've never felt smarter." He set the phone down and eased to his feet, gliding over to the doorway.

The shot had been followed by a moment of shocked silence, and then a woman started screaming. From where he was, he could see nothing of the front of the store, which was both good and bad. He couldn't see what was happening, but they couldn't know he was here.

"Shut up, bitch!" The barked order cut the wailing off in midshriek. Gabe dropped to his knees and tried to remember the layout of the store. The hallway was off to one side of the main building, which meant that, unless someone was standing at the back of the store, in direct line with the hall, they wouldn't be able to see anyone in the hall.

Drawing a quick breath, he eased his head around the door, half expecting to have it shot off. There was no one in sight. But if anyone came down the hall, he'd be a sitting duck, probably a dead one at that. A gun and a badge were unlikely to endear him to whoever had fired that shot. They might have already killed one person. Shooting a cop wasn't likely to bother them.

He drew back into the employees' lounge, his eyes scanning it for anything that might be of help. There was nothing. In the distance he could hear the wail of sirens, which meant Annie had relayed the information that shots had been fired. Probably his presence, as well. So here came the cavalry. Great, as long as their arrival didn't precipitate a slaughter.

He hesitated and then jammed his gun back into the holster. Lifting one foot, he struggled with his boots, pulling off one and then the other. Stuffing them behind a box, he shrugged out of his jacket and tucked it in with them. He sincerely hoped he would be back to get them.

In his stocking feet, he padded back to the door. Once again he eased his head around the doorway. The hall was still clear. Reaching back to pull out his gun, he slipped into the hallway. In a half crouch, he moved silently down the hallway, ducking behind one of the jewelry cases at the back of the store.

He still couldn't see anything, but the low murmur of voices became clearly audible. As he listened intently, he formed a mental picture of what was happening.

"Look what you did!" The voice was young and nervous. "We weren't goin' to shoot anybody."

"The guy came barrelin' outta there like a freight train. What was I supposed to do? Ask him to tea?" This voice was older, a little guttural.

"Shut up, both of you." There was a certain crispness to the third voice, a tone that said he expected to be obeyed. Gabe immediately pegged him as the leader.

"But, Sal, look what Joe did." That was the young one, whiny and scared.

"Shut up!"

Outside, the sirens had screamed to a halt in front and in back of the store. Gabe already knew the back door was useless. A desk and a couple of office chairs crowded the narrow hallway in front of it. Maybe they'd just redone the office and hadn't had a chance to get rid of the old furniture yet. Maybe the owner was just careless. Whatever the reason, the back door was effectively blocked.

In a crouch Gabe crept forward, halting at the end of the case, unwilling to risk crossing the gap between it and the next case. He could hear car doors slam outside. There was a vague murmur that told him the stores on either side of Hoffman's were being evacuated, the employees and customers taken out the back doors, herded into the safety of the parking lot.

"Sal, there's cops all over the place." That was the

nervous one again. Gabe marked him in his mind. Nervous people with guns were one of his least favorite things. If someone was going to go off half-cocked and start trouble, it was likely to be the nervous one. Or, obviously, the one who'd already shot the guy who'd come barreling out of the back room.

"That man is bleeding. He needs medical attention." The calm feminine tone was like a drink of cool water. Gabe recognized the voice of the little clerk with the big green eyes, sounding just as cool as if she were asking whether they'd like to pay by check or credit card.

"Let him bleed." That was Joe, the one who'd fired the shot. "Sonofabitch shouldn't'a come out shouting like that."

"I'd like to put a pressure pad on his wound," she said, ignoring the comment. Gabe didn't doubt that she was addressing Sal. "If he dies, it will be murder."

There was a moment's frozen silence while the three would-be robbers absorbed this piece of information. Gabe's fingers tightened on the gun. She was taking a risk, pushing like that. The nervous one and the guy who'd fired the shot both sounded tense.

"See what you can do for him," Sal ordered roughly.

They all seemed to be at the front of the store. Gabe's fingers tightened around the gun as he eased forward until he could look through the gap between the two cases. The wounded man lay directly in front of him. Blood had stained the front of his jacket. Probably not as bad as it looked, Gabe thought. There wasn't enough blood for the bullet to have hit an artery—didn't look as if he was in any danger of bleeding to death.

He slid back out of sight as the girl came into view. What was her name? Chastity? No, but it was something with an old-fashioned ring to it. Charity. That was it. Charity.

Why hadn't he asked her out before this? It would have been nice to have a better feel for how she was going to react in this situation. She seemed calm so far.

He heard the soft scuff of her shoes on the carpet as she approached the wounded man. Leaning his head back against the case, he debated his next move. She had probably forgotten that he was here. Was it smart to remind her? On the other hand, it might be helpful to have an ally.

Drawing a shallow breath, Gabe eased his head around the edge of the case…and looked directly into Charity's wide green eyes. She didn't look in the least surprised. She hadn't forgotten him for a minute.

"Anybody else in the back?" Sal's question was so perfectly timed, he might have been following a script.

Without so much as a flicker of an eyelash, Charity answered. "No. There's no one else in back."

"Check it out, Billy."

"Me? What if there's cops back there?" Billy asked nervously.

"If there were cops back there, we'd have been looking down the barrels of their shotguns by now," Sal said impatiently. "Just go make sure nobody else is hiding in the john."

Gabe knew that when Billy rounded the end of the last case, he had only to glance sideways to discover that there might not be cops in the back, but there was one right under his nose.

Holding his breath, he listened to the sound of Billy's footsteps, cursing the carpeting that muffled them. Praying that his timing was right, he swung into the gap between the cases just after Billy walked by it. Now he was visible only from the front.

Charity's eyes flickered up to him, her hands busy putting a pad against the oozing wound high in the unconscious man's shoulder. The lacy edge identified the makeshift bandage as a half slip.

Gabe heard Billy's boots strike the uncarpeted hallway. He could slip in behind him and eliminate at least one of the bad guys. But that would simply alert the other two to his presence and would do nothing for the remaining hostages. Just how many hostages were there?

As if she'd read his mind, Charity spoke. "You don't really need to hold all of us, you know. Why don't you let the two couples go? And Mr. Kocek needs a doctor. That would still leave you with Sally and me."

Someone—Sally, no doubt—uttered a squeaky protest. Gabe barely heard. Two couples, two employees and the wounded man. Seven hostages. More than enough to bargain with. Hearing Billy's return, he counted slowly to five before sliding back behind the case and out of sight.

Leaning his head back, he tried to decide what to do. He was right in the middle of a very nasty hostage situation with no way to communicate with the cops outside.

It was not a good situation, and he had a strong feeling that it was going to get worse.

Chapter Three

"How'd the cops get here so fast, anyway?" That was Billy, his voice stretched tight with nerves.

"Stay back from the windows, you idiot," Sal told him.

"Well, how'd they know?"

Billy moved away from the front windows, his movements quick and nervous. Charity found it difficult to take her eyes off the gun he was waving around so carelessly.

"That guy said something about a silent alarm," Joe said suddenly.

She swallowed hard and dropped her eyes to Al Kocek's still form.

"Who set off the alarm?" Billy demanded. "Couldn't'a been the old geezers, and the two of you don't work here, either." He dismissed the customers. His attention settled on Sally, who was cowering behind one of the cases, her heavily made up eyes bulging with terror. "You work here."

Charity had never in her life heard so much menace in anyone's voice. She could almost forgive Sally for her quick denial.

"It wasn't me. I wasn't anywhere near a button,"

she stammered out, her voice squeaky with fear. "It was her. Charity was right next to it. She must have set it off." One brightly lacquered nail pointed to where Charity knelt beside the wounded man.

Billy was beside her before she had a chance to do more than draw a quick breath. Grabbing her arm, he jerked her to her feet.

"Did you call the cops on us?"

The stubble of beard made him look younger, she thought, focusing her mind on that irrelevant detail. And a haircut would have gone a long way to improving his appearance. Where was Vidal Sassoon when you needed him?

"Did you push the damn button?" His fingers tightened on her arm. He gave her a rough shake. She'd have bruises tomorrow. Always supposing he didn't kill her today. "Answer me!"

"You had guns," she said finally.

"Bitch!" There was no time to avoid the blow, even if he hadn't been holding her. The back of his hand connected with her face, the force of it weighted by the gun he still held. Pain exploded through her face, radiating outward from her cheek until her whole head pounded. She would have fallen but for the hold he still had on her arm.

"You've ruined everything," he said shrilly, drawing his hand back to strike again. Over his shoulder Charity glimpsed a movement in the opening where she'd last seen Gabriel London, and her fear took on a new edge. If he moved to help her, it could set off a shoot-out that would leave all of them dead.

"Billy!" Sal's sharp voice stopped the blow. "Leave her alone."

"But she ruined everything," Billy whined. His

hand dropped but he didn't release his hold on her arm.

"Hitting her isn't going to change anything. Come here. The cops are going to be calling any minute. We've got to figure out what to do next."

Billy released her arm reluctantly, a quick slashing look telling her that he wasn't going to forget just who had set off the alarm.

Charity had to lock her knees to keep from sinking to the floor. Her pulse was pounding in her ears, throbbing in rhythm with the pain in her bruised face. She could taste the salt tang of blood from her split lip. She didn't need anyone to tell her that she'd just come close to death.

Seeing their captors huddled together working out a strategy, she dared a quick glance to the side. Gabe's eyes were on her puffy cheek, and she could sense his frustration. She wanted to give him a smile, reassure him that she was all right. But her face was too stiff to allow such a movement.

The shrill ring of the phone was startling in the tense quiet. Everyone's eyes locked on the instrument, which sat on one of the cases. Sally must have made a call and left it out, Charity thought absently. Normally the phone was out of sight. It rang again, a sharp demand for attention.

"You figure that's the cops?" Joe asked.

Sal nodded. "Bound to be. They'll want to know what we want."

"You think if we ask 'em to go away, they'll do it?" Billy giggled like a nervous schoolboy. Sal ignored him. The phone rang a third time.

"Answer the phone. You." He gestured to Charity.

"What do you want me to tell them?" she asked over the fourth ring.

"Just answer the damn phone," Joe snarled. It was obvious that the tension was getting to him.

"I'll tell you what to say once you've got them on the line," Sal told her.

Charity nodded and walked stiffly to the phone. Apparently she was about to get a crash course in hostage mediation.

GABE LEANED his shoulder against the case. Sweat trickled down his spine, though the room was not overly warm. His left thigh was starting to cramp, he'd been so still so long, and he shifted position, moving gingerly, aware that a sound could cost him his life. He rubbed at the tight muscle until it relaxed.

How long had it been? A glance at his watch confirmed that it was only five minutes later than the last time he'd looked. Not quite an hour since this situation had begun. It felt like days.

The negotiations weren't going well. In fact they were hardly going at all. He didn't have to be outside with them to know that the police were as frustrated as he was. Sal's first demand for a helicopter had been nixed when the negotiator pointed out that there was no place to land it. When he'd asked for a van, the negotiator had demanded the release of a hostage. Gabe guessed that Sal might have gone for it, but Billy and Joe adamantly opposed letting even one of the hostages go.

The last call had ended in a stalemate almost twenty minutes ago. Charity had been doing all the talking, relaying the police demands to the three would-be thieves. Gabe's admiration for her had climbed steadily as the minutes ticked by. The pressure was incredible, but her voice remained level, without a hint of the fear she must be feeling.

From where he sat, the only hostage he could see was the wounded man, who hadn't regained consciousness. His chest continued to rise and fall, his breathing reasonably steady. The others he could only hear. There was an elderly couple. The wife had asked if she could open her purse to get her husband's nitroglycerin tablets. He guessed the other couple was younger, though all he could hear was an occasional low murmur of reassurance from one to the other.

That left only the other clerk, the one who'd been so quick to inform Sal and company just who had pushed the alarm button. Gabe had a vague image of her—a brassy redhead with a rather pouty expression.

He got occasional glimpses of Charity when she came to check on the wounded man. Their eyes would meet, but she was careful to look away quickly, afraid to draw attention to his presence. Gabe's gaze lingered on the dark bruise beginning to show on her cheekbone, and his fingers tightened on the gun.

There was no reproach in her eyes, no questioning why he hadn't done anything to protect her. She knew as well as he did that the only thing he could have done was get himself killed. But that knowledge didn't stop the guilt from gnawing at Gabe's stomach. He was a police officer. His job was to defend and protect. So far he'd done precious little of either.

"Why don't they call back?" That was Billy, his voice higher and tighter than it had been the last time he spoke. "Why the hell don't they call back?"

"Chill out. They're playing a waiting game with us, that's all," Sal said.

"Well, I don't like it." Joe's voice held a ragged edge that made Gabe uneasy. Billy might sound hysterical but Joe was the one who'd shot the man who lay on the floor. "I think they're bringing in reinforcements. That's what I think."

"Maybe I don't care what you think," Sal said. For the first time, his voice was taking on an edge.

Gabe felt the adrenaline start to pump. The tension was getting to all of them. Tense people with large guns and little to lose—a potentially deadly combination. The sharp ring of the phone made him jump. From the vivid curse, he guessed he wasn't the only one it had startled.

"Answer it," Sal snarled. Gabe eased forward between the two cases. He could see the edge of Charity's skirt, a soft flow of peach cotton. She picked up the phone, cutting it off in mid-ring. Gabe listened as she relayed the conversation.

The police were willing to provide them with a van but they had to release the hostages first. Sal's reply was short and pithy—they all went together or they could take the hostages out in body bags. The negotiator suggested that a show of good faith would go a long way to resolving this situation.

And so it went, back and forth. The negotiator bargaining for time; the robbers bargaining for their freedom. The call went on, Charity's quiet voice relating the negotiator's words and repeating Sal's replies.

Gabe could feel the tension building. Something had to give soon. The hair on the back of his neck was standing on end. He had to make a conscious effort to ease his grip on the gun. In his mind he marked where the three men were, trying to hold a picture of the store layout, judging their position from the sound of their voices.

Please, God, let them hit on a compromise. The last thing they needed was for anyone to open fire in the relatively close confines of the store. Too much chance of innocent people getting shot. But something told him his prayers weren't going to be answered.

He was right.

"Screw the damned cops," Joe exploded suddenly. Gabe heard Charity's gasp and then the crash of the phone being slammed through one of the glass cases. "I can't take this no more. If they won't give us what we want, we'll just have to show them we mean business."

Gabe heard a shriek and he knew the time for waiting was over. Whatever thin thread had been holding the situation in some tattered order was broken now.

"Police. Drop your weapons." He lunged up from behind the cases, taking in the situation at a glance. One burly gunman had hold of an elderly man, a pistol pointed at his head. The other two were ranged behind him on either side of the store.

For an instant the scene was frozen, like a tableau on a stage. No one moved, no one seemed to breathe. Gabe held his weapon trained on the man holding the hostage, wondering if there was any hope that they'd simply lay down their guns as ordered. There wasn't.

"What the—" Joe, in a reckless moment, thrust the old man aside as he turned his gun toward Gabe. Gabe's bullet caught him in the throat, and the bullet that had been aimed at Gabe's head buried itself in the ceiling as Joe's finger tightened convulsively on the trigger.

Immediately two other bullets shattered the glass

counter where he'd been standing. But he was moving even as he fired, throwing himself down and to the right, his shoulder hitting the carpet as he rolled, drawing the fire farther away from the hostages. Rolling to a half crouch he snapped off another shot, the .45 slug catching a thin young man in the chest. The impact threw him backward into the front window, which shattered under the impact.

Gabe turned, rising to his feet to get the third and last gunman in his sights. But he'd misjudged. The other man had moved, even as he had. There was nothing but air where he'd been. Gabe swung around, feeling something tug his sleeve as the boom of the shot reached his ears.

And there was the third man, his face twisted with rage, his gun pointed right at Gabe's heart. For a split second, they faced each other over their drawn weapons. There was a moment, hardly more than a heartbeat, when Gabe thought the man was going to see the futility of it all; when he thought it might end right there.

Then he caught a flurry of movement out the corner of his eye. A flash of brassy red hair as one of the hostages snapped under the strain. She darted forward, shrieking mindlessly. In the instant before she came between them, the robber fired. Gabe felt the bullet brush past, a hairbreadth from his head. He dropped to his knees in a diving roll, coming up against the edge of a display case. A bullet shattered it, showering him with shards of glass. A third plowed into the wood just in front of his face.

Shaking his head, deafened by the continuous roll of sound, Gabe brought up his gun. He felt it recoil in his hand just as he heard a sharp cry.

"Sally! No!"

With horror, Gabe saw Charity stumble in front of him as she attempted to knock the other woman out of the way. Her body jerked with the impact of the bullet—his bullet. She half turned, her hands flung out, and then she crumpled to the floor.

Chapter Four

"They said she was in surgery, Gabriel. I'm sure she's goin' to be just fine." Gabe caught Annie's worried glance as she turned into the hospital parking lot, but her words didn't ease the tension that knotted his gut. Annie hadn't been there. She hadn't seen Charity fall.

He'd sleepwalked through the preliminary report. He'd answered the questions, given all the details, but his thoughts had been elsewhere—in the ambulance with Charity, in the emergency room. The paramedics had told him nothing, and he hadn't delayed their departure with questions they couldn't answer.

As soon as the investigating officers released him, Gabe headed out the door. He didn't protest when Annie took his arm and steered him away from his old Jag toward her more sedate four-door.

"Gabriel, you've got to believe she's going to be all right." She let a trace of exasperation creep into her voice as she searched for a parking place.

"Danny Androte wasn't."

"This ain't the same thing at all," Annie said. "You were shootin' at Danny Androte. This woman just happened to stumble in the way. Chances are the bullet just grazed her. She'll be just fine and she'll have an interesting story to tell her grandchildren."

Gabe didn't respond. She hadn't been there. The bullet hadn't grazed Charity. As soon as the car came to a stop, he was out the door. Swearing softly, Annie yanked the keys out of the ignition and snatched up her purse. She had to trot to catch up with Gabe's long-legged stride. She grabbed hold of his arm, pulling him to a stop.

"You go storming in there, looking like that, and the nurses will have you tranquilized and in a bed before you know what hit you."

Gabe looked at her blankly, and she clucked her tongue in exasperation, gesturing to his torn and blood-spattered sleeve. He'd allowed the paramedics to cleanse and bandage the shallow wound, but he'd refused any other treatment.

"Here. Put on your jacket, at least. You should be in bed, resting, you know," she scolded. She helped him into the jacket that someone had thoughtfully rescued from the back room of the jewelry store. Gabe sucked in a sharp breath as he eased his bandaged arm into the sleeve.

"Comb your hair," Annie ordered briskly, handing him a comb. Gabe obeyed, taming the unruly locks by feel. "There now, you look almost human."

"Thanks, Annie." He handed the comb back to her, his eyes focusing on her for the first time since the shooting.

"I'm just doing my part to uphold the reputation of the police force," she told him briskly. "Anybody who saw you would think we were all untamed wild persons." Her precise use of the non-sex-specific term drew a half smile from Gabe but he was already moving toward the hospital again.

Gabe's nose twitched as they stepped into the lobby. What was it they cleaned hospitals with to give them that odd non-smell? It was, in its own subtle way, as powerful as a whiff of ammonia.

The nurse at the desk informed them that Ms. Williams was still in surgery. It seemed to Gabe that she gave him a disapproving look, as if she knew he was responsible for Ms. Williams's condition.

Annie followed him into the waiting room. There were two people already there: a tall blond man of imposing proportions and a stunningly beautiful woman. Gabe barely noticed them.

"I didn't even know her last name until the nurse gave it to me just now." He and Annie took chairs on the opposite side of the room from the other couple.

"I don't see as how that makes any difference," Annie told him briskly.

"No, I suppose it doesn't." Gabe stared at his hands where they lay on his knees. "Did I tell you how well she handled herself? She was so calm."

"You've got to stop talking like she was dead, Gabriel."

Gabe didn't hear her. "I was going to ask her out. She had the prettiest smile. Sweet."

"You can ask her out when all this is over."

"If I'd just been a split second faster." His hand clenched into a fist on his knee.

"You can't second-guess yourself," she told him firmly. "You did what you thought was right."

Gabe didn't respond. He knew she was trying to keep him from thinking the worst. She kept telling him that it was probably a minor wound. But he knew better. Annie hadn't been there, hadn't seen the impact of the bullet.

He closed his eyes but he couldn't shut out the images. They were locked in his head, replaying over and over again like a film loop. He'd gone over it time and again, trying to see what he should have done differently.

Had he reacted too quickly? Maybe misjudged the danger to the hostages? Should he have waited to see if Joe would calm down? But if he'd waited, the old man might be dead now. Could he have prevented the shoot-out by revealing himself earlier? Would the three of them have surrendered if they'd realized there was a cop on the premises?

"Stop it." Annie reached out and caught his hand in hers, squeezing it to make sure she had his attention. "You saved several lives today. Don't you forget that."

"What if she dies?" Gabe asked her, his eyes bleak.

"She's not going to die."

He wanted to believe that, but he kept seeing Charity lying there so still and quiet, the bright tint of blood staining the carpet beneath her.

Seeing the taut line of his jaw and knowing there was nothing she could say that would make him feel any better, Annie sighed and stopped trying. Right now the only thing she could do for Gabe was to be here for him.

She got up and moved over to the coffeepot that sat on a low table. Pouring two cups, her eyes met those of the exquisite blonde, reading the banked fear in those wide green eyes. Annie gave her a half smile, offering the sort of wordless sympathy one shares with strangers caught up in the same situation.

Carrying the coffee back to their seats, she pressed one cup into Gabe's hand. He stared at it for a moment as if uncertain of its purpose and then murmured his thanks before taking a swallow.

The problem was that Gabriel London was basically too damn sensitive to make a good cop. She studied him openly, knowing he was too absorbed in his thoughts to notice. There were those who took one look at his easy smile and the casual way he approached most things and labeled him a lightweight.

But Annie knew differently. In the years they'd been partners, she'd learned that there was no one more dependable than Gabe. And there was no one less deserving of the title of lightweight. In fact it was her considered opinion that he needed to lighten up a bit.

Being a police officer was never easy. There was a reason cops had such a high divorce rate; why so many of them had drinking problems. The stress was unbelievable. If you were smart, you found a release before it reached a critical level. Whether it was racquetball or going out into the woods every weekend and getting in touch with nature, you needed something to keep you sane.

And you had to learn to go easy on yourself; to accept that all you could do was your best. Annie couldn't think of anyone more tolerant of others' failings and less tolerant of his own. Gabe expected very little of those around him and an extraordinary amount from himself.

She finished the last of her coffee. If this woman

didn't make it... She didn't want to think about what it would do to Gabe.

Gabe was aware of Annie's scrutiny, aware of her concern. He knew he should reassure her, tell her he was all right. But the truth was, he wasn't at all sure he was all right. If only Charity hadn't run between them. The other woman had been out of the way, in no danger. If Charity had just stayed where she was...

THE MINUTES ticked by, stretching into hours. Annie kept his coffee cup replenished and Gabe drank it, more to reassure her than because he wanted it. He forced himself to stop looking at his watch when he realized that less than a minute was going by between glances.

The couple across the room spoke occasionally, their voices an indistinguishable murmur. Most of the time Gabe forgot they were there.

As the hours inched by, even Annie ran out of optimistic words. The longer Charity was in surgery, the harder it was to believe her wound could be minor. Twice Gabe told Annie to go home. She ignored him, giving him a sharp look and telling him not to be a fool.

The hands on his watch had just crawled past midnight when someone at last came to the doorway of the waiting room.

"Are any of you here for Ms. Williams?" The man who spoke was short, middle-aged and paunchy. He wore surgical greens, his shoes still encased in cotton booties. He looked tired, but Gabe couldn't read anything beyond that in his eyes, no matter how desperately he tried.

Gabe jackknifed out of the chair, every muscle

tensed. His fingers tightened over the paper cup he held, crushing it. He stepped forward, but before he could say anything, the tall blond man spoke.

"I'm Brian Williams, her brother. This is our sister, Diane."

The surgeon sent a quick glance toward Gabe but didn't question his obvious interest. "I'm Dr. Lang."

"How is she?" Diane bypassed the polite introductions, asking the question on all of their minds.

"We're cautiously optimistic about your sister's condition," the surgeon told her, not in the least offended by her abruptness.

"What does that mean?" Gabe asked.

Brian and Diane Williams looked at him, surprised. All the hours they had shared the waiting room, it had never occurred to any of them that they might be waiting for the same news.

"Her condition is stable at this point."

"But?" Brian pounced on the unspoken qualifier in Dr. Lang's voice.

"There is a bullet fragment lodged very near the spine."

Annie took the ruined cup out of Gabe's hand, closing her fingers over his forearm.

"Is she paralyzed?" Was that his voice? He sounded so calm.

"We don't see any reason to expect that," Dr. Lang said cautiously. "To tell the truth, Ms. Williams has been very lucky."

"Lucky?" Diane said incredulously.

"Considering the seriousness of her wound, yes, I'd have to say your sister was lucky. The fragment near the spine is certainly a cause for concern but it's not pressing on any nerves."

"Why didn't you remove the fragment?" Brian asked.

"There's less potential for damage if we leave it alone. Once her body has had a chance to heal, I don't think she'll even notice the fragment's presence, unless she has to explain it to an X-ray technician." His half smile went unanswered.

"But you can't guarantee that," Brian said, frowning.

Dr. Lang gave him a weary smile. "Mr. Williams, medicine is not an exact science. I can tell you, based on the experiences of myself and my colleagues, it is our opinion that your sister will make a full recovery. But only time will tell for sure."

"Can we see her?" Diane asked.

"If you want to wait an hour, then perhaps for five minutes. She won't be awake, of course. But you can sit with her."

"Thank you."

"I certainly hope those thanks are deserved," Dr. Lang said, with a smile that said he was confident they were.

The waiting room was completely still after he left. For a few moments it was all anyone could do to just breathe and feel some of the tension seep away. Of course, Charity wasn't out of the woods yet, but there was reason to hope, reason to believe everything was going to be all right.

"Excuse me."

Annie's hand dropped from his arm as Gabe turned toward Charity's brother. Now that he knew who they were, he could see their resemblance to their sister.

"I don't mean to sound nosy," Brian continued with a half smile. "But who are you?"

He heard Annie catch her breath as if to caution him. But Gabe was beyond trying to think of a clever response. He said the only thing he could think of.

"I'm the man who shot her."

The stark answer wiped the cautious friendliness from Brian Williams's expression. He'd been prepared to share his relief with a friend of Charity's. He wasn't prepared to find himself face to face with the man whose bullet had put her in the hospital. His reaction was instinctive.

Gabe didn't try to avoid the punch. In his own mind he deserved that and more. Brian's fist connected with his chin with jarring force. Gabe staggered back and would have fallen if Annie hadn't grabbed his arm.

It was doubtful that Brian would have thrown another punch. The first had been more a result of tension and worry than anything else. But if he had been inclined to more violence, he didn't have a chance. With a shocked exclamation, Diane grabbed hold of his arm. Annie released Gabe, stepping in between the two men, her expression stern.

"Maybe y'all don't realize that if it weren't for my partner here, your sister and a lot of other people would be dead." In the heat of emotion, her accent thickened, making her sound more like a southern belle than a police officer.

"The police explained to us what happened," Diane said, her finger still clenched around her brother's arm. "We know it was an accident." But she avoided Gabe's eyes. Like her brother she was obviously having difficulty getting past the fact that he was the one who'd shot Charity.

Without a word Gabe turned and left. Their accusing gazes were more than his bruised soul could take. Annie gave the pair a last glance that combined sympathy and annoyance before hurrying after her partner. Catching up with him at the elevators, she threw a quick glance at his face but said nothing.

She grabbed his arm as they left the hospital, steering him in the direction of her car. Gabe followed without protest, though he'd just as soon have walked off into the night alone.

Thank God Annie didn't regard conversation as a cure-all. He leaned his head back against the seat and closed his eyes, wishing he could shut out the events of the past twenty-four hours as easily as he could shut out the freeway.

He didn't open his eyes again until he felt the car slow down for an off ramp. Opening his eyes, he realized she hadn't driven him to the station to get his car or to his own home in Pasadena. Instead they were in Glendale, heading for the house Annie shared with her husband.

"I'm really not up for company tonight, Annie." It was an effort to speak. All he wanted was to be alone.

"I'm not takin' you home, Gabriel. You'll just sit there and brood, playin' it over and over in your head, wonderin' what you should have done different."

Since that was exactly what he'd had in mind, Gabe didn't even attempt to deny it.

"Maybe that's what I need to do," he said shortly.

"I ain't havin' it. Next thing you know, you'll be throwin' your badge off some freeway bridge like a character in a Clint Eastwood movie."

Since he'd also considered doing something along

those lines, Gabe was reduced to silence. The problem with Annie was that she knew him too damned well.

"Look, I'm not going to be very good company." He made one last effort to dissuade her as she pulled into her driveway.

"Well, and here I was expectin' you to teach me to polka," she said with heavy sarcasm. "You aren't stayin' alone tonight, Gabriel. What a body needs at a time like this is good friends and a medicinal drink or two."

"Going to get me drunk?" He asked, half-smiling in spite of himself.

"It wouldn't hurt."

"Anyone ever tell you you're a pushy broad?" he asked as he pushed open the car door.

"All the time, sugar. All the time."

He followed her up the walkway to the comfortable home she shared with her husband, resigning himself to the fact that Annie was going to have her way. Maybe she was right. Maybe being alone wasn't the best idea tonight. But he doubted anything would make him forget what had happened.

No matter how many good friends were around, or how many shots of whiskey Annie managed to pour down him, nothing could blot out the memory of those seconds when he'd seen the bullet—his bullet—hit Charity. And then the bright, accusing tint of blood spilling onto her dress.

It was going to take more than company and alcohol to make him forget that.

Chapter Five

The hospital smelled just the same. That odd non-smell that was somehow more antiseptic than a whiff of pure ammonia.

Gabe's fingers tightened over the bouquet of flowers. Now that he was here, he wondered if he was crazy to have come. The last person Charity would want to see was him. He was the reason she was here.

He was determined to apologize—an empty gesture but it had to be made. Maybe he shouldn't have brought flowers. Maybe they were too frivolous. He frowned down at the bouquet of yellow roses. He'd stripped his neighbor's rose bush earlier this morning, wanting the kind of roses that had scent, rather than the hothouse sorts the florist carried. Jay would probably throttle him when he saw the denuded plant but he could worry about that later.

He stepped out of the elevator, pausing to ask directions to Ms. Williams's room. It was really a delaying tactic. He knew where her room was from his last two visits. But those times he'd talked himself out of actually seeing her. This time he intended to go through with it. The least he owed her was an apology and a chance to tell him how much she hated him.

Over a week since the shooting and still no sign of the feeling in her legs. The doctors insisted there was no reason to despair. The spine was a delicate area. It needed time to heal.

Gabe's steps dragged as he walked down the hall to Charity's room. He didn't want to see those big green eyes look at him with cold anger. Didn't want to hear her vent the rage she surely felt toward him. But he owed her that much.

He stopped outside her door, his hand so tight around the tissue-wrapped stems that his fingers ached. Like as not, she was going to throw his flowers back in his face and him out on his butt. Drawing in a deep breath, he knocked on the half-open door.

''Come in.'' Her voice was just as he remembered it. Soft, with a touch of huskiness. Gabe felt his palms break out in cold sweat. He'd rather have faced a drugged-out junkie with an AK-47 than walk through that door.

Taking a deep breath, he squared his shoulders and pushed open the door. Charity was propped up in bed, a pale pink bed jacket over her shoulders, her honey-blond hair pulled back with a matching ribbon. She was paler than he remembered, her skin almost translucent. She looked so fragile, so young.

Gabe stopped just inside the room, waiting to see the smile in her eyes change to hatred when she realized who he was.

''Mr. London.'' The smile reached her mouth, her lips curving. ''Come in.''

Gabe moved forward, walking carefully, as if the ground might shift under his feet at any moment, which was exactly how he felt. Didn't she remember what had happened?

"Hello." He stopped beside the bed. He was unable to sustain her gaze, and his eyes dropped to the roses.

"Those are beautiful," Charity said after a minute, when he showed no signs of speaking.

"They're for you." He thrust them out.

Charity took them, bent to breathe in the rich scent. "They're wonderful." When she lifted her head she was still smiling. Gabe didn't respond, only stared at her, as if he wasn't sure what he was doing here. "Would you mind putting them in water for me," she asked. "You could put them in that vase there. I think those flowers have about had it."

Gabe took the roses back from her mechanically. There was a mixed bouquet on the table next to the bed. The flowers were beginning to show their age. He dumped them into the trash and filled the vase in the little bathroom. Bringing it back into the room, he set it on the table and put the roses into it.

"They look perfect. And the scent is wonderful." She turned her head to smile at him. "Thank you, Mr. London."

"Call me Gabe," he said automatically. Shooting someone should surely put them on first-name terms, he thought, wondering if he was dreaming this visit.

Obviously she didn't remember what had happened, didn't realize that he was the one who'd shot her. He felt a wave of relief. He didn't have to see the friendliness turn to hatred, didn't have to hear her tell him that he'd destroyed her life.

"I'm the one who shot you," he said abruptly.

"I know."

Nothing changed in her eyes. She was still smiling at him. Gabe groped for something to hold on to, finally grabbing the rail at the foot of the bed.

"Don't you hate me?"

"No. Why should I?" She seemed genuinely puzzled.

"Why should you? Because it's my fault you're here. *I shot you,*" he said again, in case she hadn't heard.

"But you didn't mean to."

"That's not the point."

"It was an accident," she said, handing him the same words he'd been hearing from Annie and the police psychologist ever since the shooting. "It wasn't your fault. If it was anyone's fault, it was mine for running in front of you like an idiot."

"You were trying to save the other woman's life," Gabe said, stunned to find himself defending her to herself.

"Well, as it turned out, she wasn't the one in the way." Charity shrugged. "It was just bad timing all around."

"And that's it? You don't want to tell me you hate me? You don't want to throw something at me? Yell and scream?"

"I don't think so. Would it make you feel better if I did?" Charity smiled at him mischievously, relieved when his mouth relaxed in a rueful smile.

"I don't know. I was so sure you'd be angry. That you'd hate me. I'm not sure I know what to say. Thank you, I guess."

"You don't have to thank me."

"I wouldn't have blamed you if you'd hated me."

"Well, I don't. If it wasn't for you, that poor old

man would have been killed and probably a lot of others, including me. Besides, it's not as if I'm paralyzed for life,'' she said, hoping he couldn't hear the brittle note in her cheerful words.

"What do the doctors say?" She could hear the strain in his voice.

"Oh, you know how doctors are." Charity shrugged. Her eyes skittered over the length of her legs visible beneath the blankets, fixing on his face instead. Seeing the worry in his eyes, she forced a smile. "They tell me there's no reason why I won't walk again. It's just some bruising, I guess. As soon as it's healed, I'll be tap dancing."

The fear in her eyes brought a sharp pain to Gabe's chest. The fact that she was trying to hide it only made it more heartbreaking. He'd have given his right hand if doing so would have given her back her legs.

"Did you tap dance before?" he asked, forcing a light tone, even as his fingers tightened over the rail at the foot of the bed, the knuckles white with strain.

"No." Charity grinned at him, the expression less forced. "But when I asked the doctor if I'd be able to, he assured me I would."

"Did you tell him you hadn't been able to before?"

"No. I was all set to do my best Groucho and say 'That's funny. I couldn't before.'" Her Groucho voice was moderately dreadful but Gabe couldn't suppress a grin.

"Why didn't you?"

"He looked so serious." She sighed regretfully. "I just didn't have the heart to tell him I'd been joking."

"Probably would have done him some good to lighten up a bit," Gabe suggested.

"Probably, but I figured as long as I was stuck in this place, it wouldn't be a good idea to annoy the staff. They might do something really hideous, like bring me more than three meals a day."

"Food's that bad, huh?"

"Worse than bad." Charity shuddered, seeing the smile on his mouth slowly creep into his eyes. "It's so bland, it's deadly. After a few days of this stuff, I'd just about kill for a pizza."

Gabe's smile became a chuckle. Charity relaxed back against the pillows, taking pleasure in seeing some of the tension ease from his features.

When he'd first walked in, he'd looked like a man on his way to a firing squad. White lines of tension had bracketed his mouth and his eyes had held a look of despair that had made her heart go out to him. Now he was beginning to look like the man she remembered, the one with the easy smile that had lingered in her thoughts more than it should have.

It was odd that the nervousness she'd always felt when he came into the store seemed to have faded. What they'd gone through together had created a connection between them that left no room for nerves.

In those terrible, tense hours of waiting, listening to each attempt at negotiation fail, wondering if she was about to die, Charity had held fast to the knowledge that Gabe was there. It didn't matter that their only contact was a brief meeting of their eyes when she checked the wounded man's bandage. It didn't matter that there was little he could do. Just knowing he was there had given her something to cling to when she felt her self-control slipping away.

She'd known even then that it wasn't Gabe's badge that convinced her everything would be all right. It was Gabe himself. There was a quiet strength about him that had reassured her.

"Mr. Kocek, the man who was shot first, is going to be all right."

"I heard. That's good."

Charity's eyes searched his face, seeing the lines of strain that hadn't been there before the shooting, the tightness around his mouth. He didn't look as if he'd done much smiling lately.

"They told me that the others—the two you..." The words trailed off as she groped for the right words.

"The ones I shot?" Gabe finished for her. "They died."

"Yes." She wished she hadn't said anything. The look in his eyes was painful to see.

"Yeah, I was batting a thousand that day."

She saw his knuckles whiten where he gripped the low rail at the foot of her bed. She looked away, smoothing her hand over the covers beside her as if it was important to remove every wrinkle.

"You know, if you hadn't...done what you did, a lot more people would have died."

"Maybe." Gabe shrugged. "It's a little hard to feel good when two men are lying in the morgue and you're here, like this." He gestured to her legs.

"You did the right thing," she said, her soft voice firm. "You didn't see them the way I did. They would have shot that poor old man. And it wouldn't have stopped there."

"That's what I tell myself." Gabe's mouth twisted ruefully. "Sometimes I almost believe it."

"You should believe it all the time."

Gabe only shrugged again, but the lines that bracketed his mouth were less deep, his eyes a little less bleak. Inside he was marveling at her generosity of spirit. She was lying in a hospital bed—where he'd put her—without the use of her legs, and yet she was concerned that he not feel guilty.

She should have hated him. Instead, she was trying to make him feel better. It didn't ease his gut-deep guilt. Nothing could. But he felt his interest in her deepen.

They talked, more easily than either of them would have expected. Gabe had spent some time in the hospital when he had his appendix removed, and they compared notes, coming to the conclusion that hospitals had their good points but the food definitely wasn't one of them. Neither could explain why the nurses woke you to take a sleeping pill.

Gabe's description of the lengths to which he'd gone to try and get a full night's sleep made Charity laugh, something she hadn't done much of the past few days.

He didn't stay long. Charity murmured a protest when he said it was time he left. In between bouts of sleep, the days had been longer than she would have thought possible.

"I don't want to tire you," he said.

"I'm not tired." But a yawn punctuated the sentence. Seeing Gabe's smile, she grimaced. "All I do is sleep," she muttered crossly.

"Probably the best thing for you."

"Now you sound like my doctor. You don't have a medical degree tucked in your pocket, do you?"

"You've guessed my secret." His smile faded, his eyes searching her face. "I'd like to come again, if you wouldn't mind."

"Are you kidding? I've considered begging strangers in the hall to come and talk to me. My brother and sister come in every evening but that still leaves a lot of hours to be filled."

"What about your parents?"

"Mom and Dad are off somewhere in the African bush doing whatever one does in the African bush. They don't even know I'm in here. Which is just as well. Mom would want to dose me with some of her foul-tasting herbs and Dad would be cross-examining the doctors."

"They sound great." It wasn't hard to read through her complaints to the very real affection she felt for her parents.

"They are," she admitted, wishing suddenly that Seth and Josie Williams would walk into the room. They'd be driving her crazy inside of an hour, but there was a certain comfort in their eccentricities.

She yawned again and Gabe stood up. This time she didn't protest when he said he had to leave. No doubt he had better things to do than entertain her.

"Thank you for the flowers."

"Thank my neighbor. I stripped his rose bushes before coming over here." Gabe shrugged. "He's probably waiting for me with a shotgun. I'll have to bribe him by promising to help him haul in a load of manure next spring."

"You can assure him that they were greatly appreciated," Charity told him, reaching out to touch one soft blossom.

"That'll console him." He hesitated, pushing his hands in the pockets of his jeans, his smile fading. "Are you sure it's all right if I come again?"

"Yes. But don't feel you have to. What happened

was an accident. You weren't to blame. Besides, it isn't as if I'm stuck this way for life,'' she added with a forced smile.

Charity was torn between relief and regret when Gabe left. Regret because she didn't really expect to see him again. And relief because she didn't have to keep the happy face in place anymore—at least not until Diane and Brian came to visit in a few hours.

She watched the door close behind Gabe and closed her eyes against the sudden hot sting of tears. Tears she was determined wouldn't fall. She hadn't cried since waking up after surgery—not when they'd told her she'd been shot, and not when it had become obvious that she had no feeling in her legs.

Crying would be an admission that she was frightened. And if she was frightened, it would be an admission that she might never walk again. As long as she kept telling herself and everyone else that her paralysis was a temporary setback, she could keep from going completely crazy.

But sometimes, when she was alone, it was hard to keep the doubts at bay. There was nothing to keep her from staring at the lifeless lengths of her legs, wondering if she'd ever be able to feel them again.

Opening her eyes, Charity blinked to clear the tears from her vision. It was only natural that she'd have moments of doubt, she told herself. The important thing was to make sure that they didn't last. A positive mental attitude was vitally important to her recovery—that's what everyone said. If she heard it again, she was going to scream.

Put one of the doctors or nurses with their cheerful smiles in this bed and take all the feeling from their legs and see how long they kept a positive mental attitude. No, that wasn't fair. They were just trying to help.

She sighed, turning her head to look at the roses Gabe had brought her. Their rich scent was already filling the room, making the air less sterile. She reached out and eased one fat blossom from the vase, lifting it to her nose.

She wondered if he'd meant it when he said he'd visit again. Probably not, but it had been nice of him to say it. The rose held against her cheek, she let her eyelids drift shut.

IN FACT Gabe showed up the next day. Charity had been staring at the television mounted near the ceiling opposite her bed. But her interest in game shows was slight, to put it mildly. Diane had brought her a stack of books, but she could only read so many hours in the day. She was discovering that one of the worst things about being in the hospital was the boredom.

A small movement near the door drew her attention. She knew she had to be going over the edge when even the thought of a technician taking another blood sample was a welcome diversion. But it wasn't a technician, and she felt her heart skip a beat when she saw Gabe's lean frame.

"Is the coast clear?" he hissed before she had a chance to say anything. *Clear for what?* She nodded and he disappeared back out the door. Her curiosity piqued, she dragged herself higher against the pillows, for once hardly noticing that her legs were unresponsive.

When he ducked back through the door, he was carrying a box. The flat white shape was unmistakable even if the rich scent of oregano and tomato hadn't already told her what he was carrying.

"Pizza!"

"Shh. If they catch me, there's no telling what they'll do to me. They might even make us share." He pushed the door shut with his foot. He set the box down on the rolling table at the foot of the bed and lifted the lid.

"You brought pizza." Charity's lowered voice was reverential.

Gabe grinned, pleased with her reaction. He'd had his doubts about the advisability of visiting her again. She'd said he was welcome but he hadn't quite believed her. He couldn't help but think that every time she saw him, it must be a reminder of what had happened. But there'd been nothing but welcome in her eyes.

"Pizza with the works, just like the lady ordered," he said. He reached into the sack he'd brought, coming up with two plates and a handful of napkins.

"It smells heavenly."

He lifted out a thick slice dripping with cheese and set it on a plate, which he handed to her with a flourish.

Charity picked the pizza up and bit into it, closing her eyes in ecstasy as the rich taste filled her mouth. Her tongue came out to catch a bit of sauce on her upper lip and Gabe was startled by a sudden flash of awareness.

He dropped his eyes, not wanting her to see what might be written there. He set a slice of pizza on a plate for himself, though he wasn't particularly hungry.

Careful, London, he cautioned himself. The attraction he'd felt for Charity had to be put aside—one of those sweet, foolish dreams that wasn't meant to be. She might welcome his presence now when any distraction was welcome, but there'd come a time when he was only a reminder of a painful and frightening episode in her life. If that time came when she was walking again, he'd bow out of her life without regrets.

He suppressed the doubting voice that suggested that the regrets were likely to be fierce and hard to shake off.

"Something wrong with your pizza?" Charity's question brought Gabe's head up to meet her quizzical expression.

"I always consider the first bite very carefully," he told her condescendingly. "There's an art to these things."

"Of course there is," she agreed. "And the most important aspect is how fast you can eat. Otherwise, someone else gets more. Another slice, please, garçon." Grinning, she handed him her empty plate.

Gabe pushed away the uneasiness he felt and settled down to a serious competition. At the moment the most important thing was to see her smiling.

"I CAN'T BELIEVE that guy had the nerve to visit you!" Brian Williams scowled at his youngest sister, who returned the look calmly. It was a source of unending wonderment to her that this certified genius who was revolutionizing the computer industry had a temper more suited to a guard dog.

There was none of the stereotypical computer nerd about Brian. No glasses, no hump-shouldered posture from too many hours at a keyboard, no ink stains on his shirt pocket. He actually looked more like an athlete, which he was, than a computer whiz.

"I don't see any reason why Gabe shouldn't visit," Charity said calmly.

"No reason?" Brian's blue eyes expressed his amazement. "Would you explain it to her?" he appealed to Diane and then gave Charity the explanation before Diane could say anything. "The man shot you. It's his fault you're in here. His fault you can't walk."

"Temporarily," Charity corrected, her voice tight. "Temporarily can't walk."

Brian paused, realizing how tactless his words had been. "Of course it's temporary," he said gruffly. "But that's not the point."

"No it isn't," Charity agreed. "Even if the paralysis were permanent, it still wouldn't be Gabe's fault. You weren't there, Brian. You don't know what the situation was. He risked his life to keep those men from shooting any of the hostages."

"Yeah, right. So they didn't shoot them. He did," Brian said with heavy sarcasm.

"It was an accident. I've told you that before. I'm the one who got in the way. If I'd stayed where I was, this wouldn't have happened."

"You were trying to save that woman's life," Brian said, leaping to her defense.

"And he was trying to save all our lives." She lifted her hand when he would have continued. "I don't want to hear any more about it, Brian. I know you're worried about me and I appreciate it, but I like Gabe and if he wants to visit, he's welcome."

Brian shut his mouth with an audible snap, glaring at her. Charity returned the look calmly. After a moment he looked away, muttering something about stubborn women and people who didn't know what was good for them.

"I'm going to get a cup of that stuff they call coffee," he announced abruptly. Charity watched him leave the room and turned to look at Diane.

"Don't start," she warned. "There's nothing wrong with Gabe coming to see me."

"Of course not, Char." But Diane's beautiful eyes showed her concern. "We just don't want to see you hurt. After all, Mom and Dad aren't here and we're the only family you've got."

"If you're trying to tell me that Mom and Dad wouldn't approve of Gabe, I don't buy it. Mom would have baked him some of her inedible whole-wheat oatmeal surprise cookies and Dad would want to know his opinion of teaching Latin in high school."

"Probably," Diane admitted, smiling reluctantly. The truth was, their parents had never met anyone they didn't approve of. They could have found something good in Jack the Ripper.

"It *wasn't* Gabe's fault," Charity said for what felt like the hundredth time.

"I know. I really do," she emphasized, catching Charity's disbelieving look. "I just worry that…well, you've got to admit you're sort of vulnerable right now." She spoke slowly, choosing her words with care. "I don't want to see you hurt, Charity. Neither does Brian."

"You think I might be reading too much into Gabe's visits?" Unconsciously Charity reached for the teddy bear Gabe had brought only that afternoon, saying he'd thought the bear looked like it needed some company. She kneaded her fingers in the soft, dark fur.

"This is the guy you mentioned the day before… before this happened." Diane's graceful gesture encompassed Charity's useless legs. "When we were having tea and I was bugging you about not dating. You said there was a man you found attractive. I remember the name, Gabriel London."

Charity frowned, trying to remember the conversation. That quiet afternoon seemed a hundred years ago. Yes, she remembered mentioning Gabe, but it had been just in passing. He'd popped into her head for some reason when Diane was urging her to date more.

"Just because I mentioned him, said he was attractive, doesn't mean I'm stupid enough to think the man is in love with me," Charity protested. "I know he's only visiting because he feels guilty."

"I'm sure he likes you," Diane protested.

"Sure he does. That's my problem, remember? Men always *like* me." Charity rolled her eyes to show that it didn't bother her a bit. "The only reason he isn't telling me about his girlfriend is because he feels sorry for me."

"Does he have a girlfriend?" Diane asked, and Charity knew she was hoping he did. If Gabe was already involved, there'd be less chance of her getting hurt.

"I'm sure he does." She shrugged, ignoring the small ache the idea brought to her heart. "A man like Gabe isn't likely to be running loose." She plucked restlessly at one stuffed ear, wishing Diane would stop looking at her with that worried expression.

She wasn't a child who still believed in fairy tales. She knew perfectly well that once she was walking again, Gabriel London would walk right out of her life. But in the meantime, there was nothing wrong with enjoying his company. He made her laugh. These days, that counted for quite a lot.

It wasn't as if she were going to do something stupid...like fall in love with him.

"YOU CAN'T GO back to your apartment, Char. Be reasonable."

Gabe paused outside Charity's room. In the week he'd been visiting, he hadn't run into her sister or her brother, but it looked as if that was about to change.

"I don't see why not," Charity said, and Gabe wondered if it was his imagination that put an audible strain in her voice.

"How about the fact that there's a flight of stairs leading up to it? You can't manage those in a...in a wheelchair." Diane stumbled over the word.

Gabe winced at the mental image of Charity in a wheelchair. His hands clenched into fists in the pockets of his light jacket. There was still no feeling in her legs. The doctor claimed that it was just a matter of time. Her body had taken a tremendous shock, it needed time to heal. She couldn't be impatient.

Easy to say if you weren't the one facing a wheelchair, Gabe thought fiercely. It wasn't right that Charity should suffer like this. It was his mistake, his misjudgment that had put her there. If he'd just shot a split second sooner or later...

"Since I don't plan on going anywhere, I don't see that it matters." Gabe dragged his attention back to the conversation on which he was eavesdropping.

"You can't just shut yourself up in that apartment," Diane protested.

"Well, I'm not likely to be taking any long trips

anytime soon,'' Charity pointed out, her voice beginning to sound a little ragged around the edges.

It was the sound of that stress that brought Gabe into the room. He'd gotten to know her in the past few days. He'd admired her determined cheerfulness even while he wondered what it cost her to smile when she must be screaming with fear and anger inside. He couldn't stand to hear the strain in her voice that said she was close to losing that control.

"Hi. Not interrupting, am I?'' Both women turned to look at him as he pushed open the door. The brother wasn't there, he saw at a glance. A man the size of Brian Williams would be a little hard to overlook.

"Gabe.'' Charity's smile told him she was grateful for the interruption. "I thought you said you wouldn't be able to get in today.''

"Well, there was a break I hadn't expected so I thought I'd drop by.''

"I'm glad you did. I don't think you know my sister, Diane. Diane, this is Gabriel London.''

"Actually, we've met,'' Gabe said, his eyes meeting Diane's and seeing the uneasiness there.

"You did?'' Charity glanced at her sister, surprised that Diane hadn't mentioned meeting Gabe. "When?''

"The night you were brought in,'' Diane said. "Gabe was in the waiting room. With a friend of his,'' she added. "A very pretty woman.''

Gabe wasn't sure just what the glance she threw Charity was meant to convey, but he didn't want Charity to get the wrong idea about Annie.

"My partner,'' he said easily. "She and her husband are friends of mine, as well.'' That should clear up any lingering impression that Annie was more than a friend, he thought. Though why it should seem important, he couldn't have said.

"Oh." The flat syllable could have meant anything, but Gabe had the feeling Diane Williams didn't like hearing that Annie was nothing but a friend, and a married one at that. He could ponder the reasons she might feel that way later.

"I thought I heard you talking about going home," he said to Charity. "Are they releasing you?"

"In a couple of days. There's really no reason for me to stay in the hospital. It's just a matter of waiting now. I can do the physical therapy as an out patient."

"Are you going back to your apartment?"

"She can't. There's about a thousand stairs leading up to her apartment. Maybe you can make her see reason," Diane said, willing to apply to any port in a storm.

"I'm not coming to stay with you," Charity told her, irritated. "The carpets in that apartment are about six inches thick. If I have to learn to use a damned wheelchair, I'm not going to do it on those carpets."

"I'll tear the stupid things up."

"I'm sure your landlord would love that. Besides, quite frankly, a week of living with you and we'd be at each other's throats. I love you dearly, Diane, but you are not my idea of a great roommate."

"I have a cleaning service," Diane said huffily.

"No cleaning service in the world could keep up with you." Charity reached out and caught her older sister's hand. "I really do appreciate the offer, but I need peace and quiet right now and those are not things I associate with you."

Diane looked as if she wanted to argue but

couldn't. "Well, fine then. Don't stay with me. But you'll go back to your apartment and shut yourself in like a hermit over my dead body."

"I don't want to be a hermit," Charity said. "But it's the most practical arrangement. When Brian gets back from Europe, he can help me get upstairs and then he can take me to physical therapy a couple of times a week. He might as well use those muscles for something besides lifting barbells."

"I don't like it," Diane said sullenly.

"I don't, either." It was obvious that they'd forgotten Gabe's presence, from the surprised expressions they turned on him.

"Don't you start," Charity wailed in exasperation.

He shrugged. "Sorry. But I don't think it's a good idea. An apartment whose access is only by stairs is dangerous. What if there was a fire?"

"Exactly," Diane said in triumph, glad to have an argument Charity couldn't dismiss.

"Do you have a better idea," Charity asked sarcastically.

"Actually I do. You can move in with me."

Chapter Six

"What?" Charity and Diane spoke simultaneously, giving the word a stereo effect.

"Move in with me," Gabe repeated. "It's the perfect solution."

"I don't see how," Diane said, obviously removing him from her list of allies.

"That's because you haven't seen my place," Gabe said without rancor.

"Gabe, it's awfully nice of you to offer but you don't have to—"

"I know I don't have to," he interrupted. "I want to."

"But—"

"Before you start making objections, let me explain why it would be so ideal."

Charity subsided but her expression remained doubtful. Diane didn't even bother to look that positive. Gabe felt like an insurance salesman pitching a policy to a resistant client.

"I've got a house in Pasadena—a good neighborhood. It's one story, all hardwood floors. There're three bedrooms and two baths so we wouldn't get in each other's way."

"It sounds lovely but I don't—"

"There's also a pool out back that you could use for physical therapy. You wouldn't have to come to the hospital all the time, and my next door neighbor is a doctor," he added as a final incentive.

Diane's expression had gone from total rejection to interest. He could see that she liked the idea of having a doctor next door. Charity didn't look any more convinced than she had when he started.

"It's really nice of you, Gabe," she said. "But there's no reason for you to disarrange your life. My apartment isn't as bad as Diane makes it sound. And if it really won't do, then I can find someplace else."

"Why find someplace else when my place is so close to ideal?"

His hands braced on the foot of her bed, he leaned forward. It was important to him to get her to agree to this. She might *say* that it wasn't his fault that she still couldn't walk, but he would never believe it. He'd fired the shot that had put her in this hospital bed. There was a fragment of his bullet still inside her.

If he could help her, even in so small a way as giving her a place to stay, it might make it a little easier for him to sleep at night.

"You know, Charity, he could be right," Diane said thoughtfully. Charity gave her sister a surprised look. Wasn't it Diane who'd urged her to be careful about getting involved with Gabe? Seeing Charity's expression, Diane shrugged defensively.

"Well, it seems like a reasonable solution. There's no stairs to worry about and the pool would mean you could probably do more physical therapy than if you had to come into the hospital for it every time."

"I could stay with Brian," Charity suggested desperately, feeling as if a gentle trap was closing around her.

"Brian's place isn't big enough to swing a cat," Diane reminded her. "Besides, his hours are far from normal. He's as likely to be working at three in the morning as he is to be sleeping."

"I don't want to be in your way," Charity said, giving Gabe a pleading look.

"You wouldn't be," he assured her, knowing it wasn't what she wanted to hear. If she stayed with him, he could keep an eye on her, make sure she had everything she needed. Maybe in some small way, he could make up for putting her in here.

Charity looked from Gabe to Diane, seeing her fate already decided in their eyes. Staring down at the outline of her lifeless legs, she wanted to scream and pound her fists against the unresponsive flesh, demand that the feeling come back so that she didn't have to depend on other people.

She wanted to insist on going back to her apartment, her nice, safe little apartment where everything would be familiar and normal. Only nothing was going to be normal until she could walk again. If she went back to her apartment, Gabe and Diane were both going to worry about her—Brian, too, when he came home. They'd feel obligated to check on her, to make sure she had everything she needed.

She sighed. Realistically she knew they were right. Walling herself up in her apartment wasn't going to make everything right again. And staying with Gabe would give him a chance to ease some of the guilt he shouldn't be feeling in the first place.

"If you're absolutely sure I wouldn't be in your

way,'' she said slowly, lifting her eyes to meet Gabe's. His smile made her heart beat just a little faster than it should, a reminder that this move had some inherent dangers. She was going to have to be careful that while she was regaining the use of her legs she didn't lose her heart.

"I DON'T KNOW, sugar. You sure this is a good idea?" Annie frowned at Gabe.

"It's a great idea. I've got plenty of room and she needs a place to stay. What could be simpler?"

"You don't think maybe you're carrying this whole guilt thing a bit too far?" she asked, settling into her favorite perch on the corner of his desk.

"She can't walk because of me, Annie."

"Now, don't go getting your dander up, Gabriel." She lifted a soothing hand.

Gabe closed his eyes for a moment and drew a deep breath, forcing the tension out of his shoulders. There was no reason to snap at Annie. She was just concerned about him.

He opened his eyes and gave her an apologetic smile. "Sorry."

"That's okay. What good are friends if you can't snap at them now and then?"

"That's an interesting view of friendship," he said, stretching his legs out and crossing them at the ankles.

There were any number of reports sitting on his desk awaiting his attention. In twenty minutes they were supposed to observe a lineup, and in an hour they had to go convince a store owner to testify against a suspect they'd arrested.

At the moment the only thing Gabe could think of was the fact that he was picking Charity up at the hospital this afternoon and taking her back to his house. He'd done everything he could think of to prepare the place for her to manage from the wheelchair.

"What time do you pick her up?" Annie asked, as if she'd read his thoughts.

"Five. I borrowed Levowitz's van so there'd be room to get the wheelchair in with no problem. Her sister will be coming back with us, too. I'm going to have to do something about a car," he said, frowning. "The Jag isn't going to cut it."

Annie gave him a sharp look. "Not that I wouldn't love to see you get rid of that old heap of junk," she said carefully. "But don't you think getting a new car is carrying this whole thing a bit far? The shooting was an accident, Gabriel. You wouldn't be human if you didn't feel bad about what happened, but don't go rearranging your whole life."

"Charity's whole life has been rearranged," he said shortly, wishing she'd quit looking at him like he needed a few more sessions with the police psychiatrist.

"I'm not denyin' that. But you can't make her well, Gabriel. And puttin' bars up in your house and ramps on the steps and gettin' rid of your car ain't goin' to make her walk. Only time'll help that."

"I know that," he said impatiently. "Look, everybody is busy telling me that it's not my fault she can't walk and maybe you're all right. But it *feels* like it was my fault, and if I can help her by giving her a place to stay while she gets well, I don't see anything wrong with that."

"Of course not. If it'll make you stop beatin' yourself up, then I'm all for it. I just don't want to see you get hurt."

"I'm not going to," he said grumpily, tired of having his motives questioned. He was simply helping a friend. There was nothing all that complex about it.

CHARITY SMOOTHED her fingers nervously over the skirt of her dress, checking that it was lying smooth over her knees. Diane had brought the dress to the hospital yesterday. The full skirt draped over her legs, falling almost to her ankles when she was seated, which of course was the only position she was in lately, she thought painfully.

She'd thought she was anxious to leave the hospital, until the time actually came to get dressed and pack. Then she'd suddenly realized how safe and secure she felt there. No one stared at her when the nurses wheeled her down the halls because chances were they were in a wheelchair, too. No one stared and wondered what was wrong with her. They had their own problems to deal with.

But once she left the hospital, she wouldn't be normal anymore. She'd be in the real world where people who walked were normal and people in wheelchairs were something less.

It took all her willpower not to beg the doctor to let her stay, just another day or two. If she willed it hard enough, surely she could get the feeling back in her legs. He was wrong in thinking she was ready to leave. She wasn't ready at all. She wanted to stay here where she was safe and insulated.

As long as she was in the hospital, her paralysis was a temporary thing. Once she left, she'd be forced to start learning to manage in the real world. And every new skill she picked up, every problem she conquered, would be another sign that she wasn't ever going to walk again. It was as if learning to cope without the use of her legs would cut her off from ever using them again.

But there was no way she could explain her confused fears to anyone else. And even if she could make them understand, she couldn't expect them to keep her in the hospital just because she was afraid to leave.

So she'd struggled into the dress, trying not to look at her legs even when she had to lift them to put them in place. She hated touching them, hated feeling the lifelessness of them. That was something else she hadn't told anyone.

No matter how hard she tried, she couldn't make the connection between these unresponsive limbs and *her* legs. *Her* legs moved. She could feel blood pumping through them and hot and cold air against them. She could feel the swish of a skirt or the scrape of shrub brushing against them.

Now, sitting in her room, waiting for Diane, she smoothed her skirt again, unable to feel the pressure of her hand against her knee. If it hadn't been for the fact that she could see her legs, could touch them, she wouldn't have known they were there.

She looked away from them, fighting back tears. She had to believe that she was going to walk again. If she didn't believe that, then she would surely go crazy. The only thing that kept her sane was the thought that this whole thing was just a temporary nightmare. Soon the world would be back to normal. She'd be able to go on with her life again.

She heard Diane's voice greeting one of the nurses and forced the fears into the back of her mind, tilting her mouth up in a smile that didn't reach her eyes. If she could just keep pretending everything was going to be all right, then surely it would be.

Perhaps Diane sensed her nervousness or maybe she was uncertain about this move herself. She kept up a cheerful patter all the way to the lobby, talking to the nurse who was pushing Charity's wheelchair when Charity's responses were slow in coming.

Charity could feel her stomach starting to churn as the elevator door slid open and she was wheeled out into the lobby. The light seemed much too bright and there were far too many people. She knotted her hands together on the arms of the wheelchair, fighting the urge to beg the nurse to take her back to her room.

They stopped at the lobby desk where one of the volunteers cut the plastic I.D. band from her wrist, making a small ceremony out of it. The woman probably thought she was going to get up out of the wheelchair as soon as she was wheeled outside, Charity thought. She had no way of knowing that for her, leaving the hospital was more frightening than staying.

Stop feeling sorry for yourself, she ordered herself sternly. *It could certainly be worse.*

At the moment that was cold comfort indeed.

The doors whisked open with an electric whoosh and Charity was outside for the first time in two weeks. The air was hot and dry, tightening the skin on her cheeks, harsh to lungs accustomed to the air-conditioned atmosphere of the hospital. She squinted against the sun that poured over the pavement beyond the sheltered area in front of the hospital.

A slightly scruffy blue van pulled up in front of them, blocking her view of the circular drive. The driver's door slammed and then Gabe was walking around the front of the vehicle, his long stride filling Charity with a sense of her own inadequacy.

She looked up at Diane, her hand reaching up to clutch her sister's sleeve, ready to go back into the safety of the hospital, anything to keep from having to face a normal, *walking* world.

"Madam, your chariot awaits." Gabe stopped in front of her and swept a theatrical bow, one hand extended toward her, a pure white rose held in his long fingers.

"Oh." Charity's hand trembled slightly as she reached to take it from him. "It's beautiful," she said softly, raising it to her face.

"Its beauty pales before thine," he told her, pressing one hand to his heart and giving her such a soulful look that laughter dried the tears trembling on her lashes.

She felt better suddenly. Looking into his eyes, the fear receded. Somehow it was hard to be afraid when Gabe was there.

"Thank you, Gabe."

"De nada," he said, shrugging as he straightened. "I raided Jay's prize rose bushes again."

"Won't he be upset?" Charity knew that Jay Baldwin was the doctor who lived next door to Gabe and a good friend as well as neighbor.

"Not if no one tells him who did it," Gabe said, with a smile.

"My lips are sealed," she assured him.

The nurse wheeled her over the curb where the van waited. Gabe pulled open the door, and Charity stared at the step as if it were a viper. How many times had she stepped in or out of cars in her lifetime and never given it a thought?

But Gabe didn't give her a chance to dwell on the fact that she couldn't take the step for herself.

"Allow me." Bending, he scooped her out of the wheelchair and into his arms as if she weighed next to nothing.

Startled, Charity's wide eyes met his, only inches away. She couldn't feel the arm under her legs, of course, but she could feel the one across her back, hard and strong, as if he could hold her forever.

Even more startling than the easy strength with which he held her was the sudden awareness she felt, a tingle that started in the pit of her stomach and worked its way up to catch in her throat.

For a moment Gabe's arms tightened around her, his eyes more gold than green, and she wondered if he felt the same shiver of awareness. His eyes dropped to her mouth and she felt the impact of that glance as if it was a kiss. Her breath caught, her heart beating too quickly.

The sound of a car horn in the street broke the fragile tension. Gabe blinked, his hands shifting as he turned toward the van. An instant later he'd set her on the seat. Charity felt a real sense of loss when he drew away.

She shook her head. It wouldn't do to start imagining things. She had enough problems without adding a pathetic crush on Gabriel London to them. This was exactly what Diane had warned her about, and she'd dismissed the warnings. Now she knew she had to be on her guard. It shouldn't be hard to remember just why Gabe was so concerned. All she had to do was look down at her legs to be reminded.

GABE HANDED CHARITY the end of the shoulder seat belt, smiling in response to her murmured thanks. He

wondered what had put that sudden bleak look in her
eyes. Not that she didn't have reason enough. But a
moment before, when he'd been holding her in his
arms, her eyes had been full of promise, deep green
and warm, like a tropical sea.

He shook his head as he walked around the front
of the van. The only thing he needed to be concerned
about at this point was getting Charity home and getting her well. The fact that holding her had been like
holding a piece of heaven was not important right
now.

NO ONE HAD much to say during the drive to Gabe's
house. Gabe pretended to concentrate on his driving.
Charity stared out the window, pretending that nothing was wrong, that she'd be able to get out of the
van without help. Seated in the back, Diane stared at
the wheelchair folded into the space next to her, wishing she could just slide open the door and push it out
onto the freeway, along with her sister's need for it.

The house was, just as Gabe had said, in a nice
neighborhood, middle-class and tidy—the sort of
place where children played in the streets, moving out
of the way of the van before reclaiming the best skate-
boarding surface around.

Gabe pulled into his drive and shut off the van. For
the space of several seconds, no one said anything. It
was as if they were all just realizing that this was
really happening.

Charity's fingers knotted together in her lap. She
couldn't do it. If she'd thought it was hard to leave
the hospital, it was nothing compared to the thought
of getting out of this van. Gabe would put her in the

wheelchair and everyone would be able to see that she couldn't walk.

"We're here," Gabe announced in a tone of forced good cheer.

"It's very nice," Diane said.

Charity didn't add anything to the stilted conversation. Her chest felt tight, as if all the air was being cut off. She couldn't do this. They were all wrong to say that she was ready to leave the hospital. They had to take her back. Right this minute.

She looked at Gabe, ready to ask him to turn the van around, when the passenger door was pulled open.

"You all turned to statues or what?" Startled, Charity turned to look at the owner of the gravelly voice. Seated in the van, she looked slightly downward into a pair of deep brown eyes set in a square-jawed face. He wasn't handsome, not by any standard, but there was a sort of homely appeal in his features.

"I'm Jay Baldwin, Gabe's neighbor." He held out his hand and Charity took it automatically. "And the owner of the rose bush that came from," he added, gesturing to the rose that lay in her lap. He shot Gabe a threatening look. "I was thinking of calling the police to report the theft but I had a feeling they already knew."

"It was on my side of the fence," Gabe said virtuously.

"Funny, that bush is a good five feet from the fence."

"It sprawls," Gabe said.

"Ha. It would have to crawl to get that far."

Jay tugged open the back door, his eyes skimming

over Diane's perfection with apparent indifference. "You must be the sister," he said, reaching for the wheelchair.

It was a new and not particularly welcome experience for Diane to hear herself described—and dismissed—as "the sister."

"Diane Williams," she said, but he only nodded as he lifted the chair out, unfolding it with a few practiced moves. It was obvious that he didn't care to pursue the acquaintance any further.

"You're not going to be able to maneuver in and out of a high seat like this on your own," Jay said, opening Charity's door. She unbuckled her seat belt in automatic obedience to his gesture and found herself unceremoniously lifted and set in the chair with a minimum of fuss.

There was no opportunity to say that she didn't need to worry about getting in and out of the van because she was going back to the safety of the hospital. No chance to feel self-conscious or awkward. One minute she was sitting in the van, the next she was being wheeled up the concrete walkway.

"Gabe's house is better for wheelchair access than most but you'll still have to learn how to handle this thing."

"I don't want to learn how to handle it," she snapped. They were the first words she'd spoken since Jay's arrival.

"Of course you don't." Jay shoved open the front door and pushed her into a wide entryway. "Nobody does, but you're luckier than most."

"Lucky?" At the moment she wasn't feeling particularly lucky.

"It's only temporary for you."

Charity felt a weight slip from her shoulders. Of course it was only temporary. She'd lost sight of that today. She'd begun to think she was always going to be in this chair.

She turned to grin up into Jay's square face. "Thank you."

"Don't mention it." He grinned down at her, the expression transforming his features from homely to roguishly attractive. Diane, walking in the front door, caught sight of him and stopped so abruptly that Gabe, following on her heels, bumped into her. Diane blinked, a slightly dazed look in her eyes as she moved out of the doorway.

For the next thirty minutes Gabe showed Charity around the house, familiarizing her with the layout as well as the changes he'd made to make it easier for her to manage on her own. Since she'd already rejected the idea of a live-in aide, he'd made a few strategic modifications.

Bars had been installed in the bathrooms, as well as a hanging bar over her bed so that she could pull herself up and get into the wheelchair without having to call for help. There was one step leading down into the living room and he'd installed a ramp over that so that there wasn't any room in the house where her wheelchair wouldn't go easily.

The only blight on the tour was the antipathy between Diane and Jay. When it came up that Diane had been a model, Jay's upper lip had shown a faint but definite tendency to curl.

"How interesting," he said with total insincerity. *Airhead,* his eyes said.

"I'm sure being a doctor is much more interesting," Diane snapped. *Prig,* her eyes flashed back.

From then on, any conversation that involved the two of them was more in the nature of a verbal boxing match.

Ordinarily Charity would have been intrigued by any man who didn't simply fall head over heels for her sister. That Jay Baldwin, who was not particularly tall, dark or handsome, showed no sign of succumbing to Diane's fatal charm would have amused her no end.

At the moment, nerves and the exhaustion of her first day out of the hospital were catching up with her. She'd never have believed how tired she could get after only a few hours out of bed, and all of them spent sitting down, at that. But tired she was, bone deep and muscle weary.

When Gabe noticed her pallor and suggested that she ought to get to bed, she didn't even bother to put up a token argument. Nor did she protest when Diane offered to help her into bed. She'd practiced getting in and out of the wheelchair at the hospital; remembering to set the brake, lifting first one leg and then the other off the footrests, then using her arms to pull herself into the bed. But tonight she wasn't sure she had the strength to make the switch from chair to bed.

Once she'd managed to convince Diane that she was really and truly settled in and didn't need her big sister to spend the night holding her hand, Charity was alone. She listened to the murmur of voices from the living room as Diane and Jay bade Gabe goodnight. She felt more isolated and alone than she'd ever felt in her life.

Pressing the back of her arm over her eyes, she forced back the frightened tears. Crying never did anything but make her eyes red.

"Charity?" Gabe's voice was quiet as he tapped on the door. Sniffing, she wiped her eyes and dragged herself higher against the pillows before calling to him to come in.

"I just wanted to make sure you have everything you need." He stayed near the door, his hands pushed into the pockets of his jeans.

"Everything," she said and then winced at the forced cheerfulness in her voice.

"The bell there is in case you need me." He nodded to the decorative brass bell that stood on the nightstand.

"Oh. How thoughtful." She reached out to pick it up and the clapper pinged gently. She held it against her chest.

Gabe was relieved to see a genuine smile light her face. She looked so small lying there in her pink nightgown, her hair drawn back from her face. He'd had to push his hands in his pockets to keep from gathering her up in his arms and kissing the uncertainty from her eyes.

"I'm a light sleeper," he said when the silence threatened to stretch too long. "The least sound will wake me."

"That must make you uncomfortable to sleep with," Charity said without thinking. Hearing her words, she stared at him, eyes round, her fair skin flushing.

"I haven't had too many complaints," Gabe said slowly, his mouth curving in a suggestive grin.

"No, I don't suppose you have." And then she flushed even deeper. It had to be the shock of leaving the hospital that had addled her brain, she thought, wondering if this was a good time to fake amnesia and pretend to forget the past few minutes.

Gabe sensed her embarrassment and swallowed the comment he'd been about to make. If she got any redder, she was likely to explode. But she looked less waiflike than she had a few minutes ago.

"Well, I'll let you get to sleep," he said briskly. "Just remember to ring if you need me. Good night."

"Good night." Charity watched the door close behind him and waited for the loneliness to close in around her again. But it didn't. Rubbing her thumb lightly over the polished brass surface of the bell, she felt her mouth curve in a smile. She didn't feel alone anymore.

Chapter Seven

When Charity woke the next morning, for one blissful moment she didn't remember where she was or why she was there. Sunlight poured in through the window, spilling across the bed. From where she lay, she could see a slice of bright blue sky and a fluffy white cloud.

Maybe because for the first time since the robbery she was waking in a home, not a hospital room, her first urge was to get up and go to the window. She wanted to throw it open and draw in a deep breath of fresh air.

She threw back the covers, eager to do just that. And reality came crashing over her, shattering the sparkling mood, making the blue sky seem gray and overcast. Instead of sitting up and swinging her legs off the bed, she was stuck lying there like a bundle of old rags.

The disappointment was so acute, she felt tears burn her eyes. She forced them back and drew in a deep breath. Crying wasn't going to change things, she reminded herself briskly. The doctors said she just needed time to heal. If she kept up with her physical therapy and clung to that hope, she'd be walking again before she knew it.

Shoving the covers out of the way, Charity reached for the bar Gabe had hung over her bed and pulled herself into a sitting position. Glaring at the wheelchair, she began the rather arduous task of getting herself ready to face the day.

Well, there was one thing for sure, she thought an hour later, she certainly wasn't going to be making any impulsive trips anywhere. Just getting washed and dressed had taken more time than she'd ever dreamed.

Her back hurt with the strain of constantly stretching for things that were just out of reach. Her arms ached with the effort of compensating for all the things her legs would no longer do. Too bad she'd never learned to walk on her hands, she thought with a touch of black humor.

Now that she was dressed, she wasn't at all sure she wanted to leave the dubious sanctuary of her room. Gabe had told her that he was taking a couple of days' leave to make sure she got settled in. She appreciated his concern though she would have preferred some time alone to find out just how awkward she was going to be. But she could hardly have told him to stay away. After all, it was his house.

Charity eyed the plain wooden door like a track star eyeing the high hurdle. She could do this. After all, it wasn't as if Gabe hadn't already seen her in the wheelchair. She just had to go out and smile and show him that she was capable of managing on her own—she hoped—and he could go on about his own business. He probably had all sorts of things he wanted to do around the house.

BUT IT SEEMED that all Gabe had to do was watch over his house guest, which he did quite thoroughly. From the moment Charity pushed the wheelchair into the kitchen were he'd been drinking coffee, there wasn't a need he didn't anticipate.

He got a box of cereal from the cupboard for her, though it was on a shelf low enough for her to reach and he'd already told her that she was to make herself completely at home. He got the milk from the refrigerator before she had a chance to think of it. The sugar appeared as if by magic, as did a glass of juice and a slice of buttered toast, neither of which she particularly wanted.

When she was finished, he cleared the table. When she mentioned that she might go out on the patio, he opened the sliding door for her. Once outside, she drew a deep breath of fresh air, relieved to be alone. Until she happened to glance back at the house and saw Gabe sitting in a chair by the window, reading the paper in a place that just happened to put him where he could keep an eye on her.

Charity turned her head to hide a grin. She suspected he was going to drive her crazy, but there was something rather sweet about his concern.

GABE TRIED to concentrate on the paper but found his attention drifting to the patio. Was it warm enough for her to be out there, he wondered, frowning. Maybe she should have a wrap of some sort. The fact that the temperature was hovering in the mid-seventies and he was wearing running shorts and a T-shirt didn't register with him.

She was sitting awfully still. Was she in pain? Maybe trying to hide it? He'd already learned that

Charity was quite adept at concealing what she was feeling. He hadn't known her long but circumstances had accelerated their acquaintance a bit.

She'd looked so frightened yesterday when he picked her up at the hospital. He'd taken one look at those wide green eyes and wanted to snatch her up and hold her close, promising that nothing would ever hurt her again.

He shifted uneasily, frowning at the newspaper he wasn't reading. He wondered if Annie was right—if maybe he was letting his feelings of guilt get twisted into something more dangerous.

The problem was that he *liked* Charity. The guilt was still there, gnawing in his gut every time he looked at her in that wheelchair. But it wasn't just guilt that had made him open his home. Nor was it guilt alone that made him want to put his arms around her and protect her.

He liked her. Worse, he was attracted to her. And it wasn't just those wide green eyes or the inviting fullness of her lower lip, though he had to be honest and say that those attributes didn't hurt. But there was more to it than that.

He liked the way her eyes could smile, even when her mouth didn't move. He liked the way she didn't have to fill every moment with conversation. He liked the way she nibbled her lower lip when she was thinking. In fact he liked just about everything he'd learned about her. He wished now that he had followed his impulse to ask her out months before this whole nightmare started.

Charity had wheeled the chair over to a rather scraggly planter box that sat on one corner of the patio and was nipping faded petunia blossoms from the plants. Somehow Gabe doubted that she was paying any more attention to what she was doing than he was to the paper he was supposedly reading.

A stray shaft of sunlight found its way through the louvered overhang and caught in her hair, turning it to pure gold. She looked rather like an angel he'd seen in a painting once, all soft and gentle. It was a wonder that a woman with so much to offer wasn't already involved with someone.

How do you know she isn't?

The paper crackled a protest as Gabe bundled it shut, his brows hooked in a frown. It had never occurred to him that Charity might be involved with someone, but there was no reason why she shouldn't be. The thought was not at all pleasant.

Of course, if there was someone in her life, surely he would have been to see her while she was in the hospital. He would have been consulted about her move into another man's house.

Unless the scum had deserted her when she didn't immediately regain the use of her legs. Maybe he'd been afraid she'd be permanently paralyzed, and he'd cut and run just when she needed him most.

Gabe's scowl grew fierce. Charity certainly deserved better than a guy like that. He was just contemplating the great pleasure it would give him to plant his fist squarely in the unknown boyfriend's face when it suddenly occurred to him that he didn't even know there *was* a boyfriend. He was furious with a man who might not even exist.

He shook his head and ran his fingers through his hair, rumpling it into even shaggier waves. God, this past couple of weeks must have taken a bigger toll than he'd thought. His imagination was getting out of hand.

He looked at Charity again, shooting to his feet when he saw her leaning forward, trying to turn on the outlet that fed water to a leaky length of hose. He all but sprinted through the kitchen and onto the patio. Didn't she realize she could fall?

"Here. Let me help with that."

Charity glanced up, startled by his sudden appearance. "I can get it."

"You shouldn't have to." Gabe took the hose from her and turned the outlet on with a quick twist. Water shot out the end of the hose as well as in delicate streams from several leaks along its length. "Where did you want it?"

"I just thought I'd put a little water on these petunias, if you don't mind. They looked a little dry."

"Probably extremely dry," he said, setting the end of the hose in the planter she'd indicated. "I'm afraid I'm not much of a gardener. Jay had some extra plants and he stuck them in here. I just don't remember to water them."

Looking at the desiccated soil, Charity thought that was self-evident. The Gobi Desert probably had a similar water content.

Gabe stood next to her, watching the water run into the planter. But she knew he was really waiting to see if she was going to do anything else that might require his assistance, like maybe blowing her nose.

He'd been hovering like a mother hen all morning. She appreciated his concern, really she did, but she wasn't *completely* helpless, and having him lurking over her shoulder was going to drive her crazy.

"Are you hungry or anything?" Gabe asked.

"I just ate," she reminded him, torn between the urge to laugh and the urge to hit him. Did he have to stand there looking so damned healthy? She felt frustrated and unattractive enough without him standing around looking so...so male.

"Yeah. Right." Gabe stared at the hose again. "You're not too cold or anything are you?" He gave her an anxious look.

"It's seventy-five degrees out here."

"Right. You're probably not cold."

"No, I'm not."

Silence while they both stared at the hose again. Charity waited.

"Are you thirsty? I could get you something to drink."

"No, thank you."

She'd thought that she had her voice under control, no hint of the fact that she was grinding her teeth allowed to show. But Gabe seemed to sense something. He shot her a quick look.

"Am I hovering?" he asked after a moment.

Charity considered saying no. She considered it for all of five seconds. But the thought of having him lurk over her every minute of the day brought thoughts of actual violence to mind. For his safety as well as her sanity, they had to come to some sort of understanding.

"Yes," she said, letting out the breath she'd been holding.

"Am I driving you crazy?"

"Yes." But she softened the affirmative with a smile. "It's not that I don't appreciate it," she added quickly. "I mean, it's nice that you're so concerned and all but..."

"But you're going to hit me if I don't go away," he finished for her, his mouth curving in a rueful smile.

"Well, not too hard."

He hooked one foot around a battered lawn chair and dragged it across the cement. Sitting down, he stretched his long legs out in front of him, meeting her eyes with an apologetic smile.

"Sorry."

"Don't be." Charity was relieved that he was taking it so well. After all, he'd been trying to be helpful. It seemed rather ungrateful of her to complain.

"I just want to be sure that you know I'm here in case you need anything."

"Believe me, I know you're here."

Gabe laughed. "That bad, huh?"

"No, not really. It's just that I'm a little self-conscious about…about this thing," she said, running her fingers over the arm of the wheelchair.

"You seem to be managing pretty well."

"Thanks." She sighed, wishing she could appreciate the compliment. She didn't want to manage the wheelchair pretty well. She wanted to be rid of the thing.

Staring out at the back lawn, still green from the winter's rains, she wanted to feel the grass under her bare feet. Hell, at the moment she'd settle for being able to feel her feet at all.

Maybe she sighed or perhaps Gabe read some of what she was feeling in her expression.

"You know, you don't have to pretend that everything is great all the time," he said quietly. "If you ever want to scream or throw things, don't feel you have to pull back because of me."

Charity's startled eyes met his. Sometimes it seemed as if he knew her; knew what she was thinking, better than he had any right to. For a moment she wanted to take him at his word, wanted to let some of her fears and frustrations out.

But she stifled the urge. She couldn't admit how frightened she was that the paralysis *wasn't* temporary, that she'd *never* walk again. She had to believe she was going to walk, had to believe that she was only trapped in the hateful chair for a short time. Admitting to fear would be admitting there was something to be afraid of. And there wasn't. This was all temporary. It had to be.

"I'm not really the screaming, throwing things type," she said lightly.

Gabe nodded, wondering if she was even aware of the way her hand was clenched into a fist on the arm of the chair. But he wasn't going to be the one to point it out to her. He knew what it was to cling to the ragged edge of control; to feel that if you let go, just for an instant, you'd somehow never find your way back to sanity again.

"I meant it when I said you were to consider this your home," he said.

"I know you did. I appreciate it." She also appreciated the change of topic. It would be all too easy to let go of her feelings of fear and anger, but she wasn't sure she'd be able to get them under control again if she ever once loosened her rigid hold on her emotions.

"Don't hesitate to change things around, if you need to," Gabe continued, watching the water run into the petunias.

"Well, I don't think I'm up for any heavy-duty

furniture moving,'' she said dryly, hitting the chair lightly for emphasis.

"I can move furniture, if you want something changed.''

"Thanks, but I don't think that will be necessary.''

"And feel free to invite people over, friends or whatever,'' he said with a vague wave of his hand.

"That's generous of you, but I doubt if I'm going to feel much like entertaining.'' She rubbed the arms of the wheelchair absently.

"I just thought there might be someone you wanted to see.'' Gabe slanted her a sharp look and then returned his attention to the flowers. "I mean, someone special. A boyfriend, maybe.''

The words were not quite a question, but Charity answered as if they were. "There's no one special.''

Gabe felt a wave of relief. Strictly because he hadn't liked to think of her being deserted by someone she cared about, he told himself.

Charity stared at the redwood fence that surrounded the yard, wondering if what she'd said was entirely true. Could she really say there was no one special in her life? Her feelings for Gabriel London were perilously close to special.

What a disaster that would be; to fall in love with a man who felt, at best, friendship, and at worst, pity. Not that she was going to do anything that stupid. It was her legs that were paralyzed not her common sense.

CHARITY WAS AMAZED by how quickly life settled into a routine of sorts. It seemed that she was living proof of the endless human capacity to adapt.

Gabe stayed home for two more days, managing to

resist the urge to hover. She was reluctant to admit it, even to herself, but Charity was glad to know he was there, just in case. Of course, she would have just about died rather than call on him for help, but it was nice to know that in an emergency there was someone there.

It surprised her to realize how quickly they'd established a certain routine. Gabe was up long before Charity made it out of the bedroom, and he had coffee brewing and breakfast made. He either ate breakfast with her or sat with her while she ate.

That half hour first thing in the morning was one of the few things she looked forward to. The more she knew Gabe, the more she liked him—his sense of humor, his ability to laugh at himself.

Most of all she liked their breakfasts together, because it was one of the rare occasions when she could almost feel normal. Sitting at the table made it possible to forget that she was sitting in a wheelchair; that she could not just get up and walk away at the end of the meal.

Moments like that were few and something to be treasured.

LIFE SETTLED into certain patterns. There was a comforting rhythm to the days. It was something to cling to when her mind began to drift to less pleasant thoughts, like the fact that her legs were still unresponsive.

Most of the time she managed to keep her spirits up. She tried to focus on how lucky she was to be alive at all. There were compensations. If it hadn't been for the shooting, she would never have gotten to know Gabe London as anything more than an attractive man who came into the jewelry store.

And while she might regret the circumstances, she couldn't regret her growing relationship with Gabe. On closer acquaintance, he was, if possible, even more attractive than when he was merely a customer. The charm that was so readily apparent was more than skin-deep.

He'd told her to treat his home as her own. It was more than a polite offer. From the moment she moved in, he acted as if the house was as much hers as it was his. Not once did he make her feel like an unwanted guest. It might have been a guilty conscience that drove him to offer her a place to stay, but you'd never know it. She was to make herself comfortable, he'd said.

But how could she feel comfortable in his home when she wasn't even comfortable in her own body? The question made Charity sigh. She'd been out of the hospital for a week now, and despite daily sessions with either the physical therapist or Diane, there was still no feeling in her legs.

Patience, everyone kept counseling. She had to give her body time to heal. In time she'd regain the feeling in her legs. She'd always considered herself an unusually patient person but she was finding it a difficult quality to hold on to.

Looking out the open window, she watched Gabe pushing an old-fashioned reel mower across the lawn. The soft clickety-clack of the reels and the rich scent of freshly cut grass filled the air.

Charity blinked back tears. She could go out on the patio where she could really savor the scent. If she wanted, she knew Gabe would wheel the chair out onto the grass for her or carry her out and set her on the sweet green lawn.

But she didn't want to be settled onto the grass like an infant. She wanted to run across it, feel it cool and soft beneath her bare feet. She wanted to roll on it; dance on it; revel in the feel of it. Instead she was trapped in this damned chair.

She knotted her hand into a fist, pounding it lightly against the arm of the wheelchair. Anger was good, the therapist had told her. Anger and frustration could be turned into determination. Despair was something else entirely, though. Despair was self-defeating, the first stage of giving up.

Easy for the therapist to say, Charity thought irritably, turning away from the window. She had two perfectly good legs. What did she know of how it felt to look at your legs and wonder if you were ever going to stand on them again.

"Stop feeling sorry for yourself," she whispered, trying to banish the dark mood. "You'll walk again. It's just a matter of time."

She thrust her fingers through her honey-colored hair, massaging the ache that had settled into the back of her neck. Most of the time she managed to keep a positive attitude; to believe everything was going to be all right. She'd smiled and looked cheerful until her face ached.

Everyone seemed to accept her good cheer at face value. Except maybe Gabe. Sometimes she caught him looking at her with something in his eyes that made her wonder if he saw through to the fear she was trying so hard to keep at bay.

She suspected that Gabe saw a great deal more than most people. That lazy smile and those never-quite-serious eyes made it easy to think of him as a light-weight. But you couldn't live with someone without getting to know them and the Gabriel London she was coming to know was a man of deep feeling.

A man who stirred her emotions far more deeply than was wise. Charity rubbed her fingers absently along the arm of the wheelchair. She was beginning to fear that while she was regaining the use of her legs, she was losing her heart.

Chapter Eight

The house was early-morning quiet. Outside, the sun had barely crept over the horizon and the birds were just starting to wake up, sending out an occasional sleepy chirp to test the day.

Charity guided her wheelchair noiselessly down the hall. She breathed a little easier once she'd turned into the living room. Making her way across the smooth expanse of hardwood floor, she eased over the threshold that divided the kitchen from the living room.

Stopping in the middle of the kitchen, she let her hands relax on the wheels of the chair, grinning like a child who'd just given her teacher the slip. She'd been staying here for almost two weeks and this was the first time she'd managed to get up before Gabe. It seemed a sort of triumph. Of course, he'd worked until after midnight the night before, so she'd had a definite edge.

But she'd learned to enjoy what few successes she could. God knows, there hadn't been many of them lately. She rubbed absently at the aching muscles in her arms, her eyes on her unresponsive legs.

Two weeks out of the hospital, and all she had to show for it was a growing set of muscles in her arms.

As she'd told Diane, she was going to have an upper torso like Arnold Swarzennegger and a lower body like PeeWee Herman in a few more weeks.

Diane had laughed, but was quick to say that in a few more weeks, she'd no doubt be walking again. Charity had smiled and let her sister think the words were reassuring. The truth was, it was getting harder and harder to believe that she was going to walk again.

"Stop it," she muttered out loud. It was thoughts like that that had kept her awake most of the night. Those same thoughts led to nothing but despair. She *had* to believe she was going to walk again. If she didn't hold on to that hope, she wasn't sure she could go on.

Drawing a deep breath, she squared her shoulders. It was going to be a wonderful day and she was going to enjoy it if it killed her. Her determination made Charity smile. That was a great attitude: have fun or die.

Still smiling, she wheeled her chair over to the counter. Coffee would help her mood. Nothing like a little caffeine to get the blood moving. Too little sleep, too much worrying, she scolded herself as she put the filter in place and scooped coffee into it.

A few minutes later the heady scent of brewing coffee filled the kitchen, lightening her mood. Life couldn't be a total loss as long as she could make a decent cup of coffee. Of course, she could only manage that much because Gabe had rearranged his kitchen to make things more accessible to her.

But that was dwelling on the negative, she reminded herself briskly. And she had to try and remember the positive. Like how kind Gabe had been.

And how lucky she was to have a friend like him. Because he'd definitely become a friend these past weeks, and she believed that he felt the same way about her.

Charity poured herself a cup of rich, dark coffee, cradling it between her palms for a moment, as if the warmth of the cup could chase away the inner chill that never seemed far away these days.

Sipping the coffee, she suddenly thought that the perfect accompaniment to an early-morning cup of coffee would be a muffin, fresh and warm from the oven. A quick search of the cupboards told her that muffins were not among the things that Gabe stocked, not even a box of muffin mix. But he did have all the ingredients to make them from scratch.

Charity hesitated. One thing she'd learned was that the average kitchen was not set up for someone trapped in a wheelchair. The counters were too high, the majority of cupboards were out of reach. Other than making herself a sandwich or heating a can of soup, she hadn't tried to do any cooking.

Gabe had been cooking dinner. Or Diane brought something with her that could be reheated. Once Jay had ordered a pizza and joined them for dinner. Diane had stayed that night, and she and Jay had taken verbal shots at each other all night.

Maybe she should just forget about muffins, Charity thought uneasily. Or she could view it as a challenge, her more adventuresome side suggested. A chance to prove that she wasn't completely helpless. Think how nice it would be to present Gabe with homemade muffins fresh from the oven.

He'd done so much for her. She knew that he felt as if there was nothing he could do for her that would make up for the fact that it was his bullet that had injured her. But she didn't feel that way, and it would be a pleasant change to be on the giving side. Muffins could hardly compare to his opening his home to a virtual stranger, but it was the best she could offer at the moment.

She found a recipe in the one cookbook Gabe owned and began to methodically gather ingredients. A bowl, measuring spoons wedged in the back of a drawer, baking powder, sugar, eggs and milk—all were neatly lined up on the counter. The only thing she was missing was the flour.

She reached up to catch the bottom of an upper cabinet door with her fingertips, tugging it open. There was the flour, sitting smugly on the bottom shelf, just a few inches back from the edge. Charity stretched her arm up, but she could just brush the side of the canister.

She scowled up at the cabinet. She had everything she needed to make muffins but the flour, and she wasn't about to be stymied now. She'd started this to prove that she wasn't totally helpless. She couldn't give up at the first obstacle.

She set the brake on the wheelchair so it couldn't slide out from under her. Bracing her left arm on the counter, she levered her body up, stretching her right arm toward the elusive flour. Her left arm trembled under her weight, but she was determined not to give up.

Her fingers closed around the canister, and she grinned, but it was to be a fleeting triumph. Just as she tugged the canister off the shelf, her left arm caved in under the strain. Startled, she cried out as her arm collapsed, depositing her roughly back into the chair.

She lost her grip on the metal canister, which fell to the counter, somehow losing its lid in the process, bouncing off the carton of eggs and then tumbling against the milk carton. Charity made a futile grab for the canister as it rolled off the counter and onto the floor, spreading a dusty white cloud behind it.

For an instant all she could do was stare at the disaster. There was flour everywhere. All over the counters, all over the floor, all over her. She didn't doubt that the eggs were all broken and there was a pool of milk spreading across the counter in a slow white tide.

"What happened?" Gabe, no doubt alerted by the crashing of the canister, skidded into the kitchen doorway, clad in a pair of briefs and carrying a .38.

A quick glance was enough to show him that Charity was not in danger, and he slid the gun back into its holster.

"Are you okay?" He set the holster down out of reach of the flour that was still drifting through the air and moved toward her. "Charity?"

She said nothing. She couldn't have gotten words out past the choking knot in her throat. It was a simple little task. She hadn't been trying to run a marathon or lift a Volkswagon. She'd just wanted to prove that she wasn't completely helpless.

"Charity? Are you okay?" He'd stopped next to the wheelchair, his bare feet leaving footprints on the flour-dusted floor. She saw his hand come out, and she jerked back as if his touch would burn.

"Don't touch me!" she snapped.

She tried to move the chair back, wanting only to

put distance between herself and Gabe's kindness. But the brake was still on and her quick twist of the wheels did nothing but sting her palms. It was the final straw. Not only had she proven—to herself and the entire world—that she was too helpless even to feed herself, but now she couldn't even run her damned wheelchair.

"No, I am not okay," she said tightly. Her hands were clenched into fists in her lap. "I can't walk. I'm paralyzed and I'll probably always be paralyzed."

"Don't say that!"

"Why not?" she cried, her eyes filling with hot tears. "It's the truth! Everyone keeps telling me to have patience, that the feeling will come back in my legs. Well, it hasn't come back. It's never coming back. I'm going to be stuck in this damned chair for the rest of my life."

Tears blurring her vision, she pounded her fists against her thighs, feeling the impact only in her hands. "I hate my legs! I hate them. I hate them." Her voice cracked on a sob.

"Stop it!" Gabe crouched down beside the chair, catching her hands in his. "Stop talking like that."

"Why? It's the truth. I'm never going to walk again. I know it."

"You don't know anything of the kind," he barked, his fingers tightening over hers. "You're scared and you're frustrated but you're going to get past this and you're going to keep on fighting."

"No, I'm not. I'm tired of fighting." It was nothing more than the truth. All the anger had gone out of her, leaving her weary and hopeless. She let her hands stay in his because it was too much of an effort to pull them away. What difference did it make whether or not he held her hands? What difference did anything make?

"I'm paralyzed and I might as well start accepting it."

Gabe dropped her hands, reaching up to catch her shoulders in his, giving her a quick shake. Charity's startled green eyes met his, almost pure gold with emotion.

"If you say that one more time, I'm going to shake you until your teeth rattle," he told her. His tone was so fierce that she believed him.

"It's true," she whispered, her eyes dropping away from his.

"No, it's not." One hand left her shoulder to cup her chin, tilting her face up until she was forced to meet his eyes. "You're going to walk again. You just have to be patient."

"I'm sick of being patient." She would have turned her head away but he refused to release her, holding her as much with the strength of his gaze as with his grip on her chin.

"You're going to walk again, Charity." He said each word slowly and distinctly, his eyes steady on hers, willing her to believe him, to believe in herself.

"You don't know that," she muttered.

"Sure I do. Have any of the doctors told you differently? Have any of them said you won't walk?"

"No."

"Then what makes you think that's the case?"

"It's been so long, Gabe. And I still can't feel anything." Despite her determination not to cry again, new tears burned her eyes.

"I know." He slid his hand to the back of her neck, drawing her forward until her forehead rested against his. The despair in her eyes, in her voice, broke his heart. He'd have traded places with her in an instant if he were given the chance.

It was like acid in his gut to see her cry and know the tears were his doing. It was his mistake that had put her in the wheelchair she hated so passionately. Part of his bullet was still lodged near her spine. And if, God forbid, she never walked again, it would be because of him.

It was hard enough to see her struggling to stay cheerful, keeping the fear at bay by pretending it didn't exist. But it was ten times worse to see her like this, so full of despair.

"I know you're going to walk again, Charity," he said huskily. "If you don't believe the doctors, believe me. You're too strong to give up."

"I don't feel strong," she said on a sigh. But that wasn't quite true. With Gabe holding her, she did feel strong.

"You can't give up. You've got too much fight for that."

"Maybe." But he'd won and they both knew it. Her momentary urge to give up the battle was gone, chased away by his determination. "I'm sorry I acted like such an idiot."

"You're entitled to act like an idiot, once in a while."

"Gee, thanks."

"You're welcome." He drew back, smiling into her eyes.

Charity returned the smile, feeling her heart beat a little faster. It didn't seem fair that he should be so attractive first thing in the morning.

"You have flour on your face," Gabe said, brushing his fingers over her cheek. She felt the light touch shiver through her.

"So do you." She drew one finger across the light dusting of powder on his cheek.

Their eyes met and suddenly neither of them was smiling. A fine tension hummed between them, an awareness that couldn't be ignored.

"You know, you have the most beautiful smile." He brushed his thumb over her mouth, stealing her breath away.

"I do?"

"I think half the reason I was buying those crystals was because it gave me an excuse to come into the store and see you smile."

"It was?" His words stole what little breath his touch had left her. "You thought about me?"

"More than I liked to admit. I could have bought those little animals somewhere else and paid less for them, you know." His thumb stroked across her lower lip and her mouth parted.

"I didn't know."

"But they just didn't look as beautiful as they did when you were holding them."

Gabe leaned forward...to kiss her? And did she move to meet him?

A car backfired on the street outside, the explosion of sound shattering the fine tension of the moment. Charity sat back in her chair and Gabe eased back onto his heels, his hands sliding away from her. She felt an actual pang of loss.

Gabe looked away, groping for something to break the tension that still hummed between them. For the first time he really absorbed the disaster that was the kitchen.

"What were you trying to do?"

"Make muffins?" Charity offered, her eyes following his to the flour-strewn counters and floor. Anything was safer than looking at the long body clad in nothing but a pair of plain white briefs.

"I think you're supposed to use a bowl," he suggested, his eyes settling on the counter where milk and egg had mixed with the flour.

"No. Really?" Charity widened her eyes in shock.

"Well, I'm not sure, but it seems to me that it might be a little easier." Gabe stood up and Charity jerked her eyes away from him. She wished he'd go and put a robe on. And she wished he'd stay just as he was.

She cleared her throat, banishing thoughts of cool sheets and Gabe's lean body stretched out next to her. "I guess I'll have to keep that in mind," she said, keeping her tone light.

"You look like an extra in a haunted house movie," he said, after studying her for a moment.

"Do I?" She brought her hand up to her face, drawing it away covered in flour. Her clothes were also dusted with white powder.

"You know, maybe it's a little late to mention this, but I don't think I own a muffin pan."

Charity raised her head to look at him. "You mean, even if I hadn't made this mess, there wouldn't have been anything to bake the muffins in?"

"I think I've got a loaf pan," he offered with an apologetic shrug.

"A loaf of muffins?"

"Well, a loaf is better than none," he said seriously. The tuck that appeared in his cheek matched the laughter in his eyes.

Charity returned his smile. A few minutes ago she'd felt as if she might never have anything to smile about again. But Gabe had made it impossible for her to hold on to her depression. He'd buoyed her up again, given her the determination to keep fighting.

"Thank you, Gabe."

"For what?" He'd been dusting flour from his hands, and her quiet words brought his questioning eyes to hers. "For not having a muffin pan?"

"No. For making me laugh. For giving me a place to stay. For…being there." She lifted her shoulders in a shrug. Her eyes dropped away from his, suddenly afraid that she was starting to sound maudlin.

There was a moment of silence and then Gabe reached out and stroked his fingers over her cheek. "You don't owe me any thanks, Charity. Believe me. But if you want to thank me, just don't quit fighting."

"I won't."

Charity looked up into his eyes, feeling the light touch all through her body. If he kept looking at her like that, she'd probably promise to drag herself over hot coals. Gabe drew his hand away and Charity lowered her eyes, afraid of what he might see if she continued to look at him.

It was just the circumstances, she reminded herself. She certainly wasn't doing anything stupid…like falling in love with Gabriel London.

"DON'T MISUNDERSTAND ME, I have nothing against fashion." Jay reached for a second piece of pizza.

"You just think anyone involved in it is an airhead and a parasite," Diane ground out, her eyes spitting fire.

"I didn't say that." His tone was perfectly polite

but somehow managed to convey his opinion—his low opinion—quite well.

"Have another glass of wine, Diane?" That was Charity, doing her best to pour oil—or in this case, a cheap Chianti—on troubled waters.

"Thank you." Diane barely glanced at her sister as she bit into a slice of pizza with a fervor that made Charity suspect she'd rather be biting into Jay Baldwin.

Seeking help, Charity met Gabe's eyes, but he looked more wickedly amused than concerned. She had to admit that there was a certain humor in the situation. She'd never seen anyone whose mere presence could annoy her sister so.

Maybe it was the fact that Jay was so blatantly immune to Diane's beauty. Not that Diane was overly vain, but her face and body had been turning heads since puberty. Charity suspected that it piqued her a bit to find Jay so indifferent.

Whatever the reason, the two of them were like oil and water or, more accurately, like the Gingham Dog and the Calico Cat. If they were left in a room alone, Charity wouldn't have been surprised to come back and find they'd torn each other to pieces. It seemed only the presence of witnesses that kept them from each other's throats.

"Fashion is a very important part of society," Diane said to no one in particular. "You can tell a lot about someone by the way they dress."

"It seems to me to be rather shallow to judge people by the clothes on their backs," Jay said, speaking apparently to his glass of wine.

"Well, not all of us are gifted with the ability to

read people's minds," Diane said with awful sarcasm. "Some of us have to rely on external clues."

Jay's eyes skimmed over her emerald-green silk top and the chunky earrings that would have looked too heavy on anyone else but managed to look exotic and interesting on Diane. He took note of her carefully tousled hair and perfectly manicured nails. A quick sweeping glance and then he returned his attention to the half-eaten pizza.

"With some people, the external is all there is."

There was a moment of taut silence. Diane sat back in her chair. Her mouth opened and then shut as she sought the words to express the anger that turned her eyes emerald green.

"Have you heard from Brian?" Charity asked, thrusting herself verbally between the two combatants.

"What do you think of the Dodgers this year?" Gabe spoke simultaneously.

For the rest of the meal, Jay and Diane spoke to each other only when absolutely necessary and then with scrupulous politeness.

"I don't know what it is with those two," Charity said as the door closed behind her sister. Jay had left soon after the pizza was finished. He had to be at the office early. Diane had lingered, playing a desultory game of checkers with her sister.

"Hate at first sight," Gabe suggested, coming back into the living room and sinking onto the sofa. "Instant incompatibility."

"It must be. Diane thinks Jay is an uptight prig." She set the checkers in their box, folding up the game board to go on top of them.

"Jay thinks she's a complete airhead, so I'd guess they're about even."

"It's strange. I think Jay is the first man I've ever seen who didn't fall for Diane the minute he saw her."

"She's a beautiful woman," Gabe agreed.

"Yes, she is." Charity slid the lid on the box of checkers with a snap.

Gabe picked up a magazine and opened it. Charity wheeled her chair over to a low cupboard and slid the checkers box back into place.

Of course he thought Diane was beautiful. She *was* beautiful. She clicked the cupboard door shut, resisting the urge to slam it. She was glad he liked Diane. Glad Diane liked him. Think how uncomfortable it would have been if Diane were at odds with him as she was with Jay.

And if Gabe wanted to date her sister? The thought brought a sharp stab of pain to her chest that she promptly dismissed as too much rich food. That would be just fine, too. And all she'd need was someplace to celebrate while Gabe and Diane were out together. Someplace like a haunted crypt or maybe a nice, dank root cellar.

Not that she'd be jealous or anything. After all, it would be foolish to be jealous of her sister dating her friend. And that's all Gabe was to her. Just a friend.

Now if only she could convince her heart of that.

Chapter Nine

In the week following the flour fiasco and Jay and Diane's near fistfight over the pizza, Charity approached her physical therapy sessions with new determination. It was a battle she had to win.

There was a new closeness in her relationship with Gabe. He'd seen her without the cheerful facade she kept firmly in place for the rest of the world. Charity had faced her despair and realized that admitting to fear wasn't the same as giving in to it.

The physical therapist came by three days a week, putting Charity's legs through a series of exercises designed to keep the muscles from atrophying from lack of use. Diane drove from her studio in Beverly Hills three days a week to help her sister go through a simpler series of exercises.

Charity felt guilty about taking Diane away from her work, but need outweighed guilt. With every day that passed without any movement in her legs, the knot in her stomach grew just a bit larger, a bit harder to ignore. All the reassurance in the world that her body just needed time to heal, wasn't enough to drive away the fears that sometimes kept her awake at night.

During the day she could keep her fears at bay. She tried to keep busy, doing what housework she could, reading, watching television, teaching herself to knit. She couldn't have said just what she was making, but anything that filled her time and occupied her mind was something to be treasured.

It wasn't during the day that her fears threatened to overwhelm her. It was in the hours just before dawn when she'd wake up and there was nothing there to distract her. Hovering in the darkness between night and day, her fears had full rein.

Staring at a darkened ceiling, she tried to imagine spending the rest of her life in a wheelchair. She told herself briskly that many people managed to live happy, fulfilled lives with handicaps much greater than a simple loss of mobility.

She'd read articles about people who refused to let a handicap destroy their lives. It was so much a matter of attitude. You had to make up your mind that life was to be lived, no matter what.

But all the pep talks in the world couldn't drive away the fear that gnawed at her. She clung to her doctor's assurances that there was no reason she wouldn't walk again, but even those began to sound hollow at four o'clock in the morning.

More than once she reached for the little brass bell Gabe had placed by her bed. If she rang it, he'd come in and chase the fears away. Just having him near would force them into perspective. But she never picked up the bell.

Her emotions were already too wrapped up in Gabriel London. A few weeks ago he'd been nothing more than an attractive man who occasionally shopped in the jewelry store where she worked. In a short space of time, he'd rescued her from gunmen, brightened her otherwise tedious stay in the hospital and become her roommate and her friend. Now she was very much afraid that he might become something more.

She already depended on him too much—for companionship and support. She couldn't ask him to chase away her night fears, though she didn't doubt that he'd do it without complaint.

So she lay awake, battling the doubts and fears alone, determined that they wouldn't beat her. So far she was winning the fight.

CHARITY LOOKED UP as a shadow blocked the sun. She'd been sitting by the pool, staring at the cool blue water. Diane had called to say that her car was giving her problems and she didn't dare make the trip from Beverly Hills to Pasadena.

Charity had assured her that she could skip their session for today. The therapist would be by tomorrow. A small voice suggested that the exercise sessions didn't seem to be doing any good, anyway— what difference did it make if she skipped one? But she suppressed the negative thought.

At least the therapy sessions made her feel as if she was doing something. They gave her something concrete to do toward her recovery. And she was determined to make a recovery.

"Ready for a swim?"

Gabe moved so that he was standing in front of her. Before, he'd been nothing more than a silhouette against the sun. Without the sun in her eyes, Charity had a full view of him.

He was wearing nothing but a pair of black swim

trunks—nothing exotic—just perfectly ordinary swim trunks. She swallowed hard. It wasn't as if she hadn't seen him without a shirt before. Or for that matter, without his pants. The morning she'd coated the kitchen with flour, he'd been wearing only briefs, which certainly hadn't concealed any more than the trunks did.

But that morning she'd been more than a little distraught, and though she'd noticed his lack of clothing, it hadn't had the impact it was having now.

She swallowed again, her eyes traveling over muscled shoulders and chest, following the dusting of curling hair that arrowed across his stomach to disappear into the top of his trunks. Her eyes skittered over that all-too-tantalizing garment to trail down a pair of long, muscled legs, ending at bare feet planted solidly on the concrete that surrounded the pool.

She kept her eyes on those feet. It was safer than looking anywhere else.

"Charity? Did you fall asleep on me?"

Asleep? Not likely. Not with her pulse doing double-time. She blinked and slowly raised her eyes to his face. He was giving her a quizzical look, his brows raised in question.

"I'm not asleep." She cleared her throat, trying to look as if she weren't wondering what it would feel like to run her fingers through the hair on his chest.

"Good. I thought I'd lost you for a minute there."

"Sorry, I guess my mind wandered off. What did you say?"

"I asked if you were ready for a swim."

"A swim?" She looked from him to the pool and then back at him. "You mean, you and me? In the pool?"

"That's where people generally swim. I know Diane can't make it today, and I don't have anything else to do this afternoon."

Charity was already shaking her head. "I don't think so." It was one thing to let the therapist or Diane help her. It was something else altogether to think of getting into the water with Gabe.

"Come on. I'm a good swimmer." He crouched down in front of her, his smile coaxing. "You can trust me."

"I do trust you."

"Then what's the problem?"

"You must have something you'd rather do. You don't want to waste your time watching me flounder around."

"I told you, I don't have anything else to do. Come on, you don't want to miss a session, do you? The weather is perfect for swimming. It's over ninety. Think how good the water would feel."

Charity hesitated, looking from his coaxing smile to the water lapping quietly in the pool. It was true, the water would feel wonderful. And the pool was the only place where she felt almost normal. The buoyancy of the water helped to compensate for her useless legs, giving her a temporary illusion of normalcy.

"You don't know any of the exercises," she said.

"You can show me what to do."

She hesitated. It was true that the thought of getting into the cool water was tempting. But she wasn't at all sure she was prepared to have Gabe's hands on her. She never gave a thought to the fact that Diane or the therapist was touching her, but she couldn't imagine being so indifferent to Gabe's touch.

"Come on." Gabe sat back on his heels in front

of her, his smile reassuring. "I'll take good care of you. You couldn't be in safer hands."

"Really?" She felt herself weakening under the combined temptation of the pool and his eyes.

"Sure. I was a lifeguard one summer in Santa Monica."

"Did you ever get in the water, or did you just sit up there in your little tower ogling all the girls in their bikinis?"

"I was devoted to my job," he said self-righteously. "The bikinis were merely a side benefit."

"Right." Charity's expression conveyed her doubts about this noble claim.

"Are you going to get in the pool or just sit there casting aspersions on my character?"

Charity hesitated, but she knew what the end result was going to be. She was acting like an idiot. Gabe was nothing but a friend. It made no difference whether it was him helping her with her exercises or Diane. Okay, so Diane didn't have all those sexy muscles and Diane didn't put butterflies in her stomach. But those were minor details.

So Gabe was an attractive man. That didn't mean anything.

Nothing except that he made her heart beat too fast and her palms feel damp.

"Is it that hard to make a decision?" he asked, sounding vaguely hurt.

"No. No, of course not. I really appreciate the offer. If you're sure you don't mind."

"I don't mind."

A few minutes later Charity was chest-deep in the pool. Water wings helped keep her afloat. The first time she'd gotten in the pool, she'd been terrified. She'd felt completely helpless outside the hated security of the wheelchair.

It hadn't taken long for her to come to appreciate the benefits of working in the pool. With the water supporting her, it was almost possible to forget that her legs didn't work.

For all that he'd used humor to coax her into the pool, Gabe was completely serious when it came to the simple exercises she usually did in the water.

Charity had been nervous about having him touch her, but it wasn't long before she genuinely forgot whose hands were guiding and supporting her. There was nothing personal or sexual in his touch, nothing to hint that he even saw her as female.

In fact his attitude was so impersonal Charity wondered if she should be insulted.

But once the official reason for spending a hot afternoon in the water had been satisfied, Gabe's serious demeanor vanished.

"You know, if I'd known you guys were having this much fun out here, I'd have made it a point to get more afternoons off."

He let Charity float free, the water wings supporting her weight. He stretched out on his back, closing his eyes against the sun that poured down out of a cloudless sky.

"You're lucky to have a pool like this," Charity said, tilting her face to the sun. "There's a pool at my apartment building but it's small. When the weather is like this, everyone crowds into it."

"My grandparents put this pool in because they wanted my mother to be an Olympic swimmer."

"And was she?" Charity was suddenly aware of how little she knew about him.

"No. She never made it that far."

"Were her parents disappointed?"

"Not to the point of disowning her. After I was born, they had hopes for me."

"Did you compete?"

"In school. But I never had the kind of drive it takes to go for the Olympics. You've got to want it more than anything else."

"And you wanted to be a police officer."

"Well, first I wanted to be a fireman. That was when I was five. Then I was going to be a cowboy. When I was about twelve, I was going to be the next Hank Aaron."

"So when did you decide to be a cop?"

"About the time I got out of college and realized that there were limited choices for someone with a degree in history."

"You could have gone into teaching."

"I thought about it but I never saw myself standing in a classroom, trying to drum history into a bunch of kids who'd rather be anywhere else."

"So what made you decide to be a cop?" Charity persisted.

"Would you believe an ad on television? I was trying to figure out what the hell to do with a history degree and the rest of my life, and I saw this ad about the joys of being a security guard. But I decided to go them one better and entered the academy."

"You must like it, to have stayed with it for twelve years."

"It has its moments," he said slowly.

"You sound doubtful." Charity shot him a quick look.

"I don't think *like* is exactly the word I'd use," he said. "It can be incredibly fulfilling and incredibly frustrating, all at the same time. It's great when you help someone or arrest someone who's hurt other people. But often as not, they're back on the street in a matter of weeks, sometimes in a matter of hours. It tends to shake your faith in the system."

"You sound a little burned out."

"Sometimes," he admitted, hearing the weariness in his voice.

"What about your parents? Where are they?" Seeing Gabe's eyes were closed, Charity let her eyes linger on him, enjoying the sight of his relaxed body. He might have been asleep but for the occasional movement of his hands through the water, keeping him afloat.

"Mom died eight years ago and Dad moved to Wyoming. He's raising horses."

"Sounds nice."

"He's been after me to join him."

"Are you going to?"

"I don't know." Gabe was surprised to hear his own words. He'd convinced himself that the idea of moving to Wyoming to join his dad was nothing more than a premature mid-life crisis. Shaking his head, he changed the subject.

"What about you? What do you plan to do when you grow up?" He shot her a quick grin.

"I don't know. I guess I'm not all that ambitious. I liked working at the jewelry store. Mr. Hoffman visited me in the hospital and told me I can come back whenever I want."

"Will you?"

"I don't know." She sighed. "I just never had a driving ambition to be anything in particular. Diane always knew she wanted to design clothes. Becoming a model was just a way to earn money and get the connections she needed. And Brian is such a brain that he's managed to work in two or three life goals already. Sometimes it makes me tired just to think about it."

"And what do you want?"

"Besides being able to walk again?" She lifted her shoulders. "Not much. A home. Someone special in my life. Maybe a child." She shrugged again, her smile self-deprecating. "Nothing all that exciting, I'm afraid."

"Excitement isn't all it's cracked up to be. I think what you want is pretty much what everyone wants. It's just that these days we all make it so much more complicated than it has to be."

Conversation slowed after that. With the hot sun beating down and the gentle motion of the water lulling them, talk seemed too much of an effort. A jet flew over, so high it was little more than a shadow against the bright blue of the sky.

Charity watched it, wondering where it was headed. Wouldn't it be wonderful to be on that plane, going somewhere far away, leaving all her troubles behind. Her mouth twisted. That was funny—trying to run away from paralysis.

But she didn't feel particularly amused. She felt her relaxed mood draining away, threatening to turn into depression. But not today. Not right now. She wasn't going to think about her unresponsive legs or the possibility that she might not walk again.

Gabe gave a startled gasp as a miniature tidal wave of cold water splashed onto his sun-warmed stomach. Folding up like a pocket knife, he went under but only for a second.

He surfaced instantly, tossing his hair back from his face, his eyes seeking the source of the pool's sudden turbulence. Charity looked back at him, her green eyes wide and innocent, but he wasn't fooled.

"You tried to drown me."

"*Moi?* I wouldn't do anything like that."

"Then where did that wave come from?"

"Perhaps an asteroid fell in the pool?" Charity suggested.

"Doesn't seem likely." He paddled forward until he could stand on the bottom. Charity used her arms to ease herself backward in the water.

"How about an earthquake? They can slosh the water right out of a pool."

"Odd that the water only seemed to slosh over me." He advanced and she retreated.

"Maybe it was a very small earthquake. Localized." She bit her lip to hold back a smile.

"With an epicenter right under my pool?" Gabe thought he'd never seen her look more beautiful than she did right now, her eyes sparkling with mischief, her face lightly flushed with sun.

"Maybe you have a fault line under your pool," she offered. "Southern California is riddled with them. Maybe there's a branch of the San Andreas fault right under us now."

"Maybe. Or maybe it wasn't an earthquake at all." He stopped in front of her, scowling fiercely. But his eyes were laughing, and the tuck in one cheek told her he was trying not to smile.

"Well, if it wasn't an earthquake and it wasn't an asteroid, what do you think it might have been?"

"I have my theories," he said darkly. He drew back his hand and Charity had only a moment to draw in a quick breath before he skimmed it across the surface, sending a sheet of water ahead of it. Her eyes squeezed shut as the water cascaded over her face.

"That was totally uncalled for," she protested, wiping the water out of her eyes.

"I'm sorry." His grin made the apology seem less than sincere. "I have this terrible twitch in my arm sometimes. Did I splash you?"

"Not at all." She brought both hands together in front of her, pushing them forward in a movement that simultaneously sent a wave of water toward Gabe's smiling face and pushed her back out of reach.

It was not, perhaps, the most vigorous game of water warfare she'd ever played, limited as her movements were. The game consisted in large part of her trying to splash Gabe before he could duck. The fact that he could have easily swum out of reach seemed irrelevant.

For the first time since the shooting, Charity completely forgot about her injury. Buoyed by the water, bathed in the warmth of Gabe's laughter, she felt young, happy and, most of all, normal. This was one place where it didn't matter whether or not her legs worked. Or so she almost managed to convince herself.

Gabe had ducked underwater, and she turned to look for him. But she hadn't realized how close to the edge she was. The side of the pool loomed inches away, startling her into flailing backward, off balance, her movements clumsy.

For an instant she sank under the surface of the pool. The water closed over her head, and for one horrible moment she felt totally helpless. She'd been swimming since she was a child, and she couldn't possibly have counted the number of times Diane or Brian had dunked her or she'd gone underwater on her own.

But this time was different. This time there'd be no pushing up off the bottom, no quick kick to send her upward into the air, as there would have been if she'd had the use of her legs.

The water wings were forgotten. The fact that Gabe would hardly stand by and let her drown was forgotten. For that one horrible moment she was completely alone and completely helpless.

The water wings brought her to surface almost instantly and she drew in a gasping breath. But it wasn't enough to be back on the surface. She wanted out of the deceptively inviting water. She wanted the safety of her wheelchair, no matter how hateful it was.

Gabe was standing less than two feet away, the water lapping just short of his collarbone. He must have seen the panic on her face because his smile disappeared and he reached out to catch her arms.

"What's wrong? Are you in pain?"

Charity wrapped her fingers around his forearms, clinging to the sturdy support. The five feet of water beneath her suddenly felt endless.

"I want to get out," she said breathlessly.

"What happened?" Unconsciously Gabe drew her closer, his hands sliding up to her shoulders.

"I want out," she repeated. Near hysteria tightened her voice. "Now."

"Okay. It's all right." Gabe's voice dropped to a

soothing murmur. His hands shifted and Charity clutched at him, her nails digging into his arms.

"Don't let go of me!"

Immediately he had her wrapped against him, his arms strong and hard against her back. "I won't let go. What happened?"

"I went under." She pressed her forehead to his shoulder, struggling to tamp down the panic that threatened to choke her.

"I was right here," he reminded her, one hand moving soothingly up and down her spine.

"I couldn't breathe and I couldn't swim." Tears burned at the back of her eyes.

"I wouldn't let anything happen to you."

"I know." With his arms holding her close, Charity felt the panic receding. Of course he wouldn't have let her drown.

"I just felt so helpless," she whispered.

Gabe's arms tightened around her for a moment, and then he eased her back far enough to cup one hand under her chin, tilting her face up to his.

"I'm never going to let anything happen to you, Charity."

She closed her eyes as his thumb brushed across her cheek. His mouth followed the same path, soft kisses drying the tears from her skin. Charity shivered.

Any remaining wisps of fear were rapidly edged out by the warmth of his kisses. His mouth touched the corner of hers and she forgot how to breathe. For the space of several heartbeats neither of them moved.

Charity's hands shifted restlessly on his shoulders. As if it was the signal he'd been waiting for, Gabe's mouth settled over hers.

What had begun as gentle comfort turned to white heat in the space of a breath. His lips were cool and damp, but there was nothing cool about the feelings they stirred.

Charity's hands slid upward, her fingers disappearing into his thick wet hair. Gabe's hand tightened in her hair, tilting her head to deepen the kiss. When he drew back, Charity could feel his heart pounding against her breast. No doubt he could feel her heartbeat, the rhythm quick and hard.

She dragged her eyes open to stare up at him. His face was so close she could see the tiny gold lines that radiated out through the green of his eyes. Those eyes were searching her face, looking for something. She didn't need a mirror to know what he saw. Her eyes must be as dazed as she felt, her cheeks flushed, her mouth half-parted as if in invitation.

It was an invitation he didn't hesitate to accept, and Charity let out a soft sigh of pleasure as his mouth closed over hers again. His tongue dragged along her lower lip. With a delicious shudder she opened her mouth to him, her tongue coming up to twine with his.

The sun beat down on them, but its heat paled before the sudden fire burning between them. It was as if all the tensions of the past weeks had suddenly found release.

One of Gabe's hands stroked up and down her spine, leaving hot trails of awareness everywhere he touched. Charity drew closer, pressing herself against him as if he could somehow absorb her into himself.

Never in her life had she experienced a hunger like the one suddenly burning in the pit of her stomach. She couldn't get enough of him—his touch, his taste, the feel of his mouth, the silkiness of his hair beneath her fingers. And Gabe seemed to feel a similar hunger.

Afterward she wondered what would have happened if a shriek of laughter hadn't suddenly sliced through the still afternoon. The laughter was followed by a loud splash from next door. Obviously the neighbors were taking advantage of their pool.

The sound cut between them like a hot knife through butter. Gabe jerked back, his eyes locked in hers, his chest expanding as he drew a deep breath. Charity stared at him for a moment and then looked away, afraid of what he might see in her eyes; afraid of what she might see if she looked in her heart.

A light breeze skimmed across the water, and she shivered as it touched her wet shoulders.

''I...I think I'd like to get out now,'' she murmured without looking at him.

His hands were on her upper arms, and she felt his fingers tighten for a moment as if he might have protested. But if the thought occurred to him, he changed his mind. Without a word he guided her to the edge of the pool.

Charity gasped, her fingers clutching his shoulders for balance as he put his hands to her waist and lifted her to sit on the warm concrete.

She tried not to notice the way the water cascaded off his back and shoulders as he heaved himself out of the pool next to her. She tried not to notice how easily he lifted her, easing her down in the wheelchair. Most of all she tried not to notice how badly she wanted to run her fingers over the broad muscles of his chest.

Seated once again in the wheelchair, she felt the

loss of that momentary illusion of normalcy the pool had given her. Staring down at her legs, she reminded herself that Gabe wouldn't have looked at her twice if it hadn't been for the shooting. And he wouldn't have kissed her if she hadn't been wrapped around him like a wet dishrag.

But the reasons for the kiss weren't as important as making sure that he knew she wasn't expecting anything to change because of it. She reached up to take the towel Gabe was handing her, forcing a wide smile.

"Well, that was certainly a surprise." Yes, that was just the right note of cheerful unconcern, she thought.

"I suppose you could call it that," he said slowly, picking up a second towel and rubbing it slowly over his chest. Charity dragged her eyes away from the motion, scrubbing her own towel over her arms.

"And you don't have to worry about me thinking this changes anything," she continued.

"I don't?"

"Of course not. It's my legs that don't work, not my brain, Gabe." She shot him a quick, smiling glance, her eyes darting away almost before they reached his face.

"I never thought there was anything wrong with your brain."

"Good. Because there isn't. I know what just happened."

Gabe finished drying his torso and then draped the towel around his neck, holding one end in each hand, his gaze questioning as he looked down at her.

"You want to explain it to me?"

"Proximity." She threw him another of those quick, meaningless smiles.

"Proximity." He repeated evenly.

"That's right. I *was* practically plastered to you," she said, as if he might have forgotten just how close they'd been.

Not bloody likely, Gabe thought. Not when he could still feel the imprint of her slim body against his chest. Not when his hands could still feel her damp skin sliding under them. No, he didn't need to be reminded of how close they'd been.

"Proximity," he said again, his voice expressionless.

"That's right." Charity watched uneasily as he sat down on the end of a redwood chaise lounge.

"So you figure that I'd have kissed any woman I happened to find plastered to my chest?"

Put that way it didn't sound terribly flattering to either of them. Charity flushed and shifted uneasily in the chair.

"That's not what I meant."

"Then what did you mean?"

"It's just that we've been spending a lot of time together these past couple of weeks, what with me living in your house and all. And I know you worry about me, about my walking again, I mean."

"What does that have to do with us kissing just now?"

"Well, you haven't gone out at all. Dated, I mean." She let her voice trail off, staring miserably at the cement decking.

Gabe's brows rose. "So I kissed you because I haven't been going out with other women? That's not very flattering, Charity. It makes me sound like an oversexed moron."

"That's not what I meant." Her head jerked up,

her expression worried until she caught the humor in his eyes. Her mouth curved in a rueful smile. "I didn't mean to put it quite that way."

"So you *do* think I'm an oversexed moron but you didn't want to actually say that," Gabe asked helpfully.

"Well, not the oversexed part at least."

"Gee, thanks."

"I just worry that you're putting your life on hold for me," she said on a more serious note. "You don't have to sit around with me every night. I mean, if you want to go out with…with someone, you should go."

"Maybe I like sitting around with you," he suggested. The look Charity threw him told him she certainly wasn't going to believe that, even for a moment. Gabe didn't pursue the issue.

"I just don't want you to feel like you have to hover over me. I'm doing just fine. I'm going to get my legs back," she said. The very force of her words exposed her doubts. Realizing that, she shrugged, her mouth twisting in a half smile. "And if I don't…well, at least I'll be able to park in handicapped spots without getting a ticket."

Gabe sensed she was retreating as fast as she could from the intimacy of their kiss. The unexpected surge of passion had surprised her as much as it had him. But where he had been exhilarated by the discovery, she seemed to be frightened.

Proximity. Like hell that's all it was. Proximity might have started the kiss. But it didn't explain how right she'd felt in his arms. Nor did it explain the urge he had to kiss her right now.

But this wasn't the time. He could see that quite clearly. He wouldn't force the issue. But one of these days he was going to have to show Ms. Charity Williams that proximity alone wasn't enough to spark a fire like the one that had flared between them.

Chapter Ten

"Now, you're sure you'll be okay on your own?" Gabe gave her a concerned look.

"I'll be fine," Charity assured him. "It isn't like I haven't been alone here before."

"But not at night."

"I don't think night or day makes much difference."

He shrugged into a soft corduroy jacket, still frowning. "You're sure you don't need anything before I go?"

"Nothing. Diane brought me some old Cary Grant movies. I'm going to pop some popcorn in the microwave and watch movies all evening."

"Jay is just next door if you need anything," he reminded her, as if she might forget where Jay lived.

"I know." Charity gave him what she hoped was a confident smile.

Gabe picked up his car keys but hesitated. "I won't be late."

"Stay out as late as you want," she told him.

He hovered in the doorway. "You're sure there's nothing I can get you before I leave?"

"Nothing!" she said, laughing. "Go before I call the police and have you thrown out."

"Well, if you're sure..." She picked up a pillow and held it up threateningly. "Okay, okay. I'm going. Don't forget that Jay is—"

"I know. I know. He's next door. Now get out of here."

Her exasperated smile faded as the door closed behind him. Lowering the pillow, she cradled it against her chest, listening to the sound of his car as it pulled out of the drive. The sound faded down the street and she was alone.

Not that she hadn't been alone before. As she'd pointed out to him, she'd spent a good part of most days alone. But she felt more alone now than she had since leaving the hospital. Gabe hadn't just gone out. He'd gone out on a date.

You're the one who urged him to go.

But she hadn't really expected him to take her up on it.

You told him not to let your presence interfere with his life.

But that didn't mean he had to run out and get a date two days later.

What do you care? It's not as if you're in love with him.

Of course not. She just worried about the kind of woman he might be going out with. She didn't have to be in love with Gabe to know that he was a very special man. He deserved a very special woman. What if this woman didn't appreciate how kind he was, how sensitive?

"He's only going out on a date with her," she muttered aloud. "Not marrying her."

She tossed the pillow back onto the sofa and, putting a hand on one wheel, turned the chair toward the kitchen. She wasn't going to spend the entire evening wondering about Gabe—what he was doing, who he was with. Especially not who he was with.

She was going to do exactly what she'd told Gabe she was going to do. She was going to eat too much popcorn, watch too many movies, and then she was going to go to bed and sleep soundly. She certainly wasn't going to do anything foolish, like wait up for Gabe.

THE HANDS of the small alarm clock stood straight up. Midnight. Charity rolled her head away, telling herself to go to sleep. She'd been in bed for over an hour, most of that time spent staring at the ceiling. Every time a car drove by, she tensed, waiting to see if it would pull into the drive.

It wasn't that she was waiting up for him, she told herself. It was just that she was concerned. What if he'd had an accident? Or a flat tire? Or run out of gas on the freeway?

Or decided to spend the night at his date's apartment?

She squeezed her eyes shut as if she could close out the image of Gabe holding another woman in his arms; Gabe kissing her; Gabe in bed with her.

It was none of her business. She didn't care if he was sleeping with this woman, whoever she was. Probably a bosomy brunette with big brown eyes like a cow.

Her eyes opened again to stare at the same patch of ceiling. She'd developed an intimate acquaintance with the ceiling over her bed these past few weeks.

It wasn't as if, when she couldn't sleep, it was a simple thing to just get up and wander out to the kitchen.

That was another reason sleep was proving so elusive tonight. Earlier in the afternoon she'd thought she felt something in her legs. A tingling...faint, hardly noticeable, the sensation gone almost before she realized it was there.

She hadn't mentioned it to Gabe or to Diane when she'd come by with the tapes. She didn't want to get their hopes up. She was glad now that she hadn't said anything, because there hadn't been any repetition of the feeling, if indeed, there'd *been* any feeling.

Despite her determination not to make too much of what could be nothing, Charity couldn't help but hope. It was the first time since the shooting that she'd sensed any sign of progress.

The sound of the front door opening startled her out of her thoughts. She raised herself up on her elbows, staring at the bedroom door, listening as Gabe walked across the living room and into the hallway that led to the bedrooms.

He had to walk past her room to get to his own. Charity felt her pulse speed as she listened to his quiet footsteps. He stopped outside her door and her heart skipped a beat. She stared at the door, hardly breathing, waiting. She couldn't have said what she was waiting for.

He stood there for the space of several seconds, and Charity felt the tension in every fiber of her body. What would she say if he came in? What would he say?

When he moved on, she fell back against her pillows, drawing a deep breath. His bedroom door closed with a barely audible click, and the last of the tension drained from her.

Fool. What did you think he was going to do? Come in and declare his undying love? After he just spent the evening with a dark-eyed beauty who could walk?

The tears she refused to shed burned at the back of her eyes. It was a good thing she wasn't falling in love with Gabe.

"So, HOW WAS your date?" That was good. Just the right tone of polite interest.

"It wasn't exactly a date," Gabe said, sitting down at the table, coffee cup in hand. "Beth is the sister of one of the officers I went through the academy with. She needed an escort to a business thing."

Not a date. Charity sternly squashed the little bubble of pleasure the words gave her. It didn't matter to her one way or another if it had been a date. She wouldn't let it matter.

"I've been thinking." She stirred her spoon absently in her cereal.

"A dangerous occupation at this hour of the morning." Gabe glanced at the clock, calculating how much time he had left before he had to leave for work.

"Maybe I should find somewhere else to live."

It took a moment for her words to sink in, but when they did, his eyes jerked to her. She continued to stare at her cereal.

"Why?"

"Well, it's not really fair to you, having me dumped on you like this. I mean, when I moved in, I thought I'd be walking again in a few days."

"Let me worry about what's fair to me. And you *are* going to walk again."

"I know," she said without much conviction. "And I can't let you worry about what's fair because you probably wouldn't admit it if I was cramping your style."

"Cramping my style?" He raised his brows at the phrase. "What style are we talking about? I never knew I had a style and now it's suddenly in danger of being cramped."

Charity gave a perfunctory smile but she returned doggedly to the subject. She'd spent a lot of hours thinking this out and she was determined to have her say.

"Well, like last night, for example."

"For an example of what?" Gabe thrust his fingers through his hair.

"If I hadn't been here, you might have brought Beth back with you."

"Not unless I wanted her brother to tear my head off. Joe is six foot four and *very* protective."

"Well, if it hadn't been Beth, you might have brought her back here," Charity pursued stubbornly.

"I'd have felt like a total fool taking someone else to Beth's party."

"I'm serious, Gabe."

"I can see that. What I don't see is what you're serious about."

"What if you wanted to bring a woman back here?"

"I don't."

"But what if you did?"

"Charity, would you stop worrying about my love life?" He left his seat and went over to where she was sitting. Turning the wheelchair away from the table, he sat back on his heels in front of her, putting himself at her eye level.

"Contrary to the popular image of swinging bachelors, I do not sleep with every woman I meet. Beth is a friend, nothing more. If I'd never met you, I still wouldn't have brought her back here. Does that satisfy you?"

"What if she wasn't just a friend?" Charity ran her thumb along the arm of the chair, keeping her eyes on the movement, rather than meeting his eyes.

"Charity, I have no desire to make love to another woman. At the moment the only woman I want is busy trying to throw me out of her life."

Charity's startled eyes swept to his, reading in their depths exasperation, amusement and...desire? She looked away.

"You don't have to be kind to me, Gabe."

"Kind?"

"Pretending you...want me," she said, getting the words out with difficulty.

"Why do you assume I'm pretending?"

"I know you feel bad about me being...like this." She gestured to her legs.

"I feel guilty as hell," he said bluntly. "But that doesn't mean I don't find you attractive."

She slanted him a quick look, an equal mix of vulnerability and doubt in her eyes.

"Charity, you're a beautiful, sexy woman. Why is it so hard to believe I'm attracted to you?"

Color flooded her face at his compliment but she was already shaking her head. "I'm not beautiful. And I'm certainly not sexy. Especially not stuck in this thing. You're just trying to be kind."

"Once and for all, I'm not being kind." Annoyance colored his voice. "*I* think you're beautiful and *I* find you very sexy." His hand curved around the back of her neck. Charity's startled eyes met his as he drew her forward.

"I guess maybe actions will speak louder than words," he murmured an instant before his mouth closed over hers.

The impact was the same as when he kissed her in the pool. She'd nearly managed to convince herself that she'd imagined the feelings that had flared up between them then. But it wasn't imagination that put hunger in Gabe's mouth.

Her hands came up to clutch at his shoulders—for balance, she told herself. Her mouth opened under the hungry demand of his, her fingers sliding upward to bury themselves in the softness of his hair.

When he broke the kiss a moment later, they were both out of breath. It was all Charity could do to keep from whimpering a protest. Her fingers left his hair reluctantly, dropping to rest on his shoulders.

Gabe drew back just until his eyes met hers. "Did that feel like I was just being kind?"

Dazed, she blinked at him as she struggled to sort out her thoughts. There hadn't been anything particularly kind about his kiss. Hunger, demand, maybe a touch of good old-fashioned lust but not kindness. She stared into his green-gold eyes. She wanted to believe that he could desire her, wanted it so much it made her wary.

"I—"

But whatever she'd been going to say was destined to remain unheard. The sharp ring of the doorbell cut through the tense moment. Charity jerked her hands from Gabe's shoulders as if she'd just been caught in some sin. Gabe ignored the bell a moment longer, his eyes holding hers.

"You think about it," he told her.

She swallowed hard and nodded. *As if she was likely to think of anything else.* The bell rang again, taking on an annoyed whine, as if transmitting the irritation of whoever was ringing it. Gabe shot her one last look before standing up.

"Who the hell could that be," he said to no one in particular, glancing at the clock. Eight o'clock on a weekday morning was hardly a prime visiting hour.

Charity didn't know who it could be. At the moment she wasn't entirely sure she knew who *she* was, let alone who might be at the door.

She watched as Gabe strode out of the kitchen. His hair was tousled where her hands had slid through it. She curled her fingers against her palm. She felt as if she was suddenly seeing the world with new eyes.

Gabe found her desirable. What an amazing thought. She wanted to explore it more fully. Roll it over in her mind and look at the idea from different angles. But not, apparently, right now.

"Where is my sister?" The angry question cut across her tangled thoughts. Brian. He'd left for Europe a couple of days before she was released from the hospital. Obviously he was back, and from the sound of his voice, not in a good mood.

She wheeled herself out of the kitchen. Gabe, Diane and Brian were just stepping from the entryway into the living room. Brian saw Charity first and crossed the room to crouch down beside her.

"Charity. How are you, honey?" In his eyes was

the shock of seeing her in a wheelchair for the first
time.

"I'm fine, Brian." Since he seemed reluctant to
make the first move, as if afraid she might break, she
looped her arms around his neck. He returned the hug
with gentle ferocity and she felt tears fill her eyes.
All her life Brian had been there for her.

When they were younger, he might have pulled her
hair or teased her mercilessly, but he'd also been the
first to defend her if some other little boy tried the
same tricks. He'd visited daily while she was in the
hospital. In his eyes she'd seen his frustration at not
being able to make her world right.

"When did you get home?" she asked as he released her.

"Last night."

"And he was at my place bright and early this
morning, demanding to see you," Diane put in acidly.
Early morning was not her favorite time of day.

"Well, since no one had bothered to tell me where
you were, I think my concern was not unjustified."
Brian stood up and turned to glare at Diane.

"As you can see, I'm just fine." Charity spoke
quickly to head off the argument she could see brewing between her siblings.

"I don't know that I see that at all."

"Well, the wheelchair is a temporary necessity,"
Charity said defensively, surprised by his insensitive
attitude.

"I'm not talking about the wheelchair. I'm talking
about your living arrangements. What are you doing
here…with him?"

Charity saw Gabe's brows go up at Brian's tone
but she couldn't tell whether he was annoyed or

amused that Brian had managed to make him sound like Ted Bundy.

"Gabe has been very kind in letting me stay here, Brian." But he ignored her repressive tone.

"Kind!" The word exploded out of him. "Kind! Are you crazy. He's the one who shot you. You could have died."

"I didn't die, and the shooting wasn't Gabe's fault."

"Then I'd like to know whose fault it was. He's the one who pulled the trigger."

"Stop it." Charity's tone was crisp with annoyance. "It was an accident."

"Don't worry about defending me, Charity. I don't blame your brother for feeling the way he does."

"Well, that's real gracious of you," Brian said. His angry glance took any possible compliment out of the words.

"Is this a private fight, or can anyone join?" Jay stood in the doorway, his eyes questioning as he observed the tense scene.

"Who are you?" Brian demanded, ready to add him to the list of villains.

"This is Gabe's neighbor," Diane said before anyone else could answer. "I'm surprised you're not off doing good deeds somewhere," she said to Jay, her voice dripping with acid sweetness.

"I'm surprised you're out of bed this early. I'd think you'd need all the beauty sleep you can get."

Diane sucked in a quick breath, her magnificent eyes flashing in anger. Brian, dismissing Jay as unimportant to the present conflict, turned his attention to Gabe.

"I suppose you thought you could wipe the slate

clean by offering my sister a place to stay. But it's
not that simple. I don't know how you managed to
talk her into staying with you but she's not spending
another day in this house.''

Gabe remained stubbornly silent. He'd slid his
hands into the back pockets of his jeans and was staring at the floor, his expression impossible to see.

''Brian!'' But Charity's protest was swallowed by
Diane's angry voice.

''You know what I can't stand?'' She glared at Jay.
''I can't stand self-important prigs who think that
they're more important than anyone else.''

''And I suppose you think designing clothes for
rich women to wear once then throw away is an important contribution to the world?'' Jay shot back.

''You can't just walk away from your guilt in
this,'' Brian said, ignoring the battle between Diane
and Jay. ''You're the one who pulled the trigger.
You're going to have to live with that, and you can't
make it all better by offering her a place to stay.''

Charity lifted a hand to her head, feeling a head-
ache starting to pound in her temples. Diane and Jay
were in the midst of a full-blown argument, the subject of which she couldn't quite pin down.

They'd raised their voices, either in anger or simply
to be heard over Brian's accusations. Brian had raised
his voice over theirs, which brought the noise level
up another notch.

Gabe offered not a word in his own defense, letting
Brian's words wash over him unchallenged. His complete lack of response only fueled Brian's anger.

''You may have been able to fool my sisters into
thinking you had nothing but altruistic motives, but I
know better. She's moving out today. I—''

"Quiet!"

It was amazing what results could be obtained with a single word, especially when that word was shouted. All conversation came to an abrupt halt, and there was blessed silence. All eyes turned to Charity.

Diane and Brian couldn't have looked more startled if the lampshade had suddenly spoken. Jay looked surprised, though he didn't know her well enough to be as shocked as her siblings. Gabe's head jerked up, his quizzical expression quickly changing to one of amused pride.

Charity drew a deep breath, letting the quiet wash over her.

"Are you okay, Char?" That was Brian, bending over her solicitously, his expression so anxious that she promptly forgave him for trying to run her life.

"I'm fine, Brian."

"Then why did you shout?" His concern changed to puzzlement.

"It seemed like the only way to remind you all that I was still here," she said ruefully.

"What do you mean?" Diane asked, frowning. Jay slid his hands into his pockets, his expression going from puzzled to understanding.

"It's very nice to know that all of you are so concerned about me," Charity said. "I really appreciate it but I think it would be nice if someone thought to ask *me* what I wanted to do."

"Well, of course we care what you want to do," Diane said.

"Of course we do," Brian said supportively. "As soon as we get you moved out of here, we'll settle you anywhere you like."

"Maybe she doesn't want to move out," Gabe said

quietly, speaking for the first time since the argument began.

"You stay out of this." Brian shot him an angry look. "If it wasn't for you, she—"

"Brian." Charity didn't shout this time but there was a steely note in her voice that made him break off instantly.

"If it wasn't for Gabe, I would be dead." She tilted her head back to fix her older brother with a stern look. "I've told him and I'll tell you. He has nothing to feel guilty about."

"You don't have to defend me," Gabe told her.

"Damn right, she doesn't." Brian caught Charity's eye and subsided.

"What *do* you want to do, Charity?" It was left to Jay to get back to the main question.

Charity threw a quick glance at Gabe before focusing her attention on the toes of her tennis shoes. She knew what she *wanted* to do. She just didn't know if it was the *smart* thing to do.

Remembering the steamy kiss she and Gabe had shared just before the doorbell rang, she wondered if the smart choice wouldn't be to let Brian move her out as quickly as possible.

But she didn't *want* to leave Gabe's house. She didn't want to leave Gabe. He'd said he found her attractive, desirable. If she left now, would she ever find out if he'd meant it?

"Charity?" Brian's prompting made her realize how long she'd been silent. The time had come to make a decision—right or wrong.

"If Gabe doesn't mind—"

"He doesn't," Gabe said, earning a fierce look from Brian.

"I'd like to stay here."

Chapter Eleven

"You know, there are moments—more than a few of them—when I have serious doubts about my suitability for this job." Gabe slammed his car door as he spoke.

Annie shut her own door with more control, sliding her partner a sympathetic glance. "You can only help people who want to be helped, Gabriel. You can't force people to do what's good for them. Nita has to make the decision to leave Lawrence herself. Then we can see about getting her some help."

"Why would she stay?" Gabe asked, his voice rough with frustration. "She's got family. They'd take her in."

"She thinks she loves him, sugar." Annie shrugged. "As long as she thinks that, she ain't goin' to leave him."

"Why would a nice kid like Nita hook up with a two-bit enforcer like Lawrence?" Gabe turned the key in the ignition, the movement so violent that Annie wouldn't have been surprised to see the key snap off.

"Maybe he seemed real romantic," she suggested as they pulled away from the curb.

Nita had probably already called her boyfriend to tell him that the cops had been there asking questions. If Lawrence followed his past record, he'd come home and knock Nita around a bit, blaming her for the fact that the police were on to his protection racket.

Gabe's knuckles were white where he gripped the steering wheel, imagining that it was Lawrence Moodie's neck.

"You're takin' this all a little too personal, sugar," Annie said lightly.

"How else should I take it?" he snapped, throwing her a quick, angry look as he flipped on the turn signal. "We just left a nineteen-year-old girl back there with a black eye and bruises all over her arms. And Moodie is going to show up as soon as we're gone and beat the hell out of her again. And we didn't even get anything useful out of her."

He slammed his fist against the steering wheel, the motion full of barely contained frustration.

"You're a cop, Gabriel, not God. You can't make everyone's problems right, no matter how much you'd like to."

"We're supposed to be taking people like Moodie off the street," he said tightly.

"And we will, but we can't arrest him until we've got enough evidence to build a solid case against him."

"And in the meantime, he uses a nineteen-year-old girl as a punching bag."

"Like I said, she's got to make the first move. Last time I checked, kidnappin' was still illegal, even when it's for someone's own good."

"Well, I think that's a gross oversight in the legal

codes,'' Gabe complained. But he sounded more resigned than angry.

Neither of them spoke for a few minutes. They'd been partners long enough; spent so many hours together that they were long past the need to fill the silence with conversation.

"I'm thinking about resigning," Gabe said abruptly. He glanced at Annie, judging her reaction. She looked less surprised than he felt at having actually said the words out loud.

"Have you told the captain yet?"

"No." He shot her another look, not sure whether to be annoyed or amused at her calm acceptance. Amusement seemed most appropriate. "Aren't you going to express your stunned disbelief? How much you'd like me to stay on?"

Annie's mouth curved up in a smile. "Well, I'd be lyin' if I said I hadn't seen this comin', sugar."

"Do you know how annoying it is to have spent hours agonizing over a decision only to have someone say that she knew what you were going to decide all along?"

Annie grinned at his plaintive tone. "I know. It's one of my most irritatin' habits," she drawled. "Drives Bill crazy, the way I'm always right."

"And modest, too."

Gabe felt his black mood dissolving. Annie was right. He couldn't make everyone's problems his personal responsibility. A job like this required the ability to distance yourself from the misery that was an inevitable part of the work. He was losing that ability.

"Have you decided to quit for sure?"

"I think so. I'm losing my perspective, Annie. I used to be able to take something like this mess with

Nita in stride. You do the best you can but you can't always solve the problem. You concentrate on the ones that go right, not the ones that go wrong.'' He recited the trite maxims as if they were printed on the windshield in front of them.

''You know that's the truth, sugar. You can't beat yourself up over the ones you can't help.''

''It's getting harder and harder to believe that.''

''Then it's probably time to quit before you get yourself killed tryin' to help someone who doesn't want to be helped.''

''That's what I figured.''

Annie smoothed her fingers over the crisp crease in her slacks, her expression thoughtful.

''Does this decision have anything to do with Charity Williams?''

''Indirectly,'' he said at last, aware that Annie was waiting for an answer. ''But I think this has been coming for a long time.''

The decision to leave the force *had* been a long time coming, but Gabe had expected to have more doubts when he finally made it. Instead he was filled with relief.

He wasn't sorry he'd joined the force, and he didn't regret the years he'd spent as a cop. In his more optimistic moments, he felt he'd made a difference, at least for a few people.

But the time to leave was now, while he still felt good about the job, before—as Annie had put it—he got himself killed trying to help someone who didn't want help.

How much of the decision was because of Charity, he couldn't say. Certainly she'd influenced his thinking. All the logic in the world couldn't wipe out the guilt he felt about her. He'd played the scene over in his mind a thousand times, and he honestly couldn't see what he could have done differently, but that didn't change the fact that he'd shot her.

But it wasn't just guilt over the shooting that had made him decide to leave the force. These past few weeks he'd begun to crave something more from life. Charity was the sort of woman who made a man begin to think of hearth and home, of building a life with someone, maybe even kids.

He was more than half in love with her, he admitted to himself. Her smile, her spirit, the way she kept fighting even when he could see the fear in her eyes— all of those were things he admired. But it was the moments when he saw her vulnerability that had made his heart drop into her hands.

The anger and frustration she'd felt over the debacle with the flour; the way she'd clung to him in the pool. He'd wanted nothing more than to gather her up in his arms and hold her close, promise that nothing would ever hurt her again.

Annie might have suggested that it was just his overdeveloped sense of chivalry speaking, but he didn't think it was quite that simple. He would admit that he had a tendency to want to fix the world's ills. But there was more than protectiveness in his feelings for Charity.

He cared for her. He wasn't quite ready to admit to anything deeper at this point, but he definitely cared for her. He was even starting to wonder whether or not she'd be interested in living on a ranch in Wyoming.

THREE DAYS after her brother's rather explosive visit, Charity was beginning to wonder if it had been a mistake to stay at Gabe's house. It seemed as if Gabe had been distracted ever since.

Had she misread his signals? Only a few minutes before Brian's arrival, he'd talked her out of moving out—kissed her out of it, really. Surely he hadn't changed his mind in less than five minutes. But there was no denying that even when he was home in the same room, he didn't seem to be quite there.

Charity glowered down at her unresponsive legs. He felt guilty about the shooting—he'd admitted as much. He'd also said that the guilt was separate from wanting her. But how realistic was that?

Wasn't it more likely that he'd convinced himself that he desired her? That he was trying to make her feel better about the wheelchair. Maybe he wanted her to feel that she could live a full and active life, even if she never walked again.

God knows, he had to be wondering how likely that was. With every passing day, it was getting harder and harder to believe that her paralysis was temporary.

"What are you scowling at?" Diane's question made Charity turn her head to look at her sister. Diane was sprawled in a lounger beside the pool. Her perfect size-six body was barely clad in a deceptively simple one-piece swimsuit. Her skin gleamed with layers of sun block.

She looked like an ad for the perfect "California blonde," 1990s style, minus the deep tan that would have been de rigueur in the sixties.

Charity sighed, looking down at her own pale legs. It wasn't their pallor that bothered her. If only they'd move.

"You know, if you'd stop worrying about it so much, you'd probably walk a lot sooner," Diane said, guessing the direction of her sister's thoughts.

"Thanks for the advice," Charity snapped. "When was the last time you were paralyzed?"

"You're not paralyzed." Diane swung her legs to the ground, sitting on the edge of the lounger. Reaching up, she removed her sunglasses, fixing concerned green eyes on her younger sister. "You've got to keep thinking positive."

"I'm sick and tired of thinking positive. It hasn't done me a bit of good. And I'm really tired of hearing people who are walking around on two perfectly good legs, telling me to 'think positive.'" Her voice took on a nasty, mimicking edge as she repeated the words.

"Sorry," Diane said stiffly. "I was only trying to help." She reached down to slip on her sandals. "Maybe it's time I left."

Charity watched her shrug into a gauzy beach robe and pick up the bottle of sunscreen. Her conscience nagged at her, demanding attention no matter how hard she tried to ignore it.

"Wait." She reached out to grab Diane's arm before the other woman stood up. Diane waited, her expression stiff.

"I'm the one who's sorry," Charity said. She sighed. "I seem to have developed a temper like a rabid wolf lately. I shouldn't have snapped at you like that."

She felt Diane's arm relax beneath her finger an instant before she gave the smile that had graced countless magazine covers.

"That's okay. I shouldn't spout trite phrases at you."

"Trite phrases are about all anyone can offer at this point. No." She held up her hand. "Don't tell me that I've got to keep believing I'll walk again. I *do* believe it. Sort of. Most of the time."

"Well, I believe it completely, all the time," Diane said fiercely.

"Thanks. It helps to know somebody does." She sighed again, her hand dropping away from her sister's arm as she relaxed back in the chair. "I just get so impatient," she said, half to herself.

"Of course you do. But you've got to use that impatience, make it work for you." She caught the look Charity sent her and broke off with a laugh. "Okay, so I sound like a book of maxims for salesmen. But it's true and you know it."

"I guess."

Charity was aware of Diane's concern and she tried to project a more positive attitude. She didn't know why it had gotten so difficult to maintain that image lately. A combination of Gabe's distraction and her own building frustration, maybe. Whatever it was, it wasn't Diane's fault, and she didn't want her sister to worry any more than she already did.

"You know what you need?" Diane spoke so suddenly that Charity started.

"What?" *Besides legs that worked?*

"You need to get out of this house. You haven't set foot off this lot since you got out of the hospital, except to go back to the hospital. No wonder you're feeling gloomy."

"I don't think so." Charity's hands locked on the arms of the chair.

"Of course you don't think so." Diane pursued the idea with ruthless good cheer. "You've gotten used to being here, and it feels nice and safe. But you should get out, see some new faces.''

"And watch them stare at my legs?'' Charity interrupted, not caring if she was being rude. Just the thought of going out in public was enough to make her sick to her stomach.

"No one's going to stare at your legs, Char.''

"Oh, come on.'' Charity rolled her eyes, swallowing the urge to scream a refusal. "You don't believe that any more than I do. Maybe no one would be rude enough to gawk, but they'd steal little glances at me, wondering what's wrong with me, wondering if it's something marvelously interesting and fatal.''

"I think you're underestimating people, Char.''

"No, I'm not. I'm not saying anyone would be unkind. Or that they wouldn't feel sorry for me. But it's only human to wonder about something like this.'' She thumped the chair for emphasis. "I've been on the other side, remember? You see someone with a handicap and you wonder. You pity. And you thank heavens it isn't you.''

Diane was silenced by the bitter accuracy of her words. But she wasn't quite ready to give up on getting Charity out for a little while.

"We wouldn't have to go where there were a lot of people. A restaurant, maybe, at off hours. Or even just a park.''

"No. If I was going to be in this thing permanently, you'd be right. It would be important for me to learn to cope with the limitations of the wheelchair. But I'm *not* going to be like this permanently. I'm not.''

There was steely determination in her voice. Diane's suggestion had renewed her determination to get back the use of her legs. It was all a matter of willpower and work. She was willing to put in any amount of work, and her willpower had simply needed a small boost. Diane had unwittingly given her that.

IT WAS stubborn determination not to lose even a day's work that led her to get in the pool alone the next day. The physical therapist had called to say she was going to be an hour late. Even that small delay was intolerable to Charity in her current mood.

As far as she could determine, the exercises had had no effect, but the doctors and the therapist kept telling her how important it was to maintain her muscle tone.

After assuring Mary that she wasn't upset by the delay, Charity wheeled herself out to the pool and stared at the blue water, feeling frustration building inside. It was ridiculous to think that an hour's delay in her therapy session was going to make a bit of difference. But it didn't feel like an hour. It felt like a week.

Of course, she supposed she could ask Gabe to help her. It was his day off. He'd been shut in the den all day, but she didn't doubt that he'd drop whatever he was doing to help her with her exercises. Probably hoping to get her off his hands a little quicker, she thought gloomily.

Heaven knows, since that rather steamy kiss in the kitchen, he'd hardly seemed to know who she was. No. That wasn't really fair. He certainly didn't ignore her or treat her with any less courtesy than he had before Brian's noisy visit. He just didn't seem terrifically focused at the moment.

''And it probably has absolutely nothing to do with

you,'' she told herself firmly, her voice barely audible. ''Don't be such a paranoid egotist.''

No doubt Gabe had any number of things on his mind besides her. It was silly to think that his every mood reflected something to do with her.

It wasn't only his odd mood that made her reluctant to ask him to help her with her exercises. Vivid in her memory was the first, last and only time he'd helped her. And it wasn't the fear she'd felt when she went under the water that she thought of first. It was the feel of Gabe's water-cooled skin under her palms, the heat of his mouth on hers. Just remembering made her skin tingle.

No, she wasn't going to ask Gabe to help her. Which meant she was just going to have to wait until Mary got here. Waiting an hour wouldn't kill her, even if it felt like it would.

Of course, she could go in the pool alone. There wasn't much she could do, but there were one or two exercises that she might be able to manage. Besides, it would be nice and cool in the water.

She glanced up at the pale blue sky. The temperature was hovering near ninety and the water looked awfully inviting. Her eyes fell on the bright orange life vest that she'd been wearing since the session with Gabe where she'd gotten such a fright. With the vest on, she wouldn't be in any danger.

She looked over her shoulder at the house, feeling like a teenager about to light up a forbidden cigarette. The den was on the other side of the house, which meant Gabe couldn't even see the pool if he happened to look out a window.

Not that it was any of Gabe's business, she told

herself firmly. It wasn't as if she was thinking about doing anything dangerous.

Charity reached down to scoop the lightweight life vest off the concrete. The fabric was hot under her fingers. She struggled into it, buckling it firmly in place.

One thing she'd realized in the past couple of days was that she'd been letting other people take care of her ever since the shooting. She'd completely abdicated responsibility for her life and let them make decisions for her. If it wasn't Diane, it was Gabe or the doctors or the therapist.

She set her jaw and the brake on the chair. Reaching down, she grasped first one ankle and then the other, lifting each foot off the footrest and flipping the rests up out of the way. She slid forward until she was sitting on the edge of the chair. Then she moved each leg outward until her feet hung over the water.

Sitting there, her feet hanging in thin air, she was suddenly sure that this was the stupidest thing she'd ever done in her entire life. Before she could change her mind, she used her hands to launch herself out of the chair.

It was undoubtedly the clumsiest entry anyone had ever made into a pool. She hit her legs on the edge, something she was only able to tell because the impact jarred her whole body. She landed face first in the water, feeling a moment of panic. But the life vest bobbed her upright immediately.

What if she'd injured herself when she hit the side of the pool? She wouldn't even know if she'd cut her legs. She twisted, trying to get a look at the backs of her legs but it was beyond her.

Swiping her wet hair out of her face, she told her-

self to stay calm. At worst she might have scraped
the skin a little. But she could hardly have gashed
herself to the bone on the concrete pool edging. Besides, at least she wouldn't have to worry about
sharks.

The thought made her giggle and she clapped a
hand over her mouth, wondering if she was about to
become hysterical. But she didn't feel hysterical. Now
that the initial fright had passed, she actually felt
rather proud of herself.

Dropping her hand back into the water, she laughed
aloud. Stretching her arms out, she waved her hands
back and forth, turning a full circle in the pool. The
water felt wonderful, a cool contrast to the blazing
hot sun. As always, the buoyancy of the water helped
compensate for the lack of feeling in her legs. It was
almost possible to pretend that there was nothing
wrong with them.

She tilted her head back, closing her eyes against
the sun, savoring the feel of it on her face. There was
no real point in pretending that she'd really believed
she could do any of her exercises by herself. The real
point had been to prove that she could do something
on her own, even if it was something as foolish and
essentially purposeless as getting into the pool alone.

Charity floated, letting all the tension drain out of
her. With her eyes closed, she could imagine herself
floating in some exotic island lagoon. Any minute, a
gorgeous man, wearing nothing but a pair of minus-
cule briefs would walk out of the jungle. He'd be tall
with green-gold eyes and unruly sun-streaked brown
hair. He'd smile at her and—

"What the hell do you think you're doing!"

The dream popped like a bubble pierced by a pin.

Charity had been half drowsing, but Gabe's angry voice was better than a fire siren for banishing any lingering sleepiness.

Lifting one hand to shade her eyes against the sun, she peered up at him. He stood on the edge of the pool, his hands on his hips, glaring down at her. Though his face was shadowed, she didn't need to see his expression to know that his mood was less than light. His body language was perfectly clear.

He was absolutely furious.

Chapter Twelve

"Excuse me?" She hadn't done anything wrong, she reminded herself. But it was a little hard to keep in mind when he stood there glowering down at her.

"You heard me. What the hell are you doing?"

Charity lifted her chin. She didn't particularly care for his tone.

"I'm relaxing in the pool," she said, making it clear that she thought that should have been obvious.

"Alone?"

"Unless there's someone here I hadn't noticed."

"Are you crazy?"

"I don't think so," she said stiffly.

"Well, you couldn't prove it by me."

"I don't recall asking you. What are you doing?"

He was wearing black running shorts and a dark gold polo shirt. Now he was stripping the shirt off over his head, tossing it onto the concrete.

"You're getting out," he said flatly.

"I'm not sure I want to get out," she protested.

"Tough."

He jumped into the water. The waves from his entry into the pool reached her just before he did. Charity had been prepared to protest his macho treatment but she swallowed the words when she got a good look at his face.

She'd never seen Gabe so angry. His jaw was set like granite. His eyes met hers for only an instant, but Charity felt singed by that brief look.

The water lapped around Gabe's collarbone as he stopped beside her. She expected him to take her by the arm and tow her to the side of the pool.

Once she was out of the water, she was going to explain calmly and coolly that she didn't care for his overbearing attitude. She would make it clear that just because she was staying in his house, he didn't have the right to treat her like a child. She would make him understand—

"Oh!" Gabe scooped her up in his arms and strode to the steps. Charity's arms circled his neck automatically. He carried her as easily as if she were a child, striding up the steps and onto the concrete decking.

"Put me down." She bit her lip in annoyance. She sounded like the heroine in a grade B movie. But she didn't like being so close to him. It was hard to remember how angry she was when she could feel the steady thumping of his heart against her breast.

"Gladly." But he didn't put her into her wheelchair. He set her on the redwood lounger. "Now, would you like to explain what you thought you were doing?"

"I don't think so." She dragged the tattered remnants of her dignity around her. "I don't see why you're so upset."

"Oh, you don't?" It was obvious that his brief foray into the water hadn't cooled his temper by even a degree.

"No, I don't," she snapped. "I was wearing a life

vest.'' She wrenched at the buckles of it as she spoke, tossing it onto the decking. She glared up at Gabe, furious that he'd spoiled her small triumph. ''There was nothing to worry about.''

''I had no way of knowing that.'' He stood over her, dripping wet, his anger so palpable that she wouldn't have been surprised to see the water turn to pure steam on his skin.

''Why would you think anything else?''

''I looked out the window, expecting to see you waiting for Mary. Instead, I see that—'' He thrust an accusing finger to where her wheelchair lay next to the pool. Her precipitous exit from it had tipped it onto its side.

Charity stared at it, realizing how it must have looked. From the house he couldn't have seen her in the water. All he would have seen was the overturned chair.

Illogically her anger didn't abate with the realization that he'd had reason to be worried. It had seemed such a simple thing. All she'd wanted was to do something—however minor—to exercise some tiny amount of control over her life.

She hadn't meant to worry Gabe. And what had he been doing looking out the window, anyway?

''I thought you'd fallen into the pool,'' he said.

''Well, I didn't,'' she snapped. She blinked back tears of frustration.

''I didn't know that. You could have drowned.'' He raised his voice on the last, as if she might not have grasped the possibilities.

''Maybe that would be a relief,'' Charity all but shouted, frustration bubbling up inside her.

"Don't say that." Gabe sank to his knees on the decking beside the chair. "Don't ever say that."

"Maybe it's the way I feel," she muttered without looking at him.

She hadn't realized the tears had escaped until his hand came up to brush them away. She batted his fingers aside.

"Go away."

"Hush." The sight of her tears seemed to have washed away his anger.

"Just go away," she said, trying to turn her face away. "I'm sorry you were worried. Now leave me alone."

"I wasn't worried. I was scared to death." He cupped one hand around her chin, tilting her face to his, brushing her tears away with his other hand.

"Don't be nice to me," she mumbled, feeling like a fool. If he was too nice, she was likely to burst into tears and make a total fool of herself.

"Would you rather I was mean?" Gentle amusement laced the words.

"Yes." She sighed, blinking back the tears. "It would be easier to take. I'm sorry I scared you."

"I'm sorry I yelled at you." His thumb brushed across her lips.

"I just wanted to feel like I was doing something on my own. Like I was in control of my life again." She looked into his eyes, trying to see if he understood what she was saying.

"Next time, warn me, would you?"

Warn him of what? she wondered dazedly. Was it possible to drown in someone's eyes?

His thumb brushed across her mouth again, and her lips parted, as if in answer to a silent command.

Gabe's eyes dropped to her mouth for an instant before sweeping back up to hers. His gaze was more
gold than green. She closed her eyes, unable to sustain the intensity of his look.

She felt his breath brush across her mouth an instant before his lips touched hers. Her breath left her
on a sigh, her hands moving up to clutch his bare
shoulders.

It was just as it had been before. Passion flared
between them. Rising in a quick, stunning tide that
swept her along.

His mouth slanted fiercely over hers, his tongue
sliding past the barrier of her teeth to twine over hers.
Charity welcomed the sensuous touch. Her fingers
buried themselves in the damp hair at the back of his
neck, drawing him closer.

Gabe groaned deep in his throat, his arms lifting
her further onto the lounge, his lean body following
her, half pressing her into the cushions.

Charity murmured a protest as his mouth left hers,
but it turned to a sigh of pleasure as his tongue found
the delicate curve of her ear. She arched her neck to
allow him better access as he dragged his mouth the
length of her throat, finding and testing the pulse that
beat frantically at its base.

One strong hand cupped the back of her head. The
hand that had been resting against her waist slid upward and Charity's breath caught when he boldly
cupped her breast. She stiffened, only to melt when
his thumb brushed across the taut peak of her nipple.

Her fingers tightened in his hair, dragging his
mouth back up to hers, and she heard Gabe's rumble
of approval as their lips met.

She'd never felt this kind of frantic need before.

Her whole body seemed to pulse with it. The sun that blazed down from the sky was surely no hotter than the heat they were generating between the two of them.

· Her hands slid over his sun-warmed back, feeling the muscles rippling under her fingers. She wanted him, needed him in a way she'd never needed anything before. It was as if he was a part of her, missing all her life and finally back where he belonged.

His hand left her breast, sliding along the indentation of her waist, pausing there, savoring the feel of her yielding beneath him. Charity thought she could never get enough of him, never give enough in return.

His hand slid lower, his thumb brushing over her hip bone before stroking downward.

"No!" Hands that a moment before had been holding him close were suddenly frantically pushing him away.

"What the..." Gabe's head jerked up, his eyes still dark gold with hunger.

"Don't." The choked word was all she could get out, her hands still pushing against his shoulders.

"Don't?" He shook his head, trying to clear his mind of lingering passion. "Don't what?"

"Let me go," she ordered tightly.

"What's wrong?" He still couldn't quite absorb the abrupt change in her. "Did I hurt you?"

She shook her head. "I just don't want you to touch me there."

"Where?" His brows rose as understanding came. "Your legs? You don't want me to touch your legs?"

She nodded, turning her face away. It made her feel sick even to think of him putting his hands on her legs.

"Does it hurt you?" he asked, bewildered.

"No, it doesn't hurt," she said tautly. "I can't feel anything, remember? I can't feel it when you touch me. I can't feel anything. Let me go."

"Calm down, sweetheart. There's nothing to be afraid of."

If she hadn't been so upset, she might have noticed the endearment, might have taken pleasure in his tenderness. But all she wanted was for him to go away. Something that had been so wonderful had turned to ashes.

"I don't need your pity," she told him, her voice climbing.

"Who said anything about pity? Did it feel like I was pitying you?"

"How would I know?" she snapped. "Go away."

"I'm not going to go away until you calm down and listen to me. I've touched your legs before when I picked you up and you didn't get upset."

"That was different." She refused to meet his eyes. "Get off me." How could she explain the difference to him when she couldn't even explain it to herself? And how was she supposed to explain anything at all when he was practically on top of her?

"Charity." He caught her chin in his hand, turning her face to his. His eyes were all golden green, warm with emotion.

"I'm falling in love with you."

Just one simple sentence, but Charity felt as if her world had been picked up and given a hard shake and when it was set down, it wouldn't ever be the same again. Her eyes widened in shock.

"No."

"Yes." Gabe's half-amused look hid the anxiety she was too upset to see.

"No. You're just saying that to make me feel better."

"I'm saying it because it's true. I'm falling in love with you."

"No!" She didn't want to hear it. She was afraid she might believe it. And when reality came crashing in, she wouldn't be able to deal with the heartbreak.

"I didn't mean to upset you," Gabe said, easing away from her.

"I'm not upset. And I wish you'd stop saying that," she added on a frantic note that gave the lie to her first statement.

"Okay. But not saying it doesn't mean it's not true."

"Stop it." She pushed against his shoulders, levering herself away. "You don't love me. You just think you should." She pushed again, wanting him to be gone, wanting to lock herself away somewhere. Somewhere where she didn't have to hear things that she desperately wanted to believe.

She was so focused on her emotional turmoil that she'd completely forgotten her physical limitations; forgotten legs that didn't move; forgotten everything beyond her desire to put some distance between herself and Gabe.

Her left leg shifted toward the edge of the lounger. It was only an inch, hardly enough to notice. But Charity noticed.

"Oh my God." Charity's nails dug into Gabe's shoulders, her eyes snapping to his, a mixture of hope and fear darkening them to a muddy green.

"What's wrong?" He picked up on her sudden tension, his expression changing from one of chagrined amusement to concern. "Are you hurt?"

"No." She swallowed, afraid to even voice the thought out loud. What if she'd imagined the small movement? What if she could never do it again?

"What is it Charity?" Gabe caught her arms, his eyes searching.

"My leg," she whispered. "I think it moved."

He stared at her as the realization of what this could mean swept over him. Joy blazed over his features.

"Can you do it again?" Neither of them noticed that he'd lowered his voice to match hers, as if speaking above a whisper could jeopardize the miracle that might have just occurred.

"I don't know." She could hardly get the words out past the nervousness clogging her throat. "I don't know."

"Try. Just relax and concentrate." It didn't strike either of them that the two commands were mutually exclusive.

"What if I can't do it again?" she got out. Tension had made her voice thin.

"You can." He sounded so absolutely confident that she felt her own confidence take a bound upward. "Just try."

"I can't look," she said, her eyes never leaving his. "You look."

"You couldn't talk me out of it." He grinned at her as if there was no doubt about the outcome of the next few seconds; as if her entire future wasn't on the line here. She wanted to hit him and she wanted to cling to him. Since she couldn't seem to get her fingers unpeeled from his shoulders, the latter course seemed easier.

"Give it a shot, Charity."

Easy for him to say. His whole life wasn't about to be decided. She closed her eyes, too nervous to even think of offering up a prayer. It was a simple thing, really. She'd been moving her legs all her life without giving it a thought.

She concentrated every fiber of her being on her left leg, on moving it. Even the merest fraction of an inch would do. Something, anything, to show that she hadn't dreamed the earlier movement, to show that there was reason to hope for the future.

Gabe was watching. Even if her leg twitched, he'd see it and tell her. But she didn't need him to tell her. She felt the movement. Not much, certainly—an inch or less—but it didn't matter how much she moved. Only that she'd moved her leg.

Her eyes flew open, reading the confirmation in Gabe's eyes that she didn't really need. She stared at him, hardly able to absorb the miracle.

"I moved." It wasn't a question but he answered it anyway.

"You moved."

"I think I'm going to cry." She blinked moisture from her eyes.

"No, you're not." Gabe sat up, pulling her into a sitting position. "You'll be walking before you know it. Next thing you know, you'll be running marathons. Hell, you'll probably be ready for the next Olympics."

Swept along on his extravagant vision, Charity laughed shakily. "Don't you think you're going a little overboard? I've never run a marathon in my life."

"It's never too late to start." His smile faded.

"God, Charity, this is all I've wanted since the shooting. Just to see you walk again."

"Well, I'm not walking yet." She was trying desperately to rein in her hopes. "It could have been a fluke."

"It wasn't a fluke. I can feel it in my gut." His hands slid down her arms to take hold of her fingers. "This is your big break, kid," he said, in his best imitation of a studio mogul.

"I hope so, Gabe. God, I hope so."

"I know so." In that moment, with Gabe holding her, his eyes bright with belief, Charity didn't doubt that he was right.

IF CHARITY had been determined to keep up her exercises before, she became obsessed with them now. Given even a fragment of progress, she wasn't going to let it slip away. She spent as much time at her exercises as Mary would allow.

And she made progress. Agonizingly slow at first but it *was* progress. Every tiny step forward was a triumph, even if she promptly took two steps back.

Now that she had reason to believe she really would walk again, she focused every fraction of her energy on that goal.

The more she concentrated on regaining the use of her legs, the less time she had to think about Gabe, to think about him saying he loved her. She didn't want to think about that. If she thought about it too much, she might begin to believe it, and that would almost certainly lead to nothing but heartache.

"PLEASE, DIANE. Please say you'll come and stay." Charity was not too proud to beg. Her sanity was more important than her pride. She couldn't take much more time alone in Gabe's house. It was either convince Diane to move in or she would have to move out.

"Why? Does Gabe turn into a werewolf at midnight or something?" Diane leaned back in her chair, giving her sister a suspicious look.

"Of course not. It has nothing to do with Gabe," she lied.

"Then why do you want me to move in? And wouldn't Gabe have some objections?"

"I already asked him and he said he didn't mind." Charity shifted uneasily, remembering the way his brows had risen. Something in his eyes had told her that he knew exactly why she wanted her sister to move in and that it had nothing to do with her rather tangled explanation about Diane helping with her therapy.

It had been a thin excuse at best since Gabe knew as well as she did that Diane would be gone most of the day. So unless Charity expected to work on her therapy in the middle of the night, there wasn't much by way of practical reasons for her sister to move in.

"There's no practical reason for me to move in," Diane said bluntly.

"Can't you just do it because I asked you to," Charity suggested hopefully.

"Of course." Charity had only a moment to feel relieved at her prompt agreement before Diane continued. "But if I'm going to move to Pasadena when my home and business are in Beverly Hills I don't think it's unreasonable of me to be curious about why I'm doing it. Not to mention that you're asking me to move next door to that dreadful prig of a doctor."

"Jay isn't a prig," Charity said, taking on the most minor objection first.

"You couldn't prove it by me. The man looks at me like I'm an insect."

"You just don't know how to cope when a man doesn't fall panting at your feet. It's not an uncommon experience for us mere mortals."

"I don't expect a man to pant at my feet." She caught Charity's disbelieving look and shrugged. "Okay, so maybe I've gotten used to a pant or two. But there's got to be something between panting and sneering. And don't think you're going to distract me from the point of this whole conversation," she added, fixing Charity with a stern look. "*Why* do you want me to move in?"

Charity ran her fingers along the arm of her wheelchair—the wheelchair she would soon be leaving behind.

"It's Gabe, isn't it," Diane said.

"More or less." Charity sighed. She should have known she wasn't going to be able to fob Diane off with some thin story.

"What did he do?"

"He told me he was falling in love with me."

Seeing Diane's stunned expression almost made it worth having to explain. Diane blinked, opened her mouth and closed it again and then sat staring at her as if she wasn't sure she'd heard correctly.

"Well. The beast! How dare he! Shall we call the police?"

"He is the police," Charity reminded her. She smiled at Diane's exaggerated indignation.

"That doesn't mean he can say that he's falling in love with you! What kind of a fiend would do that?"

"Okay, okay. So it doesn't seem like a serious problem to you. But it is to me."

"Why?"

"Why?" The simple question stumped her for a moment.

"Yes, why? You feel the same way about him, don't you?"

"Of course not." Her denial trailed off under Diane's stern look. "That's not the point."

"You love him. He loves you. That seems to be very much the point."

"But he *doesn't* love me," Charity cried. "That's the problem. He only *thinks* he loves me. It's really just because he feels guilty about the shooting. If it hadn't been for that, he'd never have noticed me at all."

"Why are you so sure that's all it is? You're a terrific person. Why is it so hard to believe Gabe could really be in love with you?"

Charity ran her hands restlessly over the wheels of the chair. She didn't want to hear what Diane was saying. There was nothing she'd like more to believe than that Gabe was in love with her. But all her instincts were telling her that she was going to get hurt if she didn't keep all the facts clearly in mind.

The fact was that Gabe felt guilty about her paralysis. It wouldn't have been hard to confuse some of that guilt with something that seemed like love.

"I just don't want to be here alone with him," she said finally, sidestepping Diane's question. "Will you come and stay?"

"Of course I will, Char. If it means that much to you, you know I will. But I'm going on record as saying that you're going to regret it if you walk away from this without at least giving it a chance. Gabe is a great guy and he's had the good taste to fall in love with you. Don't let him get away.''

Charity nodded. It was easier to pretend to agree with Diane than to argue. As for Gabe's feelings for her, she was going to try not to think about that until she could walk. Once she was walking again, she'd see if Gabe still thought he loved her.

Chapter Thirteen

Charity sank into the wheelchair with a bump. Her face was shiny with sweat, her arms ached from the effort of holding herself upright on the parallel bars, and her legs felt like overcooked spaghetti. But she was grinning from ear to ear. She tilted her head back to look at Diane, seeing the happy tears in her sister's eyes.

"Not bad, huh?"

"Not bad?" Diane's voice shook with emotion. "You were fantastic! I can't wait to tell Brian."

"Maybe once he hears this, he'll stop treating Gabe like a serial killer," Charity said. She wiped her face with the towel draped around her neck.

"Gabe is going to be so thrilled."

"I'm not going to tell him. Not yet."

Diane's eyes narrowed on her sister. "Why not? I know you've got some doubts about your relationship but he'll be so thrilled about this."

"I know. But it isn't like I'm *really* walking yet."

"But you're making so much progress."

"I'll tell him," Charity said. "I just want to do it in my own time and in my own way. Promise you won't say anything?"

Diane nodded reluctantly. "If that's what you want."

"It is."

"So YOU'VE really done it." Annie's words were half statement, half question.

"I handed in my resignation," Gabe confirmed. He leaned back in his desk chair and put his feet up on the corner of the desk, hands behind his head, as he grinned at her. "I am about to join the ranks of the unemployed."

"You were just waitin' until we nailed Moodie, weren't you?" Annie leaned against the side of the desk.

"Yep."

"It meant that much to you to put him away?"

"I wouldn't have felt good about leaving him on the streets."

"Because of Nita?"

"Maybe." He lowered his hands and dropped his feet from the desk. "Maybe I just wanted to go out on a positive note. And leaving Lawrence Moodie loose would *not* have been a positive note."

Annie eased one hip onto the corner of the desk. She tilted her head to one side, studying him. Gabe raised his brows. "Do I have a smut on my nose? Or are you just trying to memorize my face so you won't miss me so much when I'm gone?"

"I'm just tryin' to remember when I've seen you so relaxed. I think the last time was at Jim Briggs's weddin' when you drank half a bowl of punch and serenaded us all with your version of 'Tangerine.'"

"If you're implying that I had consumed more liquor than I could hold with dignity, I deny the charge,'' he said stiffly.

''Dignity? You and dignity weren't even kissin' cousins that night, sugar.'' She dodged the wad of paper he threw at her, grinning. ''You certainly proved you weren't the next Perry Como.''

''You know, the real question isn't why I'm resigning,'' Gabe suggested. ''The real question is how I managed to live with you as a partner all these years.''

''Just lucky, I guess.'' They grinned at each other, in perfect accord.

Annie's smile was the first to fade. ''You know, I am goin' to miss you. This place just won't be the same without you around to annoy me.''

''Maybe you'll be lucky and your next partner will be just as irritating,'' Gabe suggested.

''Impossible.''

Gabe glanced around the station house. Already he felt a certain distance from it. A good percentage of his life had been spent here—some of it good, some of it bad—and he was going to miss it. But it was time to move on. And he didn't think he'd be looking over his shoulder, wishing he'd made a different choice.

''You goin' to join your dad and become a cowpoke?'' Annie asked, breaking the slightly melancholy silence that had fallen between them.

''I've been giving it some thought. Wide-open spaces have a certain appeal after L.A.''

''You takin' Charity with you?''

Gabe shot her a sharp look, not at all fooled by her casual tone. Annie had been worried about his involvement with Charity from the beginning. She thought he was going to take a nasty fall. She could be right, he acknowledged ruefully, thinking of the distance Charity kept between them these days.

"If she'll go," he admitted slowly.

"And if she won't? Would you still go?"

"Well, that would depend on why she wouldn't go." He picked up a pencil and turned it idly between his fingers. "If she isn't too fond of Wyoming, we could work something else out. If she isn't too fond of me, then I guess there wouldn't be much reason to hang around, would there?"

"Any woman in her right mind would be glad to move anywhere with you," Annie said loyally.

"Thanks. Now if I could just be sure Charity was in her right mind."

"How's she gettin' along with learnin' to walk again and all?" Annie straightened an untidy stack of papers on his desk.

"I guess it's going pretty well." Gabe shrugged. "She doesn't discuss it with me. But I gather everyone's happy with her progress."

The truth was that Charity didn't discuss much of anything with him these days. She held Diane as a shield between them. Gabe could almost laugh at her obvious machinations to make sure they were never alone together. Almost.

"You really love her, don't you?" Annie's soft question made him realize that he'd been staring at her without really seeing her. His mouth curved in a half-embarrassed smile.

"Yeah. I really love her."

THE PROBLEM WAS how to convince Charity that he *really* did love her.

He'd never had occasion to tell a woman he loved her until now, which meant he was far from being an expert in the matter, but he hadn't expected his declaration to strike terror in Charity's heart.

That she didn't believe him was obvious. She was sure his feelings were more guilt than love. And for some reason he couldn't begin to fathom, she had the odd notion that she wasn't the type of woman he could love. It was funny, really. He'd never thought of himself as having a particular "type." Of course, now that he'd gotten to know Charity, it was perfectly obvious that she was his "type."

What wasn't so obvious was how she felt about him. There'd been moments when he was almost sure she loved him. But the rest of the time he wondered if he was just imagining that she felt the same way.

Give her time, he told himself, reining in his impatience. The past few weeks had been rough on her, to put it mildly. She'd been shot, lost her ability to walk and most of her independence. No wonder she wasn't ready to jump into a relationship. He'd wait until she was walking again before pressing the issue.

Once she was walking again, he'd be able to convince her that his feelings went far deeper than guilt. And once she understood how much he loved her... Well, he had to trust to fate for anything beyond that.

He just had to be patient.

GABE REPEATED that promise all the way home. Having made the commitment to leave the force, he wanted to run in the door, sweep Charity up in his arms and ask her what she thought of living in Wyoming. But that would be a less-than-prudent course of action, he reminded himself.

He flipped on the turn signal and eased the battered old Jag onto the off ramp. She felt something for him. She wouldn't have responded the way she had when he kissed her if she hadn't felt something. He just had to give her some time and a little space.

He'd worked late, and despite the extra hours of daylight that summer brought, it was nearly dark by the time he turned onto his street. He pulled the Jag into the drive and flicked off the engine but he didn't get out immediately. Rolling his head, he tried to ease the ache in his neck from too many hours of paper-work.

Then he sat and stared at the lights in the house as if he might find answers in their soft glow. If he could just be sure that Charity loved him, the waiting wouldn't be so difficult.

Sighing, he pushed open the car door and eased his long legs out of the low-slung car. He wasn't getting any closer to knowing her feelings by sitting in the driveway. As he shut the Jag's door, it suddenly occurred to him that Diane's compact wasn't in the drive. Nor was it parked in the street. Which meant that, chances were, she wasn't home.

Gabe slid his hands into the back pockets of his jeans and considered the idea. Charity had made it a point not to be alone with him since Diane moved in. He wasn't sure if she was afraid he'd kiss her again or that he'd tell her he loved her. He hadn't tried to force the issue.

Right now the most important thing was for her to get well. He wouldn't do anything to distract her from that. And if, when she learned to walk again, she chose to walk out of his life, he'd just have to accept it. Just as he'd accepted her need to use Diane as a shield to keep him at a distance.

But Diane wasn't home. Did that mean Charity had decided it was safe to let him a little closer? Or did it just mean that Diane had something else to do tonight?

He pulled his hands from his pockets. He wasn't going to find out anything by standing here staring at his house.

THE MINUTE Charity heard Gabe's car in the driveway, her stomach tightened. She reached up to pat her hair. Diane had twisted it into a smooth French braid at the back of her head, leaving a few tendrils loose to frame her face.

She bit her lip. Didn't most men prefer women with their hair down? Maybe the French braid was too severe. What if Gabe thought it looked overdone? She lifted her hands, on the verge of pulling the careful braid apart.

She curled her fingers into her palms, forcing herself to lower her hands. Her hair was fine. Gabe wasn't going to worry about her hairstyle. He probably didn't know a French braid from a French fry.

What was he doing out there? Had she imagined hearing his car? God knows she was nervous enough to imagine almost anything. Moving to a mirror, she checked to make sure her makeup was okay. She'd checked it less than ten minutes ago but it never hurt to be sure. She certainly didn't want to greet him with mascara smeared under her eyes or her lipstick on crooked.

She'd chewed most of the lipstick off, actually, and her fingers were trembling too much for her to risk putting on a fresh layer. Well, at least chewing her lips had given them some color.

She turned away from the mirror, smoothing her hands over the skirt of her jade-green dress. The dress had been a present from her sister. Diane's own style might lean toward the flamboyant but she knew Charity's taste was a little more traditional. Charity had fallen in love with it the moment Diane pulled it out of the box.

The bodice was a simple cut, sleeveless with a neckline that allowed a tantalizing glimpse of the upper curves of her breasts. The waist was nipped in with a matching narrow belt. From there the skirt fell in extravagantly gathered folds to just below her knees.

It was the sort of dress that never went out of style and never looked dated. Exactly the dress to wear on a night when your confidence needs every boost it could get, she told herself. She just wished her confidence felt a little more boosted.

Where was he? She glanced at the front windows, nibbling on her lower lip. Should she look and see if she'd really heard him pull in? But what if he was out there and saw her peering out the window? She'd planned this evening too carefully to spoil it just because she was impatient.

She knew exactly how she wanted him to see her when he walked in the door. Poised and confident, standing on her own two feet. She looked down at the feet in question, wiggling her toes inside her soft flats.

She didn't think she'd ever be blasé about seeing her feet planted firmly on the floor again. It was a miracle—a miracle that she'd paid for with sweat and pain and more than a few tears. Except for that first movement, every inch of progress had been fought for. But when she'd taken her first trembling step, all the agony had suddenly seemed a small price to pay.

One of the hardest parts had been not telling Gabe every detail of her progress. She knew how much her recovery meant to him, and she'd wanted to share every step of it with him.

But she was already too close to him. Charity simply didn't have the confidence Diane did that Gabe's feelings for her would survive much past her regaining the use of her legs.

Not that she expected him to throw her out of his life the minute she could walk again. It would be more gradual than that—a slow drawing-away as he realized how much of his feelings had been guilt rather than passion.

She'd accepted that that was the way it was going to be, but she'd promised herself tonight. She pressed her hand over her stomach, trying to subdue the butterflies there.

Tonight was her last night in Gabe's house, and she knew exactly how she wanted it to go. She hadn't even told Diane what she had in mind. As far as Diane knew, she just wanted a nice, romantic dinner with Gabe. She hadn't told her sister she was leaving before morning. Let Diane argue with her when Charity turned up on her doorstep tomorrow morning.

She sighed, knowing Diane was going to think she was an idiot. But really, what was so wrong with doing it this way? Better to leave now before Gabe had to ask her to go.

And if she was wrong and he really did love her?

Well, it wasn't as if she was going to refuse to see him. She was moving out, not going into hiding.

Just when she'd convinced herself that she'd imagined the sound of his car, Charity heard Gabe's key in the lock. Immediately she felt almost sick with nerves. She didn't need to look in the mirror again to know she'd paled.

She'd planned this but now that the moment had arrived, all she wanted was to beat a quick retreat. She could go and hide in her bedroom. If Gabe knocked, she could tell him she was sick—something simple and believable like the plague, maybe.

But she'd never get away before the door opened, and she did not intend his first glimpse of her on her own two feet to be her back as she scuttled out of sight. She drew a quick breath and straightened her shoulders. She leaned unobtrusively against a small side table. From the way her knees were shaking, she had some doubt about their ability to continue supporting her.

Gabe pushed open the door and stepped into the hallway. Charity heard the door click shut behind him, and her fingers tightened over the edge of the table. Maybe it hadn't been a good idea to greet him standing up. She'd wanted to show him that she was completely recovered, that there was no need for him to feel guilty anymore. But it wouldn't do much to convince him if she collapsed into a heap on the carpet.

She stiffened her knees and drew in a deep breath as she heard Gabe's footsteps crossing the foyer.

His attention was caught first by the beautifully set table. Jay and Diane had manhandled the kitchen table to its current position next to the wide back windows. They'd argued about everything from who should take which end of the table to how to get it through the doorway, but the positioning was worth listening to them.

Looking out over the backyard, with only the soft glow from the pool lights to break the darkness, it certainly had more ambience than eating in the kitchen. Diane had provided a red tablecloth, and Charity had set it with the china Gabe said had belonged to his grandmother. Two candles, as yet unlit, promised a romantic glow.

Gabe's brows rose slowly as he studied the table. The few seconds gave Charity a chance to will the strength back into her legs. His gaze left the table, shifting unerringly to where she stood across the living room.

Oddly, the first thing that struck him was that he'd never seen her looking more beautiful. The green dress made her skin look like porcelain and brought out the color of her eyes until they glowed like emeralds.

Hard on the heels of that thought was the stunning realization that she was standing. Standing. He sucked in a quick breath, feeling his heart jump in his chest. My God, she was standing! His disbelieving eyes swept over her, trying to absorb the reality of what he was seeing.

She took a step toward him, leaving the support of the small table she'd been holding. It wasn't a long step, and there was a certain stiffness in her movements that told him she didn't quite trust in the miracle.

It wasn't until she'd taken another step that the reality of it hit. He felt joy well up inside him, his chest aching with the force of it.

Charity stopped, uncertain in the face of his silence. Why didn't he say something? Do something?

"You're walking." The words taut, as if they couldn't begin to express what he wanted to say.

"Yes."

"How long?"

"A while." She linked her fingers together in front of her. Was he going to be upset that she hadn't told him sooner? "I wanted to surprise you."

"You certainly did that." There was nothing to be read from his tone, and she wondered again if she'd made a big mistake in presenting it to him this way. He moved toward her.

Charity waited. She couldn't have taken another step if her life depended on it. She felt as if she were frozen in place.

Gabe stopped in front of her, but she couldn't seem to lift her eyes from the wedge of skin left bare by his open collar. Was he furious with her? Did he think she'd kept the extent of her progress from him in an effort to keep him feeling guilty? Until this moment, it hadn't even occurred to her that it could look that way.

"Gabe, I—"

"You're walking," he said again, as if confirming it to himself. Something in his tone brought her eyes to his face, and she forgot the tangled apology she'd been going to offer. His eyes blazed with happiness— a green-gold fire that washed over her, driving out any doubts she'd had about his feelings.

He caught her hands in his, holding them out away

from her sides as he looked down at her. His blatant pleasure made it impossible to feel self-conscious.

"I can't believe it. You're walking."

His grin was infectious and Charity felt her own mouth curve upward. How could she have thought, even for a moment, that he'd be concerned with anything more than that she was walking again? The one thing she'd never doubted was that Gabe wanted, with all his heart, to see her back on her feet again.

"I'm not running marathons yet."

"It's only a matter of time." He released her hands but only to grasp her by the shoulders. "You're walking."

He couldn't seem to quite grasp the miracle, even with her standing right in front of him.

"What do the doctors say? The therapist?"

"They're delighted with my progress. I'm not quite up to speed yet but everyone is sure it's just a matter of time."

"Are *you* sure it's a matter of time?" he asked, remembering the doubts she'd had about making a recovery.

"Yes." She gave a shaky laugh. "I guess walking at all seems like such a miracle that I've just accepted that I'm going to make it all the way. In a few weeks all this will seem like a dream."

"A dream." He repeated her words, wondering if she planned on him being a part of that half-forgotten dream or a part of her future. But this wasn't the time to worry about that.

"I can't seem to grasp that you're standing here. Standing!" He ran his hands up and down her bare arms as if to reassure himself that she wasn't a figment of his imagination. He grinned down at her. "You look stunning."

"Because I'm standing?" she asked, surprised by the almost flirtatious tone of the question. Diane was the Williams sister who flirted, certainly not quiet Charity. But she didn't feel like quiet Charity tonight.

Gabe's eyes widened slightly, as if he was surprised by the question. Awareness flared to life in his gaze, followed by a warmth that made Charity's skin feel hot.

"The fact that you're standing only enhances your loveliness." There was just enough playfulness in his tone to keep the compliment from sounding exaggerated.

Charity flushed, feeling the warmth spread from her cheeks, down her throat, settling in the pit of her stomach.

"Flattery will get you an extra serving of chocolate mousse pie," she suggested.

"Chocolate mousse pie?" Gabe's eyes flicked over the beautifully arranged table—set for two, he noticed. "Where's Diane?"

"You're never going to believe it, but she and Jay went out to dinner. Together."

"The airhead and the prig?" Gabe's brows rose, expressing his amazement.

"I nearly fell over in a faint. I think they're secretly attracted to each other."

"Like gunpowder and matches," Gabe muttered. To be honest, he didn't really care if Diane and Jay tore each other to pieces. He and Charity were alone, and the walls she'd so carefully erected to keep him at a distance had vanished without a trace. For the moment he couldn't ask for anything more.

"Are you hungry?" Charity's question brought his attention back to her. He wondered if she realized his hands were still on her shoulders. Her skin felt as soft as it looked. Hungry? Yes, but food wasn't the first thing that came to mind.

"Starved," he said with a smile. It took a conscious effort to release her. "Do I have time to change?"

"Yes. I'll set dinner out."

"Do you need help?"

"No, thanks."

"You won't try to lift anything too heavy?" He hesitated, clearly doubtful about the idea of leaving her on her own.

"I cross my heart," she promised solemnly.

"If you need anything, yell."

BUT CHARITY didn't need to yell. Diane had prepared everything before she left with Jay—not on a date, she'd said plainly. All Charity had to do was warm the casserole, a delicate mixture of chicken, rice and herbs, and steam the fresh broccoli. Tossed salads and a chocolate mousse pie Diane had brought from an exclusive Beverly Hills bakery completed the menu.

It wasn't exactly Wolfgang Puck, but it was tasty and simple enough that it didn't tax either her strength or her concentration.

Gabe certainly had no complaints. He'd changed into a pair of tailored black trousers that molded his muscular thighs in a positively sinful fashion and a loose dark gold shirt that made his eyes more gold than green.

He looked devastatingly attractive, and Charity found it hard to concentrate on her meal with him sitting across the small table from her. Though Gabe made a show of eating, she had the feeling that he wasn't tasting the food any more than she was.

Now that the miracle of her being able to walk had sunk in, Gabe was beginning to wonder what this was going to mean. Certainly there was no reason for her to continue to live in his house. No reason aside from the fact that he was crazy in love with her.

Would she have gone to all this trouble if she didn't feel something for him? The dress, the dinner, making sure they were alone for the first time in ages—it was all setting the stage. But for what?

Was she going to tell him she loved him? Or was she going to tell him thanks for the place to stay and so long?

Just because she moved out, it didn't mean that he was losing her forever, he reminded himself. Unless she told him never to darken her door again, there was no reason he couldn't see her. They could go out, date, spend time together in a more normal fashion. Heaven knew, there hadn't been anything particularly normal about their relationship up until now.

AFTER THE MEAL Gabe poured coffee while she carried the dessert plates out to the living room. He followed her, surprised when she bypassed the table in favor of the thickly upholstered sofa. He set the cups on the coffee table before sinking down beside her.

"You know, I always wondered what this sofa felt like," she commented as she handed him his plate. "It looked so decadent."

"Does it live up to your expectations?" he asked, trying to read her mood. Why did he get the feeling she had more than the sofa on her mind?

"Yes." Charity took a bite of pie, wondering if when she'd regained the use of her legs, she'd lost a portion of her mind.

She'd had the evening all mapped out. There was nothing unpremeditated about it. So far everything had gone according to plan. Gabe had been thrilled to see her walking. They'd shared a lovely meal. The conversation had flowed comfortably between them, even though half the time she'd had a hard time remembering what they were talking about.

Now all that was left was the final stage of the plan. The problem was she'd never in her life tried to seduce a man, and she wasn't at all sure how to go about it. Even worse, she was beginning to have doubts about the advisability of doing it at all.

Just how did one go about making it clear that one was shamelessly eager to share a man's bed?

"The pie was marvelous," Gabe said, setting his empty plate on the coffee table. Charity stared down at her own plate, wondering when she'd finished her slice of pie.

"Yes, it was good." She set her plate down and drew in a slow breath. She was behaving like an idiot. This was the nineties. There was nothing wrong with a woman expressing her attraction to a man.

"You look like you're on your way to take a particularly nasty midterm," Gabe said.

She flushed, her confidence in her seduction skills sinking to a new low. "I was just thinking that I didn't want any coffee after all," she offered weakly. "Too much caffeine."

"Tired?" Gabe asked. He reached out one arm and pulled her close. Charity went willingly, laying her head on his shoulder. It felt wonderful to be held close to him.

"Not really," she murmured, resting her hand on his chest. No, *tired* wasn't what she felt at all. She toyed with the buttons on his shirt. Gabe stiffened as she slid the first button through the buttonhole. Keeping her cheek pressed to his shoulder, she slipped a second one loose. But his hand closed over hers when she reached for the third button.

"You could get in trouble that way," he said softly. But there was a huskiness in his voice that told her he meant just the sort of trouble she rather hoped to get into.

"I could?" She slid the button open. Her fingers rested on bare skin now. She could feel his heart beating strong and steady. A little too fast maybe?

"Charity?" Gabe's finger cupped her chin, tilting her face up until he could see her eyes.

Her color was high but she met his gaze steadily, and he felt his pulse accelerate in a way that had nothing to do with the caffeine in the two swallows of coffee he'd had.

Only a blind man could miss the invitation in her eyes. And even a blind man could read the way her fingers moved restlessly against his chest. He wanted nothing more than to accept that invitation.

How many nights had he lain awake, thinking about her being just across the hall, wondering what it would feel like to have her in his bed, her hair spread across his pillow like honey-colored silk.

But he wanted more than just a night with her. He wanted a lifetime. Seduction had been the furthest thing from his mind tonight. Okay, maybe not the *furthest* but it certainly hadn't been part of his plans.

On the other hand, her mouth looked incredibly soft. It couldn't hurt to kiss her. Just once, he promised himself.

Her lips parted under his, and Gabe forgot all about limiting himself to one kiss. It wasn't possible to kiss her just once. Not when her mouth felt made just for him. Not when her body was so soft and yielding in his arms.

Their tongues touched and withdrew, only to touch again. It was a delicate duel where the object wasn't to win or lose, only to give and receive pleasure.

Hardly conscious of his actions, Gabe shifted her to lie across his lap. She tilted her head back to grant his mouth better access to the length of her neck. He tasted the pulse that beat at the base of her throat. He kissed his way across her shoulder, dragging aside the narrow strap that supported her bodice as he went. It dropped over her arm, leaving her shoulder bare.

His mouth came back to hers, hungry for the taste of her. Charity buried her fingers in his hair, drawing him closer, her hunger as great as his. She murmured her approval as his hand settled on her knee, sliding slowly upward under the soft silk skirt.

She caught her breath as his fingers encountered the lacy edge of her panties. Gabe felt her sudden uncertainty. He drew his head back, his palm flattening against her thigh.

Her eyes were a smoky green, dark with emotion. And desire. It took a considerable effort of will not to put his mouth to hers again and forget about everything but satisfying the hunger that had been gnawing at him for weeks.

But he wanted so much more than that from Charity. He wanted her in his bed but not just for the night.

He wanted her to understand that this was more for him than a quick toss in the hay. So much more.

"Charity, I—"

"Shh." She put her fingers over his mouth, locking the words inside him. "No talk. Not tonight."

Gabe hesitated, his eyes searching hers. His instincts told him that tonight was exactly when they needed to talk. But he wasn't immune to the plea in her eyes, the invitation in her soft body.

"Later," he said softly.

"Later," she said, her agreement swallowed in the pressure of his mouth over hers.

Holding her in his arms, his mouth locked over hers, Gabe stood up from the sofa. Charity linked her hands behind his neck as he carried her into his bedroom. This was what she wanted, what she needed. And if she paid a high price for it tomorrow, it would be worth it.

Gabe set her on her feet beside the bed. His fingers moved over her hair, destroying all Diane's careful work in a matter of seconds. Charity's hair tumbled onto her shoulders in a soft honey-gold cloud. Seeing the look in his eyes, she felt truly beautiful for the first time in her life.

If she'd had any doubts about what she was doing, they were stolen away by the tenderness of Gabe's touch, the soft whisper of his voice. He explored her body with gentle thoroughness, drawing an aching response from her.

And when the time had at last come to accept him into her, Charity could no longer doubt the rightness of her choice, the absolute inevitability of this moment. This was what she'd spent a lifetime waiting for.

THIS WAS what he'd waited for all his life. Gabe felt Charity's body adjusting to him, accepting his possession. She held him as if made for only him. If he were to die at this moment, he would feel complete.

But the pleasure only built with each movement, each sigh, until at last they could climb no higher. Gabe felt the delicate contractions that took Charity, and he tumbled after her into the final moment of pleasure.

It was a long time before he gathered the strength to move and then it was only enough to ease his weight from her lax body. Her murmur of protest changed to a sigh of contentment when he slid his arm under her shoulder, pulling her against his side.

She cuddled into him, her body fitting his as if they'd been sleeping together forever. Gabe let himself drift to sleep, feeling a soul-deep contentment. They still needed to talk, but for the first time he was confident of the outcome.

They were meant to be together. She must surely realize that now.

Chapter Fourteen

When Gabe woke the next morning, his arm swept out immediately, seeking Charity's warmth. But he was alone in the bed, the sheets cold. Frowning, he opened his eyes and glanced at the clock. It was still early, just past six-thirty.

He'd looked forward to waking with Charity in his arms. But he supposed that, after being stuck in a wheelchair all these weeks, it wasn't surprising that she wouldn't be inclined to sleep late. It must still be a novelty to be able to wake up and get out of bed.

Relaxing back into the pillow, he allowed a satisfied smile to curve his mouth. It seemed foolish now to think of how worried he'd been about the future. Obviously Charity saw it as clearly as he did. Oh, the details would still be worked out, but the important thing was that she loved him.

His smile faded slightly when he remembered that she'd never said as much. But she didn't have to say the words, not when she'd given so sweetly of herself. Her love had been in her eyes, in the way she touched him.

She hadn't wanted to talk last night and maybe she'd been right. The closeness they'd shared said more than words could have. Today they'd have the words. He'd tell her that he loved her, that he'd left the force, and he'd ask her how she felt about Wyoming.

They'd talk, say all the things lovers said. And tonight he'd take her out to dinner, some elegant restaurant with a view of the city and outrageous prices.

And then they'd come home and learn all the things there hadn't been time for the night before. His smile took on a sensual edge. On the other hand, why wait until tonight?

Gabe swung his legs off the bed and lifted his robe off the back of a chair, thrusting his arms into the sleeves as he left the bedroom. He noted absently that Charity's clothes were no longer on the floor where he'd dropped them last night. He must have been sleeping like the dead to sleep through her stirring around. But then, last night was the first time he'd felt completely relaxed in a very long time.

But that feeling wasn't destined to last. It took him only a few moments to realize that the house was empty. Tightening the belt on the robe, he slid open the patio doors and walked toward the pool. The morning was already hot, promising another scorching summer day, but Gabe didn't notice the heat.

Charity wasn't in the pool and she wasn't in the house. She didn't have a car, even if she'd been up to driving it, and he doubted she'd reached that point in her recovery yet.

He strode back into the house, sliding the door shut with a snap. He was on his way into the bedroom to get dressed when he saw the note propped up on the table in front of the window. The table where they'd shared a romantic dinner the night before.

Gabe eyed the innocuous piece of paper as if it were a letter bomb. He picked it up slowly. His name was written across the front of it. He ripped it open, already sure that he wasn't going to like what it said. He was right.

Dear Gabe, I can't thank you enough for all you've done for me. Your kindness these past weeks meant a great deal to me.

His kindness! Gabe felt his temper start to simmer.

I don't want you to feel guilty about what happened. I've told you, and I meant it, that I certainly don't hold you to blame.

I hope you'll forgive my cowardice in not saying goodbye face to face. I hate goodbyes. Besides, I certainly hope we'll see each other in the future. I consider you a friend and hope you feel the same about me.

A friend? Not bloody likely. There was nothing "friendlike" about his feelings for her. And he didn't believe for a minute that she felt nothing more than friendship for him. A woman didn't respond to a friend with the kind of passion Charity had shown him last night.

I think I got all my things, but if I've forgotten anything, I'll be staying with Diane until I get a new apartment. You can contact me there.

Contact her? Right now his palm itched with the urge to make contact with her rear end.

Please don't feel as if you owe me anything because of last night. It was what I wanted.

I'd like to think all debts are paid between us.
Yours, Charity Williams.

Gabe curled his fingers slowly into a fist, crumpling the note into a ball. *All debts paid between them?* His blood pressure climbed another notch. Is that how she thought of last night? As if she were repaying his "kindness" to her? And signing it with her full name, as if he might not know who she was, otherwise.

Come to think of it, it was probably a good thing she'd put this drivel in a note. If she'd been standing in front of him spouting this sort of garbage, he might have strangled her with his bare hands.

All debts paid in full.

If she thought she could get rid of him that easily, she'd better think again.

Gabe tossed the crumpled note on the table and strode toward the bedroom. He had several things to say to Ms. Charity Williams.

"All debts paid in full," he muttered as he jerked open a drawer and pulled out a pair of briefs. Come to think of it, maybe he'd strangle her first and say what he had to say later.

GABE MADE record time getting from Pasadena to Beverly Hills. It was not yet eight o'clock when he stopped in front of Diane's apartment door. There was a bell but he ignored it in favor of the more satisfactory pleasure of banging his fist on the door.

Time hadn't cooled his temper. When the door wasn't answered soon enough, he knocked again, more forcefully. He was just considering kicking it in when he heard Diane's voice.

"I'm coming." She sounded annoyed. Unreasonably Gabe hoped he'd dragged her out of bed. She'd probably known about this insane plan of Charity's. That made her guilty by association, and getting her out of bed seemed a small punishment.

He glared at the peephole, hoping his expression was enough to intimidate her into opening the door. He heard Diane mutter his name, as if answering someone's question, and then she was fumbling with the lock.

She pulled open the door, and Gabe didn't bother to wait for an invitation before stepping past her onto the thick carpeting.

"Come in," Diane murmured, but Gabe wasn't interested in sarcasm. He wasn't interested in anything but finding Charity.

His gaze swept unseeingly over an endless expanse of hopelessly impractical snow-white carpeting. The exquisite and expensive decor was lost on him.

His gaze only stumbled when it fell on a familiar figure in an unfamiliar place. Jay Baldwin stood in the hallway he assumed led to the bedrooms. He wore his pants but nothing else, and from the rumpled condition of his brown hair, it was obvious he'd just climbed out of bed.

Gabe's eyes skimmed from his neighbor to Diane, who wore a short black silk robe. From the looks of it, she'd just climbed out of the same bed as Jay. Gabe's brows rose slightly in surprise. So Charity had been right when she said they were attracted to each other.

But the distraction was momentary. He was only interested in one thing.

"Where is she?"

Diane's brows rose, her eyes snapping with interest. She studied him for a moment as if debating whether or not to answer.

"I could just kick open every door," Gabe commented to no one in particular.

"No need to go all macho on me," Diane said, grinning. "I'm on your side. I told her she was nuts."

"It's a pity she didn't listen," he growled. "Where is she?"

"Second door on the right." Diane nodded to the hallway. Gabe strode across the living room, nodding shortly to Jay as he passed. Now that he had her almost within reach, he wasn't sure whether to air his rage or kiss her until she came to her senses and admitted she loved him.

CHARITY WAS LYING on the bed in Diane's cluttered guest room, which also functioned as her workroom. She'd been staring at the ceiling to avoid staring at the incredible disarray that filled every corner of the room.

She had to start looking for a place of her own. And a job. Mr. Hoffman had promised her that she had a job with him anytime she wanted, but she couldn't imagine going back to the jewelry store. Too many memories, of the robbery as well as of Gabe. Besides, it was time she moved on, did something else with her life.

She jerked up on the bed, her breath leaving her on a startled cry as her bedroom door slammed open.

Thoughts of burglars and banshees scattered when she saw Gabe's towering figure in the doorway.

The sight did nothing to still her pounding heartbeat. His expression alone was enough to make banshees look tame.

"G-Gabe," she stammered out.

"In the flesh," he said grimly.

"Wh-What are you doing here?"

"All the way over here, I've been considering the possibility of throttling you," he said, advancing into the room.

"Throttling me?" she squeaked, wondering if he'd lost his mind. "I don't understand. I left you a note." She eased back on the bed, wishing Diane hadn't piled so many boxes around the room that escape was impossible. Not that she was afraid of Gabe. At least, not really afraid.

"A note." He made the word an epithet. "It's a good thing you put that crap in a note. I'm not sure I could have held my temper if you'd said that garbage to my face."

This was holding his temper?

"I don't understand why you're so upset." She wanted to stand up but she could only get off the bed on the side facing Gabe, and she didn't want to get any closer to him.

Neither of them paid any attention to Jay and Diane, who were standing in the open doorway, shamelessly eavesdropping.

"You don't understand why I'm upset? Let me explain it to you," he said with awful calm. He'd moved to loom over the bed. "I went to sleep last night with a beautiful woman in my arms—a woman I've already said I love. I expected to wake up this morning with that same woman in my bed—or at least in my house. Instead I wake up to a polite little note that could have been written by a total stranger.''

"It was a perfectly good note," she offered weakly. "I meant everything I said."

He made a noise that sounded suspiciously like a growl. "All debts paid in full," he quoted, his eyes flashing fire. "Did you mean that?"

"Yes," she admitted, wondering why he should be upset that she'd told him not to feel as if he owed her anything.

"Did you sleep with me because you thought you owed me something?" he roared.

Charity gaped at him, trying to see how he could have interpreted her note to mean that. She'd tried so hard to strike just the right balance.

"I...you didn't...I meant you shouldn't feel guilty anymore," she finally got out.

"Guilty! Is that all you think I feel?"

"I—" She looked past him at Diane, her eyes pleading for help. But Diane only gave her a completely unsympathetic grin, her eyes full of laughter. Charity was on her own.

"I think you felt very guilty about the shooting," she said carefully.

"Of course I felt guilty," he snapped. "Who wouldn't? But I've already told you—several times—that my feelings for you aren't guilt. I made love to you last night because I love you. What do I have to say to get that through your head?"

Charity saw Diane beaming with approval and she felt her own cheeks warm. So much for keeping her private life private. From the look on Gabe's face, she doubted he'd have cared if they were standing in the middle of the Rose Bowl.

"I never said you didn't like me," she began, her voice dropping.

"Like you? I love you, goddammit!" he barked in a less than loverlike tone. "At the moment I'm not sure I 'like' you at all."

Her heart began to thump. Despite herself, she almost believed him. Almost. But she had to be careful. She didn't think she could bear it if she let herself believe him and then found out he'd mistaken his feelings. Better never to have him than to lose him.

"It's easy to mistake guilt and…and affection for stronger emotions. I—Gabe!" His name was a startled shriek as he bent to grab her by the shoulders. Snatching her up off the bed, his mouth covered hers before she'd had time to regain her breath.

If Charity had wanted to resist, he didn't give her a chance. He put all his hunger and need into that kiss, and she was helpless to do anything but respond.

He ended as abruptly as he'd begun. Pulling his head back, he glared at her.

"Does that feel like guilt?" he snarled.

Charity could only stare at him, trying to gather her scattered wits. His eyes were still furious. And hurt, she realized suddenly. She'd hurt him. The realization was stunning. Gabe had always seemed so self-contained, as if nothing really got through to him. It had never occurred to her that she could hurt him. That he might care enough about her to be hurt.

That he might love her?

"Oh, what's the use," Gabe muttered, taking her continued silence as a confirmation that she didn't care. He released his hold on her shoulders, and Charity sank bonelessly to the bed, trying to absorb the incredible thought that he really did love her.

It was only when he turned away from the bed that she realized he was leaving. Walking out of her life. Because he thought she didn't care.

"Wait."

Wrapped in his own hurt, Gabe didn't even hear her husky plea. But Jay did. Acting with the presence of mind that made him an excellent doctor, he reached past Diane and grabbed hold of the doorknob, shutting the door in Gabe's face.

"What the hell?" Gabe stared at the closed door, wondering what sort of game Jay was playing. All he wanted was out of there. Charity had made it plain that she didn't love him. He'd gambled that she didn't realize the strength of her feelings, and he'd lost. Now he just wanted to go beat his head on a convenient telephone pole. He reached for the doorknob.

"Gabe." He stiffened but he didn't turn around. He didn't want to see her sympathetic look. No doubt it bothered her to think that she might have hurt him.

"Forget it," he said gruffly. He tugged on the doorknob, but something was holding the door shut. Something like Jay Baldwin, he guessed. Maybe instead of beating *his* head on a telephone pole, he'd beat Jay's head on one.

"Gabe, wait. Please."

Something in her voice reached him, breathing life into the hope he was sure was completely unfounded. He released the doorknob and turned toward her.

"What?"

She was standing next to the bed, and for just a moment he savored the miracle of seeing her on her feet. Even if he never saw her again, he'd at least know she was walking.

"I didn't mean to hurt you."

"No big deal." He shrugged.

"Gabe, are you sure you love me?"

My God, did she want to rub salt in the wounds? But there was something in her eyes that told him there was more than idle curiosity behind the question. Something he was afraid to believe in. He took a step toward her.

"I love you."

"And it's not guilt or pity or anything like that?"

"I'll always feel guilty that I hurt you, Charity. But I don't pity you. And I *do* know the difference between guilt and love."

She took a hesitant step forward, her fingers twisting in the hem of her nightshirt—a battered football jersey emblazoned with a giant number one.

"I'm walking again now, and it won't be long before I'll be able to go back to work and get an apartment. You don't have to worry about me or wonder if I can get along." She seemed anxious that he understand just how well she could get along without him.

"I'm glad. But that doesn't change the way I feel about you."

"You're sure? Really, really sure?" she whispered, her heart in her eyes.

"I'm really, really sure." He stopped inches away. "I love you, Charity. Whether you ever walked or not, I love you."

"Oh." Interpreting that, quite correctly, to mean that she felt the same, Gabe caught her in his arms.

"It's just that I couldn't stand it if you changed your mind," she said, her voice muffled against his shirt.

"I'm not going to change my mind." He slid one hand into her hair, tilting her head back until her eyes met his. "Are *you* sure? You're not feeling that you owe me something for taking care of you?"

"No. I'm sure."

"You might tell me just what it is you're sure of." His smile had a wistful edge. Looking into his eyes, Charity saw a touch of uncertainty, and she realized suddenly that he was just as worried about her feelings as she had been about his. Her arms tightened around him, and she had to swallow a lump in her throat before she could get her voice out.

"I love you, Gabriel London. I love you. I love—"

Gabe's mouth smothered her words. There'd be time enough later to tell her he'd left the force, time enough to talk about Wyoming. They had the rest of their lives.

When he's bad...
he's better!

Angel and the Bad Man

Chapter One

He was a dark shadow on the twilit street.

From the toes of his worn black boots to the shaded visor of his helmet, he was dressed in unrelieved black. Even his hands were covered by black leather gloves.

If it hadn't been for the ear-rattling roar of the motorcycle he straddled, Angie might have thought him a figment of her imagination, conjured up by her urgent wish that someone would show up to help her out of her current predicament.

Of course, her thinking had been more along the lines of a *white* knight.

"Is there a problem here?" The helmet made his voice seem muffled and dark, just as the rest of him. The question was directed toward Angie but it was Billy Sikes who answered.

"Ain't nothin' here that's any of your business, man." The look he directed toward the man on the motorcycle was both warning and threat.

The stranger did not seem impressed. He turned his head to look from her to the five young toughs standing in front of her and then back to her.

"Is there a problem?" he asked again.

Angie wished he'd take off his helmet so that she could see his face. At the moment, she didn't know whether he was offering help or just a trip from the frying pan into the fire.

As if reading the uncertainty in her eyes, and guessing its cause, the stranger reached up to lift the helmet from his head. Shadow and light. The words sprang instantly to mind.

Shaggy blond hair brushed the collar of his leather jacket and the clear green of his eyes reflected the fading light. It was his eyes that decided it for her. Though she put his age at mid-thirties, his eyes were older, as if they'd seen too much. But behind the weariness was a touch of humor that appealed to her. There was something about them that made her feel warm inside. Despite the fact that he looked hardly less dangerous than the toughs facing her, she decided to take a chance on him.

"Actually I need to get to a pay phone," she said. "My car died."

"I don't see why that should be a problem. I can give you a lift."

"I'd appreciate that," Angie said gratefully.

But when she moved toward him, one of the toughs shifted to block her path. She stopped, her eyes meeting the teenager's with a calm she didn't feel. She'd hoped that, faced with something more threatening than a lone woman, they would give up the game but it didn't look as if that was going to be the case.

"Mind your own business, man," Billy told the stranger harshly. "This ain't nothin' to do with you. Just back off." Angie held her breath, wondering if the biker would abandon her to her fate. She couldn't blame him if he did. He probably hadn't counted on risking his life just to play Good Samaritan.

Moving without haste, the stranger swung his leg over the bike and stood up. He set the helmet on the bike's seat and turned to face Billy.

"I've never been very good at minding my own business," he said, sounding regretful.

Billy looked uneasy in the face of the older man's calm expression but he could hardly back down, not with his friends watching, waiting for him to show this intruder just whose turf he was on.

"Come on, Billy, let's split." That was Tony Aggretti, his dark eyes uneasy. In her position as nurse in the local clinic, Angie had helped his family more than once. He liked her and hadn't wanted to hassle her in the first place.

"We ain't splittin'," Billy snapped. "This jerk is the one who's splittin'. Maybe in a body bag." Angie caught her breath when the knife appeared in his hand, the blade gleaming in the twilight.

"You don't want to do this," the stranger said, seemingly indifferent to that length of cold steel.

"You're wrong. I'm going to enjoy this, man." With a harsh grin, Billy moved toward him. Flanking him were three of his friends. Only Tony hung back, looking upset.

Angie took a firmer hold on her purse. She wasn't going to stand by and see her would-be rescuer hurt without trying to help him. She started forward but Tony moved suddenly, catching her arms and pulling her back.

"You'll get hurt," he said sharply, holding her despite her efforts to pull away.

Angie was just about to deck him with her purse

when it became obvious that the stranger didn't need her help. Billy feinted toward him with the knife, expecting his opponent to dodge back, putting him within reach of the youth who'd moved behind him. From the way they'd fanned out, it was obviously a move they'd used successfully before. But not this time.

The stranger didn't jump back to avoid the knife. Instead, he moved forward, stepping inside Billy's slashing thrust. His hand closed around Billy's wrist in an almost casual hold. With a cry of pain, Billy dropped the blade and the stranger released his wrist, bringing his hand up in a smashing blow to the face that dropped Billy in his tracks.

Even as Billy hit the ground, his opponent was moving, spinning to face the youth who was lunging at his back. In a move so graceful it was almost balletic, his feet left the ground, one leg kicking straight out. The worn leather boot caught his attacker just under the chin. The force of the blow lifted the younger man off his feet before he collapsed on the cracked pavement.

The stranger hit the ground in a crouch, his hands lifted, his fingers crooked, his eyes on the two remaining toughs. They hung back, looking from their fallen comrades to the man facing them. His calm gaze challenged them to continue the fight to the finish.

Angie held her breath, waiting to see what would happen. Tony still held her arm but the restraint was unnecessary. Obviously, her rescuer needed no help from her.

It must have been equally obvious to his two remaining opponents. They looked from him to the fallen bodies. He wasn't even breathing hard, yet Billy and Raul lay on the ground, unconscious. It must have occurred to them that he could have killed them without exerting much more effort. Both youths raised their hands in unison and took a hasty step back.

"Hey, man, we ain't lookin' for no trouble." The blatant lie would have been funny if the situation had been less tense. Even now, it was enough to cause the stranger's mouth to twist in a wry grin.

"My mistake," he said. Angie noticed that he didn't relax his stance. "Why don't you pick up your friends and get out of here?"

The two looked more interested in a quick departure than in carrying off their friends, but perhaps they thought the stranger might pursue them if they didn't do as he said. They moved to obey, keeping a wary eye on him.

"I'm sorry, Ms. Brady," Tony muttered. Angie hadn't even noticed when he released her arm. Now she looked at him, her blue eyes cool with displeasure.

"You should choose your friends more carefully."

He ducked his head, his eyes sliding away from hers. "They ain't so bad most of the time."

"They could get you killed one of these days," she said sharply. "Your mother depends on you, Tony. She loves you. What do you think it would do to her if you got yourself killed in some street fight?"

"Hey, Aggretti! You gonna stand there makin' time with the nurse or are you gonna give us a hand with Billy and Raul?"

Tony hesitated and Angie dared to hope that she'd gotten through to him. His eyes shifted from her to where his two companions were struggling to lift their unconscious friends. When he looked back to her, she knew she'd lost.

"They're my friends," he told her, his thin shoulders lifting in a shrug. He darted off before she could say anything more.

Angie watched the three boys gather up their fallen comrades. The stranger watched, too. Though his stance seemed relaxed, she didn't doubt that, at the slightest sign of trouble, there'd be more than two to be carried off. It wasn't until the would-be toughs had disappeared around a corner that he turned to her.

"You all right?"

"Yes. Thank you for coming to my rescue."

"You're welcome."

She waited but he didn't seem to have anything to add to the polite acknowledgement. He just stood there, watching her. She cleared her throat.

"You're not hurt, are you?"

"Are you offering to bandage my wounds, Nurse?" There was a wicked gleam in his eyes that made her cheeks warm, though he'd said nothing in the least suggestive. "They did call you a nurse, didn't they?"

"Yes," she said stiffly. "I work at the Fair Street Clinic. It's a couple of blocks from here."

"I know where it is."

"Oh. Good." Something about him made her think he probably *ought* to know where the clinic was. He looked like someone who might be needing its services.

"Not a good neighborhood for a woman walking alone," he commented. "Especially this close to dark."

"You're right." Angie followed his look, seeing the shabby businesses that lined the street, closed now, iron grills drawn across their fronts. "I thought I'd be okay because most people around here know me."

"They certainly did seem to know you," he agreed.

His mock solemn look drew a half smile from Angie. "I mean, they know I'm a nurse at the clinic. That means it's in their best interest to leave me alone."

"It didn't strike your young friends that way tonight," he pointed out.

"Billy Sikes is a very bad apple," she said, sighing. "The rest of them aren't so bad. But Billy's a real troublemaker. His mother died when he was twelve and he's been living on the streets ever since. He never really had a chance."

"My heart bleeds for him." His tone was dry and the look in his eyes said that he thought she was wasting her sympathy. Well, maybe she was but she couldn't help it. Billy had had so few chances to be anything but what he was.

The silence stretched again. Around them, the street had grown darker and Angie jumped when the streetlights came on. A few years ago, someone had done a study and discovered that pink lights were more soothing than the usual white. A well-intentioned city council had voted to replace the standard lights with the softer color, hoping that the gentler illumination would help curb the burgeoning crime rate in the area.

The effect on crime had been negligible. Angie couldn't speak for how a mugger might feel but the pallid pink lighting did nothing to make her rescuer look less tough. If anything, the soft glow only emphasized the hard look of him—and the interesting angles of his face, Angie admitted reluctantly. She cleared her throat.

"Well, thank you again," she said briskly. She hitched her purse strap higher on her shoulder, preparatory to moving on her way.

"I thought you needed a lift to a pay phone."

"It's not that far to walk."

"Far enough for you to get in trouble again. Hop on and I'll give you a lift."

She looked from him to the bike and tried to picture herself perched on the wide seat behind him, her arms wrapped around his waist. She was annoyed at how easily the image came to mind.

"That's okay. I really don't mind walking."

He leaned back against the bike and crossed his arms over his chest and looked at her with those clear green eyes that seemed to see too much.

"There are three alleys between here and the nearest pay phone," he said conversationally. "It's after dark and this is not the sort of neighborhood a woman should be alone in during the day, let alone at night."

"I'll be fine," she said, trying not to notice just how dark the street had gotten. And just what sort of business was he in that he knew exactly how many alleys there were between here and the phone? What sort of business encouraged a man to count alleys?

"If you won't let me give you a lift, I'm going to have to follow along behind you, pushing my bike. It's a big bike. Do you know how much work that's going to be?" His smile was teasing but it didn't hide his determination. He had no intention of leaving her alone.

Angie tried not to feel relieved. She wanted to be annoyed with him for not doing as she'd asked. But the truth was that she was no more anxious to be alone on the sadly misnamed Fair Street than he was to leave her there.

''I suppose, after all the effort you've already expended on my behalf, it would be ungrateful of me to force you to push your bike down the street,'' she said slowly.

''Extremely ungrateful,'' he agreed.

She moved toward the bike. ''As long as you're going to give me a lift, would you mind taking me to the police station? It's only a couple of miles.''

''The police station?'' He straightened away from the bike, his eyes suddenly wary.

''Yes. My brother is a police officer, a detective,'' she added for emphasis. If he'd had any ideas beyond giving her a ride to the phone, hearing that she was a cop's sister would surely discourage them. ''If the police station is a problem, you can just drop me at the pay phone,'' she said.

''It's no problem.'' The light made it difficult to be sure but there seemed to be a gleam of wry humor in his eyes, as if there was some joke only he could see. ''At least if I take you to the station, I can be reasonably sure you're safe.''

Angie's steps slowed. The closer she got, the larger and more intimidating her rescuer and his vehicle seemed. The pinkish glow of the street lamp reflected off the shiny black paint and gleaming chrome of the bike. She eyed it uneasily. Up close it was not quite so easy to picture herself astride it.

"It doesn't bite," he said, reading her doubt.

"Are you sure? It looks like it might have teeth."

"No. Cross my heart."

Angie decided to take his word for it. It was that or walk to a phone after all. And with the last of the sunlight reduced to a hint of red on the horizon, she had no desire to walk anywhere in this neighborhood. Given a choice between the unknown man who'd come to her aid or the well-known hazards of Fair Street, her choice seemed clear.

TRAVIS MORGAN watched the expressions flicker across her face and tried to remember the last time he'd seen anyone whose thoughts were so easy to read. Every emotion was revealed in those big blue eyes—just about the prettiest eyes he'd seen recently, he thought.

And the one pair of eyes he should stay clear of, he reminded himself. He'd heard one of the young punks call her Ms. Brady. Although Brady wasn't exactly a rare name, he was willing to bet that this particular Ms. Brady was Clay Brady's sister. Clay Brady, who just happened to be an officer on the Salem, California, police department. The same Clay Brady who'd probably punch him in the lip just for looking at his sister.

"Here. Put this on." She jumped, those wide-set eyes startled and wary as he moved toward her.

"I don't need that." Her protest was muffled as he set the black helmet on her head. It was too big for her and Travis had to bite back a grin as he looked at her. With those vaguely indignant eyes staring at him from under the raised visor, she looked like a little girl who'd been bullied into playing Darth Vader in the school play.

"I'm sure your brother, the detective, would be happier if you were wearing a helmet," he told her solemnly.

"I'm sure he'd be happier still if I weren't on a motorcycle at all."

"They're much safer than people think." Travis gestured toward the motorcycle. "Your chariot awaits."

A FEW MINUTES LATER, Angie decided that a chariot might have been a safer bet. When her companion straddled the bike and then held his hand out to her, it struck her suddenly that accepting a lift on a motorcycle was hardly the same as accepting a ride in a car. True, it was probably considerably more difficult to ravish someone on a motorcycle, but she didn't believe ravishment was on his agenda anyway. That still left the undeniable intimacy of sharing a motorcycle seat with him.

"Why don't they make motorcycles with a back seat?" she muttered.

"Because they wouldn't look as cool. Give me your hand and just swing your leg over."

Angie set her hand in his, feeling his fingers close over hers. The leather glove was softer and warmer than she'd expected. There was strength in his grip. Considering the ease with which he'd dispatched Billy Sikes and company, she'd been prepared for that strength. What she hadn't been prepared for was the odd little shiver that ran down her spine.

She wanted to attribute that shiver to the cool night air or nerves. But it was June in Southern California and the temperature didn't drop just because the sun had gone down. She might have been able to convince herself that it was nerves that had caused that odd feeling if her eyes hadn't immediately—revealingly—snapped to his.

And saw a quick awareness in his green gaze.

Their eyes held for only a moment, but it was enough to acknowledge the awareness between them. Angie shifted uneasily, tensing as if to draw back but his fingers tightened over her hand, drawing her closer instead.

"There's more room than it seems," he said, pretending not to realize the real reason for her hesitation. "It's a good thing you're wearing jeans. Motorcycles aren't made for skirts."

If there'd been anything remotely personal in his voice, Angie would have jerked her hand away and taken her chances with the familiar dangers of Fair Street. But there was nothing in his tone that even hinted at that brief moment of awareness.

Telling herself that perhaps she'd imagined it, Angie allowed him to draw her forward. Awkwardly she swung her leg over the bike. She settled into the seat with something less than grace and immediately discovered that there was no way to keep a polite distance from her companion. In fact, there was no way to keep any distance at all.

Uneasy at finding herself practically plastered against his back, she scooted back, only to clutch at his waist when he shifted the bike upright and booted up the kickstand.

"Hold on to me and lean when I lean," he ordered.

"I'm not sure—" The engine started with a roar that drowned out the rest of her sentence. She had only a moment to consider the possibility that a previously unknown thread of insanity might run in her family before the bike started with a jerk.

All thoughts of keeping a decorous distance from the man in front of her disappeared instantly. Angie clutched at his waist, pressing herself against his back as if the two of them were intimate friends. The bike roared down the street, pausing at the stop sign on the corner.

"Lean into the turn," he shouted to her over his shoulder. The reminder was unnecessary. Angie was holding him so tightly that she automatically imitated his every move.

They'd gone almost a mile before she dared to open her eyes to see where they were. After years of riding within the safe confines of a car, it was a shock to see the street rushing by so closely. But not an unpleasant shock, she admitted after a moment.

In fact, there was something rather exhilarating about it. Some of that feeling could have been inspired by the man in her arms. Her hold on him tightened as the bike leaned into a turn. If she were forced to be completely honest, she'd have to admit that she didn't feel nearly as wary of him as common sense demanded.

She felt a twinge of regret when the familiar brick police station came into sight. It occurred to her suddenly that he'd known exactly where it was. He hadn't had to ask directions. She pushed aside the thought that he might have a less than desirable reason to be acquainted with the location.

The bike came to a halt in front of the building. When he shut the engine off, the sudden silence was deafening. He pushed the kickstand down and it was only when he moved to get off the bike that Angie remembered to release her hold on his waist.

When she was standing on the pavement, she reached up to remove his helmet, shaking out her hair and giving it a self-conscious pat.

"Thanks for the ride," she said when he showed no signs of speaking.

"My pleasure." He swung his leg over the bike and sat down before taking the helmet from her. In the harsh light in front of the station his hair looked white-blond and cast concealing shadows across his face. "Do you have someone who can take care of your car?"

"Yes. My brother can take a look at it tomorrow." Angie almost regretted answering in the affirmative. If she'd said no, would he have offered to help?

"Oh, yeah. The detective." The curve of his mouth was oddly rueful. "Well, I'd best be on my way." He tugged the helmet on and eased the kickstand up before reaching for the starter.

"Wait." Angie took a step toward him as a sudden thought occurred to her. "I don't even know your name."

The bike was already moving but he glanced back at her.

"Just call me Galahad," he said, his eyes gleaming with laughter beneath the raised visor.

The bike roared off, leaving Angie staring after him.

Chapter Two

"You know, I never thought you'd come back." Bill Shearson leaned back in his seat and studied his companion across the table.

"Guess that's why you're not in the business of making predictions." Travis Morgan's grin was quick and sharp, and it stopped short of his eyes, which remained an icy green.

"Guess so." Shearson laughed and reached for his wine. "I sure thought you were going to stay out once you'd got clear."

"Yeah, well, plans change." Travis shifted restlessly, and glanced around the elegant restaurant. He would have preferred to meet somewhere less public. Didn't Bill know the place was probably crawling with cops, had been since Shearson's limo had pulled up outside?

Travis's mouth twisted ruefully as he reached for his wine. Nothing had changed. Bill undoubtedly knew exactly which of the patrons were actually undercover officers. Hell, he probably had several of them on his payroll. Bill never had been one to hide his light under a barrel. In the old days, Travis had told him more than once that a man in his line of work couldn't afford to be a public figure—it made him too vulnerable. Bill had only laughed and said that's what he hired people like Travis for—to keep him from being too vulnerable.

"So, you're interested in coming home, working for me again?"

Travis dragged his thoughts back to the moment.

"More or less. I can offer you something you want."

"I already have everything I need." Shearson's eyes were cool and watchful in his thin face.

"But you're not getting it at the price I can give you."

"Really?" Shearson turned his wineglass between his fingers, his eyes on the idle movement. "And where would you be getting such a good price?"

"If I told you that, you'd have no reason to deal with me, now would you?" Travis's grin was feral, his eyes ice-cold.

"We've known each other a long time, Travis. I'd think you'd have learned that you can trust me."

"I've known you long enough to know better." There was no malice in the words, only hard fact.

Anger flared in Shearson's eyes and for a moment, Travis thought his bluntness might have cost him the deal. But Shearson grinned suddenly.

"You always were too damned honest for your own good, Travis. I've missed that these past ten years."

"I bet you have." Travis took a quick sip of wine and met the other man's eyes. "Are you interested or not?"

"Maybe. But I didn't get where I am by being in a hurry." He studied Travis through narrowed eyes.

"I'm surprised. You would never have anything to do with that end of the business. Why the change?"

"Ten years is a long time." Travis hunched his shoulders in a careless shrug. "Things change. So do people."

"I suppose they do."

Travis met the other man's eyes coolly, allowing no sign of the churning in his gut to show in his expression. This was the first step in getting what he wanted. He had to gain Shearson's trust, the way he'd had it ten years ago.

"An acquaintance saw you at the police station two days ago," Shearson said suddenly. Despite his casual tone, he was watching Travis carefully. "With a young lady."

"Yeah." Travis added nothing to the flat agreement. He wondered if the "acquaintance" was a cop on Shearson's payroll.

"A cop's sister, I believe?"

"So she said."

"Isn't that an odd choice of companions at this point in your life?"

"There were some punks hassling her. I helped her out." Travis shrugged to show how unimportant the incident had been.

"The knight errant?" Shearson raised one brow in mocking question.

"That's me, all right. Galahad." Travis had a sudden memory of saying the same thing to Angie just before he'd ridden off. Odd, how those big blue eyes had lingered in his mind. He shrugged off the memory. "Do you want what I have? Or do I look around for another buyer?"

"Where's your patience, Travis? You know I don't work like that. I'll need a little time to consider."

Time. A commodity Travis didn't want to spend. But something in Shearson's expression told him not to push. Not right now.

"Fine. I'll be in town for a while. I'm sure you know where to find me."

"I know where to find just about anything and anyone," Shearson said lightly.

Was there a veiled warning there? Travis wondered. He slid out of the booth after politely refusing Shearson's dinner invitation. This wasn't his kind of place. And he wasn't crazy about having dinner under the watchful eye of the local police, either. Shearson might enjoy being the center of attention but he was more comfortable in the shadows.

ANGIE GLANCED at the cloud-filled sky and then looked hopefully down the street. But there was no sign of her brother's car. What a day for Clay to be late. Of course, in all fairness, it wasn't his fault that a freak summer rainstorm had made an appearance. But it would have been nice if, just this once, he could have been on time.

She glanced over her shoulder at the clinic door. She could wait inside, out of the damp, but if she went back in Dr. Johnson was sure to seize the opportunity to ask her to help out—just for a few more minutes. Before she knew it, she'd find herself working until the clinic closed at seven-thirty. Hugh Johnson was a terrific doctor and she admired the dedication that led him to spend so many hours at the clinic but the man didn't understand the meaning of the words "time to go home."

Angie edged a little farther away from the glass door, preferring to take her chances with the unseasonable rain rather than risk being dragged back inside. She shifted her purse strap higher on her shoulder and peered down the street again. There was still no sign of Clay's car. A bright red 1957 T-Bird was hard to miss, especially in a neighborhood where the rusting hulks outnumbered the functioning vehicles.

A glance at her watch confirmed that Clay was overdue by a good half hour. If it were anyone but her older brother, she would have been worried. But this was Clay. Their father used to claim that being two weeks late at birth had set a precedent that Clay had never managed to overcome.

Any minute now, he'd show up, his hair disheveled, his expression harassed, full of apologies for keeping her waiting. If Angie had been a little less tired and a little less damp, the thought would have made her smile. As it was, it made her want to smack him over the head as soon as she saw him. She'd give him another ten minutes and then she was going to risk going back into the clinic to call a cab. One thing was certain, she wasn't going to walk to the nearest pay phone.

Not that last week's adventure hadn't had its interesting side, she thought with a smile. It wasn't every day that she was rescued by a man who said his name was Galahad. A man with eyes the color of pale emeralds. She'd half expected him to turn up at the clinic but she refused to admit to any feeling of disappointment when he hadn't. Maybe she imagined that spark of awareness that had seemed to flash between them. She frowned into the rain that was starting to drift down. No, she didn't think she'd imagined it. And she was almost positive that he'd felt it, too.

She sighed and pulled the edges of her light jacket closer together. It was just as well he hadn't shown up again. Considering the neighborhood and the look of him, he was probably something less than a respectable citizen. Respectable citizens generally didn't know how to defend themselves quite as well as he had.

It was a pity that none of the respectable men she knew had managed to spark more than the most anemic interest in her. And the first man in ages to send tingles up her spine had obviously forgotten her the minute he drove off.

ACTUALLY Travis hadn't forgotten her. She had, in fact, lingered in his thoughts a great deal more than he liked. It had required a considerable exercise of willpower to resist the urge to drop by the Fair Street Clinic to see if she looked as pretty in a uniform as she did in jeans.

Resist it he had, reminding himself that this was not the time to be getting involved with anyone, let alone a cop's sister. Even without Shearson's interest in their meeting, he didn't need to get involved with Clay Brady's sister. Not now. Not ever.

When he saw her standing in front of the worn brick building that housed the clinic, he reminded himself again of all the reasons it would be a mistake to pursue an acquaintance with Angie Brady. She was pressed against the wall, the narrow overhang of the roof offering scant shelter from the light drizzle.

Her car was probably still in the shop, he thought. Well, it wasn't his problem. It was also none of his business. Which didn't explain why, when he should have turned left, he found himself turning right into the clinic's tiny parking area.

Travis was still arguing with himself over the foolishness of the move while the Harley was bumping over the cracked pavement. He was mentally running through all the reasons why he should keep a healthy distance between himself and Angie Brady when he stopped the bike next to her and shut the engine off.

They stared at each other in the sudden silence. It wasn't possible but it seemed as if her eyes were even bigger and bluer than he'd remembered. And her hair was the same shining gold that he remembered seeing in pictures of angels. If ever there was someone who had no business consorting with angels, it was him. Especially such a tempting angel.

"Hi."

"Hello." Angie wondered if it was possible that she'd conjured him up out of her imagination just by thinking about him.

"Car still on the blink?" He reached up to lift the helmet from his head, propping it on one hip as he looked at her.

"The mechanic had to send for a part." She curled her fingers against the shocking urge to reach out and comb them through his hair, which had been flattened by the helmet.

"Is somebody picking you up?"

"My brother. But he's late."

"The detective? I'm shocked. What's the police department coming to?" His expression remained solemn but his eyes were smiling.

"I'm afraid the police department isn't to blame.

Clay has been late for everything since birth. He was late for that, too.''

There was a mutter of thunder and the rain increased. Angie glanced up at the sky and then looked back at the man in front of her. The gray atmosphere made his eyes seem almost emerald in contrast.

''You're getting wet,'' she pointed out.

''If it rains any harder, that roof isn't going to be enough to keep you dry.''

She shrugged. ''I can always go back inside.''

Travis nodded. Of course she could go inside. It wasn't as if she was an orphan of the storm. *You've stopped and said hello. Now, put your helmet back on and be on your way.*

''Want a ride?'' *Now; why on earth had he said that?*

''If it's not too much trouble.'' *Why don't you just throw yourself at him, Angie? I mean, don't give him a chance to change his mind or anything.*

''I just have to leave a message for my brother,'' she said.

''Sure. I'm not going anywhere.'' Travis hoped she didn't notice the touch of wry humor in his voice. Of course, he wasn't going anywhere. He was too stupid to do something that intelligent. Well, he'd just give her a lift home and then leave. No more contact. No harm done.

Angie was almost surprised to see him waiting when she stepped out of the clinic. Something in his expression had made her think that he half regretted his offer of a ride. She glanced up the street, not sure whether she hoped to see Clay's little red T-Bird or not. It was surely tempting fate to accept a ride from this man twice. She didn't even know his name, for heaven's sake.

"I don't know your name." She blurted it out as she stopped beside the bike. "I mean, I don't know your real name."

"You don't believe I'm Galahad?" he asked. "I'm crushed." But his eyes were laughing at her again and Angie found her uneasiness dissolving. It was simply impossible to be afraid of a man who could laugh without changing expression.

"I suppose your friends all call you Gal," she suggested, raising her brows.

"Not unless they want extensive dental work," he said, dryly. "Travis. Travis Morgan. At your service." He tugged off his glove and offered his hand with an air of formality that was at odds with his faded jeans and black leather jacket.

"Angie Brady."

His fingers closed over hers. The first time he'd taken her hand, she'd felt a tingle of awareness, even through the leather of his glove. But it was nothing compared to the feel of his bare skin against hers. She'd never thought of a handshake as a particularly intimate act. But then she'd never shaken hands with anyone and felt as if she'd just touched a live electrical wire.

She kept her eyes on their linked hands, afraid of what she might see in his gaze. Afraid of what she might *not* see. How embarrassing if she was the only one to feel this odd connection when she touched him. But she didn't think that was the case, not if she could judge by the way his fingers lingered around hers. A slight breathless feeling remained when he released her hand.

Be careful, she cautioned herself. *It's one thing to be attracted to the man. But she couldn't forget that she knew almost nothing about him. And what she did know, hardly suggested that he was a model citizen.*

"Here." Travis lifted his helmet and set it on her head. "If you're going to make a habit of this, I'm going to have to get an extra helmet," he murmured, his hand brushing her chin as he threaded the strap through the rings that secured it.

Angie said nothing, hoping he couldn't somehow read her mind to discover that the idea of "making a habit of this" held more appeal than it should have.

"Okay, you know the drill." Travis held out his hand and edged forward on the seat, giving her room to swing her leg over. As soon as she was settled into place, he was reminded of all the reasons why he shouldn't have stopped in the first place.

Flicking the engine on, he tried not to think about the feel of her pressed so cozily against his back. Or about how nice her arms felt circling his waist. And he wanted to believe it was his imagination that made him think he could smell a delicate perfume drifting from her skin. The kind of scent that made a man think of cool linens and hot summer nights.

Glancing at the sky, Travis wondered if there was any chance for a little sleet. Maybe that would cool his libido. The rain didn't seem to be doing the trick.

Sleet in June was too much to ask for but by the time they'd reached the end of the block, the light rain had turned into a heavy shower. Before they'd gone two miles, Angie was soaked to the skin. The helmet kept her hair dry but it didn't do anything for the rest of her.

Not that she cared. The temperature might be unseasonably cool but she'd never felt warmer. *Shared body heat,* she told herself firmly. That's all it was. But that theory didn't account for the sort of tingle she felt where her hands were pressed against his stomach. She had the urge to curl her fingers into the leather of his jacket, to feel the skin and muscle beneath.

She flushed and tried to turn her thoughts in another more suitable, direction. Such as what she was going to fix for dinner. It was her turn to cook and the weather suggested something a little more warming than sandwiches. Spaghetti? Clay would enjoy that.

Just what did Travis look like without the bulky jacket? Without a shirt? Was he as leanly muscled as he felt? Was his chest smooth or covered in crisply curling hair?

How had she gotten from pasta to chest hair?

Angie was grateful that there was no one to see her reddened cheeks. Holding Travis around the waist seemed almost as dangerous as letting go and risking a fall from the speeding bike. She'd never, in all her twenty-five years, had such thoughts about a man she barely knew. Or about one she *did* know, for that matter.

Lightning cracked, followed by a low roll of thunder and Angie suddenly found herself grinning. There was something about the scene—the motorcycle, the man, even the rain—that made her feel like someone altogether different from the sane, steady woman she'd always considered herself to be. She felt wilder, freer, more exciting somehow. It was a rather nice change. She tightened her hold on his waist and allowed herself to enjoy the wet ride.

Travis followed her shouted instructions, finally stopping the bike in front of a clapboard house that had been painted pale yellow. The house was old by Southern California standards—1920s, he guessed. With its wide front porch and crisp white trim, it would have looked perfectly at home in a small town somewhere in the Midwest.

It was exactly the kind of house he'd imagined Angie living in. Unpretentious but solid and sturdy. The kind of place where you expected to find grandparents rocking on the porch, watching their grandchildren play on the lawn.

But there were no grandparents in the Brady family. Travis had done his research and he knew the current generation was all there was. Just Brady and his sister. The same sister about whom he was having completely inappropriate thoughts. The kind of thoughts that could get him in trouble.

"Let me give you a hand." He reached back and took Angie's hand, trying not to notice the way her body slid against his as she eased off the bike.

Standing beside the motorcycle, Angie tugged off the helmet and shook her hair out. The rain had eased, at least for the moment, becoming little more than a light mist. A mist that caught all too invitingly in the pale gold of Angie's hair.

"Would you like a cup of coffee?"

"I doubt that your brother, the detective, would think it was a good idea."

"Clay would be the first to agree that a cup of coffee is the least I can offer." Travis hadn't seen Clay in years but he felt safe in predicting that he wasn't likely to agree to any such thing. "After all, you got soaked doing me a favor. Besides, he was the one who should have given me a ride home. So the offer should actually come from him.''

Travis doubted that Brady would be inclined to offer him anything more than the shortest path to the door. Not that he could blame him. If it were his sister, he'd feel the same way. Brady didn't have anything to worry about, of course. He knew well enough that he had no business pursuing Angie, especially not at this point in his life.

''Coffee sounds pretty close to heaven right now,'' he heard himself saying. But not nearly as close as her smile.

He followed her up a cement walkway made uneven by time and the roots of the massive coast oak that dominated the front yard. She was wearing jeans again and he allowed his eyes to linger on the feminine sway of her hips. That enticing movement made it difficult to remember all the excellent reasons why he shouldn't even be talking to her, let alone having coffee with her.

Rather than going in the front door, Angie led him around the side of the house to another door. Somehow, it felt just right to step into a big country kitchen. It looked like the kind of house where the kitchen would be the real center of the home.

Angie pushed open the door and stepped onto the polished wooden floor. She shrugged out of her light jacket and then turned to see that Travis was still standing on the step.

''Come on in. Don't worry about getting water on the floor. The finish is so tough I don't think anything short of an atomic blast would hurt it. I'll put some water on to boil.''

Travis hesitated another instant before stepping inside and shutting the windowed door behind him. After the cool dampness outside, the warmth of the room enveloped him as if it were a cozy blanket.

An old hunger washed over him, a hunger he'd thought long dead. When he was younger, before life knocked most of the dreams out of him, he'd fantasized about a room like this, a place that smelled of home. A place that felt warm and secure. The kind of place that practically demanded that you sink roots and build something worthwhile.

It had been a long time since he'd thought about those dreams, but they'd been niggling at the back of his mind ever since meeting Angie Brady. Which was another good reason to keep his distance from her.

"Nice house." He moved farther into the kitchen, stopping next to the oak island that sat in the middle of the room.

"My grandfather built it in 1925. Did most of the work himself." Angie's pride was obvious.

Travis leaned his hip against the island and watched as she moved around the kitchen, putting coffee in a filter and getting out mugs. It was a charmingly domestic scene. The sort he'd seen in movies but of which he'd never been a part.

When his parents were still alive, they'd spent most of their time traveling. He couldn't remember ever seeing his mother in a kitchen. He doubted if she'd have known what to do if she found herself in one. After their death in a car crash when he was twelve, he'd gone to live with his grandfather. It simply wasn't possible to picture Hiram Morgan in a scene of such cozy domesticity. Actually the word cozy and his grandfather seemed mutually exclusive.

"Have you been in Salem long?" Angie's question

dragged Travis back to the present. He blinked, banishing the memory of his grandfather's large and chilly home.

"How do you know I haven't lived here all my life?" His tone was edgier than it should have been but he found himself wondering just how much she knew about him. Had she mentioned him to her brother? Had Clay somehow recognized the description?

"I've never seen you." If Angie noticed anything unusual in his voice, her expression didn't show it. She settled on a stool across the work island from him and fixed him with those wide blue eyes that made him think of angels and church choirs and, incongruously enough, candlelit bedrooms and slow kisses.

"Do you know everyone who lives in Salem?" A raised brow emphasized the question.

"No, but I don't think I could have missed you all these years." She flushed suddenly, realizing how her words sounded. Travis's grin told her that he hadn't missed the implication that she found him memorable. "The coffee must be almost ready," she announced briskly.

Travis waited while she poured two cups of coffee. He tugged off his gloves and placed them on the counter before taking a thick mug from her. If he noticed that she was careful to keep from brushing his fingers, she couldn't tell.

"Actually I used to live here. When I was a kid. But I left years ago. Haven't been back since." It was the truth, as far as it went. He cradled the mug between his palms and smiled at her.

"It's just that your motorcycle is so distinctive. I'm

sure I'd have noticed it." *Right, Angie. As if you know a Harley Davidson from a Honda.* But Travis nodded as if willing to take her explanation at face value.

"Have you lived here all your life?"

"Except for the years I spent in college in San Diego. I suppose that seems strange these days. No one stays in the town where they were born."

"I think it sounds rather nice. It's good to have roots."

Was it her imagination or was there a trace of regret in his voice? As if he'd never had roots?

"Where are you from originally?" she asked, taking a sip of her coffee. It was a classic question in California, where almost everyone was originally from somewhere else.

"Nowhere, really. My parents traveled a lot. I was born in Africa."

"Africa?" She set her cup down and looked at him, forgetting her nervousness at this piece of information. "How long did you live there?"

"Less than a year. My earliest memories are of a station in the Australian outback. My father had decided to raise sheep. But we left before I turned five. From there, it was an ostrich farm in Wyoming. Or it might have been the botanical trek into the Himalayas. I'm not sure just what order they came in."

"It sounds fascinating."

"It had its moments," Travis admitted.

"Where else did you live?" she asked.

"It might be easier to remember where we *didn't* live. It wasn't as romantic as it sounds. A lot of the places were full of insects big enough to carry off a small animal. And the sanitation tended to be primitive, if there was any at all."

"But think of all the things you got to see," she protested. She set her elbow on the counter and leaned her chin in her palm. "And children never care about details like sanitation. They're usually quite content with the most disgusting arrangements."

"True. But I did occasionally think one of the bugs might just carry me off."

"You must have had some wonderful experiences," she said wistfully. Her eyes, as well as her words, invited him to continue talking.

Travis sipped his coffee, stalling for time. Actually he'd already told her more than most people who'd known him for years knew. There was something about those wide blue eyes that made it easy to forget the habits of a lifetime.

"It's not nearly as interesting as it sounds." He shrugged one shoulder, dismissing his peripatetic childhood. "I always thought it would be exciting to live in one place for more than a year."

"Exciting? I don't think I'd call it that but it has its good points." Angie accepted his change of subject, sensing his uneasiness in talking about himself.

"It can't be too dull or you wouldn't have stayed."

"It isn't dull." And it was showing signs of becoming downright interesting, she thought. "Is that why you came back? To put down roots?"

Roots? Travis doubted he was capable of having such a thing. Roots were for people like Angie, all sunshine and blue eyes.

"More or less," he said and asked another question before she could pursue the issue of why he'd returned to Salem.

She was telling him about her job in the clinic when the door behind him was abruptly pushed open, letting in a wave of cold air. She saw Travis tense and his right hand jerked toward the front of his jacket. It struck her suddenly that he was reaching for a weapon.

"Clay." She blurted out her brother's name, not sure if she was greeting him or warning Travis.

"Angie. What the hell were you doing? Leaving like that? Donna said you left with some guy on a motorcycle. I thought I was supposed to pick you up." Clay's scowling glance went from her to Travis's back.

"I thought you were, too," Angie said as she came around the work island. "After thirty minutes, I began to think you'd forgotten me. When I got an offer of a ride, I took it."

Her eyes met Travis's. His gaze seemed full of regret and an odd sort of acceptance. She had only an instant to wonder why before his expression became shuttered. Moving with deliberation, he set his coffee cup down and turned to face her brother.

"Clay, this is Travis Morgan. He's the man I told you about, the one who came to my rescue last week. He seems to be making a habit of it...." Her voice trailed off when she realized that neither man was listening.

"What are you doing here?" Clay demanded.

"Having a cup of coffee." Travis waved one hand lazily in the direction of the empty mug.

"Get out." The flat command held a threatening undertone.

"Clay!" Angie's shocked protest might have been inaudible for all the attention it drew.

"Not very hospitable, Brady," Travis said.

Angie was almost as bewildered by his reaction as

she was by her brother's hostility. Obviously the two of them knew each other. And Travis didn't seem at all surprised by Clay's attitude.

"Are you leaving or do I have to throw you out?" Clay asked.

"It might be interesting to see you try." Travis straightened away from the counter, a subtle tension in his stance. The change in him was abrupt and frightening. Gone was the man with the smile that started in his eyes. He looked cold and hard. And dangerous. Angie had a sudden image of the ease with which he'd taken care of Billy Sikes and his friends. She didn't know if he'd be able to handle her brother as easily but she had no desire to find out.

"Stop it!" She stepped between the two of them. "No one is going to throw anyone out." She threw her brother a fierce look. "*I* invited him here. And unless something has changed, this is still my home, too."

Clay opened his mouth to argue but Travis forestalled him. "Don't worry about it, Angel. It's not the first time I've been thrown out and it probably won't be the last."

He picked up his gloves from where he'd dropped them on the counter. Clay stepped back as Travis walked to the door. For a moment, the two men stood face-to-face. It seemed to Angie that something passed between them—some masculine understanding. It made her want to smack both of them.

Travis stopped and turned in the doorway. He was looking at Angie but she knew his words were at least partially directed at Clay.

"I'll be seeing you, Angel." A casual wave and he was gone.

There was a moment of silence and then Clay pushed the door shut. The quiet click as it settled into place was more eloquent than a slam. He turned to face her, his even features unusually hard.

"Would you like to tell me just what that was about?" Angie demanded before he could speak.

"Would you like to tell me what Morgan was doing in this house?"

"He was having coffee," she snapped. "Acting like a civilized human being, which is more than I can say for you." She snatched up the empty coffee cups and carried them to the sink, slamming them down with such force that they threatened to shatter against the thick porcelain.

"Since when do you go around inviting men like that home?" Clay demanded.

"Since 'men like that' save me from probable rape and give me rides home in the midst of a downpour." Angie flared, spinning to face him. "Since I'm a big girl and allowed to make my own decisions."

"You don't know him."

"I know that he acted like a perfect gentleman. *He* wasn't the one who stormed in here like…like…some sort of caveman. I've never been so embarrassed in all my life." *Or scared*, she added mentally. There'd been a moment when she'd thought the tense little scene was going to end in violence.

"I didn't mean to embarrass you," Clay said grudgingly.

"Well, you did a damn good job of it. What on earth was the matter with you?"

"I know Morgan."

"No kidding." She widened her eyes in mock surprise. "I'd never have guessed it. Where do you know him from?"

"We went to school together for a few years. Before he dropped out."

"Since when is being a high school dropout a crime?" she asked with heavy sarcasm.

"It's not that." Clay shrugged uneasily. "He had a bad reputation. A lot of girls. There were rumors that he was involved in some pretty ugly things after he left school."

"Rumors," she repeated flatly. "Was he arrested? Did he spend time in jail? Did you actually *see* him doing any of these 'ugly things'?"

"No," he admitted reluctantly.

"Then you don't actually *know* anything?"

"No." The admission was grudging.

"Then what's your problem?"

"He's just not a good person for you to know." He seemed to realize that, as explanations went, this one was more lame than most. "He's a bad man, Angie. In a lot of ways." His eyes met hers. "I don't want you to get hurt."

"That makes two of us." Her expression softened. There was no doubting his concern. His behavior had been unconscionable but she couldn't stay angry with him, not when he was looking at her with so much worry in his eyes.

"Travis has been nothing but kind to me, Clay. I like him." "Like" didn't quite describe the feelings he brought out in her but she wasn't going to go into that with her older brother.

"He's not a good person for you to like, sis. He's dangerous."

"I had a demonstration of that last week," she reminded him. "But I don't think he'd hurt me."

"Not physically. Maybe." It was obvious that only a sense of fair play forced Clay to concede that much.

"Well, it's a bit premature to be worrying about him hurting me in some other fashion. Besides, I probably won't even seen him again."

"Yeah. Probably." The prospect seemed to brighten his mood.

Angie turned back to the sink and twisted the water on. Staring out at the soggy lawn, she wondered if it was too much to hope that fate would throw Travis Morgan into her path a third time.

He was certainly different from anyone she'd ever known. Different and exciting. She'd never imagined herself attracted to a man like Travis—a man with such a dangerous edge. And no matter how much she wanted to dismiss Clay's concerns, she couldn't deny that Travis was dangerous.

It wasn't just the easy way he'd handled Billy Sikes and his gang last week. There was something more subtle than that, some feel about him that suggested he would be a very bad man to cross.

Angie felt a shiver run up her spine. It was not an entirely unpleasant sensation. Dangerous or not, she very much hoped that she hadn't seen the last of Travis Morgan.

Chapter Three

It seemed as if Fate was in a particularly uncooperative mood, Travis thought. Otherwise, why would she have put temptation before him so soon after he'd made up his mind to resist it?

Two days ago, when he'd left the Brady home, he'd decided that he was going to keep plenty of distance between himself and Ms. Angie Brady. The decision had little to do with her brother's hostility. The truth was, if he were her brother, he'd have felt much the same way. He just wasn't the sort of man who had any business hanging around a woman like Angie.

So, he'd had a short struggle with his conscience and decided to do the right thing and keep his distance. After all, how hard could it be? Salem wasn't a booming metropolis but it was hardly a village. In a town this size, it couldn't take much effort to avoid crossing paths with one pretty—okay, very pretty—nurse. Even one with the most beautiful blue eyes he'd ever seen.

But perhaps it was harder than it looked, he thought, slowing the Harley as he passed a supermarket, because getting out of her car and walking toward the store, was none other than the woman he'd promised himself to avoid. It was the first time he'd seen her in daylight without storm clouds softening the light. He couldn't help noticing that the bright sunshine turned her hair to pure gold.

Hardly aware of his actions, Travis turned the bike into the parking lot as Angie entered the store. It wasn't as if he was actually tracking her down, he told himself as he parked the bike. After all, a supermarket was a public place. It was hardly his fault that they happened to be shopping in the same store.

His conscience was still arguing with temptation as he pushed open the door and stepped into the store. It was a losing battle. Temptation won when he pulled a shopping cart out of the row and started through the store. He grabbed an item here and there, more or less at random. He might have to admit to himself that he'd come into the store in pursuit of Angie, but he didn't have to admit it to her. An empty cart would be a dead giveaway.

He swung around the end of the cereal aisle and stopped. Angie was studying a box of cereal, a small frown pleating her forehead. She was beautiful. She was wearing a soft dress in a blue that almost matched the color of her eyes. Her hair was caught at her nape by a chunky white clip. She looked fresh and beautiful.

And like someone who should have nothing to do with a man like himself.

He should just walk away here and now before she saw him. He'd been right to decide to stay away from her. Just as her brother had been right to tell him to get out. If he had any sense of decency, he'd stay far away—for her sake, even more than his own.

ANGIE GLANCED UP, startled, as another cart bumped solidly against hers. She felt her heart give a similar bump when she saw who the careless driver was. Travis Morgan was leaning on the handle of the other cart, grinning at her. Her fingers tightened on the cereal box, denting the cardboard.

"Hi." She could only hope that her voice didn't sound as breathless as she felt.

"Hi."

Maybe Clay was right. Maybe Travis was a bad man. Certainly there had to be something not entirely good about a man who could make a woman feel shaken and breathless in the middle of a brightly lit supermarket.

"What are you doing here?" she asked and then immediately wished she could recall the question. *What did a person usually do in a supermarket?*

"Just picking up a few things."

"Me, too." Angie swallowed and made a conscious effort to drag her eyes away from his face.

"This is rather far from home for you, isn't it?" Travis commented.

"Yes." She stared at the brightly colored box in her hands, wondering what had happened to her brain. It didn't seem to be working very well. "Actually I'm picking up some things for a local family. The Aggrettis?" She glanced at Travis to see if the name meant anything to him, hoping it wouldn't. He frowned.

"Isn't there a Tony Aggretti who runs with that lout, Billy Sikes, the one who was hassling you?"

"Tony's not a bad kid," Angie said quickly. "He's just a little mixed up at the moment."

"So was Charles Manson," Travis said cynically.

"Are you planning on taking these things to the kid's family?"

"Yes. Mrs. Aggretti can't leave the little ones."

"And I suppose they live in a lovely, safe neighborhood?" His lifted brows conveyed his doubts about that possibility.

"Actually they live in an apartment on Fifth Street." Angie lifted her chin, waiting for the argument he was undoubtedly about to give her. Fifth Street was lined with shabby buildings and even shabbier people. Muggings were so common that the victims generally didn't bother reporting them to the police.

"I was afraid of that." Travis gave her a look of exaggerated resignation. "I'll go with you."

Braced for him to try to talk her out of going, Angie was momentarily thrown off balance by his offer.

"You don't have to do that," she said automatically.

"Sure, I do. If I don't got, I'll spend the rest of my life feeling guilty for letting you go alone."

"The rest of your life?" Angie arched her brow doubtfully.

"Certainly." He gave her a wounded look that was so exaggerated, it made her laugh. It also made her give up the argument. It wasn't as if she had any real objection to his joining her.

THEY TOOK HER CAR, which she'd gotten back from the shop the day before. Travis folded his long legs into the passenger side of her compact without complaint. The little car put them practically shoulder to shoulder. Angie felt a warmth that had nothing to do with the fact that the car had been sitting in the sun.

Fifth Street was just as bad as she remembered. She wedged her car into a parking place between the rust-pitted hulk of a Ford and a shiny green Cadillac that had probably been paid for with drug money. Half a dozen young toughs lounged on the steps of nearby apartment buildings, eyeing the newcomers with sullen interest. "I hope you don't expect to see your tires when you come back out," Travis commented as he reached for the door handle.

"They won't bother my car," she said easily. "They know who I am, that I work at the clinic. They'll leave it alone."

"Right. Just like Sikes left you alone." The look he threw her spoke volumes.

"Billy Sikes is an exception. Most of the people around here know how important the clinic is. They may need us. No one wants to force us to close shop."

She slid out of the car and then leaned in to pull a sack of groceries out of the tiny back seat. After a moment, Travis followed suit. He wrapped his fist around the upper edge of the second bag and lifted it out. Let it seem like coincidence that he was keeping his right hand free. Angie might think that being a nurse gave her some sort of protection but he didn't share her confidence.

He watched her circle around the front of the car, her steps as cool and confident as if she was walking through a shopping mall. She nodded and smiled at a particularly tough-looking youth.

"How's your sister, Joseph?"

"She's doin' fine. Carrying a 4.0 average this year." His swarthy face broke into a boyish smile, and Travis revised his age estimate. Joseph couldn't be more than twenty-one or -two. Life had added years to his face.

"That's great. You tell her I said hello."

"I will, Miss Brady."

"Miss Brady?" Travis questioned as they entered the shabby apartment building. "He calls you Miss Brady?"

"His sister almost died as a result of a botched abortion. I stopped the hemorrhaging."

Travis followed her into the poorly lit stairwell. "And she's in college now?"

"In Los Angeles. She wants to be an architect."

Travis wondered how a girl raised in surroundings completely devoid of architectural inspiration should have such a dream.

"A scholarship?" he asked, trying not to wince as Angie started up a second flight of stairs.

"Partial. Joseph is picking up the slack."

"Drugs?" He felt her glance at him, as if trying to judge his feelings. He hitched the grocery sack into a better position and pretended to concentrate on the stairs.

"Not Joseph," she said emphatically. "There aren't many ways to make money around here but he's a hustler. He's doing the best he can with what life's handed him. Not like those damn parasites who bring drugs into neighborhoods like this, preying on those who live in poverty and despair."

Their arrival at the top of the stairs spared Travis having to come up with an answer. What could he have said? he wondered. Just what he needed—a woman on crusade against drugs. Damn, but he had enough complications in his life without adding Angie Brady to the list. As soon as she'd done her good deed and given the food to the Aggrettis, he was going to walk out of her life and *this* time, he was going to *stay* out.

THERE WAS definitely something wrong with the basic communications lines between his brain and his mouth, Travis thought. His brain was saying *keep your distance* and his mouth said *we could pick up some sandwiches and have lunch in the park.* The worst part of it was that he couldn't seem to regret the foolishness as much as he should.

There was something about Angie that put a dent in what had been—up until now—his excellent self-discipline. He'd come back to Salem for a purpose, one he couldn't afford to lose sight of. If there was one thing he knew how to do, it was stick to a purpose. He was nothing like his parents, always drifting from one scheme to another, never staying in one place long enough to finish what they'd started. He'd even been told a time or two that he was annoyingly single-minded.

So where did all that single-mindedness go when he was around Angie Brady?

"I haven't been here in ages. I'd forgotten how pretty it was."

Angie's remark drew Travis away from his brooding thoughts. He followed her gaze around the park. It *was* a pretty scene. It was early enough in summer that the foliage on the huge old sycamores was still fresh and green. There was still a shallow flow of water in the small stream that ran through the middle of the grassy park.

Later in the summer, the leaves would grow tired and dull and the stream would dry up. By late July, everything would be somnolent from the heat, dozing in the sun and waiting for the fall rains to start California's second cycle of growth.

"Hello? Did you fall asleep on me?" Angie's teasing question made him realize that he'd been staring at a particularly ancient sycamore. He shook off his uncharacteristically philosophical mood and turned to look at her.

"I was just thinking that I should have picked up a couple more of those brownies," he said easily.

"Not for me." Angie shook her head. "I couldn't eat another bite."

"Lightweight," he scoffed gently. He eased back until he was braced on his elbows and grinned at her. "You'd never win a pie eating contest."

"Fortunately for me, there aren't any coming up." Angie grinned at him.

He hadn't planned to ask her on a picnic, she thought. It was hard to say who'd been more surprised to hear the words coming out of his mouth. If he could have snatched them back, he would have and she knew it. A woman with any pride would have turned him down. Until recently, she would have said she had more than her fair share of pride. But there was something about Travis that made pride seem a bit less important than it had.

She shifted her position on the blanket until she could lean her back against a conveniently placed tree trunk and allowed her eyes to settle on the man in question. He was watching a mother playing with a toddler on the swing set at the other end of the park and it seemed safe enough to let her gaze linger on his profile.

She couldn't have said just what it was about him

that made it so easy to ignore her common sense
whenever he was around. Certainly he was an attractive man but she'd met other attractive men and her
heart hadn't beat any faster. There was something else
about him. He was so different from anyone else
she'd ever known. There was an edge to him, a tension that drew her in a way she'd never experienced.

But it wasn't just his green eyes or the air of danger
that attracted her. It was something a little harder to
dismiss.

"I saw you slip money to Mrs. Aggretti," she told
him. "That was very nice of you."

"It was nothing." He sat up, hunching his shoulders uneasily under the soft cotton of his shirt. "Just
a few bucks."

"Well, it's more than she had."

"Where's her husband?"

"He left her just before the baby was born. Ran
off with a waitress from the topless bar where he was
working. No one has heard from him since."

"He ought to be shot," Travis growled.

"I'll provide the bullets," she said in agreement.
She leaned forward, drawing her knees up under her
full skirt and wrapping her arms around them. The
problems of the Aggretti family really touched him.
It didn't fit with the leather jacketed, tough guy image
he projected. And it didn't fit with what Clay had said
about him.

"Clay told me I should stay away from you." She
hadn't realized what she was going to say until she
heard the words coming out. She watched Travis,
waiting for some reaction. Other than a slight deepening of the lines around his mouth, there was nothing
to be seen.

"He's probably right," he said after a moment. He glanced at her, his eyes expressionless.

"Why?" Angie frowned, annoyed by his casual response.

"Didn't he tell you why?" He reached for the leather jacket he'd discarded earlier. Angie had the strange thought that he was reaching for armor of a sort, as if the tough looking jacket shielded him from more than just a cool breeze. She caught hold of it, preventing him from putting it on.

"He said you were a bad man for a woman to know. He seemed to think you'd hurt me. I think he's wrong," she added boldly, only just then making up her mind.

Reluctantly Travis lifted his eyes to her face. Hurt her? Not willingly. But that didn't mean she wouldn't get hurt anyway. The nature of his business was such that anyone who cared about him was at risk.

"Clay said that the two of you were in school together." Angie waited for his response.

"I wouldn't put it quite that way," he said, his mouth twisting dryly. "We went to the same school for a couple of years but we hardly ran in the same crowd." He shrugged. "It was a long time ago."

"Are you wanted by the police?" The stark question drew a grim laugh from him.

"I'm not dodging arrest warrants, if that's what you mean."

"But the police are interested in you?"

"It's hard to say who they'll take an interest in," he said evasively. His eyes dropped to where her fingers were curled over the sleeve of his jacket. Her nails were cut short and unpolished. Her hands were small but there was strength in them. They were the sort of hands a man could trust. At least they would be if he could afford to trust anyone.

"You should listen to your brother, Angel." He released his hold on the jacket to take her hand in his. Running his thumb over the back of her hand, he looked for the right words to make her see how impossible a relationship between them would be.

"I've never listened to Clay before," she said lightly. "I don't see any reason to break a family tradition now."

"Some traditions are meant to be broken." But her words drew a reluctant smile from him. There was something very appealing about her determined optimism. He suspected if she were faced with a handful of lemons, Angie would do her damnedest to make lemonade. And probably succeed. But it would take more than a scoopful of sugar to sweeten his life.

"I don't think you're as bad as you'd like people to believe," she said. Tilting her head consideringly, she studied him. Travis shifted uneasily under that interested blue gaze. It made him feel like an unusual species of insect being studied beneath a microscope.

"Maybe I'm a lot worse than you think," he suggested, only half joking.

"I don't think so. I think you put up that bad boy front to keep people at a distance."

Travis moved so quickly that she had time for only a startled gasp before she found herself lying flat on her back in the cool grass. Travis's wide shoulders loomed over her, blocking out the leafy canopy above them.

"You shouldn't be so trusting," he snapped.

"Why not?" She stared up at him, her eyes startled but without fear.

Travis ground his teeth together. What was wrong with her? Any normal woman would have been trembling with fear right now. Didn't she know how vulnerable she was? How easily he could hurt her? She barely knew him. She had no business looking up at him with those big blue eyes as if she hadn't a fear in the world. His hands gentled on her arms.

"What am I going to do with you?"

"Do you have to do anything?" She reached up to brush a lock of dark gold hair from his forehead, something she'd been tempted to do almost from the moment they met.

His quick move had startled her more than she'd let on. For a moment, she'd been reminded of his capacity for violence. But it had only been for a moment. Somewhere inside her there was a deep certainty that he wouldn't hurt her. It wasn't based on logic, and it certainly wasn't based on extensive experience with the man. Logic and experience both suggested that she heed her brother's warning and keep a safe distance.

"Don't you have any sense of self-preservation?" There was an almost pleading note in the question.

"You make me sound like a gazelle trying to make friends with a tiger."

"That's not so far off," he muttered. But his eyes drifted to where the dappled sunlight turned her hair to patchy gold and convincing her to stay away from him suddenly didn't seem quite so important. It seemed more important that, even in shadow, her eyes were a clear and shining blue.

He lowered his head toward hers, seeing awareness flare in her eyes. Her fingers dug into the muscles of his upper arms, not in protest, but in approval.

''You shouldn't let me kiss you,'' he told her, his mouth a heartbeat away from hers.

''Who says I'm going to?'' she whispered breathlessly.

''Your eyes say it for you.''

Her mouth was as soft as he'd imagined it to be. Soft and warm and welcoming. Her lips carried the taste of the orange soda she'd had with lunch. Travis hadn't realized how good the sweet drink tasted until he drank it from Angie's lips. It was possible that heaven tasted like Orange Crush.

Or maybe heaven just tasted like Angie Brady, he decided, tilting his head to deepen the kiss. His tongue feathered over her lower lip and he felt more than heard her soft sigh of surrender. Her hands tightened on his arms as her mouth opened for him. Paradise beckoned. And he hadn't the strength to turn his back on it.

''Morgan.'' The voice shattered the fragile moment.

Angie felt the impact of the single word strike Travis. For a split second, he remained frozen and then his head came up, his eyes meeting hers for an instant before he rolled away from her. The move brought him to his feet, as graceful as a hunting cat.

Dazed by the abrupt change of mood, Angie sat up. She pushed her hair back from her face and looked at the two men who'd interrupted them. They were standing a few feet away, their backs to the sun, making them little more than bulky silhouettes to her.

''We got a message for you.'' It was the one on the left who spoke. Though the words were innocuous enough, there was menace in his tone.

''You could have sent a card,'' Travis said lightly.

"It's the kind of message better delivered in person," the other man told him. Angie was glad that the light prevented her from seeing his face. She had the feeling that he was smiling and she didn't think it was a particularly pleasant expression.

"Travis?" She scrambled to her feet and edged closer to him, looking for some reassurance in his eyes. It was odd how the temperature had suddenly dropped. The park that had been so pleasantly quiet a few minutes ago now seemed ominously isolated.

"Perhaps your lady friend would like to go home," the stranger suggested politely.

"I'm not going anywhere," Angie snapped, taking hold of Travis's sleeve. Whatever they had in mind, surely they wouldn't do anything as long as she was there.

"Go home, Angie." Travis lifted her hand from his arm. "Go home."

"Come with me." She lowered her voice to a whisper, looking at him with pleading eyes.

"I have business to take care of," he said, shaking his head.

"I don't think they brought their briefcases," she muttered, casting an uneasy look at the two men.

His mouth twisted in a half smile but the humor didn't reach his eyes. "Go on. It's okay."

Angie wanted to argue but she couldn't fight the command in his eyes. He looked every inch the man Clay had warned her against. The cold in his eyes sent a shiver up her spine, even though the look wasn't intended for her.

She bent down and scooped up the old blanket they'd used for their picnic and bundled it over her arm. She cast a last, uneasy look at Travis, wishing he'd leave with her, and at the same time, half frightened by the abrupt change in his expression.

Turning away, she hurried toward the car, trying not to consider that Clay might have been right. Maybe Travis Morgan *was* more than she could handle.

Chapter Four

She really didn't know Travis Morgan well enough to be worried about him, Angie reminded herself as she squinted at the faded numbers on the crumbling curbs. Their acquaintance had been eventful but brief. She knew little more about him than his name and that his parents had traveled a lot when he was young.

So the concern she felt wasn't a really *personal* kind of thing, she assured herself for at least the tenth time. She was a nurse. A certain *impersonal* concern was a natural part of her job. She just wanted to make sure he was all right. It was practically her duty, she reminded herself.

It had been three days since she and Travis had shared their picnic. Three days since she'd left him alone with those two large and distinctly hostile-looking men in dark suits.

She felt as if her life had changed in some subtle way—as if she'd changed since she met him. What was she doing? she asked herself. She was practically chasing after a man she hardly knew. But she didn't turn the car around.

Angie edged her little compact next to the curb and got out. Standing beside the car, she shaded her eyes with her hand and studied the shabby little house before her. There was nothing to distinguish it from the houses around it. The paint was peeling and the roof had an uneasy sag in the middle. The old wooden window frames had enough coats of paint to make opening them an unlikely prospect. The lawn still showed traces of green but by midsummer it would be the same tawny color as its neighbors.

The only incongruous note in the whole picture of age and decay was the solid new door on the garage. Angie smiled when she saw it. Typical of a man to add a new garage door to protect his motorcycle and let the house continue to slide into ruin. She hoped the motorcycle was all that door was protecting.

She frowned as she turned back to the car to get her tote bag. It wouldn't do to forget how little she knew about Travis. This part of town was only slightly less known for its drug problems than the area where the Aggrettis lived.

But if Travis were involved in drugs, Clay would know and he would have used words a little stronger than "bad" to describe him. Whatever his objection to Travis, she was reasonably sure that it wasn't because Travis was a criminal.

Carrying the tote bag, she made her way up the cement walk. Age and the tree roots had buckled the pavement, making it necessary to pay close attention to where she stepped. The need didn't disappear when she reached the porch steps. They had sags to match the one in the roof and Angie tested each one before trusting her weight to it.

Standing at last before the front door, she drew a deep breath and reminded herself that there was no reason she shouldn't be there. The mental pep talk did little to still the butterflies in her stomach but, ignoring them, she rapped her knuckles against the door and waited.

She'd almost decided that he wasn't home when she heard the sound of the dead bolt sliding back. The door opened and her carefully planned little speech about checking on him flew completely out of her mind.

"Are you all right?" It was a foolish question. He was most certainly *not* all right. Though he was standing in the shadows, they weren't thick enough to hide the bruises on his face.

"Angel?" It was obvious that she was about the last person he'd expected to find on his doorstep. Later, Angie suspected that it was that surprise that served to get her in the door.

"Why didn't you come into the clinic?" she demanded, stepping across the threshold without waiting for an invitation.

"For what?" Travis stepped back automatically, letting her in. He surreptitiously took the gun he'd been holding behind the door and slipped it out of sight beneath a wrinkled shirt draped over a table.

"For what?" The look she turned on him was a combination of exasperation and disbelief. "How about to have yourself patched back together?"

"I'm okay." He pulled his head back uneasily as she reached for his chin. "What are you doing?"

"I'm going to torture you," she snapped. "What do you think I'm going to do?"

"I don't know. That's why I asked. What are you doing here?"

"I was worried about you. Those two guys in the

suits didn't look particularly friendly. I wanted to make sure you were all right.''

''I'm fine.''

''And I'm Julia Roberts,'' she said, making it clear what she thought of his claim to good health.

''I thought she was a brunette.''

''And I thought you had a brain. Sit down.''

Travis sat. It was just that he'd been sleeping when she arrived, he told himself. That was why it seemed to take more effort than it was worth to argue with her. He was still groggy.

''Open your mouth.''

He did, intending to protest, only to have her shove a thermometer between his lips.

''I don't have a fever,'' he mumbled, frowning fiercely at her.

''I don't think I have much faith in your medical opinions,'' she said, reaching for his wrist. ''Any two-year-old would have had the good sense to put some antiseptic on those cuts.''

''I did,'' he protested around the thermometer.

''Well, you didn't do a very good job. The one above your left eyebrow is inflamed. Your pulse is up a bit.''

''I'm not surprised.'' He discovered it was impossible to sound really scathing while talking around a thermometer. He would have taken it out but something in the set of her face suggested that she'd simply stick it back in.

He settled for frowning at her to make his annoyance known. She seemed singularly unimpressed. She withdrew the thermometer and frowned at it before shaking it down with an efficient flick of her wrist and sliding it back into its case.

"Your temperature is normal."

"I know," he said with awful sarcasm. She ignored him.

"You're lucky I came prepared," she said, bending to rummage through the tote she'd set on the floor.

"You shouldn't be here at all." He shifted restlessly on the old sofa, looking for a spot where the springs didn't seem quite so likely to pop through the fabric. "How did you find out where I lived, anyway?"

"Mrs. Aggretti. She told me you asked her to come by and clean for you once a week and that you paid her in advance. Several weeks in advance. That was the money you gave her when we were there."

"If I'd just given it to her, it would have looked like charity," he muttered, avoiding her eyes.

Angie's critical look took in the articles of clothing that had been allowed to fall where they would. Not that the decor would have been improved much by their absence. Early American Thrift Shop was the best description she could come up with. Nothing matched anything else. In fact, most of it didn't look as if it had *ever* matched anything else.

"Well, from the looks of this place, you can certainly use a cleaning lady."

"I haven't felt much like doing spring cleaning," Travis snapped defensively.

"If you'd come into the clinic and let me patch you up when this happened, maybe you *would* have felt like it." Angie glared at him, a tube of antiseptic clutched in her hand as if she were considering stabbing him with it.

Travis was the first to see the humor in the picture they made. The storm-cloud gray eased from his eyes, leaving the clear green behind as his mouth started to curve up.

"I don't think I've ever seen anyone make medicine look quite so threatening," he said, eyeing the antiseptic uneasily.

"I don't think I've ever had a patient who was so stubborn," Angie shot back but she eased her grip on the tube.

"Pax?" He held up his hand, giving her his most appealing smile.

"Pax."

Travis tried not to wince as her fingers closed over his bruised knuckles. But he apparently wasn't as stoic as he'd hoped because Angie's forehead creased, her eyes turning dark and worried again.

"What have you done to your hand?" She was already looking at it, taking in the scraped knuckles and swollen fingers. The look she threw him was a mixture of reproach and sympathy.

"They had very hard jaws," Travis offered by way of excuse.

"Grown men should not be finding out how hard the jaws of other grown men are by getting into fights with them," she scolded. But the bite had gone out of her voice. "Besides, there were two of them."

"So I noticed."

A shaft of sunlight had managed to find its way through a crack in the dusty curtains. It fell across her hair, painting a streak of pure gold across the honey blond.

"You're lucky you weren't hurt even worse." She dabbed antiseptic on the cut above his eyebrow.

"They didn't come out of it scot-free." There was

pure, masculine satisfaction in the words. But it vanished instantly. "Ouch!"

"Sorry." She gave him a sweet, insincere smile. "I slipped."

"I thought maybe you were trying to finish what they started," he muttered, giving her a suspicious look.

"Don't be such a baby," she said briskly. "Turn your head so I can get to the cut on your chin."

Travis obeyed warily but her touch was gentle. He'd told her the truth when he said he was all right. He'd been banged up enough times to know the difference between painful but minor injuries and wounds in need of medical attention.

Still, maybe there was something to be said for medical attention, he thought, watching Angie's hair swing forward to frame her face as she leaned toward him. She was wearing the same soft perfume that she'd worn the first time they met. Wildflowers on a sunny day.

"Who were they?" Angie asked.

"Who were who?" The look she shot him said that she recognized deliberate obtuseness when she heard it.

"Those two 'business' associates of yours. The ones with the hard jaws," she clarified.

"No one important." He shrugged, trying not to wince when the movement reminded him of assorted bruises.

She was wearing a blouse of pale buttercup yellow, a plain style that tucked neatly into the waistband of an off-white skirt. The outfit was simple, clearly not designed for enticement. So why did he feel so thoroughly enticed?

"Don't you ever wear a uniform?" The question came out almost as an accusation and he saw the surprise in Angie's eyes as she answered.

"I worked the morning shift at the clinic today and I changed before I left. Is there something wrong with what I'm wearing?"

"I've just never seen you in a uniform." *And he'd never heard himself sound quite so much like a grumpy five-year-old.*

He allowed her to wrap gauze around his knuckles and tried not to wonder if the skin on her shoulders was as silky smooth as he'd imagined it to be. She was so close. He had only to reach out to be touching the buttons on her blouse.

"Take off your shirt."

"What?" His eyes jerked to hers. Was it possible that she'd read his mind?

"Take off your shirt," she repeated.

"Why?"

"Don't sound so suspicious. I'm not contemplating anything risqué."

"Too bad."

"I want to look at your ribs," she continued, ignoring his wistful comment.

"My ribs are fine." But he was reaching for the buttons on his shirt, knowing that she wasn't going to take his word for it.

"You'll forgive me if I don't accept your medical judgment."

Angie sat down on the sofa as he eased the shirt off his shoulders. Both were sitting at an angle, their knees touching. Not that it mattered, she reminded herself. Right now, Travis was only a patient. She reminded herself of that again as the shirt fell to the floor.

In her work, she'd seen her share of men's chests. She'd long since stopped seeing them as anything more than another part to be bandaged. She'd once told her friend Leigh that if Tom Selleck were to walk into the clinic she could tend to any injuries and never once notice him as a man.

Well, the jury was still out on Tom Selleck, but there was no question that her professional indifference did not hold up when it came to Travis Morgan. It had been hard enough to keep her mind on her work before he took his shirt off.

"You've got some nasty bruises," she said, aware that her voice was too breathy.

"Getting punched tends to do that to you."

The reminder of how he'd been hurt helped to steady her hands as she set them against his sides.

"Why did those men come after you?" Maybe if she focused on something unpleasant, she'd be able to forget how warm his skin felt.

"A business problem," Travis said. He sucked in a sharp breath as her fingers probed a particularly nasty bruise along his rib cage.

"What kind of business are you in that you settle problems with a fight? Most people take them to court."

"I do odds and ends. Nothing specific. I guess I'm like my father in that my attention span tends to be short so I don't stick with any one thing very long.

"Am I going to live?"

And that was all he was going to say about his "business," Angie thought. So be it. She wasn't going to pry. At least not now.

"I think you'll live. One of those ribs might be cracked." She ran her fingers along the rib in question. "It wouldn't hurt to have an X ray."

"It'll heal." He was so close, she could feel his breath stirring the tendrils of hair on her forehead.

"I could wrap it for you." Her fingers lingered on his side.

"No thanks. I'll be careful."

"Why do I doubt that?" she asked, lifting her eyes to his.

"Because you're the suspicious sort?" His hand came up to brush the hair back from her face. "When the sunlight hits your hair, it turns it the most incredible shade of gold."

"It's just blond."

"It's beautiful."

"Thank you." When had he gotten closer? He was so close that she could see the tiny gray lines that radiated out from his pupils, adding depth to the clear green of his eyes. And why were her hands still lingering on his skin?

"You know, we were interrupted the other day," he said.

"We were?" His fingers were drifting down the side of her neck. Angie swallowed hard and tried to ignore the delicious shiver that worked its way along her spine.

"Where were we?" Travis murmured, drawing closer still.

"I don't know," she lied. She could feel her pulse beating in her throat, harder and faster than it had any right to be.

"I think we were just about...here." The last word was spoken against her mouth.

Angie's eyes fell shut, her lashes suddenly much too heavy. Travis's mouth feathered over hers in a kiss as soft as a butterfly's wing. She sighed, her lips parting in an unconscious invitation. An invitation he accepted.

His hand cupped the back of her neck as his head angled to deepen the kiss. Angie felt as if her bones were melting. Her tongue came up to meet his, touching shyly and then withdrawing only to be drawn irresistibly forward again.

Her hands slipped lightly up his chest to his shoulders, her fingers curling into the corded muscles there. Her head tilted back in complete surrender as she opened herself to him.

Her rational mind could argue all it wanted that she barely knew this man, that two meetings hardly constituted enough of an acquaintance for them to be necking on the sofa like teenagers. But rational arguments couldn't compete with the way he made her feel.

Tasting her total surrender, Travis moved to pull her still closer, so close that not even a shadow could slip between them. But the movement ended abruptly when his bruised ribs protested with a sharp stab of pain.

"Damn." The word came out on a groan as he jerked back. The abrupt movement startled another groan from him.

"Are you all right? Where does it hurt?" In an instant, the passionate woman disappeared and was replaced by the nurse. The transformation made Travis want to groan again.

"I'm fine. It's my ribs that have a problem," he said ruefully.

"You should have X rays," she fretted.

"There's nothing broken. And if there were, I suspect a few more kisses like that would patch me up." He reached to pull her back into his arms, but Angie stood up and out of reach.

"I really should get going," she mumbled, pushing things back into her tote.

Travis opened his mouth to try to persuade her to stay but closed it without saying anything. She shouldn't have come here in the first place. He should have made her leave immediately. Instead, he'd let her fuss over injuries too minor to mention and he'd compounded his error by kissing her in a way that left no doubt about just how much he wanted her. Maybe he'd taken one too many blows to the head.

He stood up and followed her to the door. Angie stopped in the doorway, turning back to look at him, her expression worried.

"You'll take it easy, won't you? You need to rest those ribs."

"Yes, Nurse. I'll be good." Though he told himself not to, his hand came up, his fingers brushing over her cheek. "Thanks for the concern. It's been a long time since anyone fussed over me." *As in, never,* he thought.

"Well, everyone ought to be fussed over occasionally," she said briskly. She hesitated a moment and then rose on her toes to press a quick kiss to his mouth, drawing away before he could respond.

"Just to help the healing process," she said, her tone light, even though her cheeks were flushed.

Travis watched her walk to the curb, waiting until she was safely in her car and pulling away. He shut the door and leaned back against it, his expression thoughtful. He was probably making a big mistake. Reason said that Angie Brady was a complication he couldn't afford.

For her sake, as well as for the business he had to do in Salem, he would take care that their paths didn't cross again.

But for the first time in a very long time, he was in no mood to listen to the voice of reason. He was listening instead to gut-level instincts that told him not to walk away from this—that he'd regret it for the rest of his life if he did.

Chapter Five

Travis paced the stark room with long, restless strides. He didn't like police stations—he never had. He especially didn't like viewing them from the wrong side of a holding cell. He knew exactly what was going on but that didn't make him like it any more.

There was no clock on the wall and he wasn't wearing a watch, so he didn't know the time but he knew he'd been pacing this damn room long enough to put considerable wear on his shoes. Hell of a way to get his exercise, he thought, his mouth curving with wry humor.

Hearing the door open behind him, he spun on one heel, his expression tightening when he saw who entered.

''Brady.'' His tone was flat, his eyes cold and hard.

''Morgan.'' Clay's tone was no warmer than Travis's. He didn't say anything more, allowing the silence in the small room to thicken.

''I guess you didn't have me called in to chat about the good old days,'' Travis said finally. He pushed his hands into the pockets of his jeans and leaned his shoulders on the gray wall behind him, looking as comfortable as if he were chatting with a friend.

"Where were you yesterday?" Clay asked abruptly.

"I was around. Why are you asking?"

"Someone stole a Ferrari yesterday afternoon."

"Too bad. What does it have to do with me?" There was no sign of tension allowed to show in Travis's cool gaze.

"The theft has your fingerprints all over it."

"But does the car?" Travis lifted one brow in cool question.

"We haven't found the car yet," Clay admitted grudgingly. "But the M.O. looks like your style."

"I didn't realize you'd studied my 'style.' I'm flattered."

"Don't be," Clay snapped. "Where were you yesterday afternoon around three o'clock?"

I was kissing your sister, Travis thought. But he decided it wouldn't be politic to say as much.

"I was at home," he said.

"I suppose you just happened to be alone so there wouldn't be any witnesses who could corroborate," Clay suggested sarcastically.

"You know, jumping to conclusions can be a dangerous business."

"Are you saying you weren't alone?" Clay didn't bother to disguise the disappointment he felt at learning that Travis might have an alibi.

Travis shrugged. Damn jealous brothers all to hell. Having Brady drag him in here this way could ruin everything he'd been working toward. And if he told him that Brady's own sister was his alibi, it was only going to make the man more determined to bring him down, if not with this, then with something else.

"If you've got an alibi, you're going to need it," Clay said.

"Not unless you've got something more concrete than the fact that you don't like me." Travis straightened away from the wall, pulling his hands from his pockets, letting his temper show for the first time. "You can't keep me away from your sister by trumping up charges against me, Brady."

"I'll do whatever I have to, Morgan." Clay set his palms on the table and leaned toward Travis, his eyes an angry blue. "I don't want you near Angie."

"Too bad you don't have much to say about it," Travis said, his tone a taunt.

"You haven't changed, Morgan. I don't know how you've managed to convince Angie to give you the time of day but I'm not going to stand back and watch you use her. If I can't nail you on this theft, I'll find something else."

"Careful, *Officer* Brady." Travis's eyes were as cold as Clay's were hot. "False arrest charges won't look good on your record. You've got nothing on me and you and I both know it."

"You were part of a car-theft ring twelve years ago," Clay snapped.

"Prove it."

"You met with Shearson."

"So what? Is it illegal to have a drink with an old acquaintance?" *Damn Shearson and his need to flaunt his activities in front of the noses of the police.*

"The only acquaintances Shearson has are the flunkies who deal drugs for him."

"You're entitled to your opinion." Travis shrugged tightly.

"Stay away from my sister," Clay told him, abandoning any pretense that he wasn't personally involved.

"She's old enough to take care of herself."

"Not with you, she isn't." Clay straightened away from the table, his hands clenching into fists. "She doesn't have any more business getting involved with you than a baby has playing in the street."

Under the anger and dislike was worry. Travis had never had a sister to worry about—or anyone else, for that matter—but it wasn't difficult to empathize with what Clay was feeling. There wasn't anything Clay could say about the unsuitability of Travis's relationship with his sister that Travis hadn't already said to himself.

Feeling suddenly intensely weary, Travis thrust his fingers through his hair, wanting nothing more than to go home and take a hot shower. This arrest had probably already blown everything all to hell and there was nothing he could do about that. All he wanted was to get out of there—immediately, if not sooner.

He could just tell Brady that he'd stay away from Angie—it was what he should have done anyway. And then maybe he could go home and start figuring out how much damage had been done by his arrest. He had to call Shearson, who'd undoubtedly known about the arrest as soon as it happened.

Before he could say anything, the door opened and a thin-faced man appeared in the doorway. Clay turned, impatient at the interruption. The newcomer gestured him over.

Without seeming to pay too much attention, Travis watched the two men. Obviously *he* was the main topic of conversation. Equally obvious was the fact that Brady didn't like whatever he was hearing. Travis could see the line of his jaw harden like iron as he listened to what the other man was saying. He shot back a few rapid sentences and then turned back to Travis as the other man withdrew.

"You're free to go, Morgan." The words were so tight and hard, they practically qualified as weapons.

"Find the real thief?" Travis asked, arching one brow.

"No. The word came down to let you go. It seems you have friends."

"Everybody ought to have one or two." Even as he spoke, his mind was working furiously.

Why hadn't they just left him to deal with this on his own? Brady hadn't had enough to hold him. A few more minutes of hassle and it would have been settled. Now, Brady had proof, if he'd needed it, that Travis was a less-than-model citizen. Not that he gave a damn what Clay Brady thought of him.

But he gave more than a damn about what his sister thought, Travis admitted bleakly.

"Well, it's been swell, but I'm sure you'll understand if I cut this short." Nothing of his thoughts showed in his expression as he moved toward the door Clay had opened. They stepped into the hall together.

"This isn't over, Morgan," Clay promised tightly.

"There's somebody here to see you, Brady." A tall Hispanic officer interrupted them before Travis could respond.

"Tell them I'll be there in a minute, Martinez," Clay said without taking his eyes from Travis.

"It's your sister." His words riveted their attention

to his face. He cleared his throat uneasily. "She says this guy's got an alibi for yesterday afternoon."

"What?" The word was more an expression of disbelief than a question but Martinez answered Clay anyway.

"She says she was with him."

The words fell like a rock into a still pool, sending out waves at their impact.

Dammit, Angel, why didn't you keep your mouth shut. He'd managed to avoid mentioning her presence to her brother. There was no reason for anyone to know she'd been with him. Now, the whole world would know. Why hadn't he listened to his own excellent advice and kept his distance from her at the start? What was it about those big blue eyes and soft mouth that short-circuited his brain?

But all that showed in his expression was a sort of smirking triumph.

"I told you I had an alibi, Brady."

The look Clay turned on him should have incinerated him on the spot. When Clay turned away without a word, Travis knew it was because he didn't trust himself to speak. He followed Clay. Angie was waiting at the end of the hallway, her expression a mixture of nerves and determination.

"Hello, Angel." Travis spoke first, his tone intimate. "What's a nice girl like you doing in a place like this?"

"Making sure justice is served," Angie said, her eyes darting over him, as if to make sure he was all right.

"You can stop looking for bruises, Angie," Clay said, his voice a little too tight for humor. "I haven't used a rubber hose on a prisoner in months."

"Travis was with me yesterday afternoon," she said, not bothering to respond to Clay's comment.

"So Martinez said." Clay shot a sharp look at Travis, silently promising retribution.

"We were at his house," Angie added for good measure.

"At his house?" Clay's expression grew positively threatening.

"How did you know where I was, Angel?" Travis reached out to brush a lock of hair back from Angie's face in a move calculated to make her brother's blood pressure rise. Damn Clay Brady, anyway. Who was he to judge the rest of the world?

"Mrs. Aggretti told me. She brought the baby into the clinic this afternoon and said you'd been arrested." Angie's eyes told him that she knew exactly who his intimate little gesture had been intended to impress.

"I appreciate your coming to my rescue."

"I just wanted to make sure the police had all the facts."

"Very civic-minded of you, sis." Clay's smile was tight. "Could I speak to you for a minute?"

Angie hesitated. She didn't want to hear another lecture on Travis's unsuitability. On the other hand, maybe if she let Clay get it off his chest now, she wouldn't have to listen to it at home later. With an apologetic smile to Travis, she allowed her brother to draw her aside.

"What are you doing here?" he demanded as they stopped next to an unoccupied desk.

"I told you. I was with Travis yesterday, during the time Mrs. Aggretti said the car was stolen."

"So you rushed down here to rescue him from the evil clutches of the police?"

"No. I rushed down here to make sure you didn't throw him in jail on some trumped-up charge just to keep him away from me," she snapped.

"It wasn't a trumped-up charge." He ground out the words.

"Good." She refused to look apologetic about suggesting that he'd abuse his badge. "Is he free to go now that you know he didn't commit a crime?"

"All I *know* is that he didn't steal a car," Clay corrected her.

"Are you going to let him go?" she asked with steely emphasis.

"Unfortunately I don't have a choice. Wait." He caught her arm when she started to turn away.

"What?" Angie waited. She couldn't remember ever feeling such an enormous gap between them. Clay must have felt something of the same thing because his expression softened.

"I don't want to fight with you about this, sis."

"Good. Because I don't want to fight you."

"Can't you just take my word for it when I tell you to keep your distance from Travis Morgan?" His tone held more plea than demand.

"Not unless you can give me something a little more concrete than he's a 'bad man.'" She set her hand over his and looked up at him, trying to make him understand. "I'm a big girl, Clay. I don't need my big brother to shield me from every bump and scrape anymore. I can take care of myself. Trust me."

"It's not you I don't trust. And you're heading for a lot more than a skinned knee," Clay said, looking over her shoulder to where Travis lounged insolently against the edge of a counter.

"He's not as wicked as he looks," Angie told him, following his eyes.

"What makes you so sure?" He searched her face, finding nothing there to reassure him. She looked, he thought despairingly, much too much like a woman about to fall in love. If she wasn't already there.

"I just don't want to see you hurt," he said, knowing the words sounded lame but helpless to come up with anything stronger.

"You can't protect me forever, Clay. You've got to let me make my own mistakes. *If* this is a mistake," she added.

It was a mistake, all right, he thought as he watched his sister leave with Travis. Just as a moth hovering too close to an open flame, Angie was likely to get her wings badly singed.

TRAVIS STARED out the windshield, oblivious to his cramped legs. He was only half aware that Angie had remembered to start a conversation twice, only to give up in the face of his monosyllabic responses. He couldn't stop thinking about her expression when she'd seen him in the police station—the worry in her eyes, her anger over what seemed to her an unjust arrest.

And he couldn't forget Brady's expression as he'd looked at the two of them together. Brady was convinced that he was going to cause his sister nothing but heartache. And the hell of it was he couldn't argue otherwise.

Travis shifted restlessly in the narrow seat, his forehead pleating in a frown. It was ironic that Angie's arrival had provided him with the alibi Brady had been so sure he didn't have.

She was handy, no arguing that. If he continued to see her, he'd find his business somewhat easier. Even the fact that she was a cop's sister could be worked to his advantage.

"You're awfully quiet." The glance she slid him was questioning.

"Not much to say." Travis lifted one shoulder in a half shrug, keeping his eyes on the unimpressive view out the window.

Angie stopped the car next to the curb in front of his rented house and shut off the engine. Travis looked at the old house, suddenly noticing just how shabby it was. It had probably been a nice home when it was new but time and neglect had taken a harsh toll. It needed a good coat of paint and a new roof, he thought. Maybe a fence to take the place of the dying boxwoods that lined the cracked sidewalk.

Listen to him. He was starting to sound like Mr. Average American, worried about sprucing up the home. Only it wasn't his home, any more than any other place had ever been his home. He was just passing through this house, just as he'd passed through other houses and apartments in his time. Once this job was done, he'd be moving out and the place would be forgotten inside of a month.

"Are you okay?" Angie's worried tone made Travis realize that he'd been sitting there, staring out the window, like a man in a trance.

"Sure. I'm fine." He turned to look at her, one side of his mouth curling up in a half smile. "I really appreciate you coming to the station and the lift back here." His tone was cool, impersonal.

"I was upset when Mrs. Aggretti told me what had happened. Why didn't you tell Clay you were with me?"

"It's bad policy to tell a cop that you were with his sister when the crime in question was committed," he said, shrugging indifferently. "It tends to make them testy."

"But they would have let you go sooner."

"I didn't have anything important to do this morning anyway," he said. "Thanks again." He reached for the door handle.

"Aren't you going to invite me in?" Angie's tone was light but he heard the uncertainty behind the question.

"It's not a good time," he said coolly. "I've got things to do." He turned to look at her, steeling himself against the temptation of those big blue eyes. "Actually I'm going to be pretty busy for quite a while."

He saw the impact of the blatant brush-off in the way her eyes darkened, heard it in the soft catch of her breath. It was for the best, he reminded himself, meeting her searching look with cool indifference.

"If this is because of Clay...because of something he said to you, I'd like to point out that I'm old enough to run my own life."

"I've dealt with big brothers before, Angel. And I haven't let one scare me off yet."

"Then why are you trying to get rid of me?"

The humor in her voice couldn't hide the hurt she felt and Travis had to fight the urge to kiss that look from her eyes. Damn. When had he gotten in so deep? He hadn't known her that long. He had no business caring about her feelings as much as he did.

"Don't make a big deal out of it," he said, his tone careless enough to be an insult. "I've just got some things to do for the next few days. I'll call you."

He pushed open the door and got out of the car before those eyes of hers could make him change his mind. It was for her own good, he reminded himself as he strode up the buckled walkway. She wasn't the sort of woman who could have a casual affair and then walk away unscathed. Besides, he didn't need any distractions right now. Better to get her out of the way so he could get on with his job.

He was slipping his key into the front door before he heard Angie's car start. A moment later, she pulled away from the curb and Travis couldn't keep from turning to watch the little compact zip down the street. He watched it until it was out of sight, trying to ignore the sinking feeling that he'd just made the biggest mistake of his life.

Chapter Six

"Eight ball. Side pocket." Travis waited for his opponent's acknowledgement before he leaned down to make the shot. He eased the cue stick back and then sent it forward with a quick jab. The ball ghosted by the eight ball, barely kissing it. With an almost lazy air, the black ball rolled into the side pocket as if there'd never been any question about where it was going.

"Man, you've got the best damn luck I ever seen." The complaint was good-natured as the other man handed over the twenty dollars that had been riding on the game.

"Skill, my man. Luck doesn't make shots like that. It's pure skill."

"Well, whatever it is, I can't afford to lose any more money to you tonight. My old lady's gonna kill me as it is."

Travis grinned and waved the waitress over to order two more beers. "My treat," he told the other man. "The least I can do is buy you a drink before the funeral."

"It might help to numb the pain a little." His erstwhile opponent laughed and took the beer the waitress offered before he wandered off to watch a poker game in progress in one of the booths.

Travis chalked the end of his cue stick, his eyes skimming restlessly over the crowd that filled the Bucket of Blood. Most of them were locals. The Bucket of Blood was not the kind of establishment that made it onto lists of places to visit while in Salem.

It was a neighborhood hangout without any of the coziness that would have gone along with that title in a better neighborhood. Fistfights were the rule but they rarely amounted to much. The bartender, who was also the owner, kept a baseball bat and a shotgun behind the bar and he didn't like it when his furniture was damaged. Even the most acrimonious battle came to a screeching halt when Sal came out from behind his bar with the bat in one hand and the shotgun in the other. As far as Travis knew, he'd never used the shotgun but the same couldn't be said for the bat.

Sal's presence tended to encourage a certain amount of order if not decorum. Fights were politely moved outside if they threatened to become too vigorous.

"You could chalk your stick at my place, sugar." The woman who spoke was wearing a pair of shiny silver spandex pants and a black knit top that was hardly more than a bandage. Her heavily made-up eyes gave out an unmistakable invitation.

"No, thanks."

"I've got some real nice chalk, sugar." She walked her fingers up his arm, looking up at him from beneath a pair of false eyelashes the size of awnings. "Won't cost you as much as losing one of those silly old bets would."

"But I'm not losing." Travis grinned at her and shifted away so that her hand fell from his arm. He reached into his pocket and pulled out a five-dollar bill. "Here. Have a couple of drinks on me."

The woman looked surprised but she took the money from him with a quick gesture that said she was afraid he might change his mind if she hesitated. Travis turned back to the table as she moved away. Even if he'd been inclined to accept her invitation, an image of wide-set blue eyes and hair the color of sunshine would have intruded.

He began racking the balls, setting up a new game, wanting nothing more than to go home. Funny, how when he thought of going home, he suddenly pictured his grandfather's huge house. He'd had such high hopes when he arrived there. Despite the shock of losing his parents, there'd been a secret, guilty excitement when he thought of finally having a home—a real home. It hadn't taken him long to figure out that there was more to a home than simply staying in one place for more than a few months.

He shook off the unpleasant memories and slid the racked balls into place before lifting the rack slowly from them. It was all a long time ago and far, far away, to quote George Lucas. He had better things to think about, such as how to get one blond, blue-eyed nurse out of his thoughts.

"Quarter a ball. Your choice of games."

Travis stiffened, his fingers curling over the rack. Now he was hearing things. It had to be his imagination because there was no way on earth that Angie Brady was standing behind him, challenging him to a game of pool. No way that she was in the Bucket of Blood. No way that she'd have sought him out after the way he'd dismissed her last week. He turned slowly.

And Angie stood there smiling at him.

She was wearing jeans and a hot pink T-shirt. Her hair was caught back from her face and held at the base of her neck by a blue-and-pink polka-dot bow. She looked fresh and young and as out of place as a kitten in a mud puddle.

And he'd never seen anything more desirable in his life.

"What are you doing here?"

"I felt like a game of pool." Angie grinned at him, feeling her confidence take a much needed jump upward. She'd stopped here on an impulse when she'd seen Travis's bike out front.

She couldn't believe she was here. She'd never been in a bar like this in her life. It seemed as if, since she'd met Travis, she was doing all kinds of things she'd never considered doing before.

She'd questioned her own sanity in seeking him after the way he'd pushed her away. But for an instant she saw something in his eyes that told her she'd done the right thing.

"You play here often?" he asked, indicating their rough surroundings.

"All the time," she lied breezily. "I'm something of a pool trout, you know."

"A pool trout?" Travis's brows climbed upward, a hint of laughter in his eyes. "No kidding."

"I can see you don't believe me," she said, feigning indignation. "You think I'm lying."

"I didn't say that." But there was a suspicious tuck in his cheek that gave the lie to his serious expression.

"Are you going to play or do I have to find someone who isn't afraid of me?'' Angie tilted her chin, giving him a challenging look.

Of course he wasn't going to actually play a game of pool with her, Travis told himself. He was going to usher her politely but firmly out of the Bucket of Blood. He'd make sure she got into her car and went back where she belonged. Where she was safe.

''Eight ball. Fifty bucks a game.'' He saw Angie's eyes widen, whether at his agreement or at the stakes he couldn't tell. But she swallowed once and nodded.

''Fine. Can you give me one of those stick thingies?''

Stick thingies? Oh, they were certainly in for a challenging game. He got a cue stick off the wall rack and chalked the end before handing it to her.

''Thanks.'' Angie set the beer she'd ordered on a table nearby and took the stick from him.

''Do you want to break?'' Travis asked politely.

''No, thank you. I always have a hard time getting the balls apart.'' She smiled up at him and Travis felt something dangerously warm unfold in his chest. He turned away before he could give in to the urge to do something remarkably stupid. Something such as kissing her right in front of God and the patrons of the Bucket of Blood.

He aligned the cue ball and broke, scattering the balls across the table. The fifteen spun into a pocket but he missed the next shot. Probably because his mind was more on the woman behind him than on the game, he admitted ruefully.

''You've got solids,'' he said.

''The ones with almost no white on them?'' she asked, eyeing the table uncertainly.

''The ones with almost no white on them,'' he confirmed, biting his lip against the urge to grin. Maybe she'd described herself better than she knew when she said she was a pool trout. He suspected a fish might know just about as much about the game.

Angie circled the table warily, eyeing the balls as if they were made of plastique. When she finally settled on a shot, she edged up to the table and set her hand on the green felt, balancing the cue stick on top of her fingers in a way that was guaranteed to end in a missed shot at least, torn felt at the worst.

"You know, there are easier ways to hold a pool stick," Travis said, coming up behind her.

"There are?" She straightened and looked at him. "I've always done okay with *my* way."

"That doesn't mean it's the best way." *If she'd ever hit a ball with a hold like that, he'd eat the table.* "I could show you if you'd like."

She hesitated, as if considering and then nodded. "Okay."

It wasn't until Travis had put his hands on hers that it occurred to him that showing her how to shoot pool meant practically embracing her. With his right arm laid along hers, her back snuggled invitingly against his chest as they leaned over the table.

"Put your hand like this," he told her, trying not to notice how soft her skin was. "And hold the stick in your other hand like this."

She smelled like a spring meadow, all sunshine and flowers. It took a real effort to resist the urge to turn his face into her hair.

"Like this?" She turned her head to look at him, so close that it would take only a small movement to bring their mouths together. Travis saw his own awareness reflected in her eyes. His hands tightened over hers, his arms drew her imperceptibly closer. Another heartbeat and he'd be able to taste the sweet warmth of her lips.

"Like that." He released her as if he'd been about to embrace a cactus, stepping back for good measure. "Do you think you have it now?"

"I think so," Angie said. She cleared her throat and turned her attention back to the table. "I think I understand, now."

"Good." Travis decided it was safer not to ask just what it was she understood. He hoped it was only the hold he'd shown her.

The first shot was so easy he felt no surprise when she made it. Angie seemed as pleased as a child when the ball hit the pocket and Travis raised his beer in salute. The second shot was a little tougher but not beyond the realm of beginner's luck. The third shot was something else altogether. It was his first real clue that things might not be what they seemed.

He set his beer down and leaned forward, watching in disbelief as she banked the cue ball and sent it spinning into the four with a smooth ease that wouldn't have shamed a professional. Her smile seemed a little less childlike this time. She paused to take a swallow of beer and look at the table.

"I have a feeling I've been suckered," Travis commented, to no one in particular.

"I don't know what you mean." She blinked at him, her eyes pure innocence.

She returned to the table without waiting for an answer. Travis watched with resigned amusement as she ran the table, knocking balls into pockets with an ease that spoke of considerable practice.

"Eight ball, corner pocket," she announced confidently. He was not in the least surprised to see the eight ball disappear into the stated pocket.

"I suppose this will teach me not to be overconfident." He reached into his pocket as she approached, pulling out the required number of bills.

"I guess I did pretty good, huh?" Angie's smile was all innocence as she took the money from him and tucked it into the pocket of her jeans.

"Not bad for a pool trout," he commented dryly. "I think you got the wrong fish, by the way. Shark might be a little more accurate."

"Shark. Trout. I always get those two confused." She fluttered her lashes at him.

"One has much bigger teeth. And I think I know which one bit me." He signaled the waitress for another beer for Angie, who'd just finished hers.

"I did tell you I was good," she pointed out virtuously.

"Yeah. And you were careful to do it in a way that made sure I wouldn't believe you. Where'd you learn to play like that? And don't tell me it was the Bucket of Blood because I don't think you've set foot in here before tonight."

"Why not? Do I look out of place?"

"No more than a glass of ice water in hell." Travis grinned at her disappointed expression. Didn't she realize how her freshness stood out in the smoke-filled room? She was like a ray of sunshine in a dungeon.

"Where did you learn to play?" he asked again.

"Clay taught me. But he won't play with me anymore," she added, with a suggestion of a pout.

"I can see why," Travis said dryly.

"I could give you a chance to recoup your loss," she suggested.

"You're trying to hustle me."

"I'm just trying to be fair. Of course, if you don't think you could beat me…" She let the challenge trail off.

He should send her home, he thought. She didn't belong here any more than she belonged with him. Hadn't he been through all this last week? Playing pool with her was *not* the way to put distance between them.

"I'm not going to show you how to hold your stick this time," he warned her.

"I don't need anyone to show me how to hold a stick, Travis." The look she shot him from under her lashes gave double meaning to the words.

It was the second time in thirty minutes that he'd been more or less propositioned. But whereas the first woman had left him with nothing but a vague feeling of pity, the playful invitation in Angie's eyes had an altogether different effect.

How was he supposed to do the right thing and keep her at a distance when she gave him a look like that?

ANGIE CERTAINLY didn't need any instruction in the fine art of shooting pool. Travis understood completely why her brother no longer played with her. There was something disconcerting about competing with someone who looked like Cinderella and played like Minnesota Fats.

She insisted on referring to the solids as "the balls with hardly any white on them" and she held her stick the way a three-year-old would. But it didn't seem to matter. It was as if she charmed the balls into going where she wanted them. Not that Travis blamed them. She could have charmed him into doing just about anything she wanted.

How else could he explain the fact that he hadn't marched her out of the Bucket of Blood and sent her safely home? He'd spent the past week thinking about her far more than he had any business doing. He'd almost managed to convince himself that she was forgotten. And then she turned up where he least expected her and made him realize just how much he'd been lying to himself.

"LAST CALL." The waitress leaned one hip against the pool table, easing the weight on her feet.

"Last call?" Travis looked at her in surprise before glancing at his watch. One-thirty in the morning. He'd lost all track of time—not a healthy habit for someone in his profession. He and Angie had been playing pool since nine.

"You want another beer?" The waitress sounded impatient. Though the crowd had thinned out, there were still enough customers to make the last half hour of her shift a busy one.

"No, thanks." Travis dropped a five on her tray, a generous tip for the night's service. He nodded absently in answer to her thanks. His attention was on Angie, who was weaving her way back from the rest room.

And "weaving" was the operative word, he realized. She wasn't simply working her way between the crowded tables, she also seemed to be having some difficulty putting one foot in front of the other. How much had she had to drink tonight? He narrowed his eyes as he tried to remember. Four...maybe five beers. More than enough for someone who wasn't accustomed to drinking.

"Ready for another game?" she asked as she reached the table.

"I think it's time to call it quits," Travis said.

"I'm still two games ahead of you. Don't you want to try to even the score? Where's my drink?" She looked down, frowning when she didn't find it.

"You finished it. And I'm willing to postpone the rematch. I think it's time you went home."

"Why?" She peered up at him, her eyes ever so slightly glazed. "Afraid I'll beat you again?"

"It's possible." Though at the moment, it seemed unlikely that she could hit the broadside of a barn with a truck. When had she gotten so high? And why hadn't he realized what was happening sooner? *Because he hadn't wanted to. Because he'd been enjoying himself and he hadn't wanted the evening to end.*

"Come on. You need to get home." He found her purse and handed it to her.

"But I was having fun," she protested, looking over her shoulder at the pool table as he was ushering her out the door.

"Yes, but it's late and if I don't get you home, your brother will probably track me down and blow my head off."

"Oh, Clay." She puckered her face in a disparaging look that made Travis want to kiss her. "He's a worrywart."

"Yeah, well, if I had a sister, I'd be a worrywart, too."

"Nope. You're not the type." She spun away from him suddenly and threw her arms up as if to embrace the full moon that hung overhead. "I feel like dancing."

"Too bad. You're going home." Travis caught hold of her arm and tugged her over to where his bike was parked.

"What about my car?" She dragged back, frowning at him.

"You're the one who told me no one would bother it around here. I can't say the same about my bike. And you're in no condition to drive."

She continued to frown but allowed him to lead her to the motorcycle. Travis had carried his helmet from the bar and now he lifted it and set it over her head.

"You're really making a habit of this, you know."

"I know. Do you mind?" She looked up at him, all eyes and soft mouth and Travis had to fight the urge to kiss her.

"I don't mind," he said gruffly. God help him, he didn't mind at all.

He drove her home through streets made quiet by the late hour. Angie snuggled against his back, her arms looped intimately around his waist. It would have been easy to pretend that they were just an ordinary couple, going home after an evening with friends. They'd go up to bed and Angie would cuddle against him as she fell asleep.

It was a lovely fantasy but Travis had never been inclined to play games of pretend. He'd spent a lot of lonely hours playing pretend when he was a child and he'd soon learned that reality always came crashing back in. It hurt less if you didn't pretend in the first place.

He eased to a halt in front of Angie's house and helped her off the bike. The ride hadn't sobered her.

She stumbled on a nonexistent crack in the sidewalk and then giggled like a teenager at a slumber party.

"I think I had too much to drink," she informed him.

"So I noticed."

"I'm a little high." She seemed to think it was important to clarify her state.

"Just a little," he agreed, catching her arm when she stumbled again.

She giggled covering her mouth with one hand as she peered up at him in the moonlight. "I don't usually drink very much."

"No kidding." He sighed when she stumbled a third time. Setting one arm around her waist, he scooped her off her feet, cradling her against his chest.

"I can walk," she said. But she looped her arms around his neck and set her head on his shoulder.

"You seem to be doing a better job of falling at the moment."

He carried her up the walk, grateful that the moon was bright enough to light the way. There was a delay when he reached the door while Angie searched her purse for the keys. She found them at last, and dangled them triumphantly. Rather than wait while she attempted to insert the key in the lock, Travis set her down and did the job himself. Angie leaned against him, humming softly.

Once the door was open, he picked her up again and carried her into the entryway. There were no lights on and he could only hope that Brady was either not home or was a sound sleeper. If he found Travis carrying his half-conscious sister up the stairs, he was not going to be a happy camper.

Having negotiated the staircase, he pushed open the door Angie indicated and carried her into her bedroom. The moonlight that had been such a help outside couldn't penetrate through the curtains drawn over the windows. Rather than risk stumbling over something in the dark room, Travis lowered Angie to her feet and pushed the door shut behind them before groping for the light switch.

The switch lit a lamp that sat on an oak dresser. It illuminated a room that was pleasantly feminine without being full of ruffles and floral prints. The crisp blue-and-white stripes and light oak furniture were exactly right for Angie. The same soft practicality that he'd come to associate with her.

Angie began to slide down the door, reminding him that he wasn't here to critique the decor but to get Angie to bed. Lifting her again, he carried her to the bed and set her on her feet. Steadying her with an arm around her waist, he turned down the covers before easing her onto the bed.

She immediately flopped onto her back, throwing her arms out against the cool linens.

"I feel so good."

"Enjoy it while you can. You're probably going to feel like hell in the morning."

"Don't be a grouch." She grinned up at him and patted the bed invitingly. "Want to join me?"

Travis reached for one of her feet and began unlacing her sneaker with quick jerks. Somewhere, someone was having one hell of a good joke at his expense. *Did he want to join her?* Only about as much as he wanted to continue breathing.

When the second sneaker hit the floor, he straightened and considered her. Jeans were not the most comfortable garment to sleep in but there was a limit to his self-control. If he started removing more than her shoes, he was going to forget just how ungentlemanly it would be to take advantage of a woman who'd had too much to drink.

"Come on. Get under the covers."

Angie shifted obediently, laying her head on the pillow and allowing him to pull the covers up to her shoulders. But when he started to move away, she reached out and caught hold of his hand.

"Aren't you going to kiss me good-night?"

How was it possible for a woman to ask a question such as that and still manage to look as innocent as a child? On the other hand, how was it possible to resist the look in her eyes? It would take a stronger man than he was, Travis admitted without regret.

Her mouth was soft and warm, as sleepy as her eyes and even more tempting. It would be so easy to deepen the kiss, to take the next step and then the next....

"Go to sleep," he said as he pulled back.

She looked up at him, her eyes smoky blue and mysterious in the soft light.

"Stay with me until I fall asleep."

Travis groaned. Just what had he done to deserve this kind of torture?

"That's not a good idea, Angel." He started to move away but she tightened her hold on his hand, pulling him closer.

"Please, Travis. Just stay until I fall asleep."

"No. I can't." There were limits to his willpower and he'd just about exceeded them with that kiss.

"Don't leave me alone."

The words touched off a flood of old memories.

How many times had he asked his parents not to leave him alone in some new place? He heard the echo of those childish pleas in Angie's words and it was always followed by his mother's admonition not to be such a baby and then the closing of a door.

But this wasn't the same thing at all. He wasn't leaving Angie alone in some half-restored monastery in Thailand or a tent in South America. This was her own bedroom in the house she'd grown up in, with her brother probably asleep just down the hall. It wasn't the same thing at all.

"Please, Travis. Stay with me," she whispered again, her voice as soft as a siren's and just as irresistible.

"Just until you fall asleep," he said slowly, wondering where his sanity had gone. He looked around for a chair but she was pulling him toward the bed.

"You can lay on top of the covers," she said. She scooted into the middle of the bed to make room, looking up at him with such a bright expression that he had to believe she was either too naive or too drunk to know what she was doing.

Travis hesitated and then shrugged. "In for a penny, in for a pound," he muttered. If he was going to be tortured, he might as well be comfortable.

He stretched out gingerly, propping his shoulders against the oak headboard and setting his booted feet uneasily on top of the striped cotton spread.

"See? Isn't this better?" Angie promptly shifted over to snuggle against his side.

Better? Better than what, he wondered. It was marginally better than having bamboo shoots thrust under his fingernails. Or jumping from a plane at thirty-thousand feet without a parachute. The jury was still out on whether or not he'd prefer to walk on hot coals.

"This is nice," she murmured sleepily.

Well, "nice" was a relative term. If one considered slow torture nice, then he supposed this would qualify. He shifted lower so that she could rest her head on his shoulder. Her hair smelled of cigarette smoke from the bar but underneath that was the scent of sunshine.

Travis let his eyes drift shut. Just for a moment. As soon as he was sure she was asleep, he'd leave. He was really going to have to make her understand that she couldn't keep coming around. She was all sunshine and he was all shadow and the two simply weren't compatible.

He turned his face into her hair, his long body relaxing further into the mattress. Her brother was right when he told her that he was a bad man. And angels shouldn't mix with bad men.

Chapter Seven

Travis came awake slowly, aware that he hadn't slept long enough. Frowning, he turned his head into the pillow, courting a few more hours of sleep. The pillow shifted and murmured something low and indistinguishable. The urge for more sleep vanished instantly.

Angie. It wasn't a pillow snuggled so confidently against his shoulder. It was Angie. And he was in her bed, just where he had no business being.

Travis forced his eyes open, stifling a groan when he saw the filtered sunlight that lit the room. He should have been out of there hours ago. He hadn't planned on falling asleep. But then it seemed as if, since meeting Angie, he was doing a lot of things he hadn't planned.

Somewhere in the house, a clock started to chime. Travis listened, counting the bells. Six o'clock. He had to get out of there. The last thing he needed was to run into Clay. There would be no explaining his presence in Angie's room at this hour of the morning. Come to think of it, it would be pretty hard to explain at any hour.

Angie was lying against him, her head nestled on

his shoulder, one arm across his chest. Her hair framed her face in soft golden curls. Her cheeks were flushed with sleep and her lips were slightly parted. She looked like a tousled angel—innocence and invitation in one soft package.

Travis lifted his hand, brushing a lock of hair away from her mouth. It curled around his fingers like the most delicate of shackles. He turned his hand, noticing how the pale gold of her hair contrasted with his tanned skin. Shadow and sun. His mouth twisted and he pulled his hand away, letting the curl drift back into place. He had to get out of there before he forgot just how big the gap between them really was.

Sometime during the night, Angie must have felt too warm because she'd pushed the light covers off, shoving them in his direction. Travis found his departure slowed by the need to untangle his legs from the discarded blankets. He'd just succeeded in freeing himself when he felt Angie's arm tighten across his chest.

"Where're you going?" Angie's voice was slurred with sleep.

"It's morning. I've got to go."

"Don't want you to." She sounded like a pouty child but there was nothing childlike in the way her hand slipped inside his shirt.

"Don't." He caught her hand, pressing it flat against his chest.

"Why not?" For the first time she opened her eyes and Travis felt his determination slipping a notch—several notches.

"I shouldn't be here," he told her, but his conviction was weakened by the fact that the arm against her back was shifting her subtly closer.

"I want you here." Her hand moved against his chest and his restraining hold eased, allowing her to curl her fingers against the hair-roughened skin.

"What about your brother?" Somehow, his hand had become entangled in her hair.

"I'm a big girl, Travis." Her eyes were midnight blue and held the promise of heaven on earth.

"So you are." The words were whispered against her mouth as he abandoned all thoughts of drawing away without kissing her. He had to taste her. Just one kiss, he promised his drowning sense of self-preservation. Just one kiss and then he'd go.

If her eyes promised heaven on earth, her mouth delivered on that promise. From the moment his lips touched hers, Travis knew he was lost. Or he would have known if he'd been able to think of anything beyond how right it felt to kiss her.

IT WAS SIMILAR TO WAKING to find herself in a wonderful dream, Angie thought. With Travis next to her, his kiss the first thing she felt, she couldn't imagine a better way to wake up. It should have felt strange, having a man in the bed where she'd slept alone most of her life. If it were any other man, maybe it would have. But not with Travis.

Her breath leaving her on a sigh, she shifted, turning farther into his arms. Her hand, still inside his shirt, slipped upward until her fingers slid into the silky hair at the base of his neck.

Her mouth parted, welcoming the warm thrust of his tongue as his hand flattened against her lower back, arching her closer as he deepened the kiss. The fire that seemed to always lay between them, banked and waiting, flared to life, and what had begun as a sleepy good-morning kiss was suddenly much more, something hot and powerful.

Travis's hand found its way beneath the T-shirt Angie wore, sliding up and down the warm skin of her back. When the elastic of her bra got in the way, he flicked the hooks open without a second's thought. He had to touch her and anything that got in the way was intolerable.

His hand traced the gentle curves of her back before settling on the indentation of her waist, then new territories beckoned and it was only a moment before his hand was drifting upward, finding its way beneath the loosened scrap of lace. Angie's breath caught as his fingers brushed the lower curve of her breast. If she had any thought of protest, it was burned away in an instant.

He cupped her breast boldly, his callused thumb brushing across her nipple. Angie felt his touch at her breast but she also felt the warmth of it spread through her body, turning her skin to fire.

She was hot silk in his hands, warm and yielding. She made him want to lose himself in the heat of her and yet he found the urge to protect her was as powerful as the need to take what she offered.

He dragged his mouth from hers, staring down into her flushed face. A sensuous angel. An impossible contradiction and yet it described her perfectly. She opened her eyes, staring up at him with a dazed look of passion that made his body tighten with aching need.

He wanted her. If he'd ever allowed himself to dream, she would have been the embodiment of those dreams.

A dream he didn't dare reach for.

If he let this continue, he could destroy the very things that made him want her most. Her sweet optimism, the way she looked at life through glasses tinted a pale shade of rose, her belief that life generally worked out for the best. He didn't share her feelings but that only made him want to protect her innocence even more.

Shadow and light. Angel and the bad man. Her belief against his cynicism. They were a study in contrasts. Two sides of a coin that could never meet. At least not without one destroying the other.

"Travis?" Angie touched her fingertips to the lines that had suddenly appeared beside his mouth. "What's wrong?"

He was.

But he couldn't give her that answer. She'd only argue, try to convince him otherwise. And at the moment he was perhaps a little too willing to be convinced.

"Nothing." He forced a twisted smile as he eased his hand from her breast. He pulled her shirt back down and rolled away from her to sit on the edge of the bed.

"Nothing?" He felt her sit up behind him and almost winced when she reached out to set her hand on his shoulder. "Then why…" She let the question trail off and Travis turned to look at her.

"Why did I stop?" He finished the thought for her.

Her cheeks were flushed but she nodded, her eyes steady on his. "That's right. Why did you? I mean, you must know that I…that I wanted you." She stumbled on the confession but managed to get the words out.

Travis stared at her, seeing the vulnerability in her

eyes. He had only to say something flip and callous to devastate her, perhaps hurt her so badly that she'd stop thinking about him. He wouldn't have to worry about her turning up at his house or challenging him to a game of pool. She wouldn't come around to bandage his injuries and scold his housekeeping habits.

Just a few thoughtless words, delivered in just the right tone would end it all right there.

She drew her lower lip between her teeth in a gesture that showed how thin her casual front really was.

"This just isn't the time or place, Angel." He reached up to rub his thumb across the lip she'd been worrying. "If your brother finds me here, he's likely to shoot first and ask for an explanation much later."

"Clay isn't my keeper," she said hotly.

"No. But he's your brother and he worries about you." His mouth twisted in a rueful smile. "To tell the truth, if I were in his shoes, I'd feel the same way about you."

"I wish the two of you would stop talking like you're Charles Manson," she said. "So far, I've seen you do all sorts of terrible things, like rescuing me from a bunch of thugs and giving Mrs. Aggretti a job and driving me home in the rain. Heavens, who knows what dreadful crime you may commit next."

There was a certain anger in her eyes. Anger *for* him, not *at* him. Travis felt something shift inside, as if a long-held wall were in danger of cracking. In all his life, he'd never had anyone so unhesitatingly take his side. His parents had rarely noticed him enough to care whether he *had* a side to take and his grandfather had been of the guilty-until-proven-innocent school, especially when it came to the grandson he neither wanted nor understood.

But it didn't change anything. It didn't change what he was and it didn't change the potential for hurting her.

"You don't know me, Angel. You don't know what I'm capable of."

She reached up to catch his hand, pressing it to her cheek. "I know you're a good man, Travis, whether you believe it or not."

"I'm not totally without redeeming value but I don't think very many people have seen fit to call me a 'good' man," he said without rancor.

Shaking his head, he drew his hand out of her hold. "You're seeing what you want to see," he said as he rose. "And that's not necessarily reality."

"Then show me the reality," she said. "Show me why I shouldn't trust you. Show me why you're so sure you're bad for me. And if you can't show me, then I don't want to hear about it anymore."

Travis turned to look down at her. "Now I see how you keep your patients in line. You sound like a nanny I had when I was eight. I was scared to death of her. But you're much prettier than she was." He reached out and brushed her sleep-tousled hair back from her face. "I've got to go."

He touched his fingers to her mouth, still swollen from his kisses, then turned and walked away, knowing that if he lingered another minute he wouldn't leave at all. He refused to look back at her as he opened the door, not wanting to test his resolve. He might not have convinced her to stay away from him but at least he'd managed to walk out of there without taking advantage of her misplaced faith in him. He pulled open the door.

And found himself looking into Clay's shocked eyes.

The two of them stared at each other. For the space of a heartbeat, neither moved, both too stunned by the unexpected encounter to react. Clay recovered first, his look of shock turning to one of burning anger in the blink of an eye.

Travis had only an instant to see Clay's raised hand. He jerked his head back and the blow that should have dropped him in his tracks landed with much less force than intended. Still, it was enough to send him stumbling back against the door he hadn't had a chance to close. It flew open, revealing Angie still sitting in the middle of her rumpled bed, the imprint of two heads plain to see on the pillows.

"You sonofabitch!" Clay threw another punch, which Travis dodged.

"Cool it, man. This isn't what it looks like." Travis backed away, raising his hands in a gesture intended to calm. It didn't have any visible effect on the other man.

"You miserable, stinking scum!" Clay drew back his fist but Angie was suddenly between them.

"Stop it!"

"Don't!" Travis grabbed her by the shoulders and thrust her out of the way, afraid that Clay might not be able to pull his punch in time to avoid hitting her.

Clay's fist skimmed through the air, mere inches from where she'd been and Travis felt his heart nearly stop when he saw how close she'd come to being hurt.

"You stupid fool!" His determination to remain passive vanished in a blaze of primal anger. "Do you know what you almost did?"

"What *I* almost did?" Clay had recovered from the shock of narrowly missing his sister and he stepped forward to meet Travis's furious look. "Who the hell are you to be telling me what *I* almost did?"

"Stop it! Both of you, just stop it right now." Angie thrust herself between the two of them again, her usually gentle features hard with anger. "If either of you throws another punch, I swear I'm going to get a gun and shoot the pair of you. Do you hear me?"

She looked at both of them, letting them see the full force of the anger in her eyes.

"I hear you," Clay said sullenly. Travis only shrugged but Angie took that as agreement.

"What on earth are you doing, Clay?" Since her brother had started the fight, he bore the full brunt of her fury.

"What the hell is *he* doing?" Clay demanded, gesturing to Travis.

"That's none of your business," she told him sharply.

"None of my business?" He gave her an incredulous look. "I'm your brother."

"My brother. *Not* my keeper."

"Look, this isn't what it looks like," Travis interjected.

"We don't owe him an explanation," Angie said but he ignored the protest.

"Nothing happened last night. She'd had too much to drink so I brought her home and carried her up to bed." He dabbed at his bleeding lip with the back of his hand. "I fell asleep. End of story."

"End of story?" Clay's mood showed no sign of lightening. "I find you walking out of my sister's bedroom at six o'clock in the morning and I'm supposed to buy that you just *fell asleep?*'' His tone expressed his disbelief and Travis's back stiffened.

''That's all the explanation you're getting,'' he said flatly. ''Take it or leave it.''

''You forget. I know you, Morgan.'' He stabbed a finger in the other man's direction. ''And I don't trust you any farther than I could throw you. Not when it comes to my sister.''

''Stop it!'' Angie slapped his hand down. ''I'm not invisible here. And I'm not a child. The bottom line, Clay, is that it doesn't matter whether you believe him or not. If I want to sleep with Travis or any other man, it's none of your business.''

''But Angie, he's—''

''I don't want to hear it.'' She interrupted him with a quick, slashing motion of her hand. ''I don't want to hear another word about it.''

She turned to Travis, her eyes stormy blue with emotion. ''I think it might be better if you left.''

Travis looked from her to Clay, his eyes pale green and as cold as ice. He wiped the last of the blood from his split lip and nodded slowly.

''Sure, Angel.'' He reached out to cup his hand around the back of her neck and bent to kiss her without haste. It was less a kiss of passion than a staking of territory. It was meant as a clear message to Clay, one that couldn't be mistaken.

NEITHER ANGIE NOR CLAY spoke until they heard the sound of the front door closing quietly behind Travis.

''Angie, how…''

''I don't want to hear it, Clay.'' She cut him off ruthlessly. ''I don't want to hear another word about his being a bad man. I don't want to hear anything from you but an apology.''

''An apology!'' He stared at her in disbelief. ''You've got to be kidding. You want me to apologize? For what?''

''For acting like an ape,'' she snapped. Angie rubbed her fingers over her forehead, aware that a somewhat violent ache was starting just above her eyes.

''I reacted like any man would have. Any man who found someone leaving his sister's bedroom at six c'clock in the morning. And what did he mean when he said you'd had too much to drink?''

''Exactly what it sounds like,'' she shot back, refusing to give an inch. ''I was drunk and he brought me home and carried me up to bed. Truly villainous behavior.'' She sneered.

''Considering that he stayed in your bed, I hardly think it earns him a nomination for sainthood. Unless taking advantage of a woman who's had too much to drink has suddenly become a good deed.''

''I *asked* him to stay!'' Angie closed her eyes in pain as the sound of her own raised voice echoed inside her head like a trumpet blast in a barrel. When she opened them again, it was to find her brother staring at her in shocked disbelief.

''You *asked* him to stay?''

''Yes. And it wasn't my idea that he left when he did,'' she admitted. ''I'm sorry if that shocks you, Clay, but you've got to get used to the idea that I'm a grown woman. And who I choose to sleep with is none of your business.''

''Angie, you can't—''

"I can do anything I want," she said, interrupting him. "Back off, Clay. I mean it."

"What the hell's gotten into you." He exploded. "You barely know this man and you're talking about sleeping with him. What kind of hold does he have over you?"

"You make it sound like he's Svengali and I'm some poor country maiden under his spell." Angie thrust her sleep-tangled hair back from her face and glared at him. "He's exciting."

"So is bungee jumping," he snapped. "And it's safer."

"Maybe I'll try that next week."

They faced each other, exchanging glare for glare. It was Clay who broke the silence first.

"I've told you he's dangerous, Angie. Isn't that enough?" His expression had gone from anger to something very close to pleading.

"Maybe I *like* it that he's dangerous," she said slowly. "Maybe I like it that he's different from anyone I've ever known." She wished she understood it better herself so that she could try to make Clay understand.

"You're not some foolish teenager whose head is turned by every punk in a black leather jacket. Hell, you weren't turned on by that kind of guy when you *were* a teenager," he said, exasperated.

"Travis isn't a punk, Clay. If you weren't so determined to dislike him, maybe you'd be able to see that."

"What I see is that he blows back into town with no visible means of support and starts hitting on my sister." He exploded, losing his temper again. "And she's stupid enough to fall for that whole 'bad boy' image. I thought you were smarter than that, Angie."

"Well, I'm sorry to disappoint you," she said, sarcasm making the apology sound less than sincere. "But this is *my* life and I'm old enough to live it as I choose. Now butt out and go away."

"But—"

"Out."

Clay looked at her, gauging her determination. Angie met his eyes, hoping she didn't look as fragile as she was starting to feel. Not only was her head pounding, but her stomach was beginning to send messages that suggested it was highly displeased with last night's excesses.

"All right," he said at last. "But this discussion isn't over."

"Fine." Angie nodded and then had to close her eyes as the movement set the room swirling around her. She didn't open them again until she heard the door close behind her brother.

Blessedly alone, she groped her way to the bed and sank onto the edge of it. The pounding in her head eased somewhat once she was off her feet.

God, what a morning. How to go from dream to nightmare in ten minutes or less, she thought ruefully. Waking in Travis's arms had been wonderful. Having Clay start a fight with him had been dreadful.

Angie smoothed her hand over the pillow Travis had used, her expression softening. Leaning down, she drew in a deep breath, inhaling the faint, masculine scent that lingered on the pillowcase. If she closed her eyes, it was almost similar to having him there.

Heavens, listen to the way she was thinking. She sounded like a love-struck teenager.

Wasn't that what she was?

Angie sat bolt upright as the small voice echoed in her mind. Ignoring the fact that the abrupt movement renewed the pounding in her head, she stared at her reflection in the dresser mirror across the room. Her eyes were rounded with shock and her pallor was caused by more than the vague hangover that threatened.

Love struck? Her? With Travis?

The disjointed questions popped into her head at random. The answers were prompt and consistent. Yes. Yes. And yes.

"My God. I'm in love with him." The words were a whisper, hardly audible and yet seeming to echo like a shout.

It wasn't possible. She hardly knew him. She was too sensible to fall in love with a man she hardly knew. That was the sort of behavior to be expected from girls with more hair than sense. And even as a girl, she hadn't been the sort to get crushes and fancy herself in love with every handsome boy who came around.

She'd never have imagined herself falling in love with a man like Travis. All dark and dangerous, full of shadows and secrets.

But all the logic in the world wouldn't change the facts. She'd fallen in love with Travis Morgan. She was in love with a man about whom she knew next to nothing. She didn't even know what he did for a living, for God's sake.

Did it matter?

Still staring at her reflection, she picked up his pillow and hugged it to her chest. Did anything matter except that her heart beat faster when he was in the room? Or that she'd never felt so alive in her entire life as she had since meeting him?

She was in love. This time, she let the idea sink in. Happiness bubbled up inside her, defying the grumbling threat of a hangover.

She, Angie Brady, was in love with Travis Morgan.

She grinned at her reflection. She wanted to shout it to the world. She wanted to find Travis and throw her arms around him and tell him that she loved him.

Her smile faded. Would Travis even want to hear such a confession? It would be foolish to assume that, just because she'd realized she was in love with him, Travis felt the same way about her.

But he had to love her, she argued passionately. It wasn't possible to love someone so much and not have that love returned. Except she knew it *was* possible. Her father had loved her mother deeply and yet Evelyn Brady had had no qualms about walking out on him and their two children. Because he was boring, she'd told him with blunt cruelty.

Angie wrapped her hands around her upper arms, unconsciously hugging herself as if she could keep the cold chill of reality from intruding on her newly discovered emotions.

Just because her mother hadn't loved her father— or her children—didn't mean that Travis wouldn't love her. He *wanted* her—that much she could be sure of. Remembering the taut length of his body against hers just a short while ago in this very bed, Angie felt her confidence take a subtle swing upward.

They definitely shared that elusive thing called chemistry. Perhaps, in that chemistry, lay the seeds of an enduring relationship. It was up to her to cultivate that seed, to give it a chance to grow.

She lay back on the bed, pressing her cheek to the pillow Travis had used, her eyes both dreamy and determined. She had a pretty good idea of where to start her gardening efforts.

Chapter Eight

Travis leaned his shoulder against the warped door that led from the garage to the kitchen. It yielded grudgingly to a superior force, giving in with a squeal of hinges that suggested it might not always be so easily conquered.

He'd thought about oiling the hinges but they were as good a burglar alarm as anything he could buy. Certainly no one was going to be sneaking up on him through *this* door.

The rest of the house had its own defenses. Nothing that would seem at all out of the ordinary to a casual thief but enough to provide Travis with a warning of any intrusion, whether he was home or not.

Entering the kitchen, he automatically stepped over the buckled piece of linoleum and set a small sack of groceries on the scuffed counter. He shrugged out of his leather jacket and tossed it onto a chair before opening the refrigerator and pulling out a cold beer. Twisting off the top, he took a swallow, letting the icy liquid flow slowly down his throat.

The unusually cool, damp spring had disappeared overnight, burned away by the heat wave that announced summer's arrival. It was after nine in the evening and the temperature outside still hovered in the upper seventies. Inside the old house it was closer to eighty-five. The sun had had all day to beat down on the sagging roof. The fact that the windows were painted shut meant that not so much as a breath of air stirred in the dim rooms.

Sipping the beer, Travis emptied the sack of groceries, throwing the perishables into the refrigerator and leaving everything else sitting on the counters to be put away when the temperature dropped, maybe sometime in October.

He moved into the living room, carrying the bottle in one hand. He flicked on one lamp. The sixty-watt bulb banished only the deepest shadows but the gloom suited his mood. There was a fan in the living room and he turned it on. It didn't accomplish much beyond stirring the hot air around but it was enough to give the illusion of cooling.

Sinking into the one chair in the house that offered reasonable comfort—a black leather armchair that had seen better days—he stretched his long legs out in front of him and leaned his head back against the cracked leather. With the cold beer in his hand and the soft whir of the fan for company, he closed his eyes and tried to make his mind as blank as possible.

Immediately a pair of summer-sky-blue eyes appeared in front of him. Warm and soft and full of passion, they beckoned to him, just as her soft mouth did. He could almost taste that mouth, almost feel that hunger in her, a hunger that had nearly matched his own. And her soft, wildflower scent, the feel of her skin beneath his hands...

"Dammit!" His eyes flew open and he sat bolt upright in the chair, his hand clenched around the beer bottle. So much for relaxing. His body was as taut as a bow string.

"Idiot," he muttered as he got up. What was wrong with him, sitting here thinking about a woman and getting aroused like some randy teenager?

But not just any woman, he admitted reluctantly. And that was the heart of the problem. Unlike the teenager he'd compared himself to, he wasn't interested in any blonde with staples in her belly. He would have preferred that. Good old-fashioned, generic lust was easy enough to ignore.

What bothered him was that this was a very specific blonde that had him hard and aching. And he wasn't feeling anything as simple as lust, either. He wanted her but there was more to it than that.

And *that* was the problem.

He swigged down the last of the beer, already slightly warm, and then stalked into the kitchen for another. But the fresh, ice-cold brew did little to cool his heated thoughts. Nor did it numb his thinking to the point where he could convince himself that Angie Brady meant nothing more to him than a pleasant diversion.

The fact was he liked her. He scowled at the chipped enamel on the refrigerator door. He *cared* about her, he thought, forcing himself to be honest. He was a hairbreadth away from falling in love with her, he admitted bleakly, forcing himself to complete honesty.

Disaster. That was what it would be. Emotional suicide. For both of them. Unless he read her wrong, Angie had just about convinced herself that she was in love with him. And remembering the look in her eyes this morning, he wasn't sure "just about" was an accurate description anymore.

He wandered back into the living room, the beer forgotten in his hand. He'd told himself that she wouldn't get hurt. He was no longer at all sure that was true. If he broke it off now, she was going to be hurt. If he broke it off later, she was going to be hurt.

And if he didn't break it off?

The thought slipped in unbidden and Travis's fingers clenched around the bottle. If he didn't break it off, then he was the one who would end up paying the price. Sooner or later, Angie would figure out that he wasn't the man she'd imagined him to be and those beautiful blue eyes would look at him with the same disappointment he'd seen in his parents. Or the look of dislike with which his grandfather had always regarded him.

He took a swallow of beer, wishing it were something stronger. Something that might burn away the old memories. Memories he'd thought he put behind him a long time ago. But then Angie had a tendency to make him think of things he hadn't thought of in a long time. Things such as white picket fences and family ties. The sort of things he'd long since decided were not for him.

Travis sighed and lifted the bottle to press it against his forehead, letting the cool glass cool his skin. Too bad it couldn't do as much to cool his overheated imagination. Even knowing how foolish it was, he couldn't stop thinking about the way Angie had looked this morning, the way she'd felt in his arms.

There was no doubt about it: He had to put some distance between them. For his sake, as well as hers. Nothing but trouble could come of the two of them.

It was almost a relief when someone knocked on the door. In this neighborhood, it would likely mean trouble, but at least it was a distraction. Eager as he was for that, he didn't ignore common sense. He didn't stand right in front of the door; he approached it from the side instead.

"Yeah?" His tone was not particularly welcoming, nor was the hand that rested on the gun tucked against the small of his back.

"Travis?"

Angie.

Travis let his hand drop from the gun. What was she doing here? Had thinking about her been enough to conjure her up? The way things had been going lately, he was willing to believe it. He pulled the gun out of the waistband of his pants and put it out of reach. Then, unable to behave as reluctantly as he ought to, he pulled open the door.

In contrast to the dimly lit room, the porch was flooded with light from the new fixture Travis had put up not long after he rented the place. It sometimes paid to have a clear view of one's visitors.

The light shone off Angie's hair, turning it to pure gold.

"Hi."

"Hi." Travis cleared his throat, which seemed suddenly tight. "What are you doing here?"

"Glad to see you, too," she said with an uncertain laugh.

"Sorry." He thrust his fingers through his hair and half smiled. "I think the heat melted my brain. Come in."

He stepped back to allow her in and then shut the door behind her. Turning to look at her, he noticed that the dingy room seemed suddenly brighter, as if she carried sunshine inside.

"It is hot, isn't it?" she said.

"Yeah. It's hot." He was hardly conscious of what he was saying. He couldn't take his eyes off the bare skin of her shoulders. Talk about a melted brain. Her dress was enough to cause a permanent meltdown.

Her shoulders were completely bare except for a pair of thin straps that held up the bodice. Peacock-blue cotton molded her breasts and clung to her waist before falling in graceful folds to just above her knees. When she half turned to set her purse on the sofa, Travis could see that the thin straps crossed in the middle of her back. And that was all that covered her back.

His fingers slowly curled into the palms of his hands. He knew from personal experience just how that length of exposed skin felt. And this time, there was no annoying strap to dispose of, just that wonderful expanse of bare skin.

Her hair was caught up on top of her head in one of those soft buns that made a woman look as if she'd just stepped out of the bath and made a man think all sorts of things he shouldn't.

He swallowed hard and closed his eyes for a moment, reminding himself that, only moments ago, he'd decided that the best thing for all concerned was to keep his distance from Angie Brady. But she wasn't cooperating.

When he opened his eyes, she'd moved closer. She was close enough now that he could smell the light floral scent he'd come to associate with her, the scent that had haunted more than a few late-night dreams.

"What are you doing here?" He'd intended the

question to sound harsh and unwelcoming. But even he could hear that it fell far short of the mark.

"I came to see you." Angie reached up to brush an invisible piece of lint from his shoulder. Travis felt the light touch burn through the fabric of his shirt. He cleared his throat.

"You shouldn't have come here, Angie."

"I keep thinking about this morning," she continued as if he hadn't spoken. "About how right it felt. Having you hold me, kiss me. Touch me." The last was hardly more than a whisper and the color in her cheeks told him that the bold words did not come as easily as she pretended.

It was that soft blush that kept him from saying something harsh, something guaranteed to put an end to this foolishness. Or that's what he told himself. That explanation grew a little thin however when he realized that he'd set his hands on her shoulders.

"Angel, this will never work." His words lacked conviction, especially since his thumbs were moving lightly over the fragile length of her collarbone.

"It seems to be working pretty well so far." She'd moved closer still and was looking up at him with those big blue eyes. What was it about her eyes that made it so difficult for him to keep track of what he should do?

"You can't use me as a club to beat your brother with," he told her.

"This has nothing to do with Clay. This is just you and me." Her fingers were working loose the buttons on his shirt.

He should stop her, of course. And he would. In just a minute.

"This isn't a good idea," he whispered huskily.

His fingers had found the first of the pins that held her hair. Within seconds it was spilling over his hands, a waterfall of gold silk.

''I think it's a very good idea.'' She'd opened all the buttons she could reach before his belt blocked her path. She set her hands on his chest. Travis felt the light touch burn his skin.

She was so close, there was hardly room for a shadow between them. He could feel every breath she drew, see the tiny silver lines that spiraled through the blue of her eyes. Her scent filled his head.

He wanted her. God, how he wanted her. He'd never wanted—needed—anything in his life the way he needed Angie at this moment. She was all the things he wasn't. She completed everything he was missing. All the warmth and trust and faith he no longer felt.

His fingers slid through her hair, cupping her head, his eyes searching her face. Would it be so wrong to steal a little piece of her brightness? It was what she wanted. What he needed. Would it be so terrible to pretend? Just for a little while?

She stared into his eyes as his head lowered toward hers, her lashes lowering in the last half breath before his mouth touched hers. The battle was lost before it had begun. The moment he felt the soft warmth of her mouth, tasted her response, Travis knew there would be no turning back.

This was right, just as she'd said. This was what had to happen. Let the devil take tomorrow. Tonight he was going to taste heaven.

ANGIE HAD THOUGHT she knew what she was doing when she came here tonight. She thought it out calmly—or at least as calmly as she could when just the thought of Travis was enough to set her pulse pounding—and she made her decision. She expected some resistance on his part. He had this stupid idea that he wasn't good for her. But she'd been sure, with a deep feminine instinct she'd never realized she possessed, that he'd give in, his need as strong as hers.

What she hadn't expected was the way everything suddenly spiraled out of control the moment he touched her. It was as if she unleashed a fire, blazing hot and full of desire. There was no slow build to passion, no soft and gentle coaxing along pathways still relatively new to her.

Travis's mouth molded hers, his tongue skimming her lower lip and then plunging into her mouth as if he had to taste her or die. Angie's breath left her on a moan as impatient hands stripped the flimsy straps from her shoulders. The bodice dropped to her waist but there was no time to feel any uneasiness at being half nude in front of a man for the first time in her life because Travis's palms covered her breasts, his touch a sweet fire on her skin.

If she'd thought to feel a twinge of fear, he gave her no time for it. Her hands slid helplessly upward to cling to the strength of his shoulders as he wrapped his arms around her back, dragging her forward until they were molded together from shoulder to waist.

It wasn't until she sensed the light change against her closed eyelids that she realized he was carrying her. She opened her eyes as he set her on her feet next to a bed. His bedroom. His bed.

He released her long enough to wrench off the open shirt, tossing it behind him. Every nerve in his body screamed for him to tumble her onto the bed and ease the ache that had been gnawing at him since the day they met. But this wasn't some woman he'd picked up in a bar. This was Angie. And he was going to make it perfect for her.

"I think we need a light."

"No." Her protest was quick but not quick enough. With a click, the bedside lamp came on, banishing the shadows to the room's corners. Angie's hands came up as if to cover herself but he caught her wrists, holding her arms out to the side.

"Don't," he ordered softly. "I want to look at you."

His eyes skimmed her and the look in them made her forget her self-consciousness. The look said he found her beautiful.

"This morning, I tried to picture what you looked like. You felt so good, all soft and silky. But you're so much more beautiful than I even imagined." He released her hands, his own coming up to cup the soft mounds, his thumbs stroking over her nipples.

Angie's hands clenched in his hair as he bent and took one dusky peak into his mouth. Never in all her wildest dreams had she imagined a sensation so intense. Every nerve in her body responded to the gentle tugging of his mouth.

Just when she thought she might faint from the intensity of it, Travis lifted his head, his mouth coming down on hers as his hands slid around her back. Angie felt him working the zipper on her dress. An instant later, the light cotton started to slide down her hips. She felt a momentary panic at the thought of standing before him without even that dubious protection but it was too late. Her dress lay around her feet in a spill of peacock blue.

Travis lifted his head, his eyes catching hers in a look that made her forget her shyness, then he looked down at her nearly bare body. The hot weather had made hose unthinkable and she was clad in only a pair of scandalously small panties the same color as her discarded dress. The swatch of blue nylon and lace contrasted invitingly with her pale skin.

She saw Travis's reaction in the way the skin tightened over his cheekbones, heard it in the shallow breath he drew. And she felt more deeply feminine than she'd ever felt before. As if from outside herself, she saw her hand come out to rest on the heavy bulge at the front of his jeans. She felt him shudder in response to her light touch.

He dragged his eyes from her slender body and locked his gaze with hers as he reached for his belt. Angie let her hand drop back down to her side. The room was hot and still yet the rasp of his zipper brought goose bumps to life on her torso.

Without breaking his gaze from hers, Travis shoved his jeans and underwear down and off, kicking them aside impatiently. Angie automatically looked down. And forgot how to breathe.

She was a nurse, and as she'd told him, the male body held no surprises for her. Or so she'd thought until now. She was rapidly discovering that there was a wide gap between clinical knowledge and actually standing face-to-face with a naked, aroused man.

"Oh!" The small exclamation escaped her.

"Oh?" Travis's mouth quirked in a half smile. "Is that a good *oh* or a bad *oh?*"

"Just, oh." She dragged her gaze upward, not sure if it was nerves or lust that was making her knees weak.

"Oh." He repeated her exclamation softly, still smiling in that way that made her pulse beat much too fast.

He reached out to set one fingertip between her breasts and she was sure he must be able to feel the way her heart was pounding. He let the finger drift downward, pausing to explore the shallow indentation of her belly button before drifting to toy idly with the narrow elastic at the waist of her panties.

Angie felt her breath stop as he slid his fingers beneath the lace, easing it into the mat of golden curls. Her hands came up to grip his shoulders for support as he slipped his hand beneath the fragile layer of nylon.

"Travis." His name escaped her on a sigh as he found the damp heat of her.

"Angel." The endearment was almost a prayer as he lowered his mouth to hers.

She was all silk and fire. Satin skin and trembling warmth.

He lowered her to the bed, disposing of the last scrap of fabric that kept them apart. The day's heat that lingered in the room was nothing compared to the warmth they generated between them. Travis felt as if he couldn't get enough of her—her smell, her taste, the feel of her body against his.

And Angie seemed to feel the same way, clinging to him as if she'd never let him go. She responded to his every touch with trembling excitement; her caresses held a shy eagerness that was more arousing than the practiced touch of a courtesan.

When Travis was sure he couldn't wait another second to make her his, he stretched out one arm to the nightstand. He knocked the clock to the floor trying to find the packet he'd put there three days ago. At the time he'd recognized the irony of preparing for an event he'd sworn would never take place. Now, he was simply grateful for his own hypocrisy.

Angie flushed when she saw what he was doing but there was also a softness in her eyes that said she appreciated his thoughtfulness.

Her arms reached up to him, welcoming him into the warmth of her body. It was an invitation the hounds of hell could not have prevented Travis from accepting. His body throbbed with need. With a hunger like nothing he'd ever felt.

He tested himself against her, gauging her readiness. She moaned—a low, hungry sound in the back of her throat—and he knew he could wait no more.

He buried his hands in her hair, his mouth finding hers as he eased forward, savoring the slow sheathing of his aching need in her welcoming warmth. The last thing he'd expected was to feel the thin, unmistakable barrier that blocked his further entrance. His body went rigid with surprise and he jerked his head up, his eyes meeting hers.

"Don't go." Feeling him tense and seeing the shock in his eyes, Angie grabbed hold of his arms, her fingers digging into the corded muscles as she sought to hold him to her.

"God, Angie, why didn't you tell me?"

"It's not important," she said desperately, convinced that he was going to leave her, that she'd never find out what lay at the end of the path he'd swept her along. She lifted her legs, pressing her knees to his hips.

"Please, Travis." She had to find out what lay at

the end of the journey they'd begun. She twisted restlessly beneath him. "Don't go."

"Angel." Travis lowered his mouth to hers. "I couldn't if I wanted to." He eased himself deeper, feeling the slow, grudging yielding. He swallowed her shallow gasp of discomfort as the barrier gave way, allowing him full access to the womanly depths of her.

He dragged his mouth from hers, drawing in deep breaths as he hammered his control into place. This was for her, he reminded himself. She had gifted him with something she could give but once and he would die before he'd do anything to make her regret that gift.

THE LAST THING Angie felt was regret. Wonder, pleasure, a deep sense of fulfillment, but not regret. She felt as if she'd been waiting all her life for this moment, for this man.

Her hands moved restlessly up and down the length of Travis's back, seeking something to cling to as he began to move over her. The fire he'd built inside her licked higher, threatening to blaze out of control. She wanted to let it burn, even as she half feared being consumed by the flames. She wanted… She needed… Her head twisted against the pillow, her body growing taut as she struggled to reach some goal she could almost see but didn't understand.

"Don't fight it so hard," Travis whispered against her ear. "Relax and let it happen."

She couldn't relax. And let what happen? If he didn't stop, she was going to break apart in a million pieces. And yet, she knew if he stopped now, she'd surely die. It was so close. So very, very close.

Her hands clung to his shoulders as she felt him lift himself away from her. For a moment, she thought he was leaving her and she felt a surge of panic. He couldn't go, not until she found...not until she knew...

And then suddenly she was spinning directly into the heart of the fire. Only the fire was within her, consuming her, melting her.

Travis watched the heat run up under her skin as the climax took her. Her eyes flew wide, staring up at him with shocked wonder as her body went taut. He wanted to savor her fulfillment, to take her even farther but the delicate contractions inside her rippled over him, tumbling him headlong into the fire they'd built together.

IT WAS A LONG TIME before he gathered the strength to move off of her. She murmured a protest and tightened her arms around him.

"I'll squash you," he said, his voice husky.

"I don't care. Don't go."

"I'm not going far." He settled beside her, sliding one arm under her to pull her close.

Angie snuggled her head into his shoulder as if she'd been sleeping that way for years. Travis stroked his hand up and down her damp back. He felt deeply relaxed, a rare experience in his life. It was more than just sating the sexual hunger he'd felt since meeting Angie. It went deeper than that, as if he'd found a part of himself he hadn't even known was missing.

"You should have told me," he said.

"Then you wouldn't have made love to me." She didn't pretend not to know what he was talking about. "You'd have gone all noble on me." She tilted her head to look up at him, her eyes full of soft humor and Travis found himself wanting her all over again.

"I wouldn't be too sure of that," he admitted slowly. He reached out to stroke a damp curl back from her forehead. "I think lust might have won out over nobility."

"Lust?" She rolled onto her stomach and put her hand flat on his chest, setting her chin on that prop. "Lust?" She grinned. "I like the sound of that."

"Why?" He couldn't resist the urge to run his fingers through the tangled silk of her hair.

"Because it makes it sound as if you couldn't resist me."

"Obviously I couldn't."

"I knew you wouldn't be able to." She curled the fingers of her free hand into the mat of dark blond hair on his chest.

"You knew that, did you?"

"Of course. Didn't you know I'm irresistible?" She batted her lashes at him in a fair imitation of a femme fatale.

"I'm beginning to get that impression," he said dryly.

He couldn't ever remember having a conversation like this after sex. Generally he wanted only to fall asleep. But then, this was the first time he'd found himself in bed with Angie, and around her, nothing seemed to be as it usually was.

Angie laid her head flat against his chest, listening to the steady beat of his heart. She could feel that beat beneath her palm, too, strong and even. She closed her eyes and combed her fingers through the mat of hair on his chest.

She felt completed in a way she'd never known

before, as if a part of her that had been missing was now found. Her body was at once completely relaxed and more alive than ever before.

When she'd decided to come here and seduce Travis, she'd had a few doubts, wondering if she were making the right choice. Now it was hard to remember why she'd even wondered. Her mouth curved in a soft, secretive smile. It had been worth waiting to find out what all the hoopla was about. It had been more than worth waiting.

Travis tilted his head to look at Angie's face. She'd fallen asleep, he realized. Sprawled across his chest like a tired kitten, she was sound asleep. His mouth relaxed in a smile that would have surprised quite a few people who thought they knew him. It would have surprised him, if he'd happened to look in a mirror. Tenderness was not an emotion he generally connected with himself.

Damn, but she was beautiful. And she was his.

His arm tightened around her as he shifted her to a more comfortable position against his shoulder. She muttered something unintelligible and frowned slightly before nuzzling her face into his skin and throwing one arm across his chest.

His. Travis looked at her sleeping face and allowed a wave of purely masculine possessiveness to wash over him. Right or wrong, she belonged to him in a way no other woman ever had. In a way she could never belong to another man. No matter what happened in the future, there'd be no forgetting this night for either of them.

As if he could ever forget anything about her, he thought. What was it about her that made him feel things he'd never felt before? Reminded him of old dreams he'd thought long gone? She almost made him believe in the future again.

He rested his cheek against her head. This couldn't last, of course. Sooner or later, something would happen and she'd see him as he really was. Travis closed his eyes, blocking out the thought. He'd deal with that when the time came. But he didn't want to think about it now.

He didn't want to think about anything now except how right she felt in his arms. In his bed. He'd dared to love an angel, he thought, just on the edge of sleep. There'd be a price to pay, but for the moment, he was just going to savor the miracle of it.

Chapter Nine

"Let me drive you home."

"And have Clay shoot you on the doorstep?" Angie was smiling as she shook her head. "I'll be fine. Have you seen my other shoe?"

Travis glanced around the bedroom and lifted his bare shoulders in a shrug. "I wasn't particularly interested in your shoes earlier."

"Neither was I," she acknowledged, flushing lightly as she remembered just how little interest she'd had in anything but him. Shoes had been the least of her concerns.

She had to admit she didn't care much about finding them now. Travis was standing at the foot of the bed, wearing a pair of jeans that rode low on his hips. They were zipped but not buttoned and Angie curled her fingers into her palm against the urge to lower that zipper.

"If you keep looking at me like that, you're never going to get a chance to find your shoes."

The husky threat jerked her eyes to his face and the way he was looking at her made her flush deepen. It promised all sorts of things, promises she was tempted to take up. With an effort she forced her eyes away from the temptation.

"I've got to go to work," she said, the reminder as much for herself as for him.

"Then I guess you're going to need your shoes."

The lost shoe was finally located in the living room. It must have fallen off when he picked her up to carry her into the bedroom, she thought. She had to force her mind away from that line of thinking before she decided that going to work wasn't important.

"I'll follow you home." Travis appeared in the bedroom doorway, shrugging into a shirt.

"That's not necessary."

"I don't want you driving home alone at this hour of the morning."

"Travis, it's almost dawn. Even the bad guys are asleep by now. Besides, I'm going to be in my car and I'll lock the doors."

"I'll follow you home." There was no arguing with the flat statement but Angie tried anyway.

"It's really not..."

"Necessary," Travis finished for her. He crossed the few feet that separated them and stopped in front of her. Brushing his fingers across her cheek, he looked down at her, his eyes gray green in the dimly lit room. "I'll follow you home," he said softly.

"Okay." She'd have agreed to almost anything he said as long as he was standing so close and looking at her that way. She turned her face into his hand, her eyes half closing as his thumb brushed over her lower lip.

"You know I'm beginning to think you're not an angel," he said huskily.

"I never said I was." Her teeth nibbled his thumb

before her tongue came out to taste him. Angie felt a surge of purely feminine satisfaction at the way his eyes darkened to deep green as he watched her. He drew his hand away from her mouth, shifting it to cup the back of her neck.

"I think you're a witch," he whispered just before his mouth touched hers.

Angie melted into him, her arms coming up to circle his neck, her body pliant against his. As she'd already discovered, her self-control faded at his lightest touch. She instantly forgot about going home. If he'd picked her up and carried her back to bed, she wouldn't have offered a word of protest.

"I thought you had to go home and change for work," he murmured against her ear.

"I could call in sick," she said, feeling a delicious shiver work its way up her spine when his teeth caught her earlobe and bit gently.

"No." She could feel the effort it cost him to straighten and step away from her. Even then, he couldn't prevent his fingers from lingering in her hair. "You should get home. Your brother will be worried sick if he finds out you didn't come home last night. Chances are, this is the first place he'll look."

"I'm a little too old to be reporting in to Clay," Angie told him, her mouth tightening in annoyance. "He's going to have to get used to it because this isn't going to be the last time I spend the night with you."

She caught her breath as she realized what she'd said. The flush that rose in her cheeks was dark and painful.

"Oh, God. That sounded so presumptuous." She

pressed her hands to her hot cheeks. ''I didn't mean to assume...I mean, if you didn't want...''

''I want.'' Travis reached out and pulled her into his arms.

Angie felt the solid beat of his heart beneath her ear and felt as if she'd come home. The words ''I love you'' trembled on the tip of her tongue. But now was not the time. She knew instinctively that it would be a mistake to tell him how she felt now.

''You'd better get going,'' Travis said, after a moment, releasing her with obvious reluctance.

Angie hugged that reluctance to her as she drove home. That, and the presence of the motorcycle's headlight behind her. The eastern sky was just starting to show a hint of gray when she pulled into the driveway.

Travis had slowed the motorcycle to a stop in the street and she knew he was waiting to make sure that she got into the house safely. Once she had the front door open, she waved her arm to let him know she was safe. He lifted his hand in acknowledgement and then lifted his foot off the pavement and sent the motorcycle off down the street, the engine's roar loud in the quiet neighborhood.

Angie sneaked up the stairs to her room, glad that Clay's room was at the back of the house, where he was unlikely to have heard the bike. Closing the door of her room behind her, she wrapped her arms around her waist and leaned back against it, letting the night's memories wash over her.

Travis cared. Oh, he wasn't ready to admit it yet but she could see it in his eyes when he looked at her. And she'd felt it in his touch last night. She wasn't naive enough to think that he loved her just because he'd made love to her. But there'd been more than passion in his touch. There'd been a tenderness there, a concern that put her needs above his own. A man didn't treat a woman with such care if he didn't feel something more than simple desire for her.

Angie pushed away from the door and drifted over to the window. Opening the curtains, she stared out at the dawn just breaking over the horizon. She felt as fresh and new and full of hope as the new day.

There were still barriers between them, she thought, forcing herself to be realistic. Something inside Travis was fighting the feelings growing between them. She didn't know what it was, why he was so determined to keep her at a distance. Even after last night, she'd felt him putting up walls, trying to keep her from getting too close.

He wanted her—that much he'd been forced to admit. And he cared about her—that much she'd seen in his eyes. For now, it was enough.

TRAVIS PUSHED open the clinic door and stepped inside. There were three people in the waiting room: a mother with a fussy toddler and an old man who sat staring at the wall opposite with blank eyes.

"I need your name and the reason for your visit."

Travis turned to look at the woman who sat behind the scarred counter that served as an admittance desk. She was a heavy-set redhead in her late thirties, wearing a hot pink blouse that clashed so magnificently with her hair it was almost a fashion statement. She looked at him with curiosity, her dark eyes skimming his tall figure as if wondering what injury or illness had brought him to the Fair Street Clinic.

"I'm here to see Angie Brady," he said.

"She's with a patient." The curiosity had turned to speculation and Travis shifted uneasily beneath the questions in her eyes.

"Will she be long?"

"Probably not. I could tell her you're here, if you want."

"I'd appreciate that. Just tell her it's Travis."

"Travis." The woman repeated his name slowly, rolling it on her tongue as if trying to extract more information from that one meager tidbit.

"Anything else I should tell her?" she asked hopefully.

"No." He added nothing to the flat word and after a moment, she heaved herself up from the stool. "You can wait in the waiting room, if you like. That's what it's there for." She grinned at him, revealing a set of perfect teeth.

Judging by her reaction, there obviously weren't many men who came around asking for Angie. He tried not to feel a twinge of pleasure at the thought.

Travis glanced at the small waiting room to find that the young woman was looking at him, ignoring the child who was tugging on her skirt and whining about wanting a cookie. The old man had also shifted his attention from the empty wall to Travis, making him feel like an exhibit at the zoo.

He turned away from their curious looks, pretending enormous interest in a poster that pointed out the health hazards of cigarette smoking. Next to that was a poster detailing the terrible things that could happen when you took drugs. He wondered if the message had any impact on the kids it was intended to reach. He certainly hadn't seen much evidence that it did.

And Shearson's business didn't show any signs of slowing.

"Angie said to tell you she'd be just a couple of minutes." The receptionist's words interrupted his thinking and Travis turned to look at her.

"Thanks." Travis glanced at the waiting room and found he was still the main object of interest. "Tell her I'll wait outside, would you?"

The receptionist had followed his glance and now her eyes came back to him. She grinned. "We don't get many healthy specimens in here," she offered, by way of explanation.

"Yeah, well, I'm starting to feel like a bug under a microscope. I'll wait outside."

"I'll tell Angie."

Travis nodded his thanks and escaped outside. He preferred dealing with the heat reflected off the pavement to facing the curious stares inside. He found a shady spot near the corner of the building and settled himself on the waist-high retaining wall that marked that edge of the property.

His position allowed him to see without being easily seen. He shouldn't have come here, he thought, glancing around uncomfortably. His relationship with Angie wasn't something he wanted made known, not to Shearson or to the police. And showing up at the clinic to see her was probably a dumb move. But then, he seemed to be doing a lot of dumb things these days.

He reached into his pocket for a stick of gum, folding it into his mouth. It had only been a few hours since he followed Angie home but he'd been thinking about when he'd see her again from the moment she stepped out of his sight.

Last night had been...extraordinary. Angie had been everything he'd fantasized she would be—and more. She'd given herself to him without hesitation, offering herself with a trust that was strangely erotic. He found himself wanting to take everything she offered, yet wanting to protect her from the possible consequences of her generosity. He'd done more of the former than the latter, he admitted.

Yet he couldn't find it in him to regret the night they'd spent together. He'd done exactly what he'd sworn not to: he'd gotten involved with Angie. But he just couldn't manage to regret one of the best nights of his life.

And he didn't think Angie had any regrets, either. There was an undeniable surge of male satisfaction in remembering the soft look in her eyes after they'd made love—the look of a woman who'd been thoroughly pleasured.

Travis shifted uncomfortably and turned his thoughts in less erotic directions. He stared down at the foil gum wrapper that his fingers had been absently folding into a neat little square and tried to picture where he and Angie were going to go from here.

God, listen to him. He was actually thinking in terms of having some kind of future with this woman. For the first time since he was a teenager, he was actually thinking it might be possible to build something lasting with another person.

"What the hell are you doing here?"

The sharp question jerked Travis out of his half-formed imaginings. He lifted his head to find Clay standing in front of him, his stocky body tense, feet braced apart as if for a fight.

"I'm waiting for Angie."

Travis slipped the wrapper into his pocket but didn't stand up. It was obvious that Clay would like nothing better than to punch him in the mouth again. Ordinarily Travis would have been happy to oblige, but brawling in a parking lot wasn't going to do anybody any good and it would upset Angie.

"I told you to stay away from her," Clay said.

"I think Angie's old enough to make her own decisions."

"Not about this." Clay stared at him, worry and anger darkening his eyes. "Dammit, Morgan! I don't want to see her hurt."

"Neither do I."

"You're not doing a whole hell of a lot to prevent it. I pulled your file," he said baldly.

Travis stiffened, his eyes suddenly more gray than green. "So?"

"So, I know what you're into. I know exactly what you're doing. And I know my sister is going to get badly hurt when you get yourself arrested. Or killed." He added the last deliberately, the words a warning. "And if you manage to avoid both of those, you're going to leave without a backward glance when you've got what you want."

"Maybe I'm starting to think about settling down," Travis said slowly, only then realizing how much he wanted to believe it was possible.

"You?" Clay's tone was scornful. "You're not the type. You're going to spend your life getting into trouble, the way you always have."

"A man can change."

"Some men. But not you. You're born to trouble, Morgan. You and I both know it. I don't know where this sudden urge for roots came from but I don't want you testing the idea out on my sister. If you care for her at all, even the smallest amount, leave her alone.''

''I've never played games with anyone who didn't know the score.''

''Angie doesn't know the score,'' Clay snapped. ''And I don't want her learning it from you.''

''It's a little late for that,'' Travis muttered.

''What's that supposed to mean?'' Clay fairly bristled with hostility.

They faced each other, only a breath away from a full-blown brawl. One wrong word and Clay was going to go for his throat. Travis reminded himself of how much it would upset Angie to find him fighting with her brother and willed the tension from his shoulders.

''It means that Angie is a grown woman, not a child, and you've got to let her make her own mistakes.''

''A mistake is one thing but she's walking right into a disaster.''

''You make me sound like the Titanic,'' Travis said, trying to lighten the atmosphere. But Clay wasn't about to be humored out of his mood.

''What about Shearson? What about your involvement with him? Have you considered that Angie could get caught in the crossfire?''

Travis's expression tightened as Clay's words touched a sore spot. ''I guess that you know as well as I do that Shearson's in Tahiti until the end of the week. There's not a damn thing going to happen until he gets back.''

''And when he gets back?'' Clay pressed. ''What about Angie, then?''

"I'll make sure she's out of the picture," Travis said shortly.

"Have you told her what you're doing?"

"I haven't lied to her," Travis said evasively.

"Stay away from her," Clay said again, his eyes bright blue and determined. "I won't have her hurt because you've made a mess of your life."

"I'm not going to hurt her, dammit!" Even as he made the promise, Travis wondered if he was going to be able to keep it.

"If you hurt her, I'm going to personally tear you limb from limb." Clay's voice was low and hard.

Their eyes met, green crossing blue in a silent battle that neither could win. It occurred to Travis that there was something ironic in the fact that they were practically at each other's throats although they shared the same goal, which was simply to protect Angie.

"Clay? Travis?" Angie's anxious voice broke into the mounting tension between the two men.

Looking over Clay's shoulder, Travis saw her hurrying toward them as if her intervention might be needed at any minute. Which wasn't all that far from the truth, he admitted as she reached them.

"I wasn't expecting you, Clay." She moved past her brother to stand next to Travis.

"I was in the neighborhood and thought I'd stop and say hello. You were already in bed when I got home last night."

"Yes." She didn't bother to specify which bed she'd been in and Travis wasn't about to clarify the point.

There was an awkward silence and Travis saw Clay's eyes go from his sister's face to where her hand rested against Travis's hip, an intimacy Travis doubted she was even aware of. The same could not be said for her brother.

"Can I talk to you, Angie?"

"Not if you're just going to tell me to stay away from Travis again," she said bluntly.

From the angry flush that came up in Clay's cheeks, it was obvious that that was exactly what he'd had in mind. The look he shot Travis said that he knew exactly where to place the blame for Angie's sudden truculence.

"Angie…"

"No. I'm tired of these veiled warnings, Clay. If you've got something to say, then say it. But stop acting like an overprotective, Victorian big brother."

"Fine," he snapped, stung. "Just don't come crying to me when you find out I was right."

"I won't."

Stubbornness was obviously a family trait, Travis thought. The last thing he wanted was for Angie and Clay to back themselves into opposite corners, with him squarely in the middle. He'd already done enough damage. He didn't want to cause further tension between the two of them. Whether she knew it or not, Angie was going to need her brother's support sooner or later.

"Look, why don't you two talk this out," he said uncomfortably. "I'm really not worth all this trouble."

As an attempt to lighten the tension with a little humor, it failed abysmally. Angie's fingers hooked into the top of his belt, anchoring him in place. The look Clay shot him held no gratitude, only a bitter anger.

"I don't want to talk about it," Angie said, directing the words at her furious brother.

"You got it." Casting a fulminating look at Travis, he spun on his heel and stalked across the narrow parking lot to where his car was parked.

Neither Angie nor Travis said a word until the red T-Bird had roared out of the parking lot. It was left to Angie to break the silence.

"Honestly, from the way he treats me, you'd think I was five years old."

"He's worried about you."

"He's overbearing and obnoxious," she said, her voice still laced with annoyance.

"That, too, but he's still worried about you."

"Well, he shouldn't be. I'm a big girl now." She turned to face him. "And I'm perfectly capable of making up my own mind. Now, let's talk about something besides my overbearing brother."

"Like what?"

"Like, have you missed me?" She grinned up at him, her eyes sparkling.

"Some," he admitted, frowning as if grudging the admission.

"How much?" She was wheedling shamelessly for compliments and Travis found himself wanting to grab her up in his arms and kiss her senseless.

"Enough that I've been wondering if I should ravish you in the bushes," he admitted, raising his eyebrows lasciviously.

"Ordinarily I'd be more than happy to take you up on that offer but those bushes have some very nasty thorns."

"What are thorns when passion burns strong?" he questioned dramatically.

"They're painful. That's what they are." Her pained expression drew a laugh from him.

"You know, I've always wondered what you'd look like in a uniform," he commented, studying the plain white dress she wore with a pair of thick-soled white shoes.

"It's hardly the peak of fashion."

"It makes you look very efficient. Very nursely."

Travis found his fingers searching for the clip that pulled her hair back from her face.

"Nursely? I don't think that's a word." Angie tilted her head to allow him to pull the clip loose. Her hair tumbled over his fingers.

"It is now," he murmured, continuing the conversation, though neither of them was paying much attention to it. "You have the most beautiful hair."

"Thank you. I like yours, too." She lifted one hand to ruffle her fingers through his dark blond hair.

Unable to resist temptation another moment, Travis bent to taste the softness of her mouth. It was a slow, thorough kiss that seemed to brand her as his. Angie felt her knees weaken as her hands came up to cling to his shoulders. Travis's arms tightened around her, molding her body to his, letting her feel his arousal, showing her how much he wanted her.

When he lifted his head, she drew a deep, shaken breath. It took a real effort to force her lashes up. Travis was looking down at her with the same puzzled expression she'd seen before, as if he wasn't quite sure she belonged in his arms.

But *she* was sure and she could be patient until he figured it out.

"I have to go. Janine's assisting the doctor and there's only so much she can do."

"Okay." Travis let his hands slide from her with obvious reluctance. "What time do you get off?"

"Six." Angie took her hair clip from him.

"Do you have plans for tonight?" There was a touch of hesitancy in the question as if he wasn't sure he wanted to ask it.

"Well, I had planned to wash my hair but I'm open to a better offer." The look she gave him was pure invitation and he wasn't proof against it.

"I'm a lousy cook but I do the best take-out Chinese you've ever seen," he said.

"I like moo shoo pork and I don't like those nasty little red peppers that set fire to your mouth," she said promptly. "Shall I bring anything?"

"Just yourself." As if unable to resist the urge, his hands caught her waist, pulling her close for a kiss that threatened to dissolve every bone in her body. When he released her, Angie had to cling to his shoulder until her knees were capable of supporting her again.

"Never mind the hot peppers," she murmured. "Another kiss like that and I'm likely to go up in smoke."

Travis returned her smile with a brooding look. "I don't want to hurt you, Angel," he said slowly.

"Oh, not you, too." Exasperated, she pushed out of his arms. "It's bad enough that Clay acts like I'm a helpless child. Don't you start it, too."

"I don't think you're a child." Travis shoved his hands into his pockets and continued to look at her broodingly. "I just want to be sure you're not going into this with your eyes shut."

"It's a little late to worry about that, don't you

think? After last night?'' There was more than a trace of irritation in her question.

He flushed but continued doggedly. "Maybe but I don't want you to mistake what's between us."

"And just what *is* between us, Travis?"

Neither of them was aware that they were standing in a parking lot in broad daylight. The traffic that moved on the busy streets, the heat that radiated off of pavement and walls—all were forgotten.

"What is between us?" she asked again, trying not to let him see how much his answer mattered.

"I...want you. So much I can hardly keep my hands off you," he admitted, his mouth twisting ruefully.

"And I want you," she said. "Is that all that's between us, then? Sexual attraction?"

His eyes searched hers, his a clouded green and full of secrets, hers shining blue and demanding honesty. For a moment, she thought he was going to open up to her, to let her inside the walls he used to keep the world at bay, but then he looked away, shoving his hands into his pockets and half shrugging.

"Sex can be a pretty powerful draw," he said, at last, almost as if he were talking to himself. "Especially when it seems new and fresh."

Angie felt a surge of crisp anger. So, not only was he not going to admit that he felt anything for her, but he was going to dismiss her feelings as nothing more than sexual need. If she hadn't been so sure that he *did* care, she might have been hurt. Instead, she felt a good, healthy anger.

"Well, sex is better than nothing," she said, shrugging lightly. She felt real satisfaction when Travis's eyes jerked to her face in shock. She pretended not to notice, glancing instead at her watch. "I've got to get going."

She braced her hands on his shoulders and raised on her toes to press her mouth to his. She felt his shock as her tongue came out to trace his lower lip. His hands caught her waist, bracing her automatically as she pressed closer, her mouth opening on his.

Angie intended the kiss to punish him for dismissing their relationship as purely sexual. She wanted to leave him with a vivid reminder that the sexual pull went both ways. She wasn't the only one caught in it.

Travis groaned softly as she slid her hands into his hair and arched against him, letting him feel every soft inch of her. The blood was pounding in his body, making it difficult to remember that they were standing in plain view of anyone who happened to walk by.

His hands started to slid around her back, to draw her even closer. But she was suddenly ending the kiss and slipping away from him.

"Got to go," she said, her casual tone only slightly marred by breathlessness. "I'll see you tonight."

She darted away with a quick wave of her hand, refusing to look back. If he thought he was the only one who could play stupid games, he had another think coming.

Chapter Ten

Travis hadn't been sure what to expect from Angie. Her mood had seemed odd when they parted. There'd been a sharpness in her he'd never seen before, an edge that he hadn't expected.

But none of that was evident when she arrived on his doorstep a little after seven. Though darkness was approaching, the heat lingered and she'd changed from her uniform into a sundress with a bright floral print that skimmed her body, hinting at more than it revealed.

There was no sign of her earlier mood as they ate Chinese food and argued over the relative merits of everything from Woody Allen movies to football scholarships. Travis found himself forgetting all the reasons their involvement was doomed to failure and simply enjoyed himself.

Though he wanted to believe otherwise, there was a great deal more between them than just physical desire. Powerful as that was, it wasn't all that drew him to her. He'd never known a woman who could make him laugh as easily as Angie did, who could argue passionately and yet never let the argument become personal.

He *liked* her, dammit. And if there was more to it than that, he'd be a fool to admit it, even to himself. Especially to himself.

He was surprised to realize that it was after ten when the conversation started to lag. They had moved from the kitchen to the living room, where the fan served to at least stir the warm air, giving the illusion of cooler temperatures.

Angie was curled in the big leather chair, her legs drawn up under her skirt and Travis had the fanciful thought that she looked like a multicolored flower, her skirt forming the petals that draped gracefully across the worn black leather.

Rather than trust the sofa, which was more bare springs than cushion, Travis had chosen to sit on the floor and lean back against it, stretching his legs out along the floor. The lamp cast a single circle of light in the dim room, as soft as candlelight.

It was a comfortable quiet, the sort that happens between two people who are past the stage of needing to fill every silence that falls between them. Travis leaned his head back against the sofa, and allowed his gaze to settle on Angie.

She was curled into the chair like a cat on a favorite cushion, her body relaxed against the leather, her eyes half closed as if she might fall asleep. His gaze drifted over her face, tracing the delicate line of her brows, the gentle curve of her mouth, the stubborn strength of her jaw.

From there it was a short trip to the soft length of her throat. The V-neck of her dress left her collarbone bare and he allowed his eyes to linger on the pulse that beat in the hollow of her throat. Since her shoulders were bare, it didn't seem likely that she was wearing a bra and he couldn't prevent his gaze from moving speculatively to the fullness of her breasts beneath the thin fabric of the dress.

Aware that he was growing uncomfortably aroused, he forced his eyes away from her, focusing instead on a hairline crack that ran down the wall near the door. *Probably caused by an earthquake,* he thought, trying to convince himself that he gave a damn.

"You know, I'm really glad we had that little talk today."

Travis started, his eyes jerking back to her.

"Little talk?" he questioned, momentarily at a loss.

"Yes. The one where you explained that what we have is a strong sexual attraction and nothing more."

"I didn't say that exactly." He watched warily as she uncurled her legs and rose. He'd almost managed to forget about that talk.

"Close enough." Angie didn't seem at all upset by the memory. "It made me think."

"It did?" He wasn't at all sure he was going to like the direction in which this conversation was going.

"Yes." She lifted her arms over her head, arching her back in a stretch. Travis's eyes dropped to the proud thrust of her breasts and he felt a wave of hunger.

Angie slanted him an unreadable look from under her lashes and reached behind her back. The unmistakable hiss of a zipper being lowered made Travis's mouth go dry.

"Yes, I thought about it quite a bit this afternoon." The dress loosened around her but didn't fall.

"You did?" He was no longer at all sure what they were discussing.

"I decided that, if sex is all we have going for us, we might as well make the most of it." She loosened the tie at the back of her neck and the dress slid down her body, landing in a bright splash of color on the floor.

And Travis forgot how to breathe.

Where on earth had she found a garment like that? Did she realize that something like that could give a man a heart attack? He wasn't even conscious of standing up.

Angie watched him from under her lashes, well satisfied with the results she'd achieved. He looked as if he'd been hit in the head with a baseball bat. She'd been a little uncertain when she dragged the black silk teddy from the back of her lingerie drawer. It had been a gift from her friend Leigh two birthdays ago and she'd never had a reason to wear it. Now she was glad she'd saved it.

She'd heard it said that sex was not enough to base a relationship on and she didn't doubt the truth of that. On the other hand, she had a heart-deep belief that Travis's feelings for her ran a lot deeper than he was willing to admit. Until the day came that he could face that, she wasn't above using sex to sharpen his interest.

If Travis could have read her thoughts he would have assured her that she'd succeeded in sharpening his interest. In fact, it was so sharp at the moment that if a Sherman tank had thundered through the wall, he would barely have noticed the intrusion.

He couldn't take his eyes off the way the strapless black silk cupped her breasts. If she drew a deep breath, she was surely going to spill out. He found himself praying for her to feel breathless.

He didn't remember moving but he was suddenly standing in front of her, his hands settling on her slender waist, drawing her closer. His blood pounded in his veins but he caught the flicker of uncertainty in her eyes as she lifted her hands to his shoulders. It reminded him of just how limited her experience was.

"From innocent to seductress in twenty-four hours," he said huskily. "Quite a transition."

"I aim to please," she told him.

"If you pleased me anymore, you just might kill me." His laugh held a note of real pain. "You shouldn't spring something like that on a man."

"I'll keep that in mind in the future."

Her words brought a quick frown. "In the future." Just what was that supposed to mean? Was she going to let someone else see her in this scrap of silk nothing. The thought had his hands tightening around her waist as he dragged her closer.

"You'd better never let anyone see you in that thing but me," he whispered against her mouth. His kiss was pure masculine possessiveness staking a claim.

Angie surrendered without protest. For now she'd accept possessiveness as a step in the right direction. Given time, possessiveness could grow into something deeper and more lasting. Something like love.

Passion flared hot and fast between them, burning away everything but need and a soul-deep hunger. If Travis's fingers were impatient with the thin silk that kept him from her skin, Angie's fingers trembled in their eagerness to rid him of the layers of cloth that separated them.

Travis barely retained enough self-control to get them into the bedroom. The springs creaked a protest as they fell onto the bed. Travis twisted so that Angie landed on top of him. Winding his hands in her hair, he dragged her mouth down to his. She tasted faintly of the beer she'd had after dinner. She felt like heaven.

Heat shot through him as she shifted, straddling his thighs. His hands left her hair to grasp her hips, lifting her, positioning and sliding into the welcome sheath of her all in one move. She accepted this new position without hesitation, her calves pressing against his thighs as she sat upright, taking him deeper.

He took hold of her hips, guiding her, helping her find a rhythm. But it wasn't long before the soft ripeness of her breasts became a temptation too great to resist. He watched her, wishing there was more light so that he could see the flush that rose from her breasts to her throat when she neared completion.

Angie felt herself trembling on the brink, a heartbeat away from the peak she knew lay just out of sight. Her whole being tensed with the need to reach that goal. It was so close, so very, very close.

And then Travis's fingers were touching her where their bodies joined together, finding the very heart of her need and she was tumbling headlong into a whirlpool of pure sensation. She heard Travis groan low in his throat and his hands were suddenly gripping her hips as he arched into her.

As the sensations ebbed, she collapsed onto his chest, her breathing ragged, her whole body limp and sated. Travis's hand came up to comb through her hair and she felt a purely feminine satisfaction when she realized that his fingers were not quite steady.

She didn't know how long they lay there, still linked physically and mentally. Travis's fingers continued to move through her hair, a soft rhythmic motion that made Angie feel like a particularly well-fed cat.

"Angel?" His voice was a husky rumble under her ear. She lifted her head to look into his face.

"What?"

"It's not just sex between us." The husky admission flowed over her like a warm summer's breeze.

"I know." She didn't press for more. It was enough for now that he'd admitted that much.

ANGIE DIDN'T KNOW what time it was when the sound of a phone ringing woke her. While she was still registering the sound, Travis was out of bed and on his way into the living room. The phone cut off in mid-ring and then she heard the low murmur of his voice. The tone didn't sound urgent, though she couldn't distinguish what he was saying. It seemed as if she was still trying to clear the sleep from her eyes when he was sliding back between the sheets.

"Something wrong?" she asked as he drew her against him.

"No. Just a business call."

"At two in the morning?" She'd managed to focus on the clock next to the bed.

"It's not two in the morning all over the world," he said by way of explanation. "Go back to sleep."

Angie knew she hadn't heard the whole story but she also doubted that further questions would elicit anything but more evasions. Just what part of the world was Travis getting calls from? And what kind of work did he do that made calls in the middle of the night necessary?

Frowning slightly, she allowed her head to settle

on his shoulder, throwing one arm across his chest. One of these days, she was going to get answers to all the questions she had about him. But not tonight.

Travis listened to her quiet breathing as she slid back to sleep. Things were moving faster than he'd expected. Shearson was back from Tahiti and he wanted a meeting. It was exactly what he'd been angling toward for weeks but he couldn't help but think that the timing stank.

Just a few more days, he thought. He'd wanted just a few more days with Angie before life intruded, but tonight was all he was sure of having. In the morning, he'd tell her that he couldn't see her for a while. He turned his face into her hair, savoring the soft scent that was hers alone.

God, Clay had been right. He had no business letting things go this far. He'd allowed his hunger for her warmth to cloud his judgment. He was only now facing just how difficult it was going to be to avoid hurting her badly.

How was he supposed to make her understand?

ANGIE PULLED HER CAR into the driveway and shut the engine off but she didn't immediately get out. Instead, she leaned her forearms on the steering wheel and stared out the windshield. The sun was barely up and traces of mist lingered under the branches of the big sycamore that all but filled the backyard. By ten, the mist would be gone as the summer sun consolidated its hold on Southern California.

Angie wasn't particularly interested in the weather at the moment. Her thoughts were on the man she'd just left, the man she'd managed to fall in love with. They'd just spent a most satisfactory night together and she'd awakened to find him kissing his way up the length of her spine, an action that had led to long and eminently pleasurable lovemaking.

And yet while they were dressing he'd told her that he couldn't see her tonight. As if she'd asked! Angie frowned and drummed her fingers against the steering wheel. He'd said he had business to attend to but, as usual, he hadn't bothered to specify just what that business was. Damn, the man was frustrating.

Why couldn't she have fallen in love with an accountant? Or a doctor? Why couldn't she have fallen in love with a man whose past wasn't a state secret and who didn't have such an aversion to talking about his present?

Because she'd fallen in love with Travis. The obvious answer didn't make her feel any better. She got out of the car and strode toward the house, her heels clicking on the pavement. Mysterious phone calls before dawn and then an announcement that he wouldn't be able to see her tonight. He'd said he wasn't wanted by the police and Clay had admitted that he wasn't a criminal. Then what was he?

She pulled open the kitchen door and stepped inside before realizing the room was already occupied. Clay stood next to the coffeemaker and from the way he turned to look at her, he had heard her coming.

Their eyes met for a moment and then Clay's dropped to skim over her dress and heels. It was obvious she'd been out all night. *And none of his business,* Angie reminded herself, lifting her chin as his gaze returned to her face.

"Good morning." She spoke first, deciding to treat the situation as if there was nothing unusual about it.

"Good morning." Clay hesitated but followed her lead.

Unfortunately Angie had run out of conversational gambits. They looked at each other across a gulf—a gulf neither was quite ready to bridge. After a moment, Clay turned away, rinsing his cup in the sink before setting it in the dishwasher.

"Well, I've got to get going if I'm going to get my run in before work." His voice was too hearty and his eyes avoided her as he turned from the sink.

"Yes." She wasn't sure what she was agreeing to but it seemed as if she should say something and that was all that occurred to her.

He glanced at her again and hesitated.

"Look, I know you don't want to hear it but I can't just watch you walk into this with your eyes closed."

"My eyes are wide open, Clay." But her tone held no anger. He looked so worried. "I'm not a fool."

"I know you're not." His fingers toyed restlessly with his watchband. "But you don't have all the facts. You don't know what Travis really is."

"I know he's the man I love," she said flatly. The words sounded surprisingly natural when spoken aloud. She saw their impact on her brother. He winced, his eyes closing for a moment. When they opened again, there was something approaching despair in their depths.

"Angie, there are things about Morgan that you don't know."

"I'm sure there's a lot I don't know," she agreed readily. "But I'd rather find out from him."

"But—"

"No, Clay. Please." She stretched one hand out her expression pleading. "Unless you've got something concrete to tell me, I don't want to hear anymore. I don't want to hear what he might have been involved in when you were in high school. I don't want to hear what you suspect him of now. If you've got proof, tell me. Otherwise, leave it alone.''

Clay stared at her, frustration tying his gut in knots. He was torn between the need to protect her and his inability to reveal privileged information. There was really only one decision possible.

''Okay,'' he said tiredly. ''I'll keep my mouth shut about Morgan and let you do as you see fit.''

''Thank you.''

''But I'm still your big brother. And if you need me, I'm still here for you, just like always.''

''Just like always,'' Angie agreed softly.

He lifted one hand in farewell and walked out the door. Angie stood in the brightly lit kitchen, feeling more lonely than she'd ever felt in her life. From the time she was small, Clay had always been there for her. They'd never gone through a stage where they weren't friends, the way most brothers and sisters did.

He'd never minded her tagging along when he went fishing.It had been Clay who taught her to ride a bike. Clay who comforted her when their mother abandoned the family. When their father died, it was Clay who insisted that Angie stay with him, rather than being farmed out to more ''suitable'' care until her eighteenth birthday.

''Damn!'' She rubbed her fingers over her cheeks, unsurprised to find them damp. Her brother had always been one of her best friends. Why, all of a sudden, had he turned into something out of a Victorian novel?

Well, it would take time but he'd come around.

Sooner or later he'd understand that she had to live her own life and make her own mistakes. She refused to believe that loving Travis was a mistake.

Her steps were slow as she climbed the stairs to her room. Yesterday morning, she'd practically floated up these stairs, sure that everything was going to turn out just as it should. But Clay's attitude and the secrecy with which Travis surrounded himself had taken their toll on that optimism.

"I'm just tired," she said aloud, her voice echoing in the hallway as she paused outside her bedroom door. Tired and just a little uncertain. What had happened to her life lately? Everything had changed so quickly. She rubbed a tired hand over her face. A couple of hours sleep would help to banish her doubts, she told herself briskly, pushing open the door.

As IT TURNED OUT, she didn't have time to take a nap. Angie had no sooner stepped out of the shower than the phone range. The clinic was short on staff. Could Angie possibly come in early? She would have agreed to go in, even if she'd had other plans, but going to work just suited her mood this morning. The last thing she wanted was to have time to brood.

It was a busy day, for which Angie was grateful. She felt guilty about her gratitude. After all, a busy day in the clinic was hardly good news for the people coming in for help. But as long as she was occupied, she didn't have time to worry about the rift between her and Clay. Or to worry about just what Travis's "business" might be. Or to wonder when he'd call her. *If* he called.

Since she'd never been in love before, she'd never

realized just how vulnerable the emotion would make her feel. She was *sure* Travis cared for her—until she thought about it a little too long. And then she was equally sure that he only desired her.

Angie murmured soothingly to a crying baby who was strenuously objecting to the treatment for a nasty scratch she'd received from a cat who didn't like having its neck squeezed. Even as Angie tended to the child, her hands sure and steady, part of her mind was occupied with the age-old question: Did he love her or didn't he?

She handed the crying infant to her mother, reassuring her that no permanent damage had been done. The woman was nearly in tears as she thanked Angie. Angie saw them on their way and then went to wash up before greeting the next patient.

She was a good nurse, she thought, glaring at the bottle of antiseptic soap as if daring it to deny that fact. She'd worked hard to get her training and she'd graduated among the top ten in her class. She was a strong, modern woman, not some fainting flower.

She'd watched her friend Leigh fall in and out of love half a dozen times since they were teenagers. And she'd never understood how Leigh could let her emotions get so completely out of control every time. Surely, *she'd* never be that way, if and when she fell in love.

And here she was, in love and a quivering mass of uncertainty and insecurity. Her mouth twisted in wry humor as she dried her hands. Maybe this was her comeuppance for being so smug and superior when Leigh was in the throes of each new love affair.

"Angie, the patient in two wants a tetanus shot."

Angie turned a quick smile on Hugh Johnson as the doctor stopped to wash his hands.

"No patient *wants* a tetanus shot, Hugh. Am I going to have to sit on this one?"

"It's Mrs. Ludovich," he told her as he soaped his hands. "She cut herself and she's convinced lockjaw is only a heartbeat away."

"Lockjaw? Mrs. Ludovich?" Angie widened her eyes, picturing the elderly woman who was known for her ability to talk for half an hour without pausing for air. "Lockjaw wouldn't have a chance with her," she said.

"Probably not." Hugh Johnson's serious features creased in a rare smile. "To tell the truth, I thought of prescribing twenty-four hours of silence just to see if she could stick to it."

"Not a chance." Laughing, Angie left him and went to give Mrs. Ludovich her shot.

BY SEVEN O'CLOCK in the evening, she'd put in almost twelve hours, most of it on her feet. She'd given shots, patched minor injuries, listened sympathetically when that seemed the best medicine she could offer. Her feet hurt, her back ached and she wanted nothing so much as a hot shower and a bed. But the hours of work had served to distract her. It wasn't possible to worry about Clay and Travis and simultaneously convince a fractious toddler that a shot was really a good thing.

The clinic closed at seven-thirty, leaving the emergency room of the local hospital to pick up the burden after that. At seven-twenty, Angie was cleaning one of the examining rooms and trying to decide whether or not to stop on the way home to pick up a salad for dinner.

At seven-twenty-five, the front door flew open and the quiet was shattered by the sound of shouted demands for help, mixed with moans of pain and hysterical sobbing.

Angie flew out of the examining room, entering the waiting room hard on Hugh Johnson's heels. The room seemed full of people at first. It took several minutes for Angie to sort them out. There were two youths in their early twenties, their decorated vests identifying them as members of a local gang. Between them they held up a boy who looked no more than thirteen. Angie barely noticed the older woman behind the three, the source of the sobbing.

"What happened?" Hugh snapped out the question, even as he was reaching for the boy.

"It was an accident," one of the youths muttered, exchanging a look with his friend.

"An accident!" That was the older woman, whom Angie had already pegged as the wounded boy's mother. "They've killed him with their stupid wars. My baby, who never hurt anyone. I told you what would happen if you joined that gang. Now look at your brother!"

"Gunshot wounds," Hugh told Angie, ignoring the woman's continued recriminations. "He's lost a lot of blood."

"Can we get him to General?" The hospital was better equipped to handle a gunshot wound, but Hugh was already shaking his head.

"We've got to try to stop the bleeding, at least. We'll put him in number one. Janine, call General. Tell them what we've got."

"Yes, Doctor." Janine turned to the phone even as Hugh directed the two youths to help him get the boy into the examining room he'd indicated.

"Is he going to be all right?" That was the boy's brother as Angie urged them from the room. Looking at his white face and frightened eyes, she wanted to offer him some reassurance but there wasn't anything she could say.

"Dr. Johnson is an excellent doctor," she said. "We'll do the best we can." She pushed them from the room and turned back to where Hugh was cutting open the boy's shirt to get a better look at the wounds.

One of the most difficult lessons for any medical professional to learn is that doing their best sometimes just isn't enough. No matter how much skill and concern were brought to bear, they couldn't win every battle.

Angie and Hugh were fighting a losing battle from the beginning and they knew it. One look at the wounds and the amount of blood the boy had already lost and they both knew what his chances were. But they didn't hesitate.

They immediately went to work, attempting to stop the seemingly inexhaustible flow of blood. They'd worked together for over a year now and Angie was able to anticipate his needs before he expressed them. Moving as if they'd been choreographed, they fought to save the boy's life.

Though Angie had never heard Hugh say so much as "damn," she wasn't shocked by the steady stream of curses that left him when it became obvious that this was one battle they weren't going to win.

By the time paramedics arrived, there was nothing they could do. There'd been nothing they could have done from the start. Angie stood in one corner of the examining room, watching as they transferred the body to a stretcher and pulled the sheet up over the young face. Her hands hung limp at her sides. She couldn't think of a better place to put them.

A glance at the clock told her that barely twenty minutes had passed since she'd been thinking about what to do for dinner. Twenty minutes. It seemed like hours. Moving as if she were an old woman, she began cleaning the examining room, her movements automatic.

''Leave it.'' That was Hugh, coming back into the room. His thin body radiated defeat. ''I'll clean up.''

''I don't mind.'' Angie methodically gathered the bloodstained instruments together.

''Leave it,'' he said again. ''Go home. You've been here all day.''

''So have you,'' she pointed out.

''Yeah.'' He stared around the small room for a moment and then went to rub his fingers over his eyes. He stopped, the move uncompleted as he stared at the blood on his hands. ''Jesus, some days I hate this job.''

In the end, they cleaned up together, finding some solace in the mundane tasks. When it was done, they left the clinic, parting company without a word. There just didn't seem to be anything to say.

Angie started her car and pulled out of the parking lot but, instead of turning left toward home, she found herself turning right. The only thing she could think of was that she had to see Travis. She wanted to feel his arms around her and have him tell her that everything was going to be all right.

It no longer mattered that she didn't know how he

felt about her. She didn't care what his mysterious business was. She didn't care about anything but seeing him.

Chapter Eleven

Travis's thoughts were on the upcoming meeting with Shearson's minions. He'd spent months working toward it and he hadn't expected this break so soon. It was everything he'd worked for and it was dropping into his lap like a ripe plum.

The meeting was set for ten o'clock at a local bar. Shearson wasn't particularly concerned about whether the police found out that he was thinking of taking on a new middleman. They'd find out sooner or later anyway. The bar was public and it was noisy, and if Shearson's men were known to the police, the police were also known to them and they'd be very visible.

When someone knocked on the door, Travis's hand jerked toward the gun he wore tucked into the back of his belt. *Nervous reflex,* he told himself but he didn't release the gun. Who the hell was banging on the door now?

"Travis?" He glanced at the clock and cursed softly. He'd told Angie he couldn't see her tonight. What was she doing here?

"Travis?" She knocked again, her voice sounding thin and uncertain in a way he'd never heard before.

"Damn." He moved to the door and pulled it open, his expression less than welcoming.

But he forgot all about his irritation and the up-coming meeting when he saw her. Her hair fell in untidy straggles from where it was caught on top of her head. Her face was pale and drawn with dark hollows under her eyes. But what caught his eyes and caused his mouth to go dry with fear were the blood-stains that streaked garishly across the formerly pristine fabric of her uniform.

"My God, Angie. What happened?" He reached out and caught her in his arms, pulling her into the living room and kicking the door shut behind them.

"Oh, Travis. There was nothing we could do." The words ended on a shallow sob. Her arms came up to circle his neck and she leaned into him like a tired child.

Relieved that none of the blood was hers, Travis put his arms around Angie and drew her closer. She shuddered and began to cry softly, as if all she'd needed was his touch to release the dammed-up tears.

It took her some time to get her tears under control. By then, from her assorted muffled explanations, Travis had managed to get a fairly clear picture of what had happened to upset her so much.

Angie had no clear memory of him settling in the big leather chair and then pulling her onto his lap. She also didn't remember his pulling the pins from her hair but he must have because he was now comb-ing his fingers through it in a wonderfully soothing rhythm.

"He was so young, Travis," she whispered, her voice husky from crying.

"Try not to think about it."

"He'd lost so much blood. There just wasn't anything we could do."

"You did the best you could. It's not your fault he didn't make it."

"I know." She sighed and let her head fall against his shoulder. "It just seems like there *should* have been something we could have done. I felt so helpless. So useless."

Travis put his fingers under her chin and raised her face to his. "You did everything you could, Angie. You're not God."

"I know." She knew he was right but knowing didn't take away the feeling that she'd failed the boy.

Travis read the doubt in her eyes and knew she was a long way from accepting that there was nothing she could have done to save the boy. He cupped her face in his hands, kissing the dampness from her cheeks.

He wanted to take her hurt away, make it his own. He wanted to hold her close and make sure that nothing could ever hurt her again.

"I couldn't think of where else to come," she admitted tiredly. "I forgot that you'd said you had things to do tonight."

"That's okay." He settled her back against his shoulder and glanced at his watch. Much as he longed to let the meeting go hang, there was too much riding on it. "I have to go out in a little while," he told her.

"I should go." But she wasn't sure she had the strength to get up, let alone the energy to drive home.

"No." His arm tightened around her. "I won't be gone long. You can wait here and I'll take you home later, if you want."

"All right." Vaguely she thought that she

shouldn't agree so easily. Hadn't she spent most of the day debating his feelings for her? But that no longer seemed important. When she'd been in pain, she'd turned to him instinctively and he was there for her. Maybe that was enough for now.

"Morgan." The knock on the door shattered the peaceful atmosphere but it was the sound of his name that had an electric effect on Travis. With a low oath, he scooped her up on his lap and stood up, setting her on her feet in one smooth move. He stood beside her, every muscle taut, his eyes on the door. When she started to ask what was wrong, he lifted his hand to his mouth, silencing her.

He grabbed hold of her wrist and looked around the bare room as if seeking a place to hide her. His visitor knocked again, a little louder this time.

"Come on, Morgan. Open up." The tone was so demanding that Angie's first thought was that it was the police but something in the taut lines around Travis's eyes told her that that wasn't the case. Unless he really *was* wanted by the police.

He pulled her toward the bedroom and thrust her through the door. "Stay in here and don't say a word. No matter what you hear or think you hear, don't come out. Do you understand?"

"I understand. But what's going on?"

A third round of knocking, even more impatient than the last had him glancing over his shoulder, her question forgotten.

"If there's trouble, go out the bedroom window and run like hell. *Don't* come out. No matter what you hear. Do you understand me?"

"But what's—"

"Do you understand me?" His hands tightened on her shoulders, his eyes fierce and urgent.

"Yes." Angie felt fear uncurl in the pit of her stomach. What was going on here?

"Travis." But he was gone, drawing the door shut behind him, leaving Angie alone in the dark bedroom. Alone and scared to death.

TRAVIS FORCED his thoughts away from Angie as he moved to open the door. He couldn't afford to think of her now, couldn't afford to think of anything but the goal he'd worked so long and so hard to achieve. This visit wasn't part of the plan and he didn't particularly like surprises, not at this stage of the game. But Shearson *did* like surprises, especially when he was the one delivering them. He could only hope that this surprise was not going to be nasty.

He pulled open the door and scowled at the two men on the doorstep. One of them had unscrewed the bulb in the porch light so they stood in darkness, but enough light spilled out the door for Travis to identify them. Drasen and Sinclair. Not too fondly known as the Dragon and the Saint. Drasen for his size and fierce reputation, Sinclair for his habit of attending church faithfully every Sunday.

He'd known them both years ago. After he left, they became Shearson's right-hand men. They were quick and dangerous, giving no more thought to killing a man than most people did to blowing their nose. He wondered if he should be flattered that Shearson had sent both of them.

"What the hell are you doing here?" he demanded, taking the initiative.

"Could we discuss this inside?" Sinclair asked politely. "My companion is feeling a trifle exposed."

Travis hesitated a moment, as if considering kicking them off his porch, and then stepped back to allow them inside. "I thought we were going to meet at the Club," he said irritably, shutting the door behind his unwanted guests.

He should have been expecting this, he thought. Shearson was fond of springing surprises, frequently unpleasant ones. He believed that keeping his people off balance was good for them. Considering the success of his organization, Travis couldn't argue with the policy. He hoped that surprise was all Sinclair and Drasen had brought with them.

"We decided it was too public," Drasen said.

"I was just about to leave," Travis said, making his annoyance plain.

"And leave your guest?" Sinclair's eyes went to the bedroom door and then shifted back to Travis's face, cool and questioning.

Angie's car. Damn his stupidity. It was undoubtedly parked at the curb. And if they'd planned to show up here all along, they'd probably been watching when she arrived.

"She can wait." He shrugged to show how unimportant she was.

"A cop's sister," Sinclair commented, dashing the hope that they didn't know who she was. "A risky proposition, don't you think?"

"No." Travis met his eyes with an icy look. "Who's going to be suspicious of a guy who's dating a detective's sister?"

It was thin—it was very thin—but it was the best he could come up with spur-of-the-moment.

"Perhaps." Sinclair still looked doubtful but he was willing to let the subject go for now. "We've been told you can meet our requirements at a fair price," he continued, getting on to the reason for their meeting. "Our employer would like to see a sample of the merchandise. We have certain standards to maintain."

"I bet you do." Travis's grin was vulpine, his lean features hard in the dim light. Moving to the rickety sofa, he lifted one of the cushions and reached into a hole in the upholstery beneath. He came up with a small plastic bag and turned back to the two men.

"Not the best place of concealment," Sinclair commented.

"The cops have no reason to be interested in me." Travis lifted one shoulder to show his lack of concern. "Not yet, anyway."

Drasen took the bag from him and opened the upper corner. He licked his finger and touched the white powder it contained. Licking his finger, he frowned and then nodded. "It's pure." He resealed the bag carefully and weighed it in his hand. "There's more where this came from?"

"I can supply what you need." Travis saw the big man's eyes go to the sofa and he grinned again. "I don't keep it here, of course."

"Of course." That was Sinclair. "When can you make your first delivery?"

"I don't deal with flunkies," Travis said flatly. "If Shearson wants what I have, he can tell me himself."

It was a calculated risk. It could backfire on him. But he was suddenly impatient with all the games. He wanted this settled. He wanted to know where he stood.

Drasen stiffened, his broad features flushing with anger. Sinclair was made of cooler stuff. He merely raised one thin brow and looked almost amused. Sinclair would be the one to watch in a fight, Travis thought. He was ice cool and deadly.

"We're in a position to make you an offer, Mr. Morgan. We have all the authority."

"I deal with Shearson or I don't deal at all."

"Why?"

"I'm a cautious sort," Travis said coolly. "I figure if I'm dealing directly with the man in charge, there's less chance of a double-cross. I know him well enough to know he's not going to want to get caught in any nasty situations. If he wants what I have, he'll see me."

He could feel the adrenaline pumping through him, telling him he was on the right track. Playing along wasn't going to get him anywhere. Sheer arrogance just might.

His eyes locked with Sinclair's as the other man weighed his words and tried to decide whether he was serious. Whatever he saw must have convinced him because he lifted his narrow shoulders in a light shrug.

"We'll tell our employer what you've said. I doubt he'll agree to it."

"His choice." Travis shrugged his indifference. "I can always take my product elsewhere. He knows me well enough to know I can do it. You can take that sample to him. Tell him there's plenty more where that came from." Considering the street value of the cocaine in the bag Drasen held, it was an expensive gesture of good faith. But you didn't hook a shark without offering impressive bait.

"You seem very confident," Sinclair commented, showing a touch of curiosity.

"I know what I've got. And I know how much he wants it."

"Overconfidence can be a very dangerous thing."

"When you own a goose that lays golden eggs, there's no such thing as overconfidence."

"True." Sinclair nodded to Drasen who slipped the packet of cocaine into his inside jacket pocket. "*If* you own the only such goose," he warned. "We'll give our employer your message and get back to you."

"You do that."

Travis saw them out, feeling the adrenaline still pumping through his body. When they passed on his demand, Shearson might be annoyed but he'd also be interested. And he needed the coke. Despite Sinclair's cool facade, Travis could smell the hunger. Something had happened to their line of supply and they needed a new supplier. And they needed it now.

Grinning like a fool, he spun away from the door.

And met Angie's horrified gaze.

He'd been so focused on the battle of wits with Sinclair, he'd put her out of his mind completely. He'd concentrated completely on the task at hand, on the goal he'd been striving toward for so many months.

"You're dealing drugs."

The hushed accusation doused his euphoric mood instantly. His smile faded, replaced by an expressionless mask.

"You're dealing drugs," she said again, as if only by repeating the words could she make herself believe them. She came farther into the room, stopping a few feet away.

"Travis?" The plea in her voice went straight to his heart.

"What?" He forced himself to indifference.

"Aren't you going to say anything? There…there must be some explanation…." She let the words trail off, obviously unable to think of such an explanation herself. "Maybe I misunderstood?" she suggested hopefully.

She was all but begging him to assure her that that was the case. Travis stared at her without saying a word. He wanted to go to her, hold her, tell her that it wasn't true. But he didn't move. Wasn't this just what he'd been looking for? A way to break off with her? A way to keep her away? Keep her safe.

But not like this, a voice inside him protested. She was looking at him as if she was seeing him for the first time—and not particularly liking what she saw.

Well, he never expected to win friends with what he was doing.

But not Angie. He didn't care what anyone else believed about him, but the look in Angie's eyes was like a knife in his chest.

"You didn't misunderstand," he said finally, when the silence had stretched to breaking point.

"Oh, God." The words were more prayer than curse. She'd been pale to begin with but the last traces of color drained away, leaving her ashen. "Oh, God."

She groped for something to lean on and set her hand on the back of the leather chair, the one they'd shared just a few minutes before, when she'd sat on his lap and let him soothe some of her pain away. But he couldn't soothe this pain away.

"How could you?" she asked at last, her voice hardly more than a whisper. "You know what drugs have done to the young people in this area. You've seen what happens to them. How could you?"

"I don't sell drugs to kids," he said automatically and then immediately regretted offering such a thin defense.

"Maybe not. But *they* do."

Travis looked away from her, unable to face the bitter hurt in her face. What a mess. Why hadn't he listened to his common sense, not to mention her brother? He'd had no business getting involved with her. It had been doomed to disaster from the beginning.

"Aren't you going to say anything?"

"What do you want me to say?" he asked wearily.

"I want you to tell me this is some kind of nightmare. I want you to tell me none of this is happening."

"I wish I could." He thrust his fingers through his hair, feeling old and tired.

"How could you do this, Travis?" Her voice broke on the question and Travis felt her pain as if it were his.

All he had to do was offer her an explanation. She'd believe anything he told her, at least for now. Later, she'd start to question, first herself and then him. And what could he say?

So he stayed silent.

When it became clear that he wasn't going to answer her question, Angie felt something shatter inside her. Her faith in him, in the future, in herself. How could she have thought she was in love with this man when it was obvious she didn't know him at all?

And the most terrible thing of all was that the love didn't die now that she knew what he was.

"I love you." The words were flat, without emotion. Angie saw Travis's head jerk up, his eyes startled. She pushed her hair back from her face, trying not to remember how he'd pulled the pins out and stroked his fingers through it, comforting her grief.

"Damn you!" Her voice broke as the pain stabbed in her chest. "Damn you, Travis!" Her fingers dug into the upholstery as she bent over the back of the chair, a shudder of agony racking her body.

"Angel…" He took a step toward her, half reaching out, as if to take her in his arms.

"Don't call me that!" Angie straightened instantly, her spine rigid, her eyes fierce. "And don't you dare touch me! Not ever again. Do you hear me?"

"I hear you." He faced her across the width of the big chair. Less than three feet separated them but it might as well have been three miles.

"I may love you but it doesn't matter," she told him.

Travis wanted to tell her that it mattered a great deal to him but the tangled web of lies and half-truths that surrounded them kept him silent.

"I can't accept what you're doing," she said flatly.

"I understand." He hardly knew what he was saying. He didn't understand anything, least of all his own reaction to her words.

"I have to go." Angie pulled her gaze away from his, looking around distractedly. "I have to go," she said again, more to herself than to him.

She moved toward the door, only to have Travis's words stop her.

"What are you going to do?"

"Do?" She turned to look at him, feeling her stomach twist in pain. "What do you mean?"

"Are you going to tell your brother about this?"

What did he expect her to say? Angie stared at him, trying to read his expression. But there was nothing there to read. They might have been talking about the weather, for all the concern she could read in his face.

How could he ask her such a thing? He'd put her in a miserable position. Either she ignored the worst kind of criminal behavior, or she did what she knew was right and helped send him to prison. And he wanted to know what choice she was going to make?

Travis regretted the question as soon as it was out. Damn his quick tongue! The torture in her eyes went through him as sharp as a knife.

"I don't know," she said, her voice thin and full of pain. "I don't know." She turned and left as if afraid he might say something more.

What could he have said? Travis stared at the closed door, feeling as if he'd been swept up in a whirlwind, given a thorough shaking and then set back down again.

The sound of Angie's car pulling away from the curb shook him out of his stupor. Moving slowly, he walked to the door and flipped the dead bolt shut. He leaned his forehead against the blank panel and closed his eyes.

What a night!

Dragging himself upright, Travis moved into the kitchen and got a beer out of the refrigerator. He twisted the top off the bottle but didn't lift it to his mouth. Instead, he stared at the refrigerator door, listening to the uneven whir of its motor and tried to sort out the night's events. What should he have done differently?

He couldn't have sent Angie away when she was in such pain. Even if he'd foreseen the arrival of Drasen and Sinclair, there wasn't much he could have done to prevent it. And once they were there and Angie was there, he supposed the rest had been inevitable.

Shaking his head, he lifted the beer and took a long swallow before moving back into the living room. He pushed the switch on the fan and it started sluggishly, stirring the warm air. Next time he rented a place in the summer, he was going to make sure the windows opened, he thought absently.

She'd said she loved him.

That was the thought he'd been trying to avoid since she left. The one thing that was impossible to forget. She loved him. Somewhere, deep inside, he felt a stirring that he recognized dimly. It was a warmth he'd never felt before.

She'd said she loved him. Even when she believed he was selling drugs, she'd still loved him. Hated him, too, of course, if he could judge by her expression. But who could blame her, believing what she did?

How many years had it been since he'd thought about things such as falling in love? How old had he been when he accepted that his parents would never love him quite as much as they loved each other and their wandering life-style?

He'd long ago come to terms with reality. He simply wasn't destined for the sort of home and hearth life that drew most men sooner or later. He didn't particularly mind. Domesticity seemed vastly overrated. He liked his work, enjoyed the company of women who were no more interested in settling down than he was. It was a perfectly good life-style.

And then he'd met Angie Brady.

He'd never before realized what a lethal combination big blue eyes and sunshine-colored hair could be. Suddenly he was thinking about picket fences and how nice it would be to share his life with someone. Someone who loved him. Someone he…loved.

Someone like Angie.

It was ironic that he was only able to admit that he loved her now that he'd lost her for good. Travis sank into the big leather chair and leaned his head back, closing his eyes. How had he managed to get his life so tangled up? He'd fallen in love and been too blind to know it, he thought.

Why hadn't he told her the truth? If not at the beginning, then tonight? Because, once he told her he loved her, he wasn't at all sure he'd be able to keep his distance from her, no matter what was at stake.

He shook his head, opening his eyes to stare blindly at the water-stained wallpaper opposite. He had to let it alone. There was no explanation he could offer, at least none that she would believe.

And she was better off out of it, out of his life. Her brother had been right from the beginning: He was not the kind of man she should know. He hadn't meant to hurt her but that's what he'd done.

She loved him.

And he'd lost her.

The bottle flew across the room, shattering against the wall, the contents staining the wallpaper. Travis closed his eyes, his fingers digging into the arms of the chair as he fought the urge to get up and put his fist through a wall.

For the first time in his life, he'd had something worth fighting for. And he'd just destroyed it.

Chapter Twelve

Angie stood in the shower and let the hot water pound over her. Her throat felt tight and her eyes ached but she could find no tears. She'd shed them all earlier, crying over the patient they hadn't been able to save. She didn't have any tears left for this second, more personal death. She set one arm against the tile and leaned her forehead on it, trying to absorb what had happened.

Travis was dealing drugs.

She couldn't make the words real, no matter how many times she repeated them to herself. There was a part of her that couldn't accept their truth. It didn't matter that she'd actually heard him arranging to meet with someone to discuss a drug deal. There had to be some other explanation.

Only he hadn't offered one.

He was selling drugs. She had to face it. Accept the reality of it, no matter how much it hurt.

Almost anything else she could have found a way to accept. But not this. This was one thing she could never accept, never condone. She'd seen the results of drug abuse firsthand. She knew what it did to the people who took drugs and what it did to their families. And she had nothing but contempt for the vultures who grew rich selling their poisons to kids too young and too foolish to know better.

And Travis was one of them.

With a moan, Angie turned her face into the hot spray of water, praying that it would wash away some of the pain. But it was going to take more than water to ease this pain. She doubted anything ever would.

She shut the water off but made no move to get out of the tub. Watching rivulets of water run down the shower door, she tried to think of where she should go from here. What was she going to do? Travis had asked the question. She hadn't had an answer then and she didn't seem to be any closer to one now.

Her movements sluggish, Angie slid open the shower door and reached for a towel. She dried herself, trying to concentrate on the simple task, trying to block out everything but the necessity of blotting every drop of water from her skin.

It was as she was reaching for her robe that she caught a glimpse of her reflection in the mirror. She stopped and stared at her image. The woman in the mirror was a little paler than usual perhaps. If you looked carefully, you might notice that her eyes seemed a little haunted, a little hollow. But there was no dramatic change outside to signal the turmoil inside.

Angie pulled her robe on slowly, wondering how she could look the same when she felt like a total stranger to herself. She wasn't the same woman she'd been a few short weeks ago. Her calm, safe existence had been shattered and she couldn't even begin to imagine how she was going to pick up the pieces.

She left the bathroom and went down the hall to her bedroom. Clay's car had been gone when she got home and there was no sign that he'd come back while she was showering. She was grateful for his absence. She didn't know if she could face him without blurting out the truth about Travis. And she didn't want to do that until she was sure it was the right thing to do.

Closing her bedroom door behind her, she waited for the peace she always felt there to enfold her. She'd grown from a child to a woman in this room. It knew all her secrets, all her dreams. It had been her haven through all the usual childish trials and tribulations.

But tonight it was just a room. She didn't feel any magical easing of her pain when she entered it. And she didn't find the answers she needed in the pictures on the walls or the row of childish stuffed toys that marched along a shelf near the ceiling.

The answers she needed were only going to be found in her heart. But how was she supposed to sort them out when all she could feel was pain?

Curling up in the wing chair that had been her fifteenth birthday present from her father, Angie drew her feet up onto the seat and wrapped her arms around them, laying her head on her knees and closing her eyes, wishing she could go back to that day.

She'd been so happy. So excited. The chair had made her feel like an adult and she'd made Clay move it to every possible position in her room before she'd finally settled on a place next to the window, where she could sit and watch the world go by and feel like a lady of the manor.

In retrospect, those days seemed idyllic. She'd had the usual teenage angst and there'd been times when she was convinced she was the most miserable girl on the face of the earth—or at least in the state of California. But they'd been good times, she thought now, even if she didn't believe it then.

No matter how hard she wished, she couldn't go back to being fifteen again. She was twenty-five and she'd just found out that the man she loved was selling drugs. And what made it even more terrible was that she still loved him.

Angie squeezed her eyes shut, feeling the sting of tears for the first time. How was it possible to love someone and hate what they were? What had happened to her that she could still love him, even knowing what he was? Why didn't finding out about the drugs erase her feelings for him?

Because she couldn't forget that this was the same man who'd come to her rescue when Billy Sikes and his gang were harassing her; the same man who'd slipped money to Mrs. Aggretti and then invented a job for her so she wouldn't feel like a charity case.

Knowing what he was didn't make her forget the way his eyes could smile even when his mouth remained serious. Or the way his mouth felt on hers. She couldn't forget the way he'd made love to her, treating her as if she were the most precious thing in the world to him. Her pleasure had come before his, he'd made sure of that.

The good memories didn't suddenly vanish. If they had, she wouldn't be torturing herself over what to do now. How was it possible that everything had fallen apart so quickly?

SITTING THERE, wrapped in pain, Angie lost track of the hours. She heard Clay come in, heard his footsteps going down the hall, hesitating outside her door. She bit her lip against the urge to call out to him. Her big brother had always been able to solve her problems for her, but this was one she had to decide on her own.

After a moment, he moved on and she heard his bedroom door close behind him. And then she put her head down on her knees and let the tears flow. Because she knew there really was no decision to make. There was only one choice, at least for her. Only one choice she could live with. And that one was unbearable.

ANGIE MUST HAVE DOZED off sometime near dawn because she woke when she heard the sound of Clay's bedroom door closing. She lifted her head, grimacing as her neck twinged in protest. For one blessed moment, she didn't remember why she'd fallen asleep in the chair. But memory came crashing in on her when she heard Clay running down the stairs.

She had to talk to him. And she had to talk to him now, this morning, before she found a way to talk herself out of it. She scrambled out of the chair, stumbling as her legs, cramped from her unusual choice of beds, threatened not to support her.

Clay was making coffee when she entered the kitchen. He was dressed for his morning run in shorts and T-shirt and the look he turned on her was not particularly welcoming.

"Good morning," he said coolly, before turning back to the coffeemaker.

Angie stared at his back, confused for a moment until she remembered their quarrel over Travis. She'd forgotten all about it. That seemed like years ago.

"Can I talk to you?" she asked, her voice husky with sleep and the tears she'd shed the night before.

"I don't have much time. Is it important?" He didn't turn to look at her as he spoke. Tears started to sting her eyes and were immediately suppressed. She'd cried enough.

"Travis is dealing drugs."

The bald statement sounded even harsher in the sunny kitchen than it had when she'd said it to herself.

"What!" Coffee scattered across the counter and onto the floor as Clay spun to face her, the measure still in his hand.

"I found out last night." She wrapped her arms around her waist and looked at the floor between them.

"How did you find out?" Clay had recovered from the initial shock. He set the measure down and punched the button to turn the coffeemaker on before turning back to her.

"I went to his house. He'd told me he was going to be busy but there was a boy brought into the clinic. He'd been shot. We couldn't save him." The words caught in her throat as she remembered how helpless they'd been.

"I heard about the shooting. I didn't know he'd been taken to the clinic." Clay crossed to her and put his arms around her. "I'm sorry, Angie. That must have been hell."

"It was rough." She slid her arms around his waist and let him hold her just as he had when she'd been six years old and her dog had been hit by a car. "He was so young, Clay."

"I know, half-pint." The old endearment made her

want to break down and sob. But that wouldn't solve anything.

She drew in a deep breath and pulled away from him, her fingers tightening the belt of her robe, though it wasn't loose. It seemed to be getting harder to talk instead of easier. She let him lead her to one of the stools that sat next to the work island.

"So you went to see Morgan," he prompted gently.

"I went to see Travis," she confirmed. "I was so upset, I'd forgotten all about his saying he would be busy."

"What happened?"

"He held me and told me I'd done my best and I just had to accept that I wasn't God and couldn't save everyone." The memory stabbed at her. "He was so gentle," she whispered, more to herself than her brother.

"Then what?"

"Then, these two men showed up."

"Did you see them? Did they see you?" He sounded more like a cop than a brother and she responded automatically to his authoritative tone.

"No. Travis shoved me into the bedroom and told me not to come out, no matter what. He also said that if there was trouble I was to go out the window and run like hell," she said slowly, just now remembering his words, remembering the urgency in his face. He'd been worried about her safety, she thought. But there was no time to consider that because Clay was prodding her for the rest of the story.

"Did you hear what they were saying?"

"Some of it. They knew I was there," she said, remembering. "Maybe they saw my car. I don't know.'' She ran her fingers through her hair, wishing her brain didn't feel as if it were filled with lead.

''Travis seemed so upset that I listened at the door,'' she admitted. ''I was worried about him.'' The irony of that struck her now, sending pain knifing through her. She had been worried about a drug dealer.

''What did they say? Did you get any names?''

''I don't think they gave their names but they mentioned someone named Shearson.'' She stopped as Clay's breath hissed between his teeth. His face was set and grim, what she'd always privately called his ''cop face.''

''What is it, Clay? Do you know who Shearson is?''

''Maybe.'' He got up, avoiding her questioning look as he went to pour coffee into two mugs. Angie didn't say anything more until he'd set a cup in front of her.

''Go on,'' he ordered shortly.

''They talked and it was obvious the two men worked for this Shearson and that Travis had something they wanted.''

''Did they mention drugs?''

''Not specifically. But it was obvious what they were talking about. They asked if Travis had a sample and then a couple of minutes later one of them said 'It's pure.'''

She told him everything she remembered, including the way Travis had demanded a meeting with Shearson.

''That's about it, I guess. They said that they'd tell their boss what Travis wanted but they didn't think he'd agree to it. Travis didn't seem worried. He said

Shearson knew him well enough to know he meant what he said. And then they left.''

''Stupid,'' Clay muttered, as if to himself.

''What? What's stupid?'' Angie was getting the distinct feeling that there were two conversations going on here and that she was only hearing one of them.

''Nothing. Did you confront Travis?''

''Yes. I suppose that was stupid. I mean, obviously, he's not the man I thought he was,'' she admitted painfully. ''I suppose I should have pretended that I hadn't heard a thing.''

''What did he say?''

''Nothing.''

''Nothing?'' Clay seemed surprised. ''He didn't deny it or say he could explain?''

''He just said I hadn't misunderstood.''

''Fool,'' Clay muttered.

Angie stiffened, feeling a spurt of anger. She hadn't expected a lot of sympathy from him but neither had she expected him to be so completely insensitive to her hurt.

''I know you told me to stay away from him,'' she said stiffly. ''But I don't think 'I told you so' is going to do anyone any good at this point. And I don't particularly appreciate being called a fool, even if I was one.''

''What?'' Clay blinked and looked at her as if only just realizing she was there.

''I said, I don't like being called a fool,'' she snapped, hurt by his apparent lack of interest.

''I wasn't talking about you, half-pint. I was talking about Morgan.''

''Oh.'' She was surprised that he hadn't come up

with a stronger word to describe Travis. "Fool" seemed a mild epithet for someone who was selling drugs.

They were silent for a little while. Angie wrapped her hands around her cup, wishing the warmth of the coffee could penetrate deep enough to thaw the ice that had formed around her heart.

She'd done the right thing, she told herself. She'd done the only thing she could do. But that didn't stop her from feeling as if she'd betrayed Travis.

"What are you going to do?" she asked at last, unconsciously echoing Travis's question to her the night before.

"About Travis, you mean?"

"Yes." She ground her teeth together against the urge to beg him to let Travis go. To make him leave town but not to arrest him.

"You really love him, don't you?" Clay's eyes searched hers, reading the answer even before she spoke.

"Yes." The one word was all she could get out without risking tears.

"Oh, half-pint." He sighed, his face twisting in sympathy and Angie felt tears flood her eyes, overflowing before she could force them back.

"Damn." She dabbed at the tears with the end of her robe's belt, a completely inadequate hankie. "Damn, damn, damn. Thank you," she muttered when Clay handed her a paper towel. "I wasn't going to cry anymore. He's not worth it. I *know* he's not worth it. I don't know why I still care."

"But you do," he said, finishing for her.

"Yes." She sniffed back a new flood of tears and scrubbed her cheeks with the rough towel. "But what he's doing is wrong. I couldn't just let him get away with it, no matter how I feel about him.''

Clay frowned, looked about to say something and then changed his mind. Getting up, he went to get the coffeepot. Bringing it back, he filled both their cups before setting the pot on the tile insert in the middle of the island.

"Did you get any sleep at all last night?" he asked.

"Some." Angie shrugged, unconcerned with her lack of sleep. "Are you going to arrest him? Do you need more evidence?"

"I don't need more evidence," he said absently, staring at his coffee.

"Will I...will I have to testify against him?" Her imagination couldn't even encompass that thought.

"No. The truth is, there's more to this than you know," he said slowly, seeming to come to some decision.

"What do you mean? You didn't know about Travis, did you? You couldn't have," she said, answering her own question. "You would have said something to me if you'd known what he was doing."

"Morgan didn't try to defend himself?" he asked. "He didn't say anything at all about there maybe being more to the story than what you saw?"

"No." Angie shook her head, trying to figure out where this conversation was going. Maybe it was lack of sleep that was making it so hard to follow. "What are you getting at? Do you know something about Travis?"

"I pulled his file," he said slowly. "I was looking for something on him, something concrete enough to make you stay away from him."

"Then you *knew* about this? You knew he was

selling drugs and you didn't say anything to me?''
She stared at him in hurt disbelief.

''That's not what I found in his file.'' The reluctance in his tone made Angie suspect that there was something even worse in the file, though what could be worse than selling drugs, she couldn't imagine.

''What was in there?'' Even as she asked the question, she didn't want to hear the answer. She didn't want to know what Clay had found. Didn't want to hear what Travis had done. She wanted to throw her hands over her ears and close her eyes to shut out whatever Clay had to tell her. Instead, she sat there, staring at her brother's face with eyes that begged him to spare her any more blows.

''I shouldn't say anything,'' he said slowly. ''But I probably shouldn't have been digging through the files in the first place.''

''What has he done?'' There was a kind of despairing resignation in her tone.

''He's not a drug dealer, Angie.'' The bald statement glanced off the protective wall she'd thrown up. She stared at him without comprehension.

''He's not selling drugs,'' Clay said, more forcefully. ''What you heard—it wasn't what it seemed.''

''I heard him making a deal. He didn't deny it.'' Hadn't he understood what she'd told him?

''He didn't deny it because it would have blown his cover,'' Clay said.

''His cover?'' Angie stared at him as the meaning of those two words slowly sank in. ''His cover?''

''He's on our side.'' It was obvious that Clay didn't particularly like admitting as much.

''His cover?'' Her voice had risen. ''He's a cop?''

"He's working with the police," Clay corrected. "It's an unusual setup."

"He's not dealing drugs?" She had to hear him say it again before she dared to allow even the smallest ray of hope to penetrate the black cloud of despair. "You're sure?"

"He's not dealing drugs," Clay said, his tone definite. "He's working with us. Apparently he contacted the people we had watching Shearson and offered to use his old connection to Shearson to penetrate the organization and bring Shearson down."

"Travis used to work for a drug dealer?" Angie rubbed her fingers over her forehead, trying to still her spinning thoughts. She didn't know whether she should be feeling relieved, or angry, or hurt. All three emotions were tangled up inside her.

"When he lived in Salem before. I told you he was in trouble then," he reminded her. "There was never enough evidence to arrest him but there was never any doubt about what he was up to. Shearson was into stealing cars then and Morgan was part of the ring. He was good enough to avoid getting caught."

"He stole cars?" Angie could hear the dazed note in her voice but she couldn't seem to grasp what he was telling her. First, Clay told her that Travis wasn't a drug dealer and before she'd had a chance to feel relieved about that, he was telling her that he was a car thief.

"There was no proof," he admitted. "About ten years ago, he quit Shearson's organization and left town. That was the last I heard of him until he showed up again. Apparently, when he offered to help the police, his connections were just too good to pass up."

"So he's not dealing drugs. He's working *with* the police to try to catch this Shearson?'' She wanted everything to be stated very clearly, with no room for misunderstanding.

"That's right. But that doesn't make him Dudley Do-Right, either,'' he cautioned. "Morgan's past is checkered, to say the least. I only told you this because I didn't want you to think that you were going to have to testify against the guy. I still don't want you having anything to do with him.''

But he was talking to himself. Angie was no longer listening. Travis wasn't selling drugs. And she wasn't going to have to watch them send him to prison. Everything was going to be all right, after all.

"I'm going to kill him,'' she announced, interrupting Clay's mutterings about her staying away from Travis.

"What, now that you know he's one of the good guys, you're going to kill him?'' He looked at her, puzzled by this line of thinking.

"He should have told me.''

"No, he shouldn't have. *I* shouldn't have told you now. There's only a handful of people in this town who know about it, Angie.''

"Well, I should have been one of them,'' she said stubbornly. "He shouldn't have let me leave, thinking what I thought.''

"He did exactly what he had to.'' It was obvious that Clay didn't like making that admission but fairness dictated it.

"I told him I loved him, Clay. I told him I loved him and he still didn't say a word.'' Her tone was a mixture of hurt and anger.

"What did he say when you told him how you felt?" Clay struggled to keep his tone neutral.

"Nothing. I told him I loved him but that I couldn't accept what he was doing. And he just said he understood and let me leave."

"Angie, I don't want to argue his side—you know I don't want you involved with him—but it *is* part of his job not to tell people, even people he cares about, who he is. And he may have been trying to protect you," he added reluctantly.

"From what?"

"From what he's involved in. *Travis* may not be a drug dealer but the people he's trying to bring down are. This may have seemed the best way to keep you safe." The fact that the words were spoken somewhat grudgingly gave them more impact.

Angie nibbled on her lower lip, considering what he'd said. Yes, Travis would have let her believe he was a drug dealer if he thought it would keep her safe. How many times had he insisted that Clay was right to tell her to stay away from him? For some reason, he was convinced he was no good for her. Maybe this had been the perfect opportunity to keep her away from him, for her own good, of course.

"I'm not a child," she said, annoyed by this additional proof of male stupidity. "I don't want or need the two of you deciding what's best for me."

"Angie—"

"No." She cut him off with a sharp gesture of her hand. "I mean it, Clay. You've got to stop treating me like I'm still ten years old. No more warning me about Travis and no more extracting promises from him that he'll keep me safe."

"I've been taking care of you a long time. It's a hard habit to break."

"I know." Angie leaned toward him, putting her hand on his arm, her eyes full of love. "But I can take care of myself now."

Clay looked at her, forcing himself to see, not the child she'd been, but the woman she'd become. He felt a pang of regret. She wasn't his baby sister anymore. And she was right to demand that he treat her as an adult, capable of making her own decisions.

"You won't mind if I worry about you, will you? I'm not sure I can break that habit."

"Worry all you want but keep your mouth shut." Her smile softened the harshness of her words and Clay laughed.

"Now, all I have to do is convince Travis not to be an idiot," she said, sitting up straight on the stool.

"Stay away from Travis." Clay's tone made the words an order and Angie's head jerked toward him in disbelief.

"I thought we just settled this," she said.

"I'm not talking as your brother now, Angie. I'm talking as a police officer. Stay away from Travis."

"But he thinks I hate him," she protested.

"You can explain later. Right now, I don't want you anywhere near him, for his sake as well as yours," he added when she opened her mouth to argue. "If he cares about you, you're a distraction he can't afford."

Angie argued but Clay forced her to admit the logic in what he was saying. If Travis had to worry about her safety as well as his own it could prove fatal.

The word "fatal" was distressing. All Clay's assurances that Travis had all the protection the police could offer were scant comfort. Nor could he tell her how long it might be before the case was brought to a conclusion and she'd be able to see Travis.

By the time he announced that he had to leave for work, Angie's head was starting to spin. Too much had happened in too short a space of time. She'd plunged lower than she'd ever been in her life. And then Clay had told her that she wasn't in love with a drug dealer, after all, and she'd felt her spirits sky-rocket.

Yet she couldn't have what she wanted most of all, which was to see Travis and make things right between them. It was just a matter of time, she told herself. Patience. She just had to be patient and everything would work out right.

PATIENCE, Travis told himself. Patience was a major requirement for a job like this. He had a meeting with Shearson in a little less than six hours. Shearson had reacted exactly as he'd expected, taking the bait as neatly as a trout swallowing a fly. His police department contact hadn't been happy about the way he'd pushed the meeting. Travis suspected that his annoyance was caused by the fact that Travis had accomplished in a few weeks what the police had been trying to do for several years.

Of course, he hadn't accomplished anything yet. If there was one thing he knew about Shearson, it was that the man was unpredictable. Shearson claimed he was ready to buy the drugs, but he could just as easily be setting him up for a nasty fall. There'd been something in Sinclair's tone when he called to set up the meeting that made Travis uneasy.

But there was nothing to do now but go to the

appointed place and see what happened. And until then, all he could do was wait. Wait and think.

He stared up at the dark ceiling and wished he hadn't quit smoking five years ago. A cigarette would give him something to do right about now.

Sixteen hours since Angie had walked out. He didn't need to close his eyes to remember the way she'd looked at him, the pain in her eyes. She'd been devastated by what she thought she'd discovered. And she'd still said she loved him. Hated him, too, from the look in her eyes, but he couldn't blame her for that.

Travis put his hands under his head, and listened to the rattle of the fan that he'd moved from the living room into the bedroom with the vague hope that it would make it easier to sleep. From the sound of the motor, it wasn't going to last much longer. But then, if things worked out the way he hoped, he wasn't going to need it much longer, anyway.

He wanted this mess with Shearson settled. He wanted to get on with his life and get everything out in the open. He wanted a chance to tell Angie the truth.

A guilty conscience had driven him to approach the police. He'd offered his connections with Shearson, his knowledge of the man, as a way to atone for past sins. He certainly hadn't been expecting to fall in love. But fall in love he had, with a pair of big blue eyes and a soft smile. A cop's sister. If it hadn't been so damned tragic, it might have been funny.

If Shearson took the bait, the whole mess could be wrapped up in a matter of days. His life would be his again, the way it had been before he'd been overtaken by this sudden urge to play Good Samaritan.

He'd be able to leave this house to its gentle decline. He'd get a motel room somewhere in town and spend his time convincing Angie to forgive him. If she'd give him another chance, he'd do his damnedest to court her the way she deserved.

His mouth curved in a smile. Courting her. Yeah, he liked the sound of that. He might have been a little slow-witted about figuring it out but he'd finally realized that he loved her. And he wasn't going to walk out of her life without at least trying to put things right again.

She'd said she loved him and his angel wasn't a woman who loved lightly. Once he had a chance to explain things to her, to make her understand, she'd forgive him for not telling her the truth—at least he hoped that's what would happen.

His smile faded and was replaced by an uneasy frown. She had to forgive him. He'd waited a long time to fall in love. He wasn't going to give up on her—on them—without a fight.

Chapter Thirteen

Angie arched her back to ease the ache that had settled between her shoulders. She didn't know whether to be glad or sorry that her shift was up. She'd had almost no sleep but she didn't feel particularly tired. The events of last night and this morning made mundane concerns such as sleep unimportant.

It had been a relatively slow day at the clinic, giving Angie more time to think than she'd really wanted. Her thoughts careened back and forth, from how much she loved Travis to the way he'd let her think the worst of him. Her emotions had been no more stable than her thoughts, spinning from relief to anger without ever settling on one or the other.

She was exhausted, physically and emotionally. She wanted—needed—to see Travis, to talk to him, to try to understand what had happened, why he'd lied to her. But Clay had done a good job of convincing her that she had to keep her distance from Travis, for his sake as well as her own.

Sighing, she picked up her purse and scrambled in the bottom of it for her car keys. She tried not to think about the danger Travis might be in. She didn't need Clay to tell her that he was playing a very dangerous game. If this Shearson found out... Shivering, she closed the thought out of her mind. She had to believe that Travis knew what he was doing, that he wouldn't take any unnecessary chances. And that he'd come out safe in the end.

So she could strangle him.

"See you tomorrow, Angie." Janine lifted a hand from her typewriter to wave.

"Bye, Janine." Angie returned the wave and pushed open the door. The heat rolled over her, nearly stealing her breath. *It must be ninety-five in the shade,* she thought, lifting one hand to shield her eyes as they adjusted to the bright sunshine.

Travis's house would be baking with nothing but that inadequate fan to cool it. Not that she'd minded the heat, she admitted. They'd generated enough heat between them to make the temperature unimportant.

She wasn't going to think about that now. She didn't want to think of anything to do with Travis. Not now. Not until she'd gained a little distance from the situation and could try to figure out just what it was she felt.

"Miss Brady?" Angie was nearly to her car when she heard the hesitant call. She turned, narrowing her eyes against the sun.

A slight figure hovered near one of the shrubs that marched along the edge of the parking lot, hanging back in their shadows.

"Tony?" She moved closer, confirming her guess as to his identity. Tony Aggretti. She hadn't seen much of him since that momentous day when Travis had come to her rescue. "Hello."

"Hi." He returned her smile with a nervous grimace, his eyes darting uneasily from one side to the other.

"How's your mother?" Angie asked, wondering at the boy's obvious uneasiness. She'd only seen him once since the incident with Billy Sikes and that had been at a distance. She noticed that he'd lost weight and wondered if he was getting enough to eat.

"She's okay." He lifted his thin shoulders in a quick shrug. "You friends with that guy? The one with the bike?"

"Travis?" Angie felt all her senses snap to attention. "Yes, we're friends. Why?"

Tony shrugged again, his eyes never quite settling in one place. He looked as if he regretted having approached her, but now that Travis's name had come up, Angie had no intention of letting him go without learning what he had to say.

"What did you want to tell me, Tony?" She forced her voice to calm authority when what she really wanted to do was grab him and shake whatever it was out of him.

"He gave my mom some money," he said. "And you've been good to us. If it wasn't for the clinic, a lot of people wouldn't make it around here. Mom says you're an angel."

The compliment brought a sharp pang, reminding her of Travis. She forced a smile.

"I wouldn't go that far. What did you want to tell me, Tony?"

"That guy? The one with the bike?" She nodded and then had to tamp down the urge to scream when he hesitated yet again. Just when she was sure she was going to have to shake the information out of him, he started talking, the words tumbling over themselves as if he was afraid to slow down.

"I heard them talking and he's walkin' into a trap."

"You heard who talking?"

"I can't tell you." He gave her a pleading look. "They'd kill me if they found out I talked to you, Miss Brady."

"Okay. Just tell me what you can." Angie's nails dug holes into the leather of her purse but not a trace of urgency showed in her voice.

"Billy and me, we was…was pickin' up some stuff." From the way he hesitated, his eyes avoiding hers, Angie had a pretty good idea what the "stuff" was but now was not the time to pursue the issue.

"Go on."

"I overheard them talking about that guy. They said they told him he'd be meeting the boss but that the boss was out of the country and they were just going to take the stuff he was bringing and kill him. I think they're planning on selling it on the side and not tell their boss at all," he said shrewdly, showing an appalling knowledge of human nature for one so young.

"Where is this meeting supposed to take place, Tony? And when? Do you know when?"

"I think it's today sometime but I don't know where it is. That's the truth, Miss Brady. I told you all I know."

"That's okay. You did the right thing, Tony." She had to get to Travis, had to warn him. The rules had suddenly changed and Clay's edict had no meaning in this situation. On the other hand, maybe Clay would have a better chance of finding him in time. Yes, that was best. She'd go to Clay.

She was unaware of having spoken the thought out loud until a new voice entered the conversation.

"I don't think so, Nurse Brady." The last words were spoken with mocking emphasis that was familiar. Billy Sikes. She'd recognize that smirking tone anywhere. She started to turn to face him but the move was never completed.

"Don't!" She heard Tony's cry but there was no time to react to the warning. There was a sharp pain behind her ear and she felt her knees give way as she sank into a whirling blackness.

Her last conscious thought was that this couldn't be happening in broad daylight. And then she didn't think anything at all.

TRAVIS APPROACHED the warehouse cautiously. When Sinclair had called to say that Shearson had agreed to the meeting, Travis had had the sudden, uneasy feeling that this was going too well. Maybe he'd been too clever for his own good. But he couldn't back out now.

So he'd agreed to the meeting and gotten in touch with his contact to arrange for backup. If Shearson really did show up and they could get something on film, they might be able to nail him immediately. Getting anything on film was not going to be easy. The warehouse was in an industrial district and provided few hiding places, which was no doubt exactly why it had been chosen.

His contact had promised to have men in place. With shotgun mikes and telephoto lenses and some luck, maybe they'd get something that could be used in court. It was the luck part of it that made Travis uneasy. He'd never trusted things that depended on luck.

The warehouse looked peaceful enough, he thought. In fact, when he cut the bike's engine, the silence was practically deafening. It was a Saturday afternoon and the area was deserted. So there'd be no witnesses? he wondered.

He swung his leg over the bike and reached up to lift his helmet off, his eyes skimming the area. There was no sign of the men he'd been promised would be in position. But then, if he'd been able to see them, they wouldn't have been doing a very good job.

Setting the helmet on the bike's seat, he thrust his fingers through his hair. He needed a haircut, he thought absently, still taking stock of the area. He flexed his shoulders and resisted the urge to check the gun tucked in the small of his back. They'd be expecting him to be armed. After all, they weren't in a particularly trusting business.

He unstrapped the black briefcase from the back of the bike and walked around to the side door, as instructed. He knocked. There was only a brief wait before it was opened. Travis didn't recognize the man who opened it but he recognized the type—hired muscle, to use a phrase from an earlier era. Dangerous enough but fairly predictable. He'd do what he was told but he wasn't likely to make any rash decisions on his own.

Travis nodded and walked past, wishing he knew just what the guy had been told. It would be helpful if he knew the day's agenda, especially whether it contained any plans for bumping off upstart suppliers.

Sinclair and Drasen were waiting for him in the

center of the warehouse but there was no sign of Shearson. The building was mostly empty, although there were a few crates stacked against the wall. A white limo was parked in the center of the huge room. Sinclair leaned against the hood while Drasen stood nearby. Both turned toward him as he stepped into sight.

"Good afternoon." Sinclair's greeting was impeccably polite, his smile socially correct.

"Good afternoon." Travis grinned, letting his amusement show. He could almost come to like Sinclair, he thought. The man was an original.

"You brought what we agreed on?" Sinclair asked.

"It's here." Travis lifted the briefcase, which contained cocaine borrowed from the police evidence room. The street value was enough to allow a man to retire for life. "Where's Shearson?" He eyed the tinted windows on the limousine.

"We have the money. But before we make the exchange, we'd like to examine the merchandise. It's not that we don't trust you. It's just good business."

"Of course." Travis didn't miss the way Sinclair had avoided his question about Shearson. Nor was he unaware of the fact that he was neatly caught between the two of them in front and the goon behind him. The hair on the back of his neck was starting to stand up.

He moved forward slowly, looking for a way out of a situation that suddenly seemed most unhealthy.

"Where's Shearson? I already told you I don't deal with middlemen."

"Yes, so you said. Unfortunately Mr. Shearson was unable to attend this meeting." Sinclair shrugged apologetically. "But knowing of your aversion to dealing with—what was it you said?—ah yes, flunkies, Mr. Drasen and I have decided to oblige you by going into business for ourselves.''

''Double-crossing Shearson?'' Travis grinned, his fingers tightening over the briefcase. ''Pretty dangerous, isn't it?''

''I don't think the late Mr. Shearson will object too strenuously.''

''The *late* Mr. Shearson?'' Travis questioned sharply.

''Yes. We received word late last evening. He met with an accident while on his yacht. Most unfortunate.''

And not only for Shearson, Travis thought. He was surprised to feel a pang of real regret at the thought that Shearson was dead. He couldn't say he'd ever liked the man and he certainly hadn't trusted him but, in the old days, he'd known him intimately enough to see the humanity behind the amoral facade.

But there was no time for regrets now. He had the distinct feeling that another ''unfortunate accident'' was in his own near future, if Sinclair had his way.

''Well, I don't care what happened to Shearson,'' he said, shrugging to show his indifference. ''I'll deal with whoever is in charge.''

''How gracious of you, Mr. Morgan.'' Travis had once seen a piranha with a very similar smile. ''Perhaps if we could see your merchandise?''

''Sure.'' Travis started forward only to come to a halt as the sounds of a scuffle came from the right and a little behind him. From the quick frown that marred Sinclair's smooth features, it was clear that this hadn't been in his plans. And anything not in Sinclair's plans might be a good thing for him.

He turned his head just as a familiar figure stumbled out from between two crates.

"Angel!" The exclamation escaped him as he took a quick step toward her.

"It's a trap, Travis," she shouted as soon as she saw him. "They're going to kill you."

There was a moment of frozen silence and then it seemed as if all hell broke loose. Travis saw Billy Sikes lunge behind Angie, grabbing for her. Out the corner of his eye, he saw Drasen's hand disappear inside his coat. And then his fingers were closing over his own gun.

He fired and saw Drasen jerk with the impact of the bullet. He fired again and then stumbled back, the breath driven from him as Sinclair's bullet slammed into him. The bulletproof vest he wore under his shirt prevented penetration but it didn't do anything to lessen the impact of the slug.

And then it seemed as if it was hailing bullets. *The cavalry,* he thought whimsically. He shoved himself away from the crate he'd fallen against and threw himself toward Angie who, he noted in some surprise, had just laid out Billy Sikes with a very nice right to the jaw.

He felt the air whoosh out of her as he slammed into her, taking her to the cement floor in a rolling dive that brought them to a halt between two crates. And there they stayed frozen, Travis's body covering hers protectively.

It seemed as if the shooting went on for hours but Travis knew it could only have been a matter of a minute or two, at most. The silence returned as abruptly as it had disappeared. He lifted his head slowly, peering out at the slice of warehouse visible to him.

Billy Sikes lay sprawled on the floor, unconscious but apparently unwounded. He couldn't see Drasen but he knew he was dead—he'd seen where his bullets hit. He could see Sinclair's leg, easily recognizable by the pale gray suit he'd been wearing. *A natty dresser, Sinclair,* he thought, apropos of nothing. Or he had been. Something about the angle of that leg suggested that Sinclair wasn't going to have much use for a wardrobe anymore.

Assured that the good guys had won this one, he sat up, drawing Angie up with him.

"Are you hurt?" he asked, brushing the hair back from her face.

For answer, she drew back her fist and aimed a furious blow at his chin. Travis jerked back to avoid the blow, smacking the back of his head against the wooden crate behind him as her fist skimmed past his face.

"Damn you!" Her voice was shaking with anger. She aimed another punch. "Damn you!"

This time, he caught her hand in his, closing his fingers around her fist, his other arm sweeping around her back to pull her close.

"I'm sorry." He didn't waste time asking why she was cursing him. "I couldn't tell you."

"You let me think you were selling drugs." She got the words out, trying to push herself away from him.

"I had to. I was afraid you were going to get hurt." Travis refused to release her. If he let her go, he might never get her back again. He had to hold her, make her understand. "I was going to tell you the truth when it was over."

"Hah." The single disgusted syllable was all she had the breath for. He was holding her so close, she could hardly breathe. But he was alive and safe and holding onto her as if he'd never let her go.

She closed her eyes for a moment, the fingers of her free hand curling into the fabric of his shirt, feeling the stiffness of the body armor beneath.

"When I saw him shoot you—" She shuddered, remembering that instant. She'd never forget seeing the bullet strike him, sending him back against the packing crates. She'd felt a panicked rage she'd never known before, felt the adrenaline surge through her. "I hurt my hand punching Billy Sikes," she said suddenly.

"You knocked him out cold." Travis had released her fist and was running his fingers over her hair. "How did you get here? I nearly died when I saw you."

She felt a faint tremor in his hand and knew that the sight of her had shaken him as badly as seeing him shot had shaken her. Somewhere beyond the narrow alleyway that held them, she could hear people stirring around. Once or twice, someone called Travis's name but he didn't seem to notice and she was in no mood to point it out to him.

"Tony Aggretti came to tell me that you were walking into a trap. I was going to get Clay, but Billy knocked me out."

"I'll wring his neck." Travis's fingers found the knot behind her ear, exploring it with gentle fingers.

"Not if I wring yours first." She wasn't quite ready to give up her anger.

She leaned back, tilting her head until she could see his face. "Why didn't you tell me the truth last night?"

"I couldn't, Angel." His eyes asked her to understand. "I'd already put you in danger just by getting involved with you. Your brother was right about that—I had no business putting you in the line of fire. I knew it from the start."

"Then why did you?"

Travis hesitated, his fingers tangled in her hair, his eyes uncertain. "I couldn't seem to stay away," he admitted finally. "I kept telling myself I was going to and then I'd find some excuse to see you again."

"Why?"

She could see the answer in his eyes but she'd just spent the most miserable twenty-four hours of her life and she wasn't going to let him off the hook quite so easily. She wanted to hear him say the words, and then she'd decide whether to smack him or kiss him.

"I love you." He gave her the words without hesitation, gave her his heart without reservation. And Angie felt all the anger drain out of her.

"I should make you suffer," she whispered. But her fingers had found the hole in his shirt and she could feel the bullet buried in the vest he wore. She'd come so close to losing him, had thought she'd seen him killed right in front of her. There were still questions to be answered—some of them important.

But nothing was as important as the fact that he was here, holding her. And he was safe.

CLAY BRADY stopped and stared at the couple embracing between the packing boxes. They didn't seem to notice that they were sitting on cold, hard cement.

Obviously neither of them had heard him calling Angie's name. His heart had nearly stopped when one of the officers had told him that she'd been there during the shooting.

But she didn't seem any the worse for the wear. In fact, judging by the way her arms were linked around Morgan's neck, she was in pretty good shape. He hesitated and then turned away without disturbing them. There'd be time enough for explanations later.

"I LOVE YOU, TOO," Angie said finally, oblivious to her brother's departure. "But don't think I'm going to forgive you that easily. I'm going to make you pay for scaring me, for letting me think that you were selling drugs."

"I may not have sold drugs but I've done things you wouldn't like." The look in Travis's eyes said he was determined that there be no more lies between them.

"It doesn't matter." Angie lifted her hand to brush a lock of dark blond hair back from his forehead. "I love you. And you love me. Nothing else matters as much as that."

Travis pulled her closer, his mouth closing over hers in affirmation. He didn't care what was going on beyond this narrow little aisle between the crates. He didn't care about anything but the woman in his arms.

Angie loved him. Despite everything he'd been, everything that had happened, she loved him. She was right. Nothing mattered beyond that.

Romance is just one click away!

online book **serials**

- *Exclusive* to our web site, get caught up in both the daily and weekly online installments of new romance stories.
- Try the Writing Round Robin. Contribute a chapter to a story created by our members. Plus, winners will get prizes.

romantic **travel**

- Want to know where the best place to kiss in New York City is, or which restaurant in Los Angeles is the most romantic? Check out our Romantic Hot Spots for the scoop.
- Share your travel tips and stories with us on the romantic travel message boards.

romantic reading **library**

- Relax as you read our collection of Romantic Poetry.
- Take a peek at the Top 10 Most Romantic Lines!

Visit us online at

www.eHarlequin.com
on Women.com Networks

Back by popular demand are

DEBBIE MACOMBER's

MIDNIGHT SONS

Hard Luck, Alaska, is a town that needs women!
And the O'Halloran brothers are just
the fellows to fly them in.

Starting in March 2000 this beloved series returns
in special 2-in-1 collector's editions:

MAIL-ORDER MARRIAGES, featuring
Brides for Brothers and *The Marriage Risk*
On sale March 2000

FAMILY MEN, featuring
Daddy's Little Helper and *Because of the Baby*
On sale May 2000

THE LAST TWO BACHELORS, featuring
Falling for Him and *Ending in Marriage*
On sale July 2000

Collect and enjoy each MIDNIGHT SONS story!

Available at your favorite retail outlet.

HARLEQUIN®
Makes any time special ™

Visit us at www.eHarlequin.com

PHMS_R